Chicane

MARIE ALLEN

Unchained Love Series
Book Two

For the ones who give their whole heart and get burned for it.
You're not too much. You're the champagne.

AND YOUR VICTORY LAP IS INSIDE.

Playlist

1. this is what love feels like - JVKE
2. Sunkissed- Khai Dreams
3. Motion Picture Soundtrack - Radiohead
4. Call it fate, Call it Karma- The Strokes
5. Happens - Sampha
6. Incomplete Kisses- Sampha
7. Red Dust- James Vincent Memorrow
8. Chest Pain/I Love- Malcom Todd
9. Yes It Is- Leon Thomas
10. Only You- zekeluv & dray tyg
11. P.S I love you - Paul Partohap
12. Losing Sleep- John Newman
13. The Only Exception- Paramore
14. Lover- Taylor Swift
15. K.- Cigarettes After Sex
16. Stay Safe- Rhye
17. You - Oscar Lang
18. next to you- Jvke
19. Drunk in Love- Beyonce
20. ILYSB - LANY
22. August - No Vacation
23. home - Deyaz
24. SLOW DANCING IN THE DARK - Joji
25. I can't forget- Diego Gonzalez
26. Cherry Flavored- The Neighborhood
27. Aguacero - Bad Bunny
28. Are We Still Friends - Tyler, the creator
29. Like I want you- GIVEON
30. Freakin out on the Interstate- Briston Maroney
31. Bout me- Dom Innarella
32. Like Real People Do- Hoizer
33. Lock N Key- Anella

Jasmine

I'M NOT JEALOUS OF MY BEST FRIEND. TRULY, I'm not. I love that Alana ran off with a literal billionaire. Love that the man looks like a goddamn supermodel. Love that they're nesting in the suburbs of London and having twins like it's the final scene of a fairytale. I even love that said man is a world champion boxer—who announced his retirement tonight and skipped his own afterparty to go home to her.

More champagne for lonely girls like me, I guess.

Kais Reinhardt might be the only man on earth who ghosts his own farewell party.

And honestly? I probably shouldn't be here either. But I wasn't about to sit upstairs in the Reinhardt guest room while he and Alana kicked off his retirement with a round of celebratory baby-making reenactments.

Love the pregnancy. Love the joy. But I'd rather shit in my hands and clap than have to listen to *even one moan* of foreplay while I'm out here pretending not to want what they have.

No thanks.

Besides, having a personal driver, a security detail, and free drinks for the night courtesy of Mr. Reinhardt is the closest I'll ever get to feeling like Beyoncé. Almost as good as having someone who loves you like you're their home. Right?

"Another one of these, please." I tap my nails against my empty champagne flute.

The bartender gives me a dirty look that makes me want to knock her on the head just to fix whatever's loose behind those eyes. Why have an attitude?

"Fuck, my feet hurt," I mutter.

How many glasses have I had... four? Maybe five? I should eat something.

Shuffling through the thick crowd of the nightclub toward the appetizer table, I'm greeted by a sea of food, mostly bullshit. Someone really needs to inform the great people of London how to make empanadas or at least some damn chips and queso.

"These will have to do," I whisper to myself, shoving a mountain of cheesy fried somethings into a napkin.

"Do you always talk to yourself?" A deep, overly amused, British voice bellows from behind me.

I turn, ready to cut the speaker in half with my eyes but the words get caught in my throat. Or maybe my tongue just short-circuits. Because that voice belongs to the tall, tan, dangerously hot, mustached stranger I bumped into earlier at the concession stand at Kais' boxing match.

I'd wiggled out of our conversation then, but on a bellyful of champagne he's even worse for my willpower. All lean muscle, effortless charm, and the kind of mouth that knows it can devour you. Golden-tan skin that screams Mediterranean summers. Dark hair that's perfectly tousled, strong jaw, and those deep dimples that flash when he grins.

My eyes climb the beanstalk of a man slower than I intend, lingering a little too long on the way up.

Champagne. Blame the champagne. And the fact that no one gave me advance warning about this man being in attendance tonight.

"Man, you weren't joking when you said you'd find me again. You're starting to give me Joe Goldberg vibes, you know?" I pop a fried puff into my mouth as I turn and walk toward the open rooftop patio doors.

"I'd like to think I'm a man of my word," he says with a smile in his voice, falling into step beside me. "You should probably stop sounding so impressed...unless you're done pretending you don't want all of this." He waves a hand over himself.

"God, you're relentless." I stop, give him a slow once-over, and pop another puff into my mouth. "Pretty. But relentless. Much like Joe."

He shrugs, lips twitching into a crooked smile, "Now just call me a good boy and we're in business. This Joe a mate of yours or something?"

His grin is criminal. I blink at him. Twice.

There was no universe in which I was calling this man a *good boy*. Not out loud. Not sober. But—damn him—it still takes effort not to laugh. Or look at his mouth again.

I pop another puff and keep walking, mostly to stop myself from saying something stupid.

"No, Joe is not a *mate* of mine." I glance back at him. "What, do you live under a rock? How do you not know who Joe Goldberg is?"

He shrugs, still flashing me that smile. The kind that should come with a surgeon general label of its own. The kind that makes dentists cry from sheer admiration. The

3

kind that's *unfair* when paired with a voice in that timbre and arms like...that.

"Man, you London boys are a lost cause," I huff, dropping onto a nearby pool lounger and kicking off my heels with a sigh of pure relief. "Joe Goldberg is a stalker. From a TV show."

"Well, I suppose whether that's a compliment depends on what kind of lad you're into." He chuckles as he takes the lounger next to mine, settling in like he has nowhere better to be.

That's probably the most lethal part. There's at least a dozen celebrities packed inside this party. Super models, champagne flowing, cameras flashing, people trying to be seen. Content opportunities that could feed my followers for months if I actually cared tonight.

But this man isn't trying. He isn't posing. He's *comfortable*, like he isn't drawing attention from every girl that passes just by existing. And yet here he is. Sitting next to me. Smiling like Goldilocks after she'd found the right porridge.

I narrow my eyes at him, tossing another fried cheese ball into my cheek.

"Hm. I don't know," I drawl, slowly chewing. "I'd say you're cute enough to get away with the whole stalker thing. Might actually be kind of hot. If I'm honest."

He doesn't even blink. "Well, if that's the case, that dress you wore last Thursday? Looked amazing—but there was a weird stain on the back. Right about here," he says casually, pointing to his shoulder.

I blink. "Oh yeah? What color was my dress then?"

Unhesitatingly, he reaches over, takes a puff from my napkin, and pops it in his mouth.

"Black. Duh," he grins mid-bite. "It's your favorite color."

My eyebrows shoot up.

"Alright," I drag the word, thinning my eyes again. "Now you might have me convinced you're actually a stalker."

He laughs, fuller this time, with his whole chest.

"Still cute?" he mumbles through a full mouth of stolen food.

"Yeah," I relent, losing myself in those ridiculous brown eyes that seem to catch the light of everything, "Actually, it's still working for me."

He dusts his hands, then extends one toward me, like we haven't just spent the last five minutes flirting like drunk strangers in a rom-com bar scene.

"James."

I take it, palm sliding against his—warm, strong, and calloused. I hadn't expected that given his whole polished rich-boy vibe. "Jasmine."

There's a moment of quiet. It isn't awkward, just thick. The kind of silence where you both feel the shift in gravity. Like maybe the night has just taken an unexpected turn, and we're the only two people who notice.

He doesn't let go of my hand right away. I don't try to take it back.

And—I don't know if it's the champagne or the lonely spiral or the fact that this man looks like he's been handcrafted by my subconscious on a particularly lonely night, with a mustache so gleaming and noble I want to saddle it up and ride it... but I'm *seriously* considering doing something stupid.

Like, maybe I could actually go full cliché and try the whole *one-night-stand-with-a-stranger-in-London-after-your-best-friend's-husband-wins-a-boxing-match* thing.

Totally common.

You're not that girl, Jasmine. Don't be that girl.

But what if I want to be?

"Why are you looking at me like that?" He asks with a shit-eating grin like he knows he has me.

"How often does this whole...thing work for you?" I retort, trying to sound unimpressed as my legs practically melt beneath me.

His brows knit. "How often does *what* work for me, Jasmine?"

Oof. I love the way my name sounds coming out of him. Oh god. Pull it together.

I clear my throat, wave a vague little swirl in the air between us like I can summon a reset button. "This whole... intense eye contact, perfect smile, charming banter thing you're doing."

"Wow," he grins, brows raised. "You think I'm charming? With a perfect smile?" Then preening dramatically, he adds, "Weird way to ask, but yeah, sure. I'll marry you."

"Alright, cocky." I blow a raspberry. "I'm serious. What? This happens and the girls just go home with you?"

He gasps as if I've wounded him. "I offer you marriage and you only want to use me for my body? That's cold." He widens his eyes in mock offense.

"Oh my god," I groan, rolling my eyes.

"I'm truly appalled."

He keeps up the act placing a hand over his chest.

"How dare you objectify me in this way?"

His smile is annoying and maniacal.

"That is *not* what I meant."

I shove him lightly, trying not to laugh.

"Uh huh. That's what they all say," he mutters, before snatching the last puff from my napkin and shoving it into his mouth like he isn't committing an act of war.

I stare at him like he just murdered my firstborn. "Now you owe me food, *travieso*."

Those whiskey eyes light up. "Ooo, be careful," he says, voice a little rougher. "Mean happens to be my kink. Especially mean in whatever accent you just used right there."

My teeth sink into my bottom lip before I could help myself.

He tilts his head slightly, studying me with more interest than before. "Spanish obviously, but I can't place you. Where are you from?"

"Mmhmm." I give a confirming nod. "Miami, but my mom's from Bogota, Dad's from Mexico City."

Something dark flashes through those eyes. Then smoother: "Say it again."

That shouldn't have hit the way it did. But it does, right between the thighs.

So I repeat myself. Slower this time, on purpose. "*Travieso.*"

His gaze drops to my mouth, not looking away. The shift is subtle, but immediate. The world seems still while he savors the word. Then he mouths it back to me, like he's trying it on.

"Damn," he mutters. "Sometimes I can guess Spanish if it overlaps with Italian. But not this one." He leans in, just enough for the heat of proximity to make me conscious of the danger behind all that charm. "Don't tell me what it means though. I'd rather decide for myself."

Then he winks.

Freaking winks.

My brain goes AWOL for a full second. Every responsible thought I've ever had suddenly packs a bag and walks into the ocean. All that's left is instinct and heat and the taste of too much champagne.

Suddenly, he's on his feet. "Should we go then?"

"I'm sorry?" I nearly choke on air. "Go where?"

He laughs, brushing fried puff crumbs from his perfectly tailored pants. "To get food, Jasmine. You just asked me to dinner. You can't stand me up when I'm right here in front of you."

I blink again, trying to reboot my brain. "Ah. I see. Smooth. Eat all *my* food so you can take me out. That's a new one. I like it."

He offers his hand to help me up. And I stare at it.

Just for a moment.

Weighing my options, because my brain is taking its sweet time catching up with my body. I glance at the party behind me, then back at the man who's stretching out his hand to me like this is normal. Like we hadn't just met ten minutes ago. Like he isn't stupid hot with a stupid accent and an even *stupider* smile that makes me want to make very bad decisions in very expensive heels.

I could take his hand, pretend to be a girl who doesn't think twice before taking a hot guy home. I could be in control for once: not lead with my emotions, not fall too fast and get my heart stomped out.

Or I could tell him no and go back inside alone. Play it safe. Nurse my drink. Pretend I'm not thinking about his gorgeous face every other second.

Instead—fueled by champagne, one too many fried puffs, and exactly the right amount of flirtation—I slide my hand into his.

That perfect smile brightens.

"I think we'll be really happy together. With time, you'll learn to love me," he says as we walk toward the elevator.

I bat my lashes at him. "What do you mean by that, James?"

He glances down at me with that cocky glint in his eyes. "Our marriage, Jasmine. You gotta keep up. We have to write the story before I can read it to you in the nursing home."

God, he's either completely insane or dangerously aware of how irresistible he is. Maybe both.

The elevator doors slide open. We step inside. And, with a reckless little buzz in my blood, something in me snaps loose. The doors close with a hush and there's no turning back.

"Kiss me," I rush the words .

He blinks, smiling in confusion, like he didn't hear me quite right. "What?"

"I'm serious," I nod, bolder than I usually am, *braver* than I usually am. "While I'm not in my head."

As if I'm offering the deal of a lifetime, I turn on my heel to face him.

"I'm flying back to the US tomorrow. I can't leave London with the regret of not kissing the really hot guy who hit on me relentlessly because I got in my own way. This can't be anything real. We're just two perfect strangers. You don't *need* to know me. I don't *need* to know you. We don't *need* to fall in love. What do we have to lose but a *what if?*"

He stares at me for half a second too long. Like he's weighing two options in his mind. Slowly, his mouth pulls up at one corner.

"Alright," he shrugs.

Then, he presses the emergency stop on the elevator.

The second the brakes hit, so does he. He moves fast, with no hesitation, hands on my waist, lifting me expertly. My back hits the mirrored wall and then his mouth is on mine—warm and unapologetic and so much better than I imagine.

He kisses like he already has my blueprints. His lips are soft but demanding, plush and parted, tasting like champagne and something sweet. His tongue slides against mine and I swear to God, I feel it everywhere.

My hands fist his jacket then thread through his hair, tugging until he groans into my mouth. The sound makes my stomach flip.

He kisses me harder after that, hands splayed over my hips like he aches for me. And god, I don't want it to end. His tongue moves against mine again, slower now, more deliberate. As if he's dragging it out. Like he knows I'll be thinking about this kiss for the rest of my life.

Then, breathless, he eases me back down onto my feet, just casually rewiring my brain and shattering my entire sense of reality in under thirty seconds.

My eyes are still shut. Lips parted. Heart hammering. Somewhere between inhale and exhale, I feel him smile against my mouth.

Then comes a soft and satisfied laugh.

"See," he whispers, his breath mixing with mine. "You're learning to love me already."

The elevator jolts beneath us as he restarts it. But the spell doesn't break. Not really.

I open my eyes slowly, hands resting on my waist, trying to catch a breath. Everything in me buzzes. But James looks smug as hell. Relaxed even.

I narrow my eyes, pulse still wild. But my mind is made up, this can't end here.

I'm doing this.

Holding up a single warning finger, I say, "One night, James. That's it. Take it or leave it."

He runs a hand over his perfect jawline, then drags his thumb across his bottom lip, stalling. Or savoring. I'm too damn drunk to overanalyze.

His eyes sweep over me again, less playful now. "One night to make you fall in love with me, huh?"

The doors open with a clean chime. Cold air sweeps in. He looks at me with arrogant confidence.

"I'll take those odds." Those dimples cut deep with his bright smile.

Then, without a word, he offers his hand for the third time tonight. Palm open. A brow arched. I don't stare this time. Just slide my fingers into his, still slightly trembling.

"Good luck," I whisper.

But he's already smiling like he doesn't need it.

Jasmine 2

Thirteen months later...

> Alana: Will you let me know once you're settled? Trying really hard to balance excitement with manners over here.
> Don't want to impose on your first day, I know it's hard landing somewhere new.
> But you're going to love London. I promise.

> Me: Baby doll, you know I'm pounding on your door the first chance I get. Just pulling up now. Tell Kais thank you again for lining this up. I'll call you later.
> Love you.

> Alana: Can't wait. Love you too.
> Welcome to the neighborhood.

THE AUTUMN FOG ROLLING OVER LONDON IS A preferable view to the image burned into my brain seventy-two hours ago: my half-naked boyfriend on top of another girl.

I don't know what the hell Alana signed me up for. I just know I needed to get the hell out of Texas and she offered me an escape route.

A friend of Kais' needing a live-in caretaker. Whoever this injured guy is, he's clearly loaded, judging by the massive houses my driver is weaving past. I figure he probably won't be the worst patient I've ever cared for in my nursing career.

Taking in the view the tension in my shoulders starts to ease, just a little.

A year of flight nursing and constant travel assignments in new states, new hospitals, and new systems was exciting at first. But the chaos burned through me faster than I expected.

So, when Alana and Kais made the call, and a sweet woman named Loretta told me about the case—Jimmy, twenty-eight, concussion, fractured hip, couple busted ribs, spinal compression fracture, needed help with some basic ADLs—I figured why not.

Cakewalk, compared to the trauma cases I've chained myself to for the past year. Or the asshole professional athletes I dotted on the year before.

The car turns onto a quieter street, just off the main stretch of Hampstead Village. It's the kind of place where every door knocker probably has a history and a trust fund attached.

But the driver slows in front of what looks like the shy cousin of every mansion we'd just passed. Still cute, just less "old money," more "I pay my taxes and vote in local elections."

The building has a brick exterior with ivy creeping up the side, a little scuffed at the edges. No fancy gates, no columned entryway. Just five stories, a boxy layout, and a row of buzzers by the door.

Honestly? Kinda charming. Though definitely not what I pictured for one of Kais' friends.

A small sign near the door reads *Windsor Terrace – Flats 1–9*.

I double-check the address in my texts.

It's right.

Okay. So...apartment building. Fancy neighborhood. Regular-ish setup. I can work with this.

"Here's a few quid for you, lad," I say to the driver in my best attempt at sounding local. He gives me the most pitiful smile, like I'd just kicked his nan instead of tipping him.

Guess that one didn't land.

At the gate stand a short, fair woman with curled grey hair and red cheeks. She looks like someone who keeps sweets in her pockets and dishes out hugs without warning. Her smile promises tea, cookies, and maybe unsolicited advice.

After months away from my own family, I'm all in on the abuelita energy.

"Loretta?" I call, heaving my overpacked suitcase and duffel bag out of the taxi, then adjusting my crossbody purse across my chest.

"Yes, ma'am. Jasmine Lozano?" she replies with a warm smile.

I catch a faint tinge of an Irish accent in her voice. The warmth in it makes my nerves ease a little more.

"That's me. Nice to finally meet you." I offer a hand, but she pulls me straight into a hug.

"I'm so glad you could make it on short notice. I've done my best with Jimmy, but I've got too much on my plate managing this building, and that boy needs someone who knows more than how to slap a plaster on a bruise, if you know what I mean." She gestures toward the front door, I follow.

"Well, thank you for having me. I'm excited to be here —though you didn't exactly give me much to go on."

She swears under her breath, patting her pockets like she'd misplaced her entire life. "Forgot me bloody keys again." Giving up entirely, she runs her fingers down the row of buzzers. "This is why I've got no business caring for a broken boy."

Just then, the door flies open, a pack of small children barrel past us like they're outrunning the *Home Alone* bandits. As their little whirlwind of chaos spills into the front lawn, Loretta giggles and holds the door for me while I lug my duffel bag and overpacked suitcase through.

Inside, the building looks like it belongs to someone's granddad: solid, a little shabby, and quiet. With every step toward the elevator, the wooden floorboards creak and sigh. Soft lighting glows from wall sconces shaped like tulips. Someone's apartment on the ground floor gives off a cinnamon toast and coffee smell.

Cozy.

"Let me help you, dearie." Loretta says, relieving my shoulder of my duffel bag that I know weighs more than she does soaking wet.

She heaves a bit, but I can tell she's the type of woman that won't go down without a fight. The elevator doors groan open like they have an opinion about me being here. I lug my remaining suitcase inside, then adjust the strap of my purse, suddenly fidgety and nervous, again.

"You'll be just fine, dear," Loretta gives me a kind smile, stepping in beside me and sliding a card for the top floor.

"Jimmy's a sweetheart. I've worked for him for—oh, seven years now, I think? Wouldn't hurt a fly. Bit of a flirt, mind you, but the kind that makes you feel better about yourself, not like you need a shower. You know?"

"I know exactly what you mean," I mutter mindlessly, exhaling and closing my eyes for half a second just to get my bearings.

Maybe it's the jet lag that's got my head spinning. Or maybe it's the lingering, bile-soaked image of coming home to Milos tangled up with that bleached-out Pilates Barbie on our goddamn bed.

Yeah. That might do it.

Now I'm halfway across the world, about to move in with a total stranger for the next three months. The distance should be reassuring. But I feel... unsteady. And that's not me. I'm the confident one. The risk taker. The wild card. But today? I just feel thin.

The elevator bumps to a stop and lets out a judgmental *ding*. I straighten up, smooth out my jacket, and remind myself I'm a professional, even if I currently feel like a half-forgotten can of energy and rage.

Loretta leads me down a dim, narrow landing, stopping at a door with a tarnished brass number plate: **9.** She fishes a key from her pocket, turns the lock, and pushes the door open.

For a moment, I question if we have the wrong apartment. It's nothing like the hallway downstairs. And much more like what I'd expect from the friend of a billionaire.

The lighting is intentionally low and golden. Wood paneling lines the entry like the inside of a jewelry box, and everything smells expensive: leather, amber, and something vaguely like the expensive hotel potpourri I swipe when I'm on brand ambassador trips.

I step inside slowly, trying not to gape.

Polished herringbone floors stretch into a sun-soaked living room that looks ripped from a magazine spread. Sleek lines, jewel tones, expensive art that somehow doesn't feel try-hard. It doesn't scream wealth: it whispers it. One wall is nothing but floor-to-ceiling windows, giving a view of the green, rolling Heath and the city beyond.

Loretta walks towards a walnut bench in the hallway, dropping my duffel. "Just set your suitcase here, love. You'll have time to get settled in later. He's usually in the living room around this hour, resting his hip."

Resting his hip.

Right. The poor, tragic, flirty patient I'm now responsible for. I push aside my suitcase and follow her past the foyer.

Then I hear it—the quiet scrape of crutches against hardwood.

My stomach dips, my pulse kicks into action, like my nerves have decided to crash all at once.

He turns the corner.

Tall, tan, a bit battered, still grinning like sin.

I nearly swallow my own tongue.

Him.

The one-night-only, champagne-fueled mistake I haven't stopped thinking about for over a year, even when I was with Milos.

"James?" I whisper in disbelief.

"Jasmine?" He laughs softly, swiping a hand over his mustache that has ruined me for all other facial hair types.

For a second, we just stare at each other. My heart kicks so hard, I swear it's echoing off the damn walls.

"Wow." He cocks his head slightly, eyes raking over me like he's checking to make sure I'm real. "I knew you'd come back to me." That maddening grin widens. "Didn't think it'd take you this long, though. I would've crashed my car sooner if I knew that's all it took."

I blink at him. Open my mouth. Nothing. Try again.

"You're my patient?" I bat my lashes, stunned. "Then... who the hell is Jimmy?"

James laughs, cocky as ever, crutching his way to a stool by the marble island counter. "That's just what the beautiful Loretta calls me."

He tosses her a wink and she blushes like a schoolgirl. Even bruised and half-crippled, the man could melt a room of women without trying.

"Wait... so did you know it was me when you hired me?" My eyes dart between him and Loretta.

"No," James replies, grinning wider. "Though I wish I could own up to being that smooth. Loretta handled everything. I just knew you were a friend of Alana's, and I figured—how bad could it be?" He lets his gaze sweep over me once. Brazen and flirtatious as the night we met. "Guess I was right."

I shake my head, mostly at myself, trying to compute how any of this is real.

Work. I am here to work. Maybe he doesn't remember everything.

Loretta looks between us, squinting like she's trying to piece together a puzzle she doesn't have the reference picture for.

I force my mind back into gear, making a quick, visual assessment of him.

No brace on the hip: surgical, probably, but healing. Partial weight bearing at best. Still favoring one side. Ribs seem to be healing too, though he moves like they still ache when he breathes too deep. Bruising along the jaw, tightness in the lower back. I'd bet anything he's six- or seven-weeks post-op and already pushing past every restriction they gave him.

Great. Hot, injured, and impossible. My favorite.

"You gonna stare at me all day, or are you gonna tell me what's in the duffel bag?" James raises a brow at me, as if he can hear my internal monologue. See my desperate attempt to hold it together. "Don't get me wrong, I'd love to assume it's lingerie, but—"

"It's scrubs," I cut in flatly, stepping forward. "Because I'm your nurse. Not your groupie."

Loretta stifles a giggle then slips out the front door, as if to say, *My job here is* very *done*.

James' grin doesn't budge. "Damn. Groupie would've been more fun."

I cross my arms. "Are you always this charming with the women tasked with making sure you don't fall down the stairs?"

He leans back against the counter, all smug angles and maddening confidence. "Only the ones I've kissed in an elevator... and who moaned curses in Spanish after I smack —"

"Don't even finish that sentence Jimmy."

I raise a warning finger. My cheeks flame.

Okay, this is going to be hell.

James

3

THE FINGER COMES UP LIKE A LOADED GUN.

I almost laugh. Not because she isn't serious (she absolutely is), but because the Jasmine I remember is better at pretending than hiding.

And judging by the way she won't meet my eyes now? She remembers everything.

That makes me want to poke at her just a little more.

Worst-case scenario: she'll cuss me out in that firecracker way that drives me fucking wild.

Best-case scenario: she'll admit she's been thinking about me too.

"So, do I get to know your last name now, or have you already come to terms with taking on Del Toro since, you know... you've moved in and all?"

She lets out a breathless little laugh.

"Lozano," she rolls her eyes. "And I didn't even know *your* last name was Del Toro until this very moment, *Jimmy*. That might've helped me piece this whole thing together."

She waves a hand around like she can just swat reality away.

Honestly, I can't believe any of this either. I haven't stopped dreaming about her since the night she vanished from my bed and left nothing behind but a honey-scented pillow that I refused to wash for way too long.

Now here she is, hotter than ever in tight black athletic wear, that trademark attitude locked in and on top form.

"I'm surprised you don't remember the building," I say, unable to help myself. "Although, to be fair, you were a little... preoccupied doing other things. So maybe that part slipped your mind."

A familiar, irritated little sigh slips from her lips. She leans against the counter, flipping her dark hair so it falls in a wave down her back, longer now than it was that night.

I almost reach out to touch it.

"James," she breathes, pinching the bridge of her nose and squeezing her eyes shut.

I brace for something cunning, a signature jab, a little curse. But it doesn't come. She just looks... tired. A little worn down.

"I don't think this is a good idea," she almost whispers. "You should hire another nurse."

Yeah, right. Not in a million years. She is out of her mind if she thinks I'd let her off that easy.

I will never admit the lengths I went to find this woman after that night last year, but honestly, you can only get so far on a first name.

"Not necessary, *Nurse Lozano*." I lift my hands in surrender. "I'll behave."

She thins her eyes at me. "I'm serious, *travieso*. Let's be professional here, okay?"

There she is.

I smirk, holding back the dirty comment that wants to slip out. She remembers. That nickname: 'Trouble'. That night. It's not just me. And if I'm speculating, she doesn't mean a damn thing she's saying right now but if playing along makes her feel better about staying, I can play.

She doesn't say anything else. Just pushes off the counter and wanders further into the flat pretending she didn't just threaten to quit two minutes in.

I watch her like a man who isn't afraid of heartbreak.

The sway of her hips. The way her hand stays clenched around the strap of her handbag. How she takes in the space without really looking at anything. Those big brown eyes just skim, never settling on any one thing.

Clearly she's shaken. She doesn't want to be here. Or maybe she does. Maybe that's the problem.

Her shoulders tense when I crutch a few steps closer, as if she can feel me watching her. Like my attention rattles her the same way she's rattling the hell out of me.

I'd imagined seeing her again more times than I can count. But not like this. Not with a busted hip, two fractured ribs, a concussion, and a spine that still screams if I move wrong. Not needing help to get to the damn bathroom. Not with her looking at me like a landmine she hadn't meant to step on.

Nonetheless, having her here feels like a cosmic favor, because this woman had given me nothing but her first name and her entire fucking body that night and honestly? That's just unfair.

One-night stands have never been my style; I'm not the kind of guy who hooks up and moves on. But from the moment I first saw Jasmine at Reinhardt's boxing match, I was done for. I'm still kicking myself for not realizing how closely connected we are. If I had, I'd have done things a whole lot differently.

Jasmine finally turns to look at me and Christ, I swear my heart stutters a bit.

"You should get off your feet, James," she says gently, gesturing toward the couch. "Sit so I can get a look at you, please."

"Yes, boss." I obey, trying not to hobble too clumsily as I lower onto the sofa.

She braces me with a warm, steadying hand.

For a moment my ego flares, not wanting her to see me so weak. But I'll take this protective touch over her leaving any day of the week.

"Why are you looking at me like that?" She groans, rummaging in her bag.

"If you want me to be professional, maybe don't ask questions like that, *Jasmine.*"

She rolls her eyes, muttering "*Pendejo*" under her breath as she kneels beside me and lifts my shirt.

I click my tongue. "You love to talk dirty when you take my clothes off, huh?"

She mutters a stream of curses I only half catch, though her aggressive attempt to whisper them makes me laugh. Her fingertips graze lightly over my bruised ribs, her eyes on the bandages.

"You tore one of the Steri-Strips." She tugs on a pair of gloves. "Lay back a bit, please. I need to check the site and make sure it's healing right."

"You gonna buy me dinner first?" I nod, playing it cool but my ribs are bloody screaming.

"James," she warns.

"Hey, it's a valid question if you're trying to get into my pants, Jasmine," I say, swallowing my grin.

No smile from her, not even a twitch. She pulls the waistband of my sweats down, just enough to expose the site of injury, working with clinical tact—until her fingers brush the edge of the bandage and still.

She tries to hide it but I felt that tiny pause. She's remembering the same electric feeling of our skin touching, just like I am.

Jasmine exhales through her nose and keeps going. Peeling the dressing back with steady hands, not saying a word.

Doesn't stop my mind from remembering how her skin tasted, that honey scent I can get a whiff of from here, or the sound of her laugh when I dressed her in one of my shirts and promised to make her coffee the next morning.

"It's healing clean," she mutters. "Minimal swelling. No signs of infection." Her voice dips lower. Softer. Like she forgot she's supposed to be keeping a professional distance.

I clear my throat and try to blink back into focus.

"Thanks, doc," I manage. My voice comes out rough, broadcasting just how off-center she's got me. "That the final verdict?"

"This is the part where you say thank you and stop talking." She pulls my sweats back in place and slips off the gloves, still refusing to smile.

I flash her a slow grin, trying to bait her again, break this ice. "I'd thank you properly, but you've made it very clear we're being professional."

She gives me a look like she's considering throwing a gauze pad at my head. But then she bites back a smile—and I nearly forget how to breathe.

Fucking hell, I almost forgot how crazy that look drives me.

She pulls out a folder that Loretta left her and starts

talking (something about movement restrictions, pain meds, maybe a chart). I'm not totally listening. Not because I don't care. But because she sits just a little too close when she opens it. So close I can almost feel the heat rolling off her.

"...partial weight-bearing on the left side only." Her eyes flick up but she refocuses quickly. I'm completely gone. "You can use the crutches around the flat but no stairs unless absolutely necessary. You've got weekly physio coming on Mondays and Thursdays, and you're cleared for assisted walks, but I need to be with you."

I nod like I'm absorbing all of it. Truth is, I'd already ditched half the doctor's rules in week three. But if she wanted to read them all night, I'd happily listen.

"Got it," I say. "No stairs. No solo field trips. And you're the boss."

Her eyes narrow. "Don't start."

"I'm being serious." I keep a straight face. "You're the boss, Nurse Lozano. I'm completely at your mercy."

She gives me a look that tells me she isn't buying a word of it, but she doesn't argue. Probably because we both know who *really* has the upper hand here. And it isn't the guy with the busted spine and bruised ego.

"Well, it doesn't seem like you need me right now. Tell me where I'm sleeping, please."

I make a move to stand, only to have her palm flatten against my chest.

"Don't get up. I can find it myself. Just point me."

Her hand lingers on my chest.

Does she even realize how she's touching me?

I don't bring attention to it.

"End of the hall," I point. "Last door on the left. Might look familiar. Decent view. Fresh sheets."

That earns me a death glare. One I receive with pride.

"You gave me your room?"

I shrug. "I'd offer to share, but that might be presumptuous. The guest room is next door, though, so if you need anything at all..."

She rolls her eyes with a scoff of a laugh.

"I'm going to shower and *consider* unpacking my things," she mutters, zipping her kit bag with more force than necessary. "Don't go getting banged up in the meantime."

"No promises," I sink back against the cushions, calling after her. "I tend to get into trouble when you're not watching."

I toss her a wink just to see if she'll flinch.

She doesn't. She just flips her hair, shoots me a middle finger without missing a beat, and vanishes down the hall.

This is going to be fun.

Jasmine

4

I HEAVE MY DUFFEL ONTO THE BED.

The mattress lets out a protesting creak, echoing my feelings about this dire situation. My phone is out before I even know what I'm doing. My thumb hovering over Alana's name , white-hot with the urge to light her up for putting me in this situation.

Only... she doesn't know. Hell, I didn't know.

Of course I'd told her about that night. About *him*. At least a dozen times, all in the gossipy, half-drunken detail you only share with your best friend. I don't even think I told her his damn name for fear her husband might know him.

But how the hell was I supposed to know that the man I decided to have my first one-night stand with, was her husband's best friend?

"Fuck," I whisper-yell, pacing a quick path in front of the bed hoping it might help me make sense of what to do with all of this.

My thumb lingers over Alana's name like it might explode. I need to talk to her more than anyone—but that's

27

exactly the problem. The second I tell her that elevator guy is James, it stops being a job and starts being a situation. And I can't afford a situation. Not with her. Not with Kais. Not with myself.

What the hell am I thinking? There's no way he's spinning out about this like I am. I'm probably just a fun memory to him—one night, one hookup, one notch in a very well-worn belt.

He's charming. Relentless. Practically allergic to shame.

I know his type.

I used to be his type.

I thought I'd aged out of that game when I moved across the country for a man who swore he wanted forever.

Real fucking wrong about that one.

So fine. I can handle this.

Let him flirt. Let him smirk. Let him flash those stupid movie star teeth and throw that ridiculous wink around like confetti.

I am a professional.

A professional who seriously needs to fucking vent.

I peek into the hallway. James is still on the couch, head tipped back, fingers raking through his stupidly thick brown hair, phone pressed to his ear. He lets out a low, easy laugh to something the person on the other end of the line just said.

Probably a girl, judging by that fucking giggle.

Heat creeps across my chest. Stupid. Am I fucking jealous?

The thought makes my skin itch. I shake it off—physically, like a wet dog—close the door and walk to the ensuite bathroom. Memories of being in this room flooding my brain with every step.

Shit.

If I can't call my best friend there's at least one other girl, who shares the same genetic makeup with Alana and has held both my heart and my hair on many drunken nights last year.

Penelope. Alana's cousin and my roommate for the year I moved from Miami to Dallas.

I tap onto her contact and press call

She answers on the second ring.

"Jazzy, baby. You miss me already?" Her honey-dipped Texan twang crackles through my speaker, all sunlight and sass.

"Bitch..." I sigh with relief, leaning against the vanity.

Like clockwork, I catch the unmistakable clatter of skates in the background.

"Ooo, baby, watch your profanity." Penn drops her voice to a whisper. "You're on speaker and I've got my hands in a crying right winger's hamstring."

The man groans in response.

"My bad." I wince. "I forgot the time difference. You're in the training room right now?"

She laughs. "Yeah, but you're good, babe. Talk to me. Henry here doesn't care. Do you, Hen?"

A gruff chuckle echoes faintly. "Spill the tea, girl. I need a distraction. Penelope's being a real pain in my ass right now."

That makes me laugh for the first time since I landed at Heathrow. I turn the shower on to full blast and whisper, "As much as I'd love to, I don't want anything getting back to... you know who."

"Milos?" She spits the name like it's something bitter in her mouth, then blows a dramatic raspberry—our favorite reaction to anything icky and man-related.

"Fuck that guy. Excuse my language." A pause.

"Actually, no. Don't excuse my language. I took him off my schedule. It's bad enough I'm stuck with him as a roommate after you ran off and left me. I don't need to be massaging that asshole's calf too."

Guilt slices through me. I don't think I'll ever be able to forgive myself for putting her in that situation. First dating her coworker, now bailing across the Atlantic and leaving her with him for a roommate.

"Damn Penn..."

Henry groans loudly in the background, followed by: "Fuck Milos. I hate that prick. He's a fucking grocery stick."

Penn barks a laugh. "You heard the man."

"Talk your shit," Henry adds with a grunt, "And cuss as much as you want. It's the only language I speak."

I hesitate. But the fact that none of my ex's teammates like him—and the way my chest feels like it might explode if I don't vent—pushes me over the edge.

"Do you remember that guy I told you about?" I squeeze my eyes shut, barely hearing the shower running over the pulse in my ears. " From London. Last year."

"Mmhmm," Penn hums knowingly, followed by a soft grunt, probably elbow-deep in poor Henry's hamstring. "The one you used Milos to distract yourself from going back after?"

I can practically see her bright-ass grin through the phone.

"I did not use that man," I huff. "And since when are you opposed to using hot hockey players for emotional CPR?"

Henry chuckles in the background.

"You can use me, Penny—just please stop digging like that," he practically whimpers.

"Not a chance, Henry," Penn shoots back. "Anyway,

what about him? Don't tell me you bumped into him at the airport or somethin'."

The bathroom mirror fogs up as shower steam climbs the walls.

"Worse," I mutter, tugging my shirt over my head. "He's my patient."

The line goes quiet.

Then chaos.

"Shut. The. Heck. Up!" Penn cackles, nearly choking on her own laughter. "You manifested that mess with those crazy telenovelas you use as white noise."

"Yeah, well—now I'm fucked. Because he's still hot. Still relentless. And acting like an entire year hasn't passed—like he didn't ghost me."

Penn sucks her teeth. "Girl. Didn't you tell me you never gave him your number? Didn't tell him your last name either?"

"Damn, that ain't right." Henry moans dramatically. "You didn't give the man a fair shot—ow, Penelope!"

Sighing hard, I step out of my pants and test the water with my hand. "Damn. That is kinda fucked, isn't it? Like... I ghosted myself. Who does that?"

There's a second of silence before Penelope's voice turns softer.

"Sad girls in pretty dresses."

Well fuck, that hits me right in the chest.

"Girls who didn't want to risk getting hurt again."

Yeah. That fucking lands too.

I don't say anything for a minute. The steam wraps around me like a blanket of invisibility I didn't ask for but really need right now.

"It was supposed to be a one-time thing," I murmur. "I didn't know he was Kais' best fucking friend."

Penelope lets out an incredulous laugh. "Well, damn, babe. That changes everything. Listen—it could go one of two ways. You collect a check, maybe have a little fun, then leave. Or..."

"Or what?" I ask, stepping into the shower.

"Or you see where it goes. Could be good for you."

"Yeah, whatever. I'm not Alana." I roll my eyes, letting the water run over my hair. "I'm bringing my ass home single. She got lucky. I'm not getting my heart broken by another fuckboy."

They both laugh at that.

"She's not coming back, Penelope," Henry says in that flirtatious tone all giant men get around her. "You might as well let me move in once that little bitch Milos finally leaves. I'll keep you company."

He yelps like she hit a nerve. Knowing her she did, the girl will flirt with a little whiskey in her system but acts allergic to men sober.

I choke on a laugh, leaning further into the water, feeling just a little bit more like myself again.

"Either way," she says, her voice soft and motherly again, "don't bring your tail back here yet. Stay there. Take a breath for yourself. And don't rush it. And maybe think about taking some of those sponsorships and make something of the one point two million followers you have on social now that you've actually got the time."

Setting the phone in the soap dish, I let the hot water bite into my back until it numbs. "Yeah... maybe."

"Hey," she firms up. "You got this, babe. I'm here for you. Put sad Jazzy away and make that kitty sing again."

I snort. "Bye, hoe."

She gives me that sweet melodic laugh of hers. "Toodles, beautiful."

I hang up and toss my phone onto the towel on top of the toilet, feeling a pound lighter.

Maybe she's right. Not about James: he is still firmly off-limits. But maybe this isn't about him at all. Maybe this is about me. Finally figuring out what I want. And who I want to be without anybody else's say but mine.

Jasmine 5

"Good morning, Nurse Lozano. Did you sleep well?"

James is far too cheerful for this hour, his too-perfect smile fully deployed. Lounging theatrically on the edge of his bed like he's doing a magazine shoot.

"Good morning, James." I lean against the doorframe to his room.

This man must have a sponsorship deal with Red Energy or something—second hoodie in two days with its scarlet bull logo slapped across the front.

"So," I yawn, tugging my ponytail free from the back of my scrub top. "Breakfast? Do you have a cook, or do I do that too?"

He stands slowly, bracing on his crutches. "I'm the cook. But I'm open to requests, if you're offering them."

Great. Hot *and* can cook. As if he needs more help being dangerously irresistible.

I sigh, turning on my heel. "You're not cooking in this condition, James."

He follows, and I try very hard not to notice how good he looks doing the most mundane things like breathing.

"Have a seat. I'll make you something." I motion to the couch as we pass the living room.

"Nah," he says, hobbling after me. "I'd rather take in the rare sight of you in morning light."

There isn't a chance I survive three months of this man saying things like that.

I ignore him—barely—and open the fridge while he eases onto a stool at the kitchen island.

"What do you want to eat?" I turn, palms pressed to the counter as I hold his gaze.

His brow arches, mischief already loading in those brown eyes.

"For breakfast, travieso."

A slow, shameless grin pulls across his lips.

"You're really making this too easy, Nurse Lozano," he leans back in his stool, arms crossing over his chest in a way that highlights every inch of his very sculpted torso.

God help me. This man is the physical embodiment of every dirty dream I've ever had.

I clear my throat, trying to focus on literally anything besides the way his biceps flex in that hoodie.

"Please don't make this harder than it already is. Are you on a special diet? Macros? Any specific numbers I need to hit for... whatever it is you do?" I wave a vague hand toward the Greek statue he calls a body.

Given he's Kais Reinhardt's best friend and lives in an apartment this nice, I'd bet money he's some kind of professional athlete. Not that I'd know. Loretta was very committed to keeping those details locked up tight.

"Food delivery has become my nutritionist since I got

home from the hospital, but there's a folder in that drawer behind you that has some specifics from my team."

Called it. Very on brand for me. I can't seem to stay away from heartbreakers with teams. Yet another reason I need to keep my head on straight around this man.

A red folder with a Red Energy logo lay in the drawer.

"You really love energy drinks, don't you?" I mutter, flipping it open.

"Can't say I've ever had one, Those things'll kill your kidneys. But I like how the logo looks like it was made for my last name."

I raise an eyebrow. Del Toro: bull. Red Energy: bull logo. Of course this smug man would find that amusing. I don't give him the satisfaction of acknowledging how clever it is, choosing to thumb through the papers instead.

Macros, detailed schedules, performance tracking, muscle mass targets. Clearly, this is more than the average gym rat spreadsheet I sell alongside my workout programs. The man has more biometric data than a medical journal.

Then I flip to a page with lap times and pit strategies.

"...Is this a racing thing?" I squint at the technical jargon.

"Yeah." He doesn't elaborate.

I look up, finding James watching me, seemingly amused by my confusion.

"What, like NASCAR?"

He chokes on air. "God, no."

"So what then?" I ask, suspicious now. "You're not seriously telling me you're like... a professional go-kart driver or something?"

He blinks once. Slowly. Then cheeses like I just delivered the punchline to his new favorite joke.

"Close. Formula One."

I stare. " My dad watches that, I think. That's the one with the fancy little cars and the champagne spraying, right?"

"That's... one way to describe it." He scratches the back of his neck, clearly trying not to look smug for once.

I tilt my head, narrowing my eyes. "So, like, you actually drive them?"

His eyes cut away from mine. "When I'm not broken, yeah."

"You say that like it's casual." I point to the packet. "This has a section on your resting heart rate and bone density."

"It's a little less casual than I'd like," he mutters, grabbing a blueberry from the bowl on the counter and popping it in his mouth. "But I try not to lead with it."

"Why? Embarrassed you're a glorified Mario Kart character?" I tease.

"Mortified." He chuckles with a crooked grin.

I smile softly, turning back to the fridge. If there's one thing I can do with my eyes closed, it's whip up a macro-friendly meal that didn't taste like sadness.

"Well, you're in luck." I pull out eggs and spinach. "I make an egg white omelet that saves lives."

"Is that the one with the mustard sauce?" he asks, like he's genuinely trying to remember.

"Yes..." I pause, blinking. "How do you know that, James?"

"Saw it on your highlight reels." He shrugs me off, popping blueberries in his mouth as if that statement is casual.

"You're following me on my socials?" I step closer to the island.

"I am now that I know your last name."

He gives me a head to toe look. "Though I guess you didn't notice. Hard to catch a notification when half the planet already follows you."

"Oh, please." I roll my eyes, cracking eggs into a bowl. "Don't be dramatic, Ricky Bobby."

He snorts. "I don't know which part of that joke's more offensive—the American racing or the general plot line of that film."

That smile hits me far too low below the belt. So does the banter and the way he keeps up with my brain that runs on caffeine and movie quotes. We stare at each other a second too long.

"Well, just be happy I didn't call you Jean Girard," I rip my gaze away, yanking open the drawer to grab a knife—more for the distraction than the vegetables.

"You know." He leans back lazily in his chair, unapologetically checking me out. "If you want me to speak in a French accent and wear tight pants, you can just say that. I'll happily oblige."

I should be annoyed by how much he flirts with me no matter how many times I try to remind him that this is professional. That I'm here to do my job and not fall into his bed, again.

But truthfully, it's kind of a relief. Nice not to be the only one in this kitchen failing to keep their eyes to themselves.

I turn to the stove and pour the omelet mix into the skillet, fully aware that I'm giving him an even better view of the part of my body I fully remember him being drunkenly obsessed with.

He wants to play. I play better.

"So how did you get into racing?" I ask, glancing at him over my shoulder.

He shifts in his stool, the first hint of discomfort I've seen from him since I walked through the door. "Trying to catch up on all the pillow talk you missed out on by sneaking out before sunrise, Nurse Lozano?"

I shoot him a pointed look.

Yes, I took an uber out of here before he could wake up but I hate how he plays up our one night like I wounded him. With all this he's got going on I know that isn't true. Never is with the rich athlete type.

My mouth pops open ready to give him a piece of my mind. But then he smiles.

That's exactly what he wants, to distract me so he wouldn't have to answer that question. I keep nudging the edges of the omelet inward with my spatula. I built my entire personality on knowing when someone's deflecting. And he's waving a neon sign.

So I let the question hang, deciding to let him circle back to it on his own time, while I plate his omelet and slide it in front of him.

"Thanks," he says, in a quieter voice and takes a bite. "Fuck, that's brilliant."

"Mhm," I roll a wrist at him before pouring the rest of the omelet mix into the pan. "You're clearly ignoring my question."

"Too clever for me." He lets out a small laugh, like he knows he's been caught. "I started when I was six. Grew up in a town called Caltanissetta in Southern Italy—not quite Hampstead, but my mom did her best. Sometimes our neighbor, Turi, would watch me when she was at work. He was a mechanic. Mostly for junior league karts."

He pauses, fork halfway to his mouth, lost in the memory.

I let my eyes roam over him—his golden tan skin, those

messy but perfectly groomed chocolate curls. The inconsistency in his accent makes more sense now. Still he's so damn polished and aristocratic even wearing basic team merch he still looks like he belongs at a yacht club.

"He let me test drive the karts sometimes," James continues. "I guess he saw something in me, because one day he gave me my first kart. Convinced my mom to sign me up."

He shrugs like it's just another memory, though the way he stares down at his plate for a second too long gives him away.

"One thing led to another, and I started winning... a lot," he pauses between bites. "It meant traveling, constant attention. All the best development teams were in London, so my mom picked everything up and moved us here when I was thirteen. Got a job at the school where I met Reinhardt. I polished up my irresistible charm and heavy accent, started in F4, worked my way up. Red Energy recruited me from F2 at eighteen."

He says it all in the most rehearsed fashion but there's something in the way his shoulders drop. Not quite defeated. Just... like it stings to say it all out loud.

"What about your dad?" I flop my own omelet onto a plate and take a bite, watching him with more softness than I should allow myself to. "Was he around for any of that?"

"Neh, that part of the story's pretty short." He swallows a bite, eyes locked on his now empty plate.

Before he can say anything else, his phone buzzes on the counter.

We both glance at it.

"That'll be my trainer. He's coming by in twenty." James pushes back from the island quickly, happy to avoid my line of questioning I assume.

"Guess that's your cue to start emotionally preparing for how annoying I am during PT."

I flash a crooked smile, allowing him his flirtatious deflection and grabbing his empty plate. "You know, you might actually be more like Ricky Bobby than you realize."

"Well then," he says with a dramatic sigh, "guess it's time to shake, bake, and try not to cry too loudly."

I laugh, watching him crutch away. Only staring at his ass in those sweats for a second but not until I knew he wasn't looking... I am a professional after all.

James

6

"HEY, I THINK YOUR TRAINER'S HERE. A MAN named Zach?" Jasmine calls from the hall. I sigh, dragging my crutches under me.

Great. Time to put on a full-body demonstration of just how weak I've become. At least she already knows how strong I was *before*. I'll hang onto that while I embarrass myself through whatever medieval torture devices Zach brought with him today.

"Yep. I'm coming," I call, hopping down the hall.

"Morning, Del Toro," Zach says as he steps inside, carrying a black duffel that may as well have had "Pain" stitched across the side. Resistance bands. Foam rollers. A mat so thin it looks like false hope in vinyl form.

"You ready to suffer a little?" he grins that menacing gap-toothed smile.

"Maybe just ease up so I can impress the lady and not look like a complete knob," I mutter, sinking into the armchair with the grace of a man twice my age.

Jasmine walks out of the kitchen, big brown eyes locked on mine.

"Don't worry about what I think, James. Focus on yourself. Every rep gets you closer to the other side of this."

She hands me a blender bottle.

"What's this?" I deliberately brush my fingers against hers as I take it.

"Water. Electrolytes. Pinch of salt," she calls over her shoulder, heading back toward the kitchen.

Something is deeply troubled in me I think, because I like her looking out for me far too much.

Zach raises an eyebrow, mouthing, "Hot. Is she single?"

I shake my head. I don't know if Jasmine's seeing anyone. But even the thought of him trying anything makes my blood run hot.

He sucks his teeth. "Well, since you're already sitting, let's start with sit-to-stands."

"Sadist." I shoot him a look that promises retaliation.

He grins again. I brace my hands on either side of the chair.

Just stand.

Easy...if I weren't relying on a leg that currently felt like it belonged to someone else. My body used to react faster than my brain sent the signal for it to move. Now it hesitates, stalls, like the signal's taking a detour on the way down.

My good leg pushes. The other lights up in protest, pain like a live wire spiking up through my hip. I clench my jaw, trying to swallow my grimace.

"Don't overcompensate," Zach barks. "You're leaning too far forward."

"I'm leaning forward so I don't punch something," I hiss through my teeth.

Jasmine crosses the room and crouches on the floor beside me. Her hand lands lightly on my knee.

43

"Try pushing from your heels, not your toes," she whispers patiently. "That'll give you more leverage."

I exhale through my nose.

Reset. Try again.

This time, I make it halfway up before my balance slips and I catch myself on the armrest.

"Better. Reset and go again." Zach claps once. A physical therapist from hell, I swear.

My grip tightens on the chair.

My pride is already in shreds, so screw it. Might as well earn the bruises to match.

After about a dozen other forms of painful exertions I barely make it through, Zach moves on to pelvic tilts and core activation.

Simple enough. Lie down, feet flat, knees bent. Rock the pelvis just enough to engage the deep core muscles.

But nothing about it feels simple. I've done deadlifts heavier than my body weight. Thrown a car into a chicane at 190 kph. And here I am, struggling to tilt my goddamn hips.

"Engage the core, not the glutes," Zach yells, frustrated again.

I grit my teeth. "I *am*."

"Nope. You're cheating. You're using everything but your core. *Again*."

I try again. And fail. Again.

Jasmine kneels down beside me, brushing my hand aside and placing her own gently on my lower abdomen.

"You're compensating up here too." She presses just above my hip bone. "Try exhaling first, then tilt. Let your spine fall into the mat." Her voice is softer than Zach's— warmer, more patient. It cuts through my frustration.

I follow her cue. Breathe. Exhale. Tilt.

And it clicks, barely. But it fucking clicks.

She gives me a wide smile almost like she's proud.

"There you go." Zach claps that heavy palm noise again. "Finally," he continues, "That's real progress from last week, Del Toro. I know it doesn't feel like it, but hang in there, lad."

I close my eyes, breathing through the burn—not because the movement itself was impossible, but because it was humiliating that it even qualified as effort. That I had to work this hard for *that* little. That she had to see it.

The shame of needing her help grates against the part of me that has always been able to do everything myself. But beneath that is something else entirely.

Gratitude.

That she's here. That she isn't running from the mess of me.

Christ should I be this sappy over a one night stand?

My mind starts to race with too many thoughts. I reach for my crutches as Jasmine helps me up from the mat, her hand firm against my arm.

"When can I ditch these?" I ask Zach, lifting one crutch slightly.

"Maybe another week." Zach packs his things with a shrug. "If you keep pushing like you did today."

Like I pushed today...

I'm not even sure I can do that again. Not because it physically broke me but because it cost more than I expected. I didn't push like an athlete. I pushed like a man trying not to look weak in front of someone who suddenly matters too much.

"See you after the weekend," Zach calls out, heading to the elevator.

I give him a lazy wave and start the wince-filled trek to

the bathroom, trying not to look like a man on the verge of collapse. I need a shower. Not just for the sweat, but to rinse off the frustration sticking to every inch of me.

"Hey, slow down," Jasmine says gently behind me. Following me into my room.

"I can handle this part, Nurse Lozano." I flash her what I hope passes for a smile.

I have a dozen jokes queued up about her wanting to get me naked but the throbbing in my hip shuts down all of them before I can start.

She steps around me without a word and turns on the shower. Steam fills the room almost instantly.

"James," she whispers. Her eyes holding mine, warm and unflinching. "I can see you're in pain. And that's okay. You don't have to be strong all the time. This is my literal job. I won't even look at you." A faint smile pulls at her full lips. "Just... let me help. Please."

I exhale slowly, dragging a hand through my hair as my pride stages a final stand.

Heat sparks in my hip and I know it's be better to just take the damn help.

"Yeah. Okay." I nod. "Fine."

She takes my crutches and leans them against the wall. I shrug off my hoodie and t-shirt, then brace against the counter to push down my gym shorts.

The second I wince—just a flicker of lightning through my hip—she's there. Eyes screwed shut, squatting in front of me to tug them the rest of the way off like she's done this a hundred times before.

Probably has for sad bastards like me.

She stands, sliding an arm around my back as I hop into the shower and drop myself onto the very unsexy shower chair I can't live without.

"I'm not looking." She continues shielding her eyes with one hand as she reaches past me for soap and a loofah with the other.

I chuckle, weak but real. "Just so we're clear, this does *not* count as our first shower together."

She laughs a real giggle.

Then completely unexpectedly, kicks off her shoes, and steps into the shower behind me. Still fully clothed and getting ridiculously wet by the rainfall shower head

"Now it does," she teases, passing me a hand towel. "Here. Cover up a little so I can do my job and not have inappropriate thoughts, please."

I toss the towel over my lap and look up at her, amused. "This helps?"

She sighs like it physically pains her. "As much as it can, *travieso*."

She tries to play it off, but I caught that slip: *inappropriate thoughts.* She could've said anything else. But she didn't. And somehow, that tiny crack in her composure keeps my fading ego alive.

Jasmine scrubs my back and arms with slow, steady strokes—methodical, clinical even—but every now and then, her fingers skim a little too languorous over my skin to be anything but aware.

She hands me the loofah to scrub the more intimate parts myself, then slaps her hand over her eyes again.

"So... what made you become a nurse?" I ask, trying to sound casual.

Partly to break the awkwardness of scrubbing my junk in front of a fully clothed woman in the most unattractive manner. But mostly because I want to know everything I never got to ask.

What better time for her to be vulnerable than when I'm already stripped down, inside and out?

"You want to talk about my career choices while you scrub your ass, James?" she replies, a grin tucked into her voice.

"Couldn't think of a better time," I mutter, dragging the loofah down my side, trying not to grunt. My ribs still hate me.

She sighs, stepping around me again. "Well... it's not as interesting as your story, honestly."

I hear the snap of a bottle lid and turn just enough to glimpse her holding shampoo. "Shampoo and conditioner combo? How is that even a thing?" she mutters, half to herself.

Clearly we've both mastered the art of dodging a question. Fair play for me to push back too then.

"Don't change the subject," I tilt my head forward.

She huffs, and then her fingers are in my hair, raking from crown to nape with that gentle touch that punches the breath from my lungs.

It's nothing and everything all at once. It doesn't feel like she's just washing my hair. It feels like she's letting me fall apart a little and somehow holding the pieces steady without making a thing of it.

It's exactly what I need.

"Nursing is just what the women in my family do. My grandmothers on both sides were nurses, and so is my mom," Her voice is quiet , almost like she's afraid someone will hear her. "It was just kind of expected that I—being the only child—would carry that on."

Her hands move lower, scrubbing gently down to the nape of my neck. I tilt my head back just enough to catch her eyes. She doesn't shy away, but there's something soft and distant in her expression.

"What did you actually want to be then?"

The corner of her mouth ticks up like she might try to laugh it off, but she doesn't.

Instead, she reaches for the wall shower head and switches the water from the rainfall to rinse.

"Honestly—" she sighs, tilting my chin forward with a touch that's more careful than it needs to be, "I don't know. I never gave it much thought. I just wanted to make my family proud." She runs her fingers through my hair, rinsing away the suds in smooth motions that beg to put me to sleep. "And I do really love being able to do this," she added.

A slow smile pulls at my lips. "Take showers with broken race car drivers?"

"No, idiot." She swats my shoulder just hard enough to make me grin wider. "Helping people. When they need someone the most."

There's a weighty pause as she stands still for a moment, resting her hand near my collarbone.

"But if I'm honest," she breathes, "I don't get to spend much time doing the care part in my day-to-day. If I'm not on a trauma flight, I'm mostly just chasing alarms and trying to keep more than a dozen people alive at once in the ER. And that's... exhausting."

She turns off the water and grabs a towel, working it carefully down my back around the bruised areas. When I wobble getting up, she steadies me without a word, adjusting her grip until I'm balanced.

"So what would you do if you couldn't do this then?" I ask, watching her tuck the towel securely around my waist.

"It's dumb," She shakes her head like she's already

embarrassed by the thought, grabbing my crutches and holding them out to me.

"Look at me," I deadpan, gesturing to my ridiculous state. "I'm wrapped in a towel and using you as a human crutch. Embarrassment? We're past that."

She gives a short nod, her throat visibly working.

Then finally, with a frustrated breath: "I'd go full-time with my social platform."

I blink.

That was the dumb part?

She says it like it's something to be embarrassed about. Like choosing herself—her vision—is somehow less noble than burning out for someone else's expectations.

Clearly, I missed something. But that's not shocking—I don't run my socials, never had a reason to scroll through wellness influencers until she walked into my life. What she's doing isn't dumb.

It's brave.

And brilliant.

And anyone who makes her feel otherwise doesn't know what the fuck they're looking at. But the way she's avoiding looking at me again... seems as if she was expecting me to laugh, or judge, or write her off like what she does isn't a real job.

It makes something burn in my chest.

"Am I missing something?" I ask, crutching behind her as we move toward the bedroom.

"It's just risky," she mumbles, rifling through my drawer. Nonchalant when it's clear she just confessed to something that means everything to her.

"I mean... technically I make more with my workout program and small brand deals I have now than I do on staff at any hospital. And I do really love it: the creating, the fitness industry, the way I can actually help people make changes in their lives before disease or sickness catches them."

She pulls out a pair of briefs and kneels beside me to help me step into them. Eyes closed tight. To hide from my nudity or herself, I don't know.

"Still waiting for the embarrassing part, Jasmine," I say as she stands, tugging them up gently over my hips.

"Shorts or sweats?" She turns away quickly back to the dresser.

"Dealer's choice," I toss out, not wanting her to lose her train of thought. She grabs a pair of blue gym shorts, hesitating for a second before pulling them out.

"I don't know," she mutters. "It's not as noble as being a nurse. People make assumptions about women like me who post what I post, dress the way I do. They think it's shallow. Attention-seeking." Her voice is almost guilty again, just like it was in the shower. She helps me into the shorts, quiet a moment. "And then there's the whole disappointing-my-family part. That one's a real treat." She gives the waistband one last tug, smoothing it out, then tosses me a white t-shirt.

"Have they even seen your stuff?"

"Yeah." She huffs a small, dry laugh. "My mom calls it *cute.*"

"Cute," I repeat, letting the word sit there like the insult it is.

I tug on my shirt and bite my tongue.

What I want to say—is that I know exactly how that feels. How people look at me and see a poster boy. Pretty face in a fast car. They don't see the work it takes to sit behind that wheel. How easy it is to be replaced by the next young and hungry driver.

Nor the broken vertebrae, the months of rehab, the pressure of my entire career fate resting on whether my spine can handle 5Gs through Copse corner. They think it's glamorous. That looking good on camera means the work isn't real.

Jasmine has built something that actually matters to people, that gives her real freedom she can control. And her family calls that cute?

"You don't owe anyone your burnout just to prove your worth."

She blinks hard, clearly trying not to let me see her vulnerability. "Do you want some moisturizer or something?" she asks, eyes scanning the room as if hoping the topic might disappear.

"No, I just use body lotion."

"With a face like that?" She motions at me with an open palm, seemingly appalled. "That's criminal."

She disappears down the hall a second and comes back holding a small gold and purple container.

"Here." She scoops a dollop out with a tiny gold spoon like she was about to serve caviar.

"Just smear it in?" I ask, already knowing that's probably the wrong thing to say.

She looks personally offended. Stepping between my legs, she plucks the cream from my hand. "You can't just rub it in any kind of way. You'll encourage wrinkles, James."

Her fingertips glide easily—small, confident strokes over my cheeks, nose, jaw. It's sort of soothing. Much like everything else she's done for me today.

I laugh quietly. "I always thought I might get better looking with age. Like Antonio Banderas."

"You definitely will." She smiles easily, stepping back to

wipe her hands on a towel. "But no need to fast-track your way through the Desperado phase."

Those dark eyes hold mine for a minute. Definitely not the look of someone just doing their job. Catching herself, she tucks her hair behind her ear and steps away.

"Okay. I'm done here. No more naked confessions. I need to change out of these wet scrubs."

I rake a hand through my damp hair, still feeling the ghost of her fingertips working through it. "You really think a man can survive all this pampering and not fall a little in love?"

She rolls her eyes, half hearted as ever.

"You've done enough dangerous things, James. Don't go adding falling in love to that list," she tosses the words over her shoulder before walking out the door.

But if I'm honest, I don't think I could stop myself from falling for her even if I wanted to.

James

7

"James, amore mio, you need to eat more. You look too skinny." I smile through a sigh, adjusting the phone so my mum can see my face better.

She's got flour dusted on her apron and streaked across her cheek like a badge of honor.

"Don't roll your eyes at me, Monello. I'll fly over there and feed you myself," she warns, waving a dough-covered hand at the screen like she can actually swat me through it.

"I'm not rolling my eyes," I lie. "But if you keep threatening to weigh me down with passata, I'll never make weight for the car again."

Even through a grainy FaceTime call, my mom's death-glare has the power to cut through steel. I smile big anyway. That glare feels like home.

"I miss you too, Mama. How's the place coming along?" I shift the phone to one hand as I made my way into the kitchen.

Quietly.

Well past the time Loretta would come knocking but Jasmine isn't up yet. Probably fighting the jet lag still or just avoiding me after the intimacy of yesterday. I don't blame her.

"It's coming along," my mum grunts, slapping a stubborn mound of dough against the counter like it wronged our whole bloodline.

I set my phone against the backsplash watching her and reach for my moka pot and Barbera. Yesterday seemed to check that pillow talk box for me and Jasmine, why not make good on my coffee promise today.

"The men are finishing the roof this week." She catches a breath wiping her forehead, a sure sign whatever she's making will taste like heaven. "If I'm lucky and God is good, I'll be open by spring."

She smiles big and warm. Pride lacing every syllable.

All I can think about is how much I miss her kitchen. The smell of her cooking. Just her.

"Make sure they send the invoice to Loretta," I blink, clearing the emotion begging to crawl up my throat. "I'm still not checking emails."

"Mio figlio," she sighs, dusting flour off her hands like she can wipe away my help. "No—no. You do too much."

"I don't do enough."

"You do more than I ever ask."

"You don't ever need to ask. Just let me be your first guest. I got in on the ground floor of this whole bed and breakfast empire twenty years ago, remember?"

She chuckles, folding and kneading her dough in that same rhythm I learned before the alphabet. Taking me back like I'm six years old again, sitting on the counter with flour on my knees and stealing bites from hot pans.

"No, Tesoro. You'll be back on the grid by then. Can't have you distracted. You come when your season brings you to Monza."

I roll my eyes, brushing her off with a flick of my wrist. "I've always got time for you, Mama. You promised me *pasta con le sarde*, remember? Maybe I'll bring someone with me."

Her abrupt laugh rolls straight through the phone speaker.

"Oh no, no. Don't you go making promises you won't keep."

A door creaks open down the hall. A second later Jasmine peeks around the corner, sleep-tousled messy braid and wearing an oversized t-shirt, sweats, some homemade looking socks and that groggy little scowl I'm already too fond of.

She mouths *sorry*, eying my phone and trying to back out.

I shake my head and wave her in.

She hesitates, then shuffles closer like the floor might bite her.

"When have I ever made you a promise I didn't keep, Mama?" I say, circling back to her ludicrous statement about me not keeping promises. Not taking my eyes off flighty Jasmine as I pour two espressos from the hissing moka pot.

"Never," my mum replies warmly. "You're a good son."

I pass a cup to Jasmine. Her sleepy and warm fingers brush mine as she takes it. "Well, I've got to get ready for my meeting, Mama. I'll call you after, sì?"

She waves me off, back to assaulting dough. "Ciao, Tesoro. Ti amo."

Jasmine smiles into her cup with raised brows.

I return her smile but don't cower in embarrassment like she seems to expect I will.

"I love you too, Mama." The call ends. But Jasmine's

still eying me over the rim of her mug, like she isn't quite sure what to make of me.

"Still a hell of a sight, seeing you in the morning light." I sip my espresso with a satisfied smile and slide my phone into my pocket. "I was half-convinced you made a break for it down the fire escape by now."

Jasmine scoffs , but her gaze dips with a raised brow. Doing a quick sweep of my shirtless torso, chest to hip.

"You're not supposed to be up without your crutches," she mutters, like she didn't just check me out. "And maybe you should put a shirt on. Your schedule says you've got a meeting in less than an hour."

"You and my mother would get on like wildfire." I smirk, running a hand through my hair and giving her a better look since her eyes haven't moved. "Maybe you should meet her before the wedding. That's tradition, right?"

She laughs, low and incredulous. "You never give up, do you?"

"Not when I know it's a good bet."

She shakes her head, then tips back her espresso like it's a shot. Or maybe she just wishes it was.

"Thanks for the coffee. I'm pretty sure I'll be awake for the next three days off whatever jet fuel you brewed in there."

"Maybe that's your kryptonite. If you don't sleep, you can't sneak out." I reply, watching her walk to the sink. If she can look so can I.

She grabs my cup from my hand, sets it beside hers, then turns and hold out my crutches. Cool and composed, but blushing as red as a strawberry.

"Let's go get you dressed, Casanova."

I take the crutches from her slowly. Brushing her fingers

with mine and noting the goose bumps that trace up her arms

"You always this hands-on with your patients?"

She arches a brow and snatches her hand back. "Only the ones who flirt like it's a full-time job."

"Lucky for you, I've got excellent benefits."

Her eye roll is immediate, but she has to nip her bottom lip to stop that smile. A quiet admission she doesn't hate this as much as she pretends.

I follow her out of the kitchen, her every step intentionally casual, hands raking through her long hair like she's trying to fix it without being obvious.

It's almost comical watching her try not to like me.

THE MEETING ROOM smells like glass cleaner and tension. Chrome edges, carbon-fiber details, a Red Energy logo on the far wall so glossy it seems to reflect every light in the building .

Fredrick Lemaire, my team principal, sits at the head of the table in his signature red polo, sleeves rolled just enough to show off a vintage Heuer watch. Always on brand.

Across from him sits Patrick Holt, my performance engineer—too tall even sitting down, with that angular Alexander Skarsgård look that usually makes women stupid. His icy eyes linger on Jasmine a beat too long before he forces his attention back to the tablet in front of him.

Trying not to scowl, I settle into the chair they've left for me, hyperaware of every clumsy step it took to get here. Frederick and Patrick don't comment, but their eyes follow the crutches as I prop them against the table. We haven't spoken since the hospital, and judging by the quick glance they exchange, this isn't the recovery timeline they were banking on.

Jasmine makes a beeline for the arm chair in the corner of the room. Sitting quiet in her black scrubs, hair up, hands folded in her lap professional and unreadable. But I can feel her attention on me like a spotlight.

Lemaire doesn't acknowledge her, but Patrick keeps staring like he wants me to knock his eyes out.

"Winter testing begins February 17th," Fredrick blurts with no preamble.

"That gives us sixteen weeks." Holt adds, "And twelve until your next press obligation. Cloud Sports wants you for a pre-season piece in January. We've pushed it as far as we can."

My jaw locks. "I can handle press."

"Can you?" Lemaire asks, cocking a brow. "Because right now, all the public knows is that James Del Toro ghosted after Spa. No interviews. No footage. No statement. You let us carry the fallout."

Spa.

That damn name hits like a bullet. Every time I close my eyes, I see it. That split second when I registered the maneuver. Too tight, too quick. Just before the rear clipped and I went airborne. It wasn't a mistake. It was a move. Calculated. Vicious.

And it came from Kieran Denune, the one bastard on the grid with something personal to prove by beating me for the drivers championship and someone to impress with it. Namely, my ex.

"I'll do the interview," I say. "I'll be ready."

Lemaire glances at Holt, who pulls up a progress chart. Colored bars. Percentages. Recovery targets.

"Based on physio notes, you're pacing six to eight weeks behind what we need for early testing," Holt says, pinching and zooming. "Even if we push your simulator time to January, there's no guarantee your reflex response will be race viable."

"I've already started," I hold his gaze steady.

"This isn't about doing the work, James. It's about results." Lemaire leans forward. "We need to know right now if we're putting our weight behind you or moving on. Our reserve driver Adam is producing solid lap times. If you can't prove readiness, we'll lock him in before winter testing."

A familiar simmer starts in my chest. The slow, grating scrape of pride against panic. I'd built my life around being the one they bet on. The one they counted on. And now, they were already drafting my obituary. I'd spent the last year before my crash training Adam Perry, now what? He replaces me before I get a chance to breathe.

"You want to replace me?" I ask.

"I want a championship. And right now, we're leading in Constructors. Ollies on pace to take the Drivers. I don't need headlines. I need podiums."

He fails to mention that the lead we have is because of the three hundred points I put up before I got hurt or that even hurt I'm still leading the board which is unheard of, but that's fine.

Jasmine doesn't move. But I catch her staring at me from my periphery. That professionalism slightly cracked and her brows knotted. An appropriate response for witnessing the slow unravelling of my career that won't be fixed with electrolytes and showers I suppose.

"If you're in, I need proof. A fitness test by December.

Track sim data. Coach clearance. Otherwise, we move on." Lemaire adds.

"I'll be ready, book the test."

My words are convincing even to me for a split second. Lemaire's face doesn't change. "Then your re-evaluation is in five weeks."

"I won't miss it."

"We'll see."

Holt stands, gathering his tablet. Lemaire doesn't offer a handshake. He never does if there isn't a camera.

I stand slower, jaw tight, pride alone keeping my balance solid. Jasmine is already at my side like she knows I need out of this room. Her eyes too soft on me as if she's pitying me. And I want to run as far away from that look as possible.

I'm already losing the only part of me that ever felt worth something. The part that made me useful. To my mom. To the people who count on me. The last thing I need is the woman I let slip through my fingers giving me a look that reminds me of everything else that's falling through them too.

Jasmine

8

JAMES WAS WAY TOO DAMN QUIET IN THAT meeting. And that tiny man with the overpriced watch was a fucking asshole.

It took every ounce of professionalism I had not to hurl my phone at his smug face. It's one thing to have standards, another to deliver bad news like the person across from you isn't even worth the oxygen they're using to explain themselves.

James just took it.

Sat there and swallowed it, like he didn't even deserve to fight back. That did something to me. Lit a fuse. Watching him sit in that chair with that hurt look in his eye that will no doubt haunt me, felt like seeing someone slap an ice cream cone out of a kid's hand just for the fun of it.

He didn't say a word the whole ride home. Not a single flirty comment when we walked through the door. Just limped off to his room to "take a nap".

Yeah, sure. I'd seen that brand of self-pity before. Hell, I'd invented it. I was the queen of the mopey spiral. I don't know what gets him out of it, but I know what works for me.

An hour and too many stores later I've got it all tucked under one arm. Waitrose and American Food Store bags weigh down every one of my fingers, much like a kid refusing to make a second trip when mom calls for help with groceries.

I'm not about to let him sit in the dark and forget who the hell he is. Not on my watch.

"Fuck. Fuck. Fuck," I mutter through clenched teeth, because of course my mouth has become a third hand in the great grocery bag struggle. "I'm gonna look like a damn idiot," I groan, using my head to jab every call button like a desperate gremlin.

"Yes?" A singsong voice crackles through the speaker.

"Hi—shit, sorry." I suck in spit, slobbering down the bag handle in my mouth. "I work for the man upstairs, and I've got about six grocery bags digging into my arms and one clamped in my teeth. Is there any chance you could buzz me in before I dislocate something?"

She laughs, light and musical. "Of course, dear. Who am I to turn down a ministering angel?"

An angel? Okay, this lady's clearly unhinged.

A few seconds later, the door swings open. A petite blonde woman holding a very fresh newborn holds it open for me.

Great. I'm burdening a new mom with grocery bags and desperation.

"I'm so sorry," I mumble through the bag that was halfway to becoming a chew toy.

"Here, darling. Let me help you." She laughs and gently plucks it from my mouth with her free hand.

I exhale, muttering a flustered "Thank you. I'm really sorry," as we walk to the elevator.

"It's okay," she replies sweetly. "I've been holed up in my flat for two weeks now. Nice to stretch my legs, honestly."

I glance down at the baby in her arms, swaddled and asleep like a literal cherub.

The elevator groans open with its usual attitude, and she steps in beside me.

"Boy or girl?" I whisper, eyes on the sleeping bundle in her arms.

"Girl. Her name is Violet," she replies, grinning like the name itself is made of honey.

"Cute. My best friend just had twin boys earlier this year," I add, watching the elevator tick past each floor.

"Would your friend happen to be named Alana?"

My head tilts in confusion. "Either the universe is very small, or that's a suspiciously common name for women birthing twins in London."

She laughs, adjusting the baby gently. "I met her at women's shelter she runs with her husband. She's the one who got me and Violet here connected with the program Mr. Del Toro runs here." Her voice goes soft, full of gratitude. "Free rent in Hampstead for a year? After everything we've been through, it felt like winning the lottery."

I wince, humbled by how much I didn't know about the philanthropic gigs my best friends been up to, nor the man I'm trying very hard not to look at with hearts in my eyes. "That's incredible." I whisper, mostly to myself.

"Yeah, it is. Especially since no one in the building looks at me funny. We're all here under the same kind of circumstances, you know? Trying to start over. It's a brilliant thing Mr. Del Toro does. Good man that one. "

The elevator dings, opening with a groan and a flicker of light.

"Thank you again, really," I say as I step out. "You can just set that there."

She crouches to set down the bag. "Anything for the man upstairs—and his helping angel."

I blink, then snort at the realization. "Ah. Man upstairs. I get it. That's good."

She grins at her own mom joke and gives me a little wave as the doors slides closed.

I open the door and lug the bags into the kitchen. Still no sign of James. As nice as this place is, it's dark, too quiet, and honestly kind of depressing. Lit only by the faint twinkle of the London skyline filtering in through the windows. Not exactly the vibe I'm going for.

So, I get to work.

Operation: Get-Out-of-Depression-Free is officially underway.

I flip on a few lamps, set up a fortress of fuzzy blankets and eye masks, toss in a pair of ridiculous fuzzy socks for good measure, and lay out enough American snacks to qualify for cultural diplomacy. Cheese pizza, sour gummies, mini-Oreos, Reese's, Red Vines. The works. I even plug in my game system and cue up the lo-fi.

If this doesn't cheer him up, he might actually be broken.

I give the setup a once-over, hands on my hips, and nod to myself.

Honestly? Some of my finest work. Nurse of the year shit. Though, if I'm being really honest, I'm not showing up tonight as Nurse Lozano. He doesn't need that version of me right now.

What he needs—what I recognize all too well—is a

friend who knows how to fight sadness with snacks and distraction.

So I tiptoe past his room, change into my comfiest hoodie and sweats, then brace myself. I've officially pulled out all my best tricks.

I creep down the hall. James' door is cracked just enough to let out a sliver of warm light. A single lamp glows in the corner of his room, just as depressing as the living room was when I walked in. James is propped up in bed, eyes glued to his phone, thumb scrolling like it might keep the spiral at bay.

Ah, doom-scrolling. Dissociation 101.

"Knock, knock," I say softly.

Those dark eyes flick up. Warm brown but dulled around the edges. The kind of look you wear when you've been run over by more than just a car. A lazy almost-smirk curves one side of his mouth, but it doesn't stick.

I hate that.

"Time for evening meds, Nurse Lozano?" he asks dryly.

I bite back the grin of excitement tugging at my mouth, holding tight to what little professionalism I have left. "Nope. Are you busy?"

He deadpans. "Do I look busy?"

He flashes the game of solitaire on his phone. So, not doom-scrolling social media like a normal person in crisis. Just... solitaire. Like an old grandpa with nothing but time. While I was probably getting tagged in a hundred things right now, he was playing cards against himself.

I step in anyway, walk straight to his bedside and hold out his crutches.

"Then come with me."

He chuckles, but the sound is hollow. "I'm kinda tired. Think I'll just crash early."

"Unacceptable." I shake my head. "Let's go."

He sighs like I'm dragging him into battle, but he pushes back the covers and stands. The soft thump of his crutches follows me down the hall. He doesn't ask questions. Doesn't joke that this is some play to get in his pants.

Just silence.

And somehow, that made me want to fix this even more.

James stops as the hall breaks into the living room. His weight shifts, crutches planted, like he isn't sure he's allowed to move further in his own home. Lofi fills the quiet from the speaker under the TV.

I watch his eyes skim the fortress of pillows, the snacks, the pizza box, the controllers waiting on the armrest.

"Damn," he says finally. "You did all this for me?"

I shrug a shoulder, trying not to look as self-satisfied as I feel watching his eyes light up a little. "It was either this or stage an intervention. You're lucky I didn't show up with a priest."

He huffs a laugh, but it sounds softer than usual.

"This is..." He shakes his head like the rest of the sentence got lost somewhere in his throat. "You didn't have to."

"I know," I reply simply.

He doesn't say thank you. But the way his shoulders ease, like it isn't just a living room anymore, but somewhere safe, that says enough.

"Consider it your pre-preseason training." I hold up a Cars DVD and Mario Kart. "You want to watch a training video or jump right into simulation?"

That too perfect grin starts to creep back while he glances between the DVD case and the game controller like

I just offered him two golden roads out of hell. Or lonely solitaire.

Same thing.

"You're telling me this is rehab-approved?"

"Absolutely." I plop down onto the couch with a throw pillow in my lap. "Endorsed by the top minds in sports medicine."

He raises a brow. "Pretty sure you're making that up."

"And yet here I am." I pat the cushion next to me. "Your very own overqualified, underpaid sports psychologist-slash-pizza fairy. So, unless you'd rather go back to losing at solitaire in your sad boy cave..."

That earns me a real smile. Crooked, but real.

"You're relentless."

"You're welcome."

He eases down beside me, slower than he wants me to notice, but I pretend not to.

"Okay, rules are simple," I hand him a controller, cuing up the game with mine. "If you win, you get any of the delicious treats you see here." I wave my hand over the snack mountain. "If I win, you tell me something honest."

He gives me a sidelong look. "Define honest."

"No PR fluff. No charming bullshit everybody already knows. Actual James."

He clicks the 'A' button with a little too much force.

"Fine. But if I win, you have to call me Mario for the rest of the night." He swipes an Oreo.

I burst a laugh. "You're more of a hot Luigi, but okay."

"Hot Luigi?" His face twists like I've just offended his honor. " That's not even a compliment."

"It absolutely is. Tall, underrated, kind of sweet? Secretly the backbone of the franchise."

He shakes his head, grinning like I'd both insulted and

intrigued him. "You've put way too much thought into this."

I tick my shoulder. "Or not enough."

His elbow brushes with mine when I settle in next to him.

"Now shut up and pick your kart."

I choose not to notice the way he doesn't move to a friendly distance as I scroll through the character select screen and land on Luigi with zero hesitation. If I'm going to destroy him, might as well commit to the bit.

"Oh, come on," he groans. "You're really gonna rub it in?"

"Every. Single. Lap."

He lets out a dramatic groan, dragging his selection screen like he's dragging a cross. "Unbelievable. I'm injured. Vulnerable. And you're out here channeling a petty green plumber to destroy me."

"You make it sound like a war crime," I shoot back, watching the countdown. "Come on, the matador wants to dance with the blind shoemaker."

"How many times have you actually seen that movie? Your brain is 60% movie quotes. Should I be concerned?" he laughs, a deep and warm sound that makes my stomach flutter.

"Concerned? Babe, I'm just living my truth. I wanna go fast." I keep up the bit, speeding quick into first place, holding a red vine in my teeth like Wario's cigar.

He nudges my side, earning a giggle from me, then mutters something about how video games are an affront to realism and the laws of physics.

I let the silence hang, comfortable and fizzy, then absolutely annihilate him in the first match.

"Okay, there's no way that red shell hit me from behind

while I was boosting," he protests, pointing at the screen like it owes him an apology. "Physics. Ever heard of it?"

"Oh my god," I gasp, laughing so hard I have to put my controller down. "You're that guy—the one who blames game mechanics for sucking."

"I do not suck." He rakes a hand through his perfectly messy hair. "You've clearly sacrificed a goat or something to be this good at a game meant for *literal* children."

He bypasses the clear agreement we made on my winning and jabs the rematch button before I can even gloat properly.

Guess I'll just kick his ass again then.

"Or you're cheating," he adds like a sore loser. His eyes are narrowed on the countdown, leaned in fully gearing up for redemption and looking a lot more like himself than he was when I came home.

I can't help but smile at that.

"How, James? How am I cheating?" I lock my eyes on the screen too.

"I don't know. You're just... too calm. No one's that calm while drifting Rainbow Road."

"I'm built different."

Casually, I lob a green shell that clips him mid-air and sends him flying off the track.

His gasp so loud, so full of genuine betrayal, I snort.

"You aimed for me?" he shouts.

"It's a race," I reply sweetly, eyes not leaving the screen. "Not a group hug."

Final lap. I floor it. He tries some slick last-second mushroom boost like it might save his pride, but it's too late. I cross the finish line. Luigi does his little fist pump. Victory music. Confetti. Eternal glory.

I turn my head slowly, savoring it. "That's two for two buddy."

He drops his controller onto the couch and flops back, mortally wounded. "This is the Catalina Wine Mixer of betrayals, Jasmine."

My stomach hurts from laughing but I can't help but buy into our Will Ferrel bit.

"I know we started as foes, but after that courageous act —maybe, maybe—someday we can be best friends."

He reaches across my lap, grabbing an unearned slice of pizza. "I would follow you into the mists of Avalon, if that's what you mean," he mumbles through a bite, wiggling his eyebrows.

We both burst out laughing.

I never knew I could be so turned on by a man quoting movies back at me, but here I am. He speaks my language. The weird, obscure, quote-it-till-you-die language. And that might be more dangerous than his smile.

"I've humbled you, Dale," I sit back into the cushions, popping an Oreo into my mouth.

"Please. I'm un-humble-able." He slings an arm across the back of the couch, his flirty smirk finally returning. "But I do want a rematch."

I tilt my head, pretending to think about it like that wasn't the most fun I've had in months. "Fine. One more. But first... you owe me something."

He turns toward me, head tilted, smile lazy and way too charming for his own good. "Fine. A deal's a deal."

"Come on then. Make it good." I turn too, smiling back with the excitement you get at a slumber party.

He leans, resting his head against the couch, long legs stretched out. When he looks at me this time, something shifts. The playfulness drains away, replaced by something heavier. Something that makes my stomach kick up those butterflies again.

"That night we met..." His eyes pin mine like he's seeing it all over again. "I didn't even want to hook up with anyone."

Suddenly I need to concentrate too hard on breathing.

"I mean—until I did, obviously," he adds, flashing that crooked grin like a defense mechanism. "I've never been that guy. I was just... tired, I think. Tired of everyone wanting something from me. Of feeling used or like a stepping stone. You were the first person I'd talked to in months who didn't care who I was. Something about being with you felt like taking a breath."

My throat goes dry.

Why the hell did I ghost this man again?

"Your turn." He ticks his chin at me.

"Fair. Um..." I take a breath, picking at the hem of the blanket in my lap. "I've never done that ever—the whole one-night thing."

"Really?"

I nod, forcing myself to meet his eyes again. "I'm the type who falls too fast. Gives way too much. I've had to teach myself how to be casual." I scoff under my breath, gesturing with my eyes at the very elaborate set up around us. "Clearly, I suck at it."

His expression softens even more into something unguarded.

I reach for another cookie just to have something to do with my hands. "So... I left that night while you were asleep before I could do anything else stupid."

I don't look at him again. More like I can't look at him again.

A minute passes. Then another. The menu music loops again, soft and nostalgic. Too gentle for how loud everything suddenly feels inside me.

And then, just above a whisper, he says, "Just because you left doesn't mean it's over."

James

9

Ollie: Pint tonight? Or are you still off your tits on painkillers DelToro?

Kais: Must you get cunted at every dinner, Oliver? Isn't your wife due any day now?

Ollie: Exactly my point, lad.

Me: I'm off the meds, but I need to stay upright for when Ollie inevitably loses his seat.

Ollie: Oh piss off. I've podiumed almost every race since your little flying lesson. Good luck clawing back lead, twat.

Me: And yet I'm still 100 points ahead of you. Injured. You're welcome for the opportunity, cunt.

Kais: You're both cunts. Dinner's in an hour. Drink a pint or don't. I don't give a fuck.

OLIVER BISSET HAS BEEN THE BIGGEST PAIN IN MY ass since we were kids carting in shit gear and oversized helmets. Even back then, the little prick had more confidence than skill, but damn if he didn't catch up fast. That cocky streak of his never went away.

But it's exactly what makes him the best kind of teammate: bold on the grid, louder off it, and just consistent enough to keep the heat off my back this season.

He's been podiuming like hell lately, and while I'm the one who laid the foundation for us to take the Constructors again, I won't be the one driving it home. That stings more than I let on.

Still... I'm lucky. Most teammates want the lead seat. Ollie just wants the win. And for that, I'll put up with his mouth.

A soft knock sounds against my bedroom door.

"Yeah?" I call back.

Loretta peeks her head around the corner. Neat grey bob, cardigan buttoned just right, a smile like sunshine filtered through old linen.

"Oh, good—glad you're decent, Jimmy." She steps in with her usual no-nonsense grace.

"Evening Loretta. Aren't you a sight for sore eyes. I like the new haircut." I grin, hoping it masks the little sting of disappointment that she isn't the person I'd been hoping for on the other side of that knock.

"Oh, hush. I just ran a comb through it. I wasn't expecting to see anyone." She gives me a mock scoff, waving off the compliment, but her cheeks still pink.

"Glad you stopped by anyway." I reply, pulling open my dresser drawer.

"Well, I hate to bother you, Jimmy, but we've got a

tenant moving out. I need to know what you want to do with the open unit."

I tug my head through a fresh t-shirt, talking through the cotton. "Who's moving?"

She swipes through her phone like it holds national secrets. The amount of life she manages through her note's app is genuinely terrifying.

"Miss Cruz and her girls," Loretta says with genuine excitement. "She got offered a teaching job in Finland."

I thumb through my hangers, trying to find something that doesn't have Red Energy slapped across the chest. "Good for her. Though I'll miss that cinnamon milk drink she makes."

Loretta lets out a small laugh. "I think it's called horchata?" she whispers, widening her eyes hesitantly.

"That's the one." I snap my fingers, walking over to my wardrobe. "Her unit's the two-bedroom, yeah?"

She nods.

"Alright, let's check if anyone in the building needs the space before I offer it outside. I'll ask the Reinhardt's tonight—see if they've got someone in mind."

I settle on a heather grey Aran sweater and pull it from the hanger.

"Um... Jimmy?" Loretta clears her throat, her tone a little hesitant.

"Yeah?" I mumble, tugging the sweater over my head.

"Would it be alright if I switched to Miss Cruz's unit? My daughter's coming in for the holidays, and it would just... make things easier."

I don't even let her finish. "Loretta, you don't have to ask. I'd help you move myself if I wasn't walking like a ninety-year-old geriatric. I'll get someone on it."

"Thanks, Jimmy." She presses a hand to her chest, just

for a second, that maternal calm back in place. " I brought your mail up—I'll just leave it here."

She sets a stack of envelopes on the edge of my bedside table, then gives me one of those warm, departing smiles that never failed to brighten my day before disappearing out the door again.

I should be thanking her, really. She's been like a second mum since the day I signed the deed here, quietly holding the whole building together while I chase podiums around the world for most of the year.

This block of flats was the first thing I bought after my first season as lead driver. Kais told me real estate was the smartest move I could make if I didn't want to burn out by thirty. "Land doesn't crash," he'd said. "People always need somewhere to call home."

But truth is, I didn't buy it to make money. Not really. I just kept thinking about my mum. Twenty-four, alone, dragging suitcases through Heathrow with nothing but my karting schedule and a prayer.

She'd given up everything so I could chase something. And if owning this place means giving someone else a softer landing than we ever got, then it's worth every pound.

Partnering with Kais and Alana's non-profit last year feels like the best thing I've done with the place. Every unit goes to single mums from the women's shelter they run.

Free rent for a year. A chance to breathe.

I haven't made a pound off this place since. But on days when I wonder if I'm just a body in a car chasing champagne and points? This reminds me I'm worth something even if I never race again.

The bassline of whatever pop song Jasmine is blasting through the wall ripples down the hall, vibrating like a countdown.

I figure I have at least twenty minutes before she emerges, wrapped in perfume and sarcasm, looking like trouble I'd thank her for.

She's only been here two weeks, but I already know every one of her little quirks. The way she hums when she's thinking. The curses she whispers under her breath when she forgets her coffee on the counter and it goes cold. The way she hands me exactly what I need before I even know I need it.

And Christ , I haven't smiled this much in a year.

She's been acting differently since that meeting with Lemaire, less guarded maybe. But still a bit unreadable. I can't tell if she's pulling closer or keeping me at arm's length for both our sakes.

There are moments, quiet ones, where it feels like she sees me. Really sees me. And then the next second, she's gone, deflecting with a joke or dodging my gaze like it's dangerous.

I don't know if I've been friend-zoned or if I've just stepped into some slow burn limbo where no one wants to light the match.

I spray on the same cologne I've worn since I was nineteen. Tuscan Night. A classic. And a magnet every time I've walked into a room. Maybe tonight it'll work on the one person who keeps pretending she doesn't want to pull me in too.

The music in the hallway finally drops. Less bass and more melancholy. One of those quirks I've picked up on that means she's about to emerge.

I sit on the edge of the bed, flipping through the stack of mail Loretta left behind.

Junk.

Bills.

A catalog for watches I very much don't need.

Then—

A letter.

Addressed to me. From someone named Aurelius Del Toro.

I stare at the name like it might blink first. My father's name was Hernán Del Toro. Never met the bastard. All I know is that he left my mom alone and pregnant at sixteen, and that fact alone was enough to keep me from ever giving a shit about where he ended up.

So who the hell is Aurelius Del Toro?

I tear the envelope open and read the letter once. Then again. And again, just to be sure I'm hallucinating the burn in my chest.

Two lines hit like a fist:

Hernán's funeral was last month.

And:

All that to say—fuck that guy for hiding the fact that you're my brother. If you want to meet me, I sure as hell want to meet you.

Brother.

The word echoes, heavy. My heart slams against my ribs. Every part of me is suddenly too alert, and somehow too still.

Somewhere out there's someone with my blood in his veins. Someone who knew Hernán, who buried him. Who apparently hates him a little, too. And now wants to meet me.

I don't know what the hell I'm supposed to feel. Angry? Relieved? Like some missing part of me just sent up a flare?

All I feel is pressure. The same kind that's been sitting in my chest since Spa. Since Lemaire's deadline. Tight and unrelenting. And now this. One more thing I don't know what to do with.

I didn't even hear Jasmine walk up to the door.

"You ready, travieso?" she asks softly, her voice a gentle nudge.

I look up and for a second, I forget what the hell I was doing. Forget about the letter. The funeral. The fact that I apparently have an older brother.

She's just... standing there. Leaning against the doorframe in high-waisted jeans and a red sweater that dips just enough at the collarbone to be distracting. Her hair loosely curled, her flirty little bangs laid just right, her lips glossed, eyes calm.

And fuck me, she looks beautiful. Effortlessly beautiful. The kind that makes me forget, just for a second, that my whole world is unraveling.

I run a hand through my hair, trying to bring myself back to solid ground.

"Yeah," I reply, sliding the letter into my drawer.

"You sure you don't want your crutches?" She glances down as I stand.

"I'm good," I say, forcing a smirk. "If I lose my balance, I'll just grab your ass or something."

She chuckles, completely unfazed. I wish it wasn't so damn easy for her. Wish I could tell if that laugh means she likes it, or if I'm just entertainment.

Not that I can blame her. Flirting with her is like a reflex, but lately—since that night on the couch with the blanket and the goddamn green plumber—it's felt like more than just a game. Like I'm waiting for her to call my bluff.

"Or," she drawls, stepping closer, "instead of trying to live a replay, you could take my arm like a civilized person."

She holds out her elbow, like she's my fucking escort.

I blink at her, deadpan, before swatting it gently aside and offering her mine instead.

She slides her arm through with a smile that hits a little lower than is gentlemanly.

"This is nice," I mutter as we step into the hall.

"Not as nice as my ass apparently," she replies without missing a beat. "But you're welcome."

I snort and just like that, my pulse finally settles. She hasn't fixed anything. She doesn't even know what needs fixing. But I can't help but to be grateful she's not playing nurse tonight.

Jasmine 10

"Fuck, this place is massive,"

I mutter as James and I climb out of the cab, gravel crunching beneath our shoes. Not that we really needed the ride. I didn't realize my best friend lives a literal quarter mile down the road from me. Which only makes me feel worse for taking two weeks to come see her.

"What is this, Pemberley?" I add, eyes sweeping over the house.

I can feel James watching me, probably amused at how gobsmacked I look.

It's the kind of house that belongs in a Brontë novel. Tall and stately, with dormant rose vines clinging to old stone. A gravel path weaves through manicured hedges, and the windows all ripple slightly, like they'd been watching people come and go for centuries.

It looks like a place that has loved and lost a hundred times. Dramatic. Brooding. Stubbornly romantic.

Great, now I'm projecting my own issues onto a fucking house.

"It is really charming, isn't it?" James replies quietly, like the house might overhear."Does that make us the Bingley's, if they're the Darcys?"

"Mmm. I am a sucker for Mr.Bingley. Not gonna lie... it's cute how well you've got me pegged," I whisper.

He laughs softly, looking up at the façade, eyes warm, his arm brushing mine as he stands beside me.

Just that slight touch is enough to short-circuit half my rational thoughts. Heat licks up my thighs like a warning flare.

I've been avoiding him all week. On purpose, with discipline. Because I do *not* trust myself around this man. Not even a little. And the worst part is it gets harder every damn day.

Every little thing I learn about him dismantles my defenses one brick at a time. Every overheard call with his mom, every passing comment from a tenant in the building he owns but never brags about.

Absolutely lethal to my willpower and the very fragile vow I made not to fall for the guy.

"Are you two going to come in or hold on to your last moment of avoiding us?" Alana calls from the doorway, beaming like she already has our number.

Ever the golden-skinned, brown-eyed queen she's always been, like Princess Jasmine by way of a '90s rom-com, she stands in a cream cashmere lounge set and fuzzy slippers. One curly-haired boy balanced on her hip, a tiny Kais clone right down to the quiet intensity in his eyes.

My throat tightens instantly.

Jesus. What kind of soppy emotional bitch am I turning into?

I'm already flying up the steps before I can stop myself, arms wrapping around both of them, breathing in that familiar crème brûlée scent of her shampoo that I'd somehow forgotten I missed.

"Damn," I mumble into her cloud of chocolate curls. "You're such a fucking MILF."

She snorts, swatting my arm. "Your gross compliments are making it really hard to stay mad about you taking two weeks to get your ass over here."

Behind me, James takes the steps slower. Steadier, but I can tell by the way his jaw clenches that he's pushing it. I start to turn back to help, but he catches my eye and shakes his head with that stubborn smile. The second he reaches the top, his whole face lights up.

"There's my favorite boy. Come on, Rafi." He opens his arms and with a giggle, the curly-haired boy practically launches himself into them.

Alana smiles like this is a regular thing. "You say that to both of them, James. One day they're going to make you pick."

She waves us in, stepping back as James nuzzles Rafi, who is now gripping his cheeks with both chubby hands and squishing his face into something that makes my ovaries threaten mutiny.

"I'll never choose." James blows a raspberry into Rafi's cheek, making him dissolve into a fit of giggles.

I was *not* ready for this.

Not the softness in James' eyes. Nor how natural he looks holding a kid. Nor for how it makes him seem like someone you could build a life with.

I could build a life with, how much I want that life.

Woah, no—no Jasmine.

"Everyone's in here," Alana says, guiding us through a wide arched doorway and into what can only be described as a period piece fever dream.

The kind of living room that looks stolen straight out of a BBC adaptation of an Austen Novel. Ornate crown molding, soft drapes, and antique furniture that somehow doesn't look stuffy. The air smells like cinnamon and warm bread, and the whole house pulses with cozy, lived-in, pretty damn fancy charm.

"Hey!" A chorus of voices ring out the second we cross the threshold, like they've been waiting for us.

Kais—with that face that made you believe in impulsive marriages, part Arabian Vogue spread, part Bond villain—is sunk into a deep armchair near the hearth, cradling a nearly-asleep baby boy identical to the one in James' arms. Copy-and-pasted straight from his DNA, sleepy brown eyes and all.

A blonde man with an annoyingly perfect jawline and baby blue eyes sits nearby, slouched in a club chair like it owes him something. I recognize him from one of the racing posters at James' last meeting.

The teammate with the mouth.

On the floor beside him, a very pregnant, very glowy blonde sifting through a pile of baby clothes as if she's curating a tiny fashion show.

"James," the woman clicks her tongue, heaving herself to her feet with the grace of someone who used to be elegant and is now reluctantly waddling. "Hand him over. You shouldn't be walking around like this, let alone holding a wiggling baby."

James turns away like a toddler guarding his favorite toy. "Back off, Emilia. You're not taking my godson from me. I've been deprived for weeks. I'm making up for lost time."

He lowers himself onto the couch with a dramatic sigh, Rafi still clinging to him like a koala.

"Besides," he adds, stretching out his good leg, "I'm fine. You should be more worried about the shitheel you married. Man's got a race in two days and he's already three beers deep."

The blonde guy raises his glass in salute, scowling. "Fuck you, James. It's my first one. You just got here and you're already being a bloody prick."

"Ollie, please watch your mouth around the boys," Alana says, shooting him a look that somehow holds both mom energy and mob boss precision.

Then she turns to me, hands warm on my shoulders, her whole face brightening.

"This is my best friend, Jasmine," she announces proudly. "She's James' nurse."

Ugh.

I smile on cue, but being called James' nurse lands like a wet sock. Something about hearing it out loud, in front of strangers, makes me suddenly crave one of Ollie's beers.

Maybe two.

"Jaz, this is the lovely Emilia and..." Alana's eyes flick toward the blonde with the smirk and the pint. "Foul-mouthed Ollie."

I nod at them both, trying to focus on anything other than the words *James' nurse*, echoing in my skull like a bad ringtone.

"Lovely to meet you, Jasmine," Emilia says, her voice warm and refined. Posh Spice if she played an expecting mother in a Nancy Meyers movie. She pulls me in for a hug with surprising force.

I hug her back politely, but something inside me twists. Emilia is unfairly glowing, and obviously close with my best friend. She's settled into a life I've missed far too much of this past year.

And damn it, that stings.

I smile convincingly nonetheless and turn to Alana. "Point me to a beer, baby doll."

James raises an eyebrow, still bouncing Rafi on his good leg. "Ooo, Auntie Jazzy's being a bad girl, huh Raf?"

"I'll grab you one" Alana giggles, already moving toward the hall. "Just sit down and maybe go say hi to Zayd before he conks out."

I make my way toward Kais, arms out like a greedy toddler. "Come on, Father Bear. He hasn't seen his Tía since he popped out of his mom's coochie. Don't be stingy."

Kais lets out one of those manly, Ron Swanson-esque chuckles, kisses the top of Zayd's sleepy curls, and passes him over like a trust fall. Zayd doesn't even stir. Just melts into me, all warm footed pajamas and baby weight, his little hand fisting gently in the fabric of my sweater as I settle on the sofa beside James.

"You know, one of you is enough, Kais," I say, cradling Zayd as he burrows into my chest. "But copying yourself twice over? Feels a little arrogant, don't you think?"

"Oh, come on," Alana bellyaches, reappearing with a beer in one hand. "They look a little like me."

She hands it to me with a look of betrayal, then promptly seats herself in Kais' lap like the overstuffed floral print arm chair next to him isn't good enough.

Clearly my jealousy is turned up to a ten tonight.

Not taking his eyes off his wife, Kais says: "I was aiming for one of her. We'll fix that next time."

The way he looks at her makes my chest ache.

Arms wrapped around her waist, chin resting on her shoulder, like he needs her close as possible—like she's home for him.

It makes me crave something I'm not even sure I believe in anymore. I'd chased love enough times to know better. Fresh off a breakup when I met James. Fresh off another one when I walked back into his life. Maybe I'm the problem.

I reach for my beer as Zayd drifts back off to sleep in my arms. James bumps my shoulder with his, all casual confidence, then leans in just enough to make my pulse stutter, his voice low against my ear.

"Have a few more beers. Maybe we can replay the night we met and I can give you one of those too."

Heat bolts up my spine. I giggle before I can stop myself.

Damn it.

One sentence and he's dismantled two weeks of telling myself to keep my distance. Every time I think I have my guard up, he knocks me right back down to square one.

My eyes immediately dart to Alana. Her brows jump like she's caught the scent of gossip, eyes narrowing on me in rapid blinking suspicion.

I clear my throat, masking the sound with a cough, and chug my beer like it can drown whatever reaction just sparked to life in my bloodstream.

Thankfully, Ollie and Emilia were too distracted by the baby clothes they were rummaging through to pick up on it.

James resumes playing with Rafi like he didn't say a thing. But when I glance back at Kais and Alana, they're both watching me intently.

"So, dinner?" I ask, taking another swig of my beer and praying it might cool the blush crawling up my neck.

Alana's eyes narrow in that way they do when she knows too much.

"Yeah... dinner," she says slowly, standing with a little too much purpose. "Jazz, can you come help me in the kitchen?"

"Ooo, brilliant," Emilia chimes in from the floor, reaching up with both arms. "I've been dying to get my hands on that sleepy angel all evening."

Regrettably, I place Zayd gently in her lap, brushing his baby-soft hair from his forehead as he melts against her like warm dough. Think I could hold him all night if his mom wasn't summoning me for gossip.

Then I follow Alana, who's already striding out of the room with a mission in her step.

Once in the hallway, she tugs me forwards by my arm like she's about to perform an exorcism.

"Fuck, this kitchen is insane," I mutter as we push through the swinging door and into a cathedral of marble, brass, and exposed beams.

I've only seen this place in grainy renovation photos she'd texted me while I was busy pretending my life wasn't falling apart an ocean away. Being here in person is overwhelming in a way that has nothing to do with the imported Italian tile.

"Uh-uh." She wheels on me. "Spill. What's going on with you and James?"

I scoff. "What are you talking about, crazy ass?"

She crosses her arms, leaning a hip against the island, and gives me the stare. The one that peels you like a grape and would have made her a killer lawyer had she not given it up for a life of philanthropy and domestic bliss.

"Jazz. We're best friends, I lived in your pocket for four years. Don't even try it."

I sigh, forcing a breath through my teeth like it might deflate the tension. "Nothing is happening, Alana."

She doesn't blink.

I groan, rubbing a hand across my chest. "Okay, do you remember... hot elevator guy? From Kais' after party last year?"

"No!" Her eyes blow wide. Her hand flies over her mouth.

"Yes." I grimace.

Her jaw drops. "Mr. Best Sex of Your Life is *James*?"

"I didn't say that." I look away, fixating on the oven door, the smell of whatever Alana's cooking is suddenly very interesting.

"Oh, but you did." She beams, following me around the island like a bloodhound with a scent. "You also said, and I quote, you didn't think you'd ever actually had an orgasm before that night."

"Can you not?"

"Oh my God. You and James Del Toro." She's practically bouncing with glee now. "How did I not think to put you two together myself?"

"Wipe that look off your face." I wave a hand in her direction. "It was one night, Alana. Over a year ago. Nothing's happened since. We're just..." I struggle for the right word. "We have an understanding."

"Mmhmm." She nods, but it's the kind of nod people give when they're humoring you. "So basically, you're lying to yourself and being emotionally avoidant because you're terrified of getting hurt. Got it."

"Bitch, don't read me like that," I grumble.

She just bounces a shoulder, smug little shit.

"I know you, Jazz. And I know the look you just gave each other. You're both totally fucking gone."

She turns to the oven, pulling out two heavy, cone-shaped ceramic dishes that smell like heaven and spice.

I cross my arms, fighting the burn in my chest.

"I am not gone," I lie firmly. "In two months, I'm on the first flight back to Dallas, and James will be back to working his way through the same parade of women I know he keeps in rotation."

Alana snickers, shooting me a look over her shoulder as she pulls a tray of golden bread from the second oven.

"You must be talking about a different James," she says. "Because the one I know is the biggest lover boy on earth. He won't even go on a date unless he can, and I quote, 'see a future with her.'"

The words hit me dead center.

I've been clinging to the idea that I was just another story for him. Another chapter, easy to close. Honestly, it's the only thing keeping me from walking into his bedroom, butt naked and begging.

She studies me like she's reading the fine print of my soul, that little button nose of hers wrinkling in the way it always does when she's about to call bullshit.

"I'd say something dramatic about not hurting him—" Her hand comes to rest on my forearm. Soft, motherly in a way that makes me want to squirm. "—if I didn't think you might already feel something too."

"So I'll say this instead: don't fuck up something that could be really good just because someone else tried to break you first."

I exhale hard, more annoyed at how right she was than anything else. "Don't go all fucking Oprah on me now. I'll lose my appetite, and whatever the hell that is..." I point at the bread the looks like it was animated by studio Ghibli, "...smells too damn good to miss."

"Let's go eat, then." She smiles, that same knowing one I hate and love her for, and hands me a bread basket.

I want to tell her she's wrong. Want to look her in the eye and swear I don't feel a thing. But the truth is his laugh has been stuck in my head for days. And so has that thing he said the other night.

Just because you left doesn't mean it's over.

I take the basket. Follow her out. And whisper the lie to myself once more. Just in case it still works.

James

11

It's funny how group gatherings always gender-split like clockwork. Women in one room, men in the other. Like some primal program in the matrix.

Jasmine, Alana, and Emilia are curled up around the fire in the living room, giggling at something I can't quite hear. Jasmine's head tipped back as she laughed, eyes crinkled, bare feet tucked under her.

She looks so fucking at home, like she just belongs. Some days, it feels like she's the only one who can ever fit into my life this way.

Most days, I'm trying not to think about what happens when she leaves. When the five weeks are up and I'm still not cleared to race. When she realizes I'm just a broken driver with nothing left to offer.

I follow Kais down the hall, one sleepy boy on his shoulder, the other slumped heavily in my arms. Ollie trails behind us, dragging his feet like the fucking toddler he is.

"Kais, I don't know how you do it, mate," Ollie mutters, dropping into the recliner in the nursery. "I'm scared shitless of Emilia pushing out that boy."

"Keep your voice down, you twat," Kais whispers, setting Rafi into the crib like a man defusing a bomb.

I hold on to Zayd a bit longer. Jasmine stole all his sleepy snuggles tonight after dinner, and let's be honest, they're the best part of being a godparent to these boys. I love the way they melt into me without hesitation. Like I'm enough, exactly as I am. Every time feels like a remedy for something I've been missing.

I'd been telling myself I don't need to think about settling down yet. That racing's enough. That I've got time. But watching Kais with his boys, watching Jasmine light up when she held them... I'm not sure I believe that anymore.

"Since when are you scared of anything, Oliver?" I mumble, finally lowering Zayd into the other crib.

"Oh, I don't know, you fuckin' bellend," Ollie snaps. "Maybe since you almost bloody died and left the entire team on my shoulders three months before my wife has our first baby."

The words hit harder than he probably meant to. Or maybe he meant to. Ollie doesn't usually aim unless he's trying to wound.

"Why the fuck do you two bicker like toddlers," Kais grumbles, leaning against Zayd's crib, arms crossed, eyes flicking between the both of us. "You're a team, yeah?"

We both nod, sheepish.

"Then act like one," he whisper-yells. Quiet enough not to wake the boys. Hard enough to make us both stand straight. "Right now, Ollie, you're picking up extra weight because your teammate can't. And when you're half-dead from sleep and nappies and colic, James'll have to return the favor."

He rolls his shoulder, exhaling hard.

"It's no different from what you'll do for your wife.

She's about to give you the best fuckin' gift of your life, and she'll need you to carry the load when she can't. So don't be a fuckin' cunt about it. Suck it up. Step the fuck up."

Ollie actually has nothing to say for once.

And I swear, if I wasn't holding back a sigh of relief, I might have applauded.

I don't have it in me to fight back. Not when part of me agrees with Ollie. I did leave him holding the bag. Carrying a team that was built around me, all while waiting to see if his best mate would even make it back. And now his wife's about to give birth and I'm still broken.

Still useless.

"Yeah, you're right, mate."Ollie rakes a hand over his reddened face. "I'm being a wee bit of a cunt?"

I wince. "Just a bit, lad."

He stands, giving me a hard slap on the back. His version of an apology.

"Alright, that's enough. Don't start fuckin' kissin' now," Kais mutters, waving us off.

That pulls a schoolboy laugh from both of us.

Ollie gently moves his hand to my shoulder. "So, how's it lookin'? You think you're coming back? Or are you really gonna stick me with that kid Perry forever?"

"Physically?" I exhale, dragging a hand through my hair. "Better than expected. But I'm more worried about my head than my body. You're only as good as your last race, you know?"

Kais' brow pulls tight. "That's bullshit."

I look over to him.

"You start tellin' yourself that and you might as well not get in the fuckin' car again."

"He's right." Ollie nods, serious now. "That's not you,

lad. You're ruthless on the grid. Always have been. Find that again. Stop tucking your tail."

He flops back into the recliner, expression hard. "You really gonna let that wanker Kieran end your fuckin' career?"

I turn back to watch Rafi as if that could shield me from the question. I know they're both right. Doesn't mean I want to hear it.

Everyone on the grid's got guns for me, and fair enough. I've led the boards with a hundred-point gap every season. On the rare occasion, and I mean *rare*, that I don't win, I still podium. So yeah, beating me? It's a fuckin' achievement.

A headline.

And Kieran Denune has been clawing for one all season. Probably thinks he's the main character now, since he's dating my ex, Francesca. The same one who cheated on me with him a few months before I met Jasmine. I guess causing my crash wasn't enough of an ego boost for him.

I sigh, heavy and tired. "Fuck that guy."

They both laugh, amused and immediate.

"Exactly, mate. Fuck that guy," Ollie says, shaking his head. "He's got a fire up his ass lately, but only because I've boxed the cunt out every race since Spa. No way I'm letting that prick take the drivers' championship. Especially not with his seat up next year. Delancey's already sniffing around other drivers."

I shrug, not mentioning that I'm one of the other drivers Delancey keeps coming after even while I'm hurt. Neither me nor Ollie would dream of racing for another team.

"Yeah, well, maybe he should worry more about that than posting shit about me on Frenchie's stories."

Kais' eyes narrow. "You still follow her?"

"No, I barely get on socials," I mutter. "Doesn't stop every keyboard warrior from shoving it in my face when I do."

I hate that it still gets under my skin. One post slips through my well-crafted blocks and I'm right back there. Second-best and watching Francesca rewrite history as though I was always a pawn.

For the last two weeks, I've kept telling myself Jasmine's different from Frenchie. And she is. Entirely.

But sometimes she does this thing. Keeps just enough distance to make me chase that feels like Francesca's same game. And I can't lie, that gets in my head. Gets all those insecure parts of me that feel inadequate going.

Because I've played this game of back and forth before. And last time, I lost a hell of a lot more than just a girl. Every insecurity I've got is telling me to let her go.

But I fucking can't.

Not yet. Not when part of me already feels like she's the one thing I don't want to lose in all this. And that's what scares me most.

"Who gives a fuck about bloody internet trolls?" Ollie snorts. "Aren't you shagging that mad fit nurse downstairs anyway?"

I shoot him a look. "Oi. You just said you weren't gonna be a prick."

Kais, of course, doesn't miss a beat. "No, I'm with Ollie on this one. I picked up on that too. You lot where giggling and makin' eyes on my sofa all night."

"Ollie," A soft knock sounds at the open nursery door behind me. Emilia.

Thank Christ.

"We should head out." she says, leaning in the doorway. "I nearly passed out in the armchair downstairs."

"You got it, babe. Goodnight, boys." Ollie smiles, then pushes up from the recliner, giving me a smirk that promises he won't be dropping the Jasmine thing as he passes.

I straighten up, ready to follow Ollie out and dodge Kais' knowing glare too.

"I should probably head out too," I nod toward the twins. "Give you lovebirds some time while they're knocked."

"Right. Give *us* some time." Kais huffs a quiet laugh and walks in front of me

He doesn't leave right away. Just stands there, one hand braced on the doorframe, like he's deciding whether to give me shit or bite his tongue.

"Oi," I drawl. "You alright?"

He looks at me for a half second.

"You're gonna come back. Not for them. Not to prove some petty shit. For you."

"Would be a waste of all those years of Reinhardt sponsorships if I didn't come back," I scrub a hand over my chin. "I'd hate for you to start underground fighting again just to recoup the investment."

The joke lands flat because it isn't really a joke.

Kais funded my F3 season when no one else would bet on a broke kid from Sicily whose mum cleaned classrooms to pay rent. He'd believed in me before I'd given him any reason to. And now I'm terrified I'm about to prove everyone else right: that after all, I wasn't worth the investment.

Kais stares at me like he's deciding if that was supposed to be a compliment or a cry for help.

"You're shit at keeping your word," he grouses.

"I'm not bringing it up. But you can't blame me for feeling a bit nostalgic when you start getting all motivational on me." I hold his intense stare, almost wanting to joke but honesty wells in me. "I wouldn't have gotten to where I am if you hadn't believed in me the way you did back then. You're one of three people I don't want to disappoint when I'm out there... maybe four now."

He grunts, his usual contemplative noise. "Jasmine?"

I nod.

"Fuck what I did when we were kids. You are where you are because you were fuckin' made for it." He takes a deep breath. "And if you're serious about starting something with her, that's all the more reason to get your bloody head right."

I shift my weight. "Right, so what you're saying is... I should stop spiraling and start winning again. For love. Can I at least cry dramatically in the rain once before I sort myself out?"

"You're an idiot." He shakes his head, walking out the room.

"Yeah," I mutter, following him out. "But I'm your idiot. And technically your investment, so I fully expect one of these little talks once a quarter."

He pauses again, just briefly, like something tugged at him on the way out. Then, deadly serious, he says, "She's good for you. Don't fuck it up."

That lands harder than I expected it would.

Not just because it's Kais saying it, but because the man used to act allergic to relationships then eloped with Alana after a month of knowing her and never looked back. He's last person on earth I'd expect to turn into a romantic, and yet here he was, living proof it could work when you knew. When it was right.

I try to play it off.

"You mean that? Or is this a test because she's your missus' best friend and you'll have me assassinated if I blow it?"

He doesn't even blink. "Both."

Then he claps a hand on my shoulder and disappears down the hall without another word.

Easy for him to say. He's not the one trying to unlearn what it feels like to be a fucking fool.

12

"WELL, THAT WAS FUN,"

Jasmine says, standing by the shoe rack in the hall as she unzips a boot.

"It was. I don't think I'll ever get my fill of those crispy honey puffs Alana makes."

"It's a wonder how you have a body like that with as much as you love food," she laughs, taking off her coat to reveal that cheeky red jumper again with its maddening dip down her chest.

She's already walking over to my bedroom doorway, and I might be dreaming, because for the first time in days she seems to not be completely avoiding me. Which makes me way giddier than it reasonably should.

"It's a love language for me," I reply, tugging off my sweater, which conveniently drags my t-shirt with it. I'm almost certain I hear that little cough she does when she's trying to act unaffected. When I glance up, I catch the flicker in her dark eyes before she looks away.

"Interesting," she says, leaning against the doorframe, eyes fixed on me.

"What?" I smirk. "You checking me out or judging my passion for honey puffs?"

"You should learn to keep a shirt on if you don't want to be checked out, travieso." She huffs, biting back a smile with that signature eye roll that will probably kill me one day.

I move toward the dresser for sweatpants but wince slightly. I've been dressing myself for a week but the long evening without crutches is catching up to me.

Jasmine notices immediately, stepping closer.

"Here, let me." She helps me into my sweats and a fresh t-shirt without closing her eyes as she usually does.

Then, like it's nothing, she hops onto my bed.

My bed.

She bounces once, grins like it's hers, and suddenly I don't know where the hell to put my hands. I watch her, heart pounding in a way I'd never admit out loud.

She isn't running tonight. She's right here, like she doesn't want to be anywhere else. I don't know what the hell changed, but I'll take it as a small opening.

I drop down next to her. Slow and not smooth in the least, but I'd take the pain ten times over if it means I get to stay this close to her.

"So you're admitting to checking me out and climbing into my bed?" I ask, smirking. "Not sure if I should feel flattered or concerned that you only like me when you've been drinking."

"I didn't even finish the one beer Alana gave me," she huffs, rolling her eyes and laying back, arms tucked behind her head. "So do with that what you will."

This woman. Reckless words. My bed. And me, idiot enough to want something real when I know how this ends. All of it way too dangerous to mess with right now.

I can't help but do it anyway.

"I'll just take it as an open invitation to start planning the wedding, then." I match her position, arms behind my head, attempting to act like my heart isn't trying to beat its way out of my chest.

She lets out a soft laugh but doesn't fire back this time. No snark. No comeback. Just quiet.

And that, that's the moment everything seems to shift. The air between us stretches, pulls tight like it's waiting for one of us to breathe too loud. I turn my head slightly, studying the curve of her profile in the dim light. She looks relaxed, but I know better. She only gets this still when she's thinking too hard.

And then, softly, almost like a secret:

"James?"

"Jasmine?" I match her tone, low and drawn out.

She turns her head just slightly, enough for me to see the glint in her doe eyes when she says, "Tell me something real."

I let out a breathy laugh, trying to keep things light. "I thought we only do that when there's pizza and plumbers involved?"

She doesn't laugh this time. Just the smallest curve at her lips before it fades again.

"Please." She adds, her eyes soft, almost like this new vulnerability we share with each other means more than she'll say.

It hits like pulling 5Gs through a turn.

I think she needs this. Not the flirty jokes, not the chase, but this. Something honest. For me to meet her in a place she doesn't let other people see.

I draw in a slow breath, recentering myself. "I just found out I have a brother."

She turns toward me, her brows knitting together. Focused on me in a way that makes my chest clench.

"I thought you were an only child?"

"Yeah, me too" I exhale, feeling the burn I'd pushed down since I shoved the letter in my nightstand.

"I got a letter today. I stare up at the ceiling. Seems safer than looking at her. "Turns out my dad was married at some point. Had my brother eight years before my mom had me, never told anyone. I guess he passed away last month, and his son, my brother, found a bunch of letters from my mum. Things my dad kept hidden away. Now he wants to meet."

Jasmine shifts, propping herself up on her elbows to look at me. Closer now. Eyes locked on mine.

"Fuck," she breathes. "That's a lot."

I nod, holding her gaze longer than I probably should when she's close enough to pull in.

"Are you okay?"

"Yeah," I say quietly. "I've never met my dad. Never wanted to. So that part doesn't really get to me." I hesitate, thumb brushing the blanket underneath me. "It's more the brother bit. Knowing he's out there. Someone I've never met, never even had the chance to know... That part bothers me."

She tilts her head, softening her whole expression. "What's his name?"

"Aurelius Del Toro."

"Jesus." She breathes a quiet laugh. " That name sounds like a fucking warrior king."

"I know, right?" I laugh too. "What's worse is, the guy's apparently some big-time legendary rugby player."

She shakes her head, a smile living on her glossy lips. "Of course he is. I really hope he didn't lead with that."

I chuckle, settling a little more into the mattress. "No. That bit just came up when I googled him."

She watches me, eyes bouncing between mine. "So... are you going to meet him?"

"Maybe," I shrug. "He only lives two hours away. Which is kind of far, but reasonable enough."

"I'm sorry, what?" She snorts. "Two hours is nothing. Some people drive that to work every day in the states." She leans in a little, her tone shifting, more optimistic now. Which is great because I am not. "You should meet him. You've got a couple days until your next PT, and this is probably the last bit of quiet you'll get before everything starts back up again with your test and all that."

I turn, resting my weight on one hand to face her. "What if he's an asshole?"

She mirrors my position. "Then I'll personally kick his ass for you. Or shave off his beard. Because with a name like that? I know he has one."

We both laugh.

"He does, but I can't really judge him though," I wince at myself. "I am a mustached race car driver."

Jasmine laughs harder, scrunching her nose in the most adorable manner. "No, I guess you really can't. But it's more of a hot-boy mustache than, like, a full-blown caricature."

She leans in closer again. Closer than before. And for a second, it feels like time stops. She's right here. So close, I can feel the warmth of her breath. So close, one tilt forward and her lips would be on mine.

Without a thought I reach out and tuck a loose strand of hair behind her ear.

She stills. Her eyes holding mine, wide and warm, something unreadable in them, but she holds them there for just a moment, drops them to my lips and back up again.

Then she clears her throat and pulls back, laying down again, biting her lip like she didn't feel the same thing I did.

"Let's do it. I'll drive you," she says, breaking the silence like it didn't just try to swallow us whole.

"Yeah. Maybe," I mutter, standing, needing the space. "He left a phone number. Maybe I'll give him a call."

I offer my hand to help her up. She hesitates a second, then takes it. Her fingers hold mine just a little too long. Or maybe I'm just going mad and reading into everything more than I should.

"Just let me know. You know where to find me." She smiles, but it doesn't quite reach her eyes. Something seems off, like part of her I thought I had when she walked in here has already gone somewhere else.

"I do, Nurse Lozano. Goodnight," I force a grin to hide the crack in my chest.

She pauses in the doorway, one hand on the frame like she might turn back. Like she's holding something in her mouth and can't decide whether to spit it out or swallow it.

"James?" she says softly.

"Jasmine?" I reply, trying not to look too deeply in those eyes again.

She holds my gaze anyway. "Thank you. For telling me that."

Then she smiles, barely, and disappears into the hallway like a ghost.

I let out a breath that hurts more than it helps. Because part of me, stupid, hopeful, already-too-attached, has been waiting for a sign. Something to tell me she feels what I do. And maybe that soft little "thank you" isn't nothing. Maybe it's a crack in the door.

Jasmine

13

I AM OFFICIALLY THE BIGGEST CHICKENSHIT OF the century.

I had my mind made up. The other night was going to be the night I finally stopped hiding. The night I stopped running from what I want while pretending it was self-preservation.

Spoiler alert: I'm not preserving anything. I'm just exhausting myself.

I was there. In his room. In his bed. With James looking at me with those stupidly gorgeous eyes like he saw me—and the second he touched me, I bailed.

Classic.

And now it's been an awkward week of me running to my room or the gym the second he doesn't need me to be Nurse Lozano.

"Asshole," I curse myself, shoving yet another pair of pants I probably don't need into a bag that's supposed to be for an overnight stay at James' brother's house in a place called Bath.

Bath. Weird name. Gorgeous photos. Kind of a fairy

tale. It's always been my dream: hop around England, take in the sights: Castles, old pubs, rehabbed bed and breakfasts. Eat fries and laugh poshly as I call them chips. I thought this job would be my chance to do that. Instead, I'm apparently falling for my patient like a fucking idiot.

My phone buzzes across the nightstand.

Penelope Cameron.

"Hello, beautiful!" Penelope beams in that thick Texas twang of hers, way too bright for how early it is. Her big blue eyes glitter through the screen.

"Morning, Penn," I grumble, zipping my bag.

"Ew, what's with the attitude? I was calling with good news, but maybe I'll wait until Jasmine Lozano re-enters the building."

I roll my eyes. "Sorry. I'm just... kicking my own ass a bit this morning."

"Mmmm" She pouts dramatically. "So that's code for you're still playin' games with that gorgeous man."

"I am not playing games, Penelope. I'm just trying not to get the last shred of a heart I have stomped the fuck out." I drop back onto the bed in sheer emotional exhaustion.

"Sugar, it sounds to me like you're the one doing the stompin'. You sound miserable." She arches a perfect eyebrow.

"I'm fine." I wave her off. "I'll pull it together. What's the news?"

Penelope sucks her teeth. "I'm lettin' this little mood of yours slide for now because I know you're talkin' more mess to yourself than anyone else ever could. On a lighter note..." She lights up. "Would you be interested in a collaboration with OneActive?"

I stand up straighter. "Wait, what? Of course I would. How?"

She leans in, lowering her voice. "They're the new sponsor for the Comets, and their rep mentioned looking for fitness influencers with a strong social presence. Naturally, Milos is the only player we've got with any real pull, but when I brought up your name, the rep knew exactly who you were. He wants to set up a meeting this week."

"Penn, that's amazing."

"I know, right? No more vitamin gummies for you, baby. This is the big leagues."

I exhale. "I'm heading out of town, though. Might be gone a few days."

"Even better," she grins. "Make 'em wait, babe. Makes you look in demand. Can I pass your info along?"

I should be excited. This is exactly the kind of opportunity I said I wanted. So why does it feel like I'm too wrapped up in James to even think straight?

Between his PT sessions, worrying about his test deadline, and trying not to fall for him completely, I've barely managed more than a single gummy vitamin ad since I got here. My mom would probably say I'm finally focusing on "real" work for once, but that thought just makes everything feel more complicated.

"Yeah. Please. And... thanks, Pretty Penny. Sorry for being an ass."

She waves it off. "Girl, it's gonna take more than a funky attitude to get rid of me. But can I give you a piece of advice?"

"Hit me."

She softens. "Closing yourself off doesn't stop you from getting your heart broken. You're doing a good enough job of that all on your own. All you're really doing is eliminating the possibility of receiving the love you actually deserve."

I let out a sigh. "I swear, you Cameron girls need your own damn talk show."

She smiles like she can see straight through me. "Toodles, babe."

The screen goes dark. I stare at my reflection in it: the crease between my brows that will call for Botox if I don't ease up, the pathetic frown on my face.

God, I hate those little Oprah bitches.

A soft knock pulls me from my thoughts.

"You ready?" James asks gently, looking effortlessly hot dressed down in a navy sweatsuit and his favorite baseball cap, the one with a little rip in the brim he swears gives it character.

He's been distant and withdrawn since the night I almost kissed him. Probably exhausted by my mixed signals. I would be.

"Yeah." I nod, grabbing my bag from the bed and following him. "Are you?"

He shrugs. No flirtation, no grin. That alone tells me he isn't.

"I packed road trip snacks," I offer, trying to lighten the weird quiet between us as we walk to the elevator.

He perks up, just a little. "Any of those crunchy, spicy chips?"

The elevator door slides open.

"I love that you never know the actual name of anything. Everything's just a description to you." I laugh as we step inside.

"You always know exactly what I mean though, Nurse Lozano."

I shoot him a look. I hate when he calls me that. It

always feels too pointed, too formal. Like when someone uses your full name because they're pissed.

"Ooh, I almost forgot," he says, digging into his bag. "You nearly left behind your gummy vitamin things. I tossed them in with my stuff."

I snort. "I don't take those. That was for an ad deal. Contract's up now."

He laughs as we step out on the ground floor. "Nice to know you're promoting products you believe in so strongly."

I swat his arm. "Hey, everybody's gotta start somewhere. And I'll have you know I'm taking a meeting with OneActive next week."

I toss my hair over my shoulder like it's already a done deal, following him out the front door.

He stops dead in his tracks.

"Jasmine, that's a huge deal. They're the main sponsor for Fargo's racing team."

I shake my head. "I mean, maybe. It probably won't turn into anything, but it makes me feel less crazy for putting so much into my platform."

His eyes pin mine.

"It will turn into something. That's not even a question. But you need to figure out what you want going into that meeting. Don't undersell yourself. You're worth way more than they're gonna offer you at first. Fight for that."

I blink at him. "Okay, wow. You've been hanging out with Alana too much. You're starting to sound just like her."

He laughs, shaking his head as he veers toward the back of the building. "Good. You need more people around you who actually value you."

Goddamn.

I don't say anything, but I felt his words settle deep in my chest. Like a truth that'd been waiting to be said for years.

He clicks a button in his pocket, and a garage door opens to reveal two cars: a cherry-red Ferrari, sleek enough to flirt, and an army green vintage Defender truck that looks like it eats Ferraris for breakfast.

Of course. This is where he lets the money show. Not in watches or suits or whatever else rich men flex with, but here. In engines and horsepower and machines that make him feel something. It's the only place I've ever seen him indulge without apology.

James circles to the back of the Defender and tosses his bag in.

I hold out my hand. "Keys."

"Yeah, okay." He raises a brow, laughing under his breath. " I can drive, Jasmine."

"You're not cleared to drive for another week, James. Cough 'em up."

He narrows his eyes on me, a slow grin tugging at his mouth. "Can you even drive stick?"

"You should know the answer to that," I step closer, dropping my voice. "Unless you've forgotten."

His mouth opens, probably for a comeback, but I'm faster. I toss my bag into the back and snatch the keys right out of his hand while he's still stuck in neutral.

His boyish laugh follows as he steps right up behind me, his voice gravelly and way too pleased with himself.

"Other side, Jasmine. Unless you're standing over here to jog my memory."

I turn, slow and smug, and tap him on the cheek. "There he is. For a minute, I thought I lost you."

He shakes his head, still grinning as he climbs into the passenger seat.

God, I want to lean into this so bad. It could be so easy. We never stop laughing when we're together...until I kill the mood with my bullshit.

Nope. Not today. I'm going to actually try. Actually take my friend's advice and lean in... at least a little.

James adjusts his seat with a grunt, fiddling with the lumbar support, muttering something about "not trusting anyone with this spine".

I crank the engine with one dramatic flourish. "You good, Grandpa? Want me to grab you a neck pillow?"

"Just get us there alive, please," he says, buckling in. "And don't scratch my girl."

I tap the wheel and pull off. "She's in safe hands."

He glances at me, then at the car. "Not sure who you mean by that, but I'll take it as a reassurance."

My stomach flips.

There it is. The flirt I've been dodging all week. And for once, I don't hate myself for wanting it. I should fire back. Take Penelope's advice and say something equally flirty like I want to. B

ut my throat goes tight and all I can manage is pretending I don't feel that comment everywhere.

I connect my phone to Bluetooth and scroll through playlists.

James groans. "Don't tell me we're starting the morning with one of your emotional damage compilations."

"Not this time." I keep scrolling, trying to pretend I'm not overthinking every option.

Everything feels too flirty, too aggressive, too obvious. I sigh and tap shuffle.

The smooth, melancholy voice of Tyler, the Creator filled the car.

Are we still friends? Can we be friends?

James choked on a laugh.

"Seriously?"

"What?" I keep my eyes on the road and pretend I don't notice the irony.

"This is your vibe right now? Mournful friendship angst?" he teases. "Should I be worried?"

"I didn't pick it on purpose." My fingers itch to skip it.

"Sure you didn't. You just subconsciously felt the need to emotionally destroy us before we even hit the highway."

I roll my eyes. "You're so dramatic."

"You picked a song that literally asks if we're still friends. That's not subtle, Jasmine." He says through a laugh.

"No, *shuffle* picked the song. I'm ignoring you now." I tuck my smile under my teeth.

"You can't. We're in a car. Together. Trapped."

"Then feel free to jump out anytime."

He laughs, and despite the awkward song, I smile. James has that kind of laugh that can sneak under your skin and soften everything in its path.

The song plays on. And neither of us say anything for a while after that.

The Defender rolls over the open road, bumping beneath us as trees blur past. James' hand rests loosely on the armrest, his fingers tap gently to the rhythm like he doesn't whatever weight was on him before we left was ignorable for now. My eyes are on the road, but I can feel him sneaking glances at me. Quiet ones, like he's trying not to look like he's staring.

I hit a dip in the road a little too fast, and the truck jolts.

"Jesus," he laughs, steadying himself.

His hand instinctively reaches out, bracing against the only thing within reach.

My thigh.

He freezes the second he realizes. His palm is warm and wide, it's truly unfair how good it feels.

Slowly, he starts to pull away, cautious, hesitant, but I move first. Without thinking, without overanalyzing for once, I reach down and cover his hand with mine, gently pressing it there.

Just holding on.

James stills completely. I feel him look at me, see the question in his gaze.

Carefully, slowly, he turns his palm up beneath my hand, threading his fingers lightly through mine, locking us together.

His voice comes quieter, warm and teasing but underscored with something deeper.

"So, are we still friends?"

My chest tightens. I breathe out carefully, eyes still fixed ahead. "Maybe something like that."

He hums softly, thumb brushing gently over my knuckles. "I think I like this kind of friendship."

I tighten my fingers around his just slightly, letting myself lean in, enough for him to notice.

"Me too," I mutter. "Don't let it go to your head, though."

"Too late, Jazz." He chuckles under his breath, settling deeper into his seat without releasing my hand.

The song fades out, leaving us in the quiet of the road and the warmth of each other's touch.

Don't say goodbye...

James

I DON'T KNOW WHAT I EXPECTED FROM AURELIUS Del Toro, but a literal cottage in the countryside with a garden and steam rising from the kitchen window sure as hell wasn't it.

The truck rumbles over gravel as we pull down a narrow lane. Ahead of us sits a weathered brick cottage, tucked behind a crooked fence and flanked by a garden that looks half-forgotten and somehow perfect. Endless hibernating rose bushes, overgrown trellises, a small glass hot house, and raised garden beds made of logs.

It's the kind of place that doesn't feel temporary but kept. Steady in a way that settles my anxiety about meeting the man inside into something closer to stillness.

Jasmine shifts beside me, throwing the truck into park.

"You ready?" she asks softly, her big brown eyes holding mine like she wants to take some of the pressure I'm feeling onto herself.

The doubt I've carried over the last week of her avoiding me still sits in the back of my mind. But this is louder. Her looking at me like I matter. Like she genuinely wants to help carry whatever I'm feeling. Maybe I don't need to figure out which version is real right now. Maybe I can just let this one be enough.

I nod and follow her out of the lorry, every step toward the front door making this feel more nerve wrecking.

Jasmine lifts her hand to knock, but the door opens before she can make contact.

He doesn't swing it wide. No grand gesture. Just unlatches it and stands there like he knew the exact second we'd arrive.

Aurelius Del Toro.

Taller than I expected. Easily a few inches taller than me, but broader. Covered in tattoos and built like he'd been chiseled out of something heavier than stone. His shoulders fill the doorframe, his posture easy but with that athletic always ready form. Like he knows how to hit and how to hold back. Makes sense with the whole rugby bit.

He's wearing a simple black long sleeve t-shirt and jeans that look like they'll stay standing when he takes them off. His hair's shaggy and dark brown like mine, pushed back like he hasn't bothered with it, still damp near the ends. Like he rinsed off in a sink or walked through the rain without flinching.

But most impressive of all is his beard. Full, unapologetic, and intimidating in a way that shouldn't look nice and yet somehow does.

He doesn't speak right away. Just looks between the two of us, eyes landing on me like he's checking for resemblance. Not in the face, but in the posture, I think.

I stand a little straighter. Can't help it. The man looks like he wrestles bears for cardio, and even though my spine is barely held together by prayers and spite, something in me needs him to see I'm Del Toro enough.

To see I can chop wood too. Or split boulders with my hands. Eat nails. Hell, whatever he does that makes him look like Zeus left Olympus to play Mother Goose.

"You're early," he grunts, finally. The voice matches everything else about him. Rough. Deep. Like he'd been etched from granite and learned to talk anyway.

I should respond. Introduce myself like a normal person. But I can't get any words out. What am I supposed to say? Hi, I'm the brother you didn't know existed until a month ago?

Before I can spiral further, Jasmine steps forward with that nurse-on-duty smile that makes her seem composed even when I know she isn't.

"Hi. Jasmine Lozano," she says brightly, offering her hand. "I'm James' nurse. Just here to make sure he doesn't trip and sue someone."

I glare at her.

Really?

"Good" Aurelius nods once. "He looks like the dramatic type."

I blink. Then laugh, actually laugh, because something about the way he said that was deadpan in a way I understand completely.

Okay, we have the same sense of humor. That has to count for something.

He steps aside, gesturing us in with a tilt of his head.

"Soup's ready."

Not hello. Not come in. Just *Soup's ready*. Like this is the most normal thing. And somehow... I think I need that.

The inside of the house is just as Beatrix Potter as the outside. In no way does it look like this would be this guy's house. But watching him move through the place, I get it.

This is his refuge. The place where he can drop everything and just be whoever he is.

Jasmine makes me feel like that. That night with the snacks and video games, when she made my living room into a little fortress where I didn't have to be anything but myself. No performance. No pressure. Just... there. I could live forever in that feeling.

The table is already set, steam rising from a pot on the stove. Like he's been waiting. Like he gives a shit, though his grunting tells me he won't say that out loud.

"You allergic to vegetables?" he asks, ladling thick stew into deep ceramic bowls. His tone is gruff, eyes darting between me and Jasmine.

"Nope," Jasmine answers. "And before you ask if I'm gluten-free or vegan, I love meat and bread, and anything that makes a meal worth eating."

He lets out a masculine chuckle. More thunder than laughter.

"Me and you are gonna get along just fine," he rumbles.

"I think we are too, Aurelio," she says easily, accepting a bowl and sliding it toward me.

Wait. Did she just give him a nickname? And he didn't flinch. He just softened like she'd been calling him that his whole life.

What the actual fuck? I've been terrified about this moment for days, and she just walks in and makes it look easy.

They grab bowls of their own and sit at a little wooden table with mismatched chairs nestled by the back door. I sit across from Aurelius, next to Jasmine. None of us talk for a few minutes, just the sound of spoons clinking and hot stew being blown cool.

And damn I think this is the best stew I've had in my life.

"Did you make this?" I ask eventually, too impressed to keep quiet.

"Yep." He gives a curt nod, slurping a bite. "And I'll do you one better. I hunted the bison and grew the veg in my garden this summer."

I squint at him.

"The bison?"

He smirks. "Nah, just takin the piss. It's from the market. But the veg is legit. Got a five-foot courgette out in the hothouse right now."

"No fucking way." I narrow my eyes at him just in case he's bullshitting again.

"Absolutely, mate. Wanna come see it?"

"Yeah," I'm already rising. "Absolutely I do."

He's out the door before I can grab my bowl.

"You coming?" I ask Jasmine.

She smiles faintly, tucking her hair behind her ear. "You go. I need to take a call anyway."

Her fingers brush over mine. Then barely a squeeze, but it lingers. Long enough to say, *I see you. I want this for you.* Long enough to make me wish we were alone again.

But she lets me go.

And I let her—even though I really don't want to.

"This thing is fuckin' massive," I circle the vegetable that's roughly the size of Jasmine.

Aurelius chuckles. That thunder-god sound I'm too quickly growing fond of.

"It's not worth shit for eating," he says, scooping another spoonful of stew into his mouth as he leans on the hothouse doorway. "But it'll win at the town harvest fair."

The entire yard is packed. Wild bushes, neat rows of vegetables. Ornate pots line the walkway with trees nearly ready to be pulled in before the frost comes. A fact I only know because my mom keeps her fruit trees the same way.

"This place is incredible." I step back out into the yard. "Did you do all this yourself?"

"Nah." He pauses. "My grandmother. I guess she's yours too. Odessa Del Toro. Our dad's mom. She raised me here."

His eyes drift toward the far hedgerow, exhaling roughly.

"She passed a few years back. I let the place sit too long after that. Lost some good rose bushes because of it."

He gives a thoughtful grunt. "Moved back in after my divorce. Been trying to bring it back to life ever since. It's not what she had it at, but... close enough."

He rolls his shoulders like the memory settled uncomfortably there.

Odessa Del Toro. Just hearing her name, hearing him say it like it ties us together...makes me feel less like a stray, more like someone who might belong.

"You have kids?" I venture, a little tentative.

"Nah. Would love one." His mouth curves, not with amusement. "But my ex was a pain in the ass. Wasn't into the whole family thing. Took off with the gaffer from my old club. Had a few with him."

I let out a pained chuckle. "Sounds like a Del Toro curse then."

His gaze flicks to mine, a faint smirk in it.

"The nurse?" he nods toward the house.

"Nah," I shake my head. "My ex cheated on me with the twat who caused my wreck."

He scratches at his beard, letting out a dry laugh. "Yup. That'll do it."

It hits me then. How different our lives are, but how similar the bruises feel. Same ache, different shape. And somehow, that makes me feel closer to him than I'd expected.

I finish my stew while the air hangs quiet and peaceful between us, like a welcome into his world in its own right.

Then Aurelius claps a heavy hand on my shoulder, firm and warm.

"You know, I almost didn't send that letter, lad. Thought you might be a proper prick." He takes a heavy breath. "But I'm glad I did."

I slap a hand to his back in return. Something unspoken clicks into place between us.

"I'm glad you did too, Ari."

I try for my own rendition of a nickname for him.

He snorts but doesn't protest the name. "You staying the weekend then?"

I shrug. "I was thinking just the night."

He grunts. "Right. That's what I told myself too."

We both laugh, the kind that eases the awkwardness of it all a bit more.

"Come on," he says, already turning toward the house. "Let's grab that pretty friend of yours. I'll show you where you're sleeping."

He gives my shoulder one last firm squeeze before heading for the door. And for some reason I can't explain it feels like we'd known each other years rather than moments.

Jasmine

"WELL, AT LEAST IT'S NOT ONE BED. THOUGH THAT would be pretty on brand for our kind of luck." I laugh nervously, eyeing the questionable bunk beds in James' brother's annex, a converted garage barely the size of a walk-in closet.

"I take it you want to be on top?" James grins wickedly

I cut my eyes at him. "I don't think your hip would allow much else, Grandpa."

While I toss my bag onto the small sofa tucked beneath the window, James leans against a wooden post that looks like it's holding the whole ceiling together by mere suggestion.

"Ari invited us to the pub with him," he says. "You up to it?"

"You should go. Just you and him. I'll hang back; maybe finally read the book I've been pretending to carry around for three weeks."

His brow furrows. "Nah. I'm not letting you retreat back to ignoring me."

"I'm not ignoring you," I scoff. "I'm giving you space to connect with your brother, James."

He flashes me that cocky knowing smile.

"I can do that with you there, Jasmine. He should probably get to know you too, yeah?"

I thin my eyes, knowing exactly where he's going with this.

"Let me guess. Because of the wedding?" I say sarcastically.

He laughs, then slides an arm around my shoulders, warm and easy, like touch is just our thing now.

Maybe it's becoming our thing. The hand holding in the truck. The literal fight I had to put up against myself not to reach for him again, to give him the space he needs to process this entire situation.

"I was going to say because you're his guest," he whispers into my ear, "but I'll take that too."

"Travieso," I shake my head as he pulls me out the door.

THE EARLY EVENING air carries a faint chill, just enough to raise goosebumps along my arm That in-between kind of cold, not quite night, not quite day, swathed in a haze of soft blue light. A low fogs settled along the cobblestones, turning the street into something half-forgotten and magical, under the slow bloom of the street lamps.

James and I trail behind the behemoth he calls his brother, our steps quieter, slower. Like we're walking through the pauses between moments.

James' gait is steady, less pained. He's made leaps and bounds in his recovery, which is almost bittersweet. I love to see him better, but every steady step reminds me how much closer I am to going back home.

"Cold?" He asks, sliding his arm around me before I can answer. His palm moves in slow circles over my shoulder, rubbing warmth into the space just beneath my skin.

I lean in, wrapping my arm around his waist.

For warmth. Obviously. Nothing more.

He dips his head a little, breath brushing against the shell of my ear. "Afraid you'll lose your footing?"

I nod. "Exactly. Glad you're so sturdy these days."

The truth is, ever since his hand found mine in that ridiculously big truck earlier, each touch has made the next one feel inevitable. Like I'm sliding down a hill I can't climb back up.

But is this the right moment to be free falling?

"This is it," Aurelius announces, nodding toward an unassuming stone building with a weathered wooden sign swinging above the door. A blackbird with a monocle carved into the wood.

The Blackbird Pub.

James and I step in first, the warm uproar of voices, clinking glasses, and noisy heat washing over us. A few heads turn. Then a few more.

And then:

"Aye! Del Toro!" someone bellows.

For a moment, I think they mean Aurelius. But then the cheers grow louder, more pointed, and the clapping starts on James' back, his shoulders, anywhere people can reach.

"Drinks on the house for our champion!" the bartender roars, grinning as he rings a brass bell mounted to the wall.

I blink as people surge toward James, cheering and calling his name.

"Aurelius, you didn't say you knew our Champ!" Someone shouts from across the bar.

Aurelius just laughs, slinging a thick arm around James and pulling him in like he's always been there.

"Turns out the little shit's my brother."

James smiles so wide it looks like it catches him off guard. He tugs his hat lower as if to hide the way he lit up at the words, but it doesn't work.

Not even a little.

My heart warms at the sight of him like this. Bright up from the inside out. Happiness looks good on James. Better than the quiet stress he's been carrying lately.

Ever since that first meeting with his team principle, it's lived in the lines around his eyes, in the way his jaw stays locked like he's bracing for something.

I don't know shit about Formula One. Honestly, I used to think it was just a bunch of rich adrenaline junkies showing off in circles. But one late night and a quick Google search of James Del Toro shut me up real quick.

Four-time Drivers' Champion. Undefeated through ten straight races this season. The kind of prodigy headlines are made of. Until Belgium. Until the wreck that could've killed him.

That might still end his career.

So, yeah. Seeing him here tonight, smiling like nothing's broken, like nothing's chasing him, that feels like a big fucking win. Maybe not the one he's after, but still the kind that matters.

"Here you are, dear." The bartender slides a bird-shaped glass across the counter, frothy and filled to the brim.

"Thank you," I wrap both hands around it.

The old man smiles bright, nodding toward James across the room. "You're a much prettier match than that

Francesca girl they always showed him with. Never looked too happy, that one."

I bat my eyes like there's something in them and force a tight-lipped smile like I wasn't just punched in the stomach with a name I'd purposely avoided Googling.

Thanks for that, sir. Really. Nothing says cheers to the night like dragging ghosts to the party.

I don't want to know about her. Swore I couldn't care less. If it ended, it ended. People break up every day. But still, some nosy, insecure corner of me curled around the curiosity like it was a bruise worth pressing.

Across the pub, James and Aurelius are still surrounded. Pats on the back, clinking glasses, raucous laughter bouncing off the walls.

They look like brothers. Really look like it, not just in their dark features. Both of them carry the same easy confidence, the same way of holding themselves in a room.

Watching them together, side by side like they've known each other for years instead of hours, make something warm take residence in my heart. This was what he needed. I'm not going to interrupt that.

James catches my eye. I lift my beer and mouth *"I'm going to sit"*, gesturing toward the back. He holds my gaze before Aurelius tugs his shoulder in laughter saying something that ropes him back in the conversation. And I saunter over to a little table nestled in the corner, shadowed by tall bookshelves and a crackling fireplace.

I tuck myself into a chair pressed against the far wall. Then, feeling safely hidden by the shelves behind me, I pull my phone out. One leg curled up, my cheek finding the warmth of my knee through the cold denim of my jeans as I type the name I hadn't dared search until now.

Francesca "Frenchie" Vanderbilt.

A banner greets me: **Follows you.**

Of course she does.

I glance up, instinctively, as if someone might catch me mid-snoop even though James is still on the other side of the pub and thoroughly distracted.

"Interesting," I mutter, clicking into her profile.

I'm a girl's girl. Always have been. I hate when women are pitted against each other like prizes. But that doesn't mean I'm immune to the sting.

And this woman is really fucking hot.

Ethereal in that undone, Kate Moss kind of way. Smoky eyes, high cheekbones. Dressed in vintage leather jackets and posed with champagne on rooftops. A different brand entirely. I'm more Paola Turbay on her loudest day. Fire and hips and several inches shorter. The polar opposite of this blue-blooded girl, different enough to make me question what James sees in me if this is his type.

And I hate that feeling.

Scrolling deeper, I see pictures of her in Delancey's paddock with another driver. Kieran, I think is the guy's name. Hard to tell with the helmet on and my very limited knowledge of this whole world she looks like she was born for.

Figures she's with another driver. Apparently, her type is fast cars and faster men.

There's a story there. Has to be. There are like twenty F1 drivers, there must be drama when they date each other's exes.

"You wanna play darts, or are you glued to that thing?"

James' voice catches me off guard, way too close.

I click the screen off like I've been caught stealing and tuck it into my back pocket.

He's right in front of me with that maddening dimpled

grin and his hat turned backward like he needs to garnish how hot he is.

"Excuse me, Champ. I was just waiting for your fan club to calm down."

I take a long sip of the beer I've forgotten, making a face. Lukewarm and flat. Fitting.

"I don't even know how to play darts," I add, setting my beer back down.

"I'll teach you," he says simply. Like it isn't up for discussion.

Before I can protest, he grabs my hand and tugs me toward the boards in the other corner of the room.

"James," I complain, half-laughing, half-serious. "Shouldn't you be doing this with Aurelio, not me?"

He plucks a dart from the board and turns toward me, full of that calm, unbothered confidence.

"I am doing exactly what I should be doing."

He leans in, voice dropping. "Besides, he's knee-deep in some worm compost monologue I'd rather not get dragged into."

James presses a dart into my hand, then circles behind me. Lining his tall, taught body up with mine and guiding my arm into place. His hand slides around my waist, settling just beneath the hem of my crop top, fingers spreading wide against my bare skin.

Breathing quickly becomes a foreign concept.

His other hand covers mine, adjusting my grip as if this was nothing but darts. But I'm about two seconds from forgetting my own name. My pulse thunders in my ears, every inch of my body suddenly aware of him.

Of the ache between my thighs with the memory of what he feels like against me.

I close my eyes, just trying to center myself, but all I can smell is him. That cologne he wears every time we go out somewhere. It's an act of war on my self-control at this point.

"You have to open your eyes, Jasmine," he laughs softly in my ear.

"Shut up, James." I mumble, peeking through one eye. "I'm finding my concentration."

He peers down, giving me that *'I know you're lying'* look.

"Right then. Just focus on where you want the dart to land, pull back, and follow through with your fingertip."

His voice drops, every word skimming my skin.

"Got it." I shake my head, trying to ignore how close his breath is against my neck. "Now stop trying to feel me up and let me throw."

I bump my hips into him, and he doesn't miss a beat. His hand meets my ass with a quick, unfair tap before stepping back and muttering "Yes ma'am."

Heat crawls up my neck, bringing with it another memory of him I've tried to suppress for over a year now. I clear my throat and channel my frustration into my throw.

The dart lands clean on the black ring just outside the center.

"See?" I turn, grinning. "I'm a natural."

He laughs, brown eyes gleaming. "Alright. Shall we wager something then?"

I cross my arms. "Name the stakes, Champ."

"You win," he steps closer, "I'll finally have a beer with you."

I arch a brow, pulse kicking up. "And if you win?"

That perfect smile curves slow. "Then you have to dance with me."

My stomach drops. God, he's good at this.

"You're assuming I'll say no without a bet?"

He shrugs, eyes flicking to my mouth and back up again. "I'm hoping you'll surprise me."

I don't answer. Just turn back to the board with a cocky grin.

"I'm full of surprises, Champ."

The dart leaves my hand and strikes the twenty.

He steps up beside me, not even looking at the board. "So am I."

Then, without breaking eye contact, he hits a fucking bullseye.

We didn't stop after one round. Or two. Or six. He kept winning, and I kept letting him until somehow we were both flushed and a little buzzed, arguing over whether his last shot was a double twenty or just dumb luck.

I don't remember when we started to dance. Only that the music was slow, and he pulled me close without asking. And I didn't want to pull away.

The pub thinned. The air turned golden and warm. Somewhere between laughter and another pint we forgot to keep track of time.

It was the kind of night that didn't need music to feel like a slow song.

Jasmine 16

"WE STAYED WAY TOO LONG," I MUTTER AS WE stumble out onto the rain-slick cobblestones, the cold biting at my ankles. Aurelius bowed out an hour ago, smart enough to know when to quit.

James and I? Not so much.

"I'm definitely going to regret that third pint," I add.

James chuckled beside me, his shoulder brushing mine with every step.

"You regret nothing. You danced. You hit a bullseye. You introduced my brother to a pickle back he'll probably ferment cucumbers for by next weekend."

"The bartender had a real time learning that one." I snort. "But you know what? I'll never get over the fact that Aurelio clips rose bushes and talks to animals."

"Like a tattooed Snow White," James says. "You don't suppose that makes us the dwarves he shoved into the annex?"

"Oh god," I gasp dramatically. "The other five are probably fertilizing his human size vegetables."

We both break into laughter, the breathless, clutch-your-stomach laughter that makes it hard to walk straight. Or maybe that's the alcohol.

Hard to tell.

The air is crisp; the cobblestones are slick with mist that makes my heels feel like ice-skates. Just enough of a hazard to justify the way I lean into James' side, without have to admit to the many other ways I want touch.

"God, I'm freezing. And before you suggest it, no." I point a finger at James. "I'm not gonna wear one of your stupid racing hoodies to bed again."

"You say that like it's not your favorite piece of clothing." James grins, slinging his arm over my shoulders and pulling me closer.

"Only because it smells like expensive soap and poor decision-making."

"You're welcome." He laughs. "You know, you're always freezing. If I recall correctly, that was the same excuse you used to cuddle up to me on a night like this before. I very vividly remember you tucking those icy feet of yours under my legs while you snored."

I gasp exaggeratedly. "I do not snore."

His grin is insufferable. "Like a motorboat."

Rolling my eyes, I loop my arms around his back without thinking—whether it's the beer or the night or just him, I don't care anymore. It feels good. He feels good.

The lights from Aurelius' cottage spill a yellow glow across the gravel driveway as we wander past it, the windows still fogged with warmth and whatever soup he'd put on to simmer before we left. The guy really loves soup.

"You think he's still up?" I say in a tipsy hush like we're teenagers sneaking in.

"Yeah," James whispers back, tugging me in a little closer. "Probably shitting out all that pickle juice."

We both crack up again just as we pass through the garden gate. The path to the annex twinkles with string lights, glowing like something out of a fairytale— if fairytales had tiny annexes and bison stew and giant men named Aurelius who kept compost journals.

"How's your hip?" I ask, suddenly aware of how much I've leaned on him the entire walk back. How natural it had felt. How much I didn't want to stop. How I hoped I didn't cause him pain by forgetting the entire reason I'm here.

He stops walking, turning to face me, but doesn't let me go. Just shifts closer, hands settling at my hips with a kind of focus that makes my heart trip over itself.

"Depends who's asking," he says, voice low, eyes softening. That flicker of intensity returning. "Are you Jasmine," he adds, "or Nurse Lozano right now?"

I rest a hand against his chest, right over the slow thud of his heart.

"Nurse Lozano clocked out the second she agreed to go to a bar with you, James." I surprise myself with my own honesty and make a mental note that I need to stop drinking around this guy.

He nods like he'd been waiting to hear that. Then reaches up with one hand, gently sweeping my bangs from my eyes, then tucks another behind my ear.

My breath picks up. His fingers linger at the nape of my neck, thumb brushing the edge of my cheekbone, trailing slowly down the line of my jaw until he tilts my chin up.

I can't breathe. But I don't think I want to.

Those dark eyes stay on mine as he dips forward. Slow and patient, giving me every possible out. Every second to pull away.

I don't.

I rise to meet him. Thread my fingers through his thick hair. Pull him into me and press my lips to his.

He deepens it instantly, his mouth claiming mine like a man out of air. I breathe him in too, every nerve lit up. His tongue sliding over mine while his other hand moves from my hip to cradle my face, like he can't decide where he wants to touch me more. My hips shift into his as if they're drawn by gravity, every inch of me already knowing the shape of him.

And I'm not thinking anymore.

I'm burning for him.

With an urgency we both move toward the annex without breaking apart. We barely make it to the door before my back hits it with a rattling thud, his body pressing into mine, mouth trailing from my lips to my jaw, then lower. Dragging heat down the line of my throat.

"Fuck—" I gasp, fumbling blindly for the door handle as he sucks gently at the place just beneath my ear, like he wants to write his name on it.

My fingers scrape against wood. James groans against me, his hands slide around my hips, tightly gripping my entire ass. His mouth hovers just above mine, breath shallow.

A soft moan escapes me.

"We're not even inside—don't start that yet," he growls, voice frayed. "You gotta earn that, Jas."

"You have no idea how many ways I'm already planning to do exactly that," I pant.

A pleased grin splits his lips, then he kisses me again. Rougher this time, desperate, like he can't help himself.

Then—

"Jamsey boy, that you mate?" Ari's voice rings out from

across the yard. Too far, or maybe too drunk, to see what he's just interrupted.

"Bastard," James groans into my mouth, forehead dropping to mine with a breathless laugh. His chest rises against mine, still caught between tension and want. He braces one hand on the doorframe, the other running through his already-mussed hair.

"Yeah, was just heading to bed," he calls back, squinting like that might earn us privacy.

"Come in for a second!" Ari shouts. "Got something to show you. Bring Jazz!"

James lets out a slow exhale. Dropping his head as if he's physically reeling himself back in. A conflicted smirk pulls at the corner of his mouth, but his eyes stay locked on mine. Still dark, still intoxicated from that kiss.

"You should go," I whisper, pressing a hand to his chest. Steadying both of us. "He sounds excited."

He doesn't move right away; just looks at me with the same yearning I'm feeling. This can wait. But this new relationship with his brother that will last long after I'm gone is more important.

So, I yell back to Aurelius, "He's coming, but I'm going to bed, Aurelio."

James stares at me, those gorgeous eyes studying mine.

"This isn't done," he says quietly, thumb brushing my bottom lip like a promise. "I'll be back."

I nod once. "I seem to recall you being a man of your word."

His laugh lights up his whole face before he kisses me again. Just once. Soft. Tender. But I still feel it in the backs of my knees.

"Don't go to sleep," he whispers into my ear, then disappears down the path, leaving me with lips still tingling and the quiet realization I'm not getting a minute's sleep tonight.

THIS HAS TO BE IT. What all the books and movies try to capture. What my best friend felt that made forever sound like the easy part. What made Sylvia Plath write like love could both save you and swallow you whole.

This feeling makes everyone before James feel like a fucking joke. Like filler scenes. Like I'd been rehearsing lines for a role I was never meant to play until now. This might finally, fucking finally be it for me.

I replay the kiss again and again as I peel off my jeans with their grass-dampened cuffs and kick off my heels. It loops in my head like a highlight reel. His mouth, his hands, the way he kissed me like he'd been waiting forever for me.

Why the hell did I torture myself for so long? I could almost feel how long he'd been holding back, waiting for me to just let go. And yeah, maybe the beers blurred the edges a bit, but everything about that kiss screamed otherwise.

I pull one of his hoodies over my head, the one I've grown way too fond of in the evenings and just swore to him I wouldn't wear again. The fabric is warm from the heater, comforting like it holds the shape of his body. It smells like him too, I'd almost think he sprayed it with that damn cologne so it does.

The little annex creaks with the wind as it brushes past the windows, rattling the panes just enough to remind me I'm still here. Still wrapped in this strange little in-between of a night that hasn't quite ended yet.

I drop down onto the small sofa, pulling my legs beneath me as I scroll through my texts. My fingers itch to call Alana or Penn, but they'd probably murder me if I rang them at this hour.

Instead, I thumb through my camera roll, smiling like an idiot at the dozen selfies I took with James at the bar. Most were blurry or mid-laugh. A few had that classic red-light warmth from the fireplace we'd been sitting by. But my favorite, the one I keep circling back to, is the one Aurelius snapped.

Me and James, tucked into that little corner table. I'm mid-laugh, head thrown back, absolutely cackling because James ruined a perfectly good picture by sticking his finger in my nose at the last second.

Would it be too bold to post it?

No. Fuck that.

I've never seen myself look this happy. Not once.

Not even when I was with Milos. And yeah, he looked good on paper. Said the right things, made long-term plans, kissed my father's ass at dinner. But none of that mattered, not when he turned around and shattered it all.

Love doesn't cheat. Love doesn't lie straight to your face, then act like you were the one who couldn't handle commitment. That wasn't love. That was a performance. Compatibility dressed up in a tux and smiling for photos.

This—whatever this is—feels like the thing that burns all the fake almosts down.

It's terrifying how much I feel. How much I want to stay. How, for the first time since walking through James' door, I'm not scanning for the emergency exit.

I should be scared out of my fucking mind. But I'm not. I'm here. Barefoot. Wearing his hoodie. Laughing at a photo where he's picking my nose like a menace, and I look happier than I've ever looked in my life. Drunk on whatever this is and waiting for him to come back.

So, fuck it. Why not post it?

The moment I open my socials, Francesca's profile stares back at me like it's been lying in wait. I'd totally forgotten I'd been snooping, like any of it fucking matters. I go to swipe away, shut it down before I can give it power.

But something catches my eye before I can look away.

I wasn't searching for it. I wasn't trying to ruin the best night I've had in... maybe ever.

But there it is. Just posted less than an hour ago.

A photo.

Post race. Late sunlight. Francesca in a white dress and red lipstick, laughing into James' neck. His nose is nuzzled in her hair, smiling. His hands on her waist in that possessive, intimate way that felt all too familiar. It doesn't look posed. Just captured. Like someone had stumbled onto something private and beautiful and hit save. The kind of moment you don't fake.

Exactly like the photo of us in the pub.

And maybe that's what makes it worse. Because mine feels like something brand new. Like a secret I'm not ready to say out loud yet. And hers looks like something that had already been loved, lived in, maybe even mourned.

Maybe not over.

Caption: *"Some things are worth fighting for. Some people are worth coming back to."*

It doesn't say they're still together. But it says enough to make me feel like I might just be a rebound. I hate how fast my heart drops. As if it just figured out it was on borrowed time.

And I hate, *hate*, that their picture looks like the mirror version of ours, that it makes us look like the copy.

My chest pulls tight. The afterglow of the night fizzles into something cold that burrows a pit in my stomach. I try to tell myself it was just a memory. That people in these kinds of circles post things all the time for attention. It's no use. I went from glowing to gutted in record time, my brain starting to rewrite everything.

What if I was just a soft place to land? A placeholder until whatever they had worked itself out?

I click out of the app and climb into bed before I can answer that.

I don't know how long I laid there, just staring into the dark, willing sleep to take the edge off. But my thoughts wouldn't stop spinning. Not after that post. Not after that kiss.

And fuck, I was doing it again. Falling too hard and too fast. Wrong, again. Like I'd been with every guy before who made me feel like maybe this time would be different.

The door creaks open. Slow and careful. Light from the garden lights paints across the wall in front of me.

"Jasmine?" James whispers.

I don't answer. Just keep still. Letting the weight of the duvet and the ache in my chest do their job.

The air shifts as he moves through the room. One foot, then the other. The rustle of fabric. The floorboards soft beneath his weight. I can hear it in his breath, like doesn't want to shatter whatever sleep he thinks I might be clinging to.

I keep my back to him. Eyes screwed shut. Breathing even. Maybe I can fool both of us.

Then the lower bunk creaks beneath me. He's either sitting or lying down. I can't tell. But I feel him there. Close, but too far. The silence between us is loaded.

And I hold still like my life depends on it. It feels like it does. I want to blame the buzz, but I'm certain if I uttered a single word it'll come out teary and desperate. Two things I've never been and can't afford to be if I want to make it out of London in one piece. Or at least the appearance of one.

The room stays still, just the sound of his breath and the faint rustle of leaves outside, the wind pressing gently against the windows like it wants in.

Then, quietly, so quietly it feels like it isn't meant for me at all, James speaks.

"I don't know if you're asleep... or just ignoring me because you might be scared of this."

He pauses, and I can hear the shift in his breathing. The weight of the silence pressing down on him.

"Honestly... I am too."

He waits like he hopes I might say something.

"But I've never felt this way about anyone in my life. And I won't walk away from it. I'll wait forever for you if I have to."

My heart physically aches.

I don't move. Don't breathe. Because if I do, I won't stop. I'll crawl right into that bunk and tell him I feel it too. That I've been feeling it. That I've only felt it when I'm with him. But I can't trust that. Can't trust myself. Doesn't matter how different this felt. Doesn't matter that my heart is screaming "he's the one."

I know better. I know how hard James loves. I need to lead with logic for once in my life. She's been there before I ever showed up, written into the margins of his life like a name that never really fades.

And I'm the afterthought pretending not to look like one.

James

17

I BARELY SLEPT. NOT FROM LACK OF TRYING, because I really fucking tried, but because I spent the whole night fighting the urge to lift Jasmine from her bunk and pull her into mine.

Christ, the one time I actually want a cliché, I get bunk beds.

Aurelius could've waited 'til morning to show me Polaroids of every relative I've never met, but still, hanging with him like that? Pretty fucking cool. And after everything that happened with Jasmine last night, there's no way in hell she can go back to pretending we're nothing.

Now comes the awkward so-we-almost-hooked-up-but-my-brother-interrupted-so-what-are-we? conversation.

Sort of stings to know I'd already have the answer if she'd stayed up a minute longer. If she'd gotten that door open a second sooner.

My phone buzzes on the floor beside the bunk, pulling my attention from hope to pure fucking dread.

This is the reason I never managed my own social media or

turned on news notifications. But even with my do not disturb settings maxed out, the one I knew would be coming eventually leaked through. There, lit up in the smug little banner:

Kieran Denune Spotted at Red Energy HQ - Contract Talks Heating Up?

I stare at the headline until the screen goes dark. Then stare some more.

I try to convince myself that this is what the media does when a driver is in contracts. Every little crumb becomes a trade or someone losing their seat.

But the truth is I have no goddamn clue what's going to happen to my spot. Kieran's wanted to drive for Red Energy since his rookie season, and after that shit he pulled in Spa, I'm certain there's nothing he wouldn't do to make that happen.

I swipe the notification away and delete all my social apps from my phone without another thought. He wants my seat? He can fight me for it when I'm cleared.

I toss the phone onto the bed and rub a hand over my face, willing the tension out of my shoulders. I don't even need to look up to know Jasmine's bed is empty. After weeks of having her close, I've started to notice when she isn't. Like some part of me is always tracking her.

And the glow from Ari's kitchen window tells me exactly where she'll be. After pulling on sweats and the hoodie she'd slept in, still holding her warmth, I head out into the fog.

The early morning air is thick and quiet, all birdsong and dew-slick grass. I get why my brother loves this place. It feels like it has nothing to prove. I understand now what he meant yesterday. About coming for one night and never leaving.

It's not the cottage or the roses. It's this stillness. The way it lets you stop running without feeling like you're giving up. Part of me wants to stay. To let Kieran have it. To see what it feels like to just be somewhere without a clock ticking down.

"How do you stand to sleep that long?" Ari asks the second I open the kitchen door, he's already parked at the table in front of a skyscraper stack of pancakes.

"How do you stand not sleeping at all? We went to bed, what, two hours ago?" I groan, my voice coming out rough and half-asleep, which pretty much proves my point.

Closing the door behind me I shake my head at him, then turn, finding her. Fully dressed. Cooking like she'd already lived an entire day without me.

Her eyes meet mine for a second, dark and guarded, then flick away just as fast as she catches her finger on the edge of a hot cast iron skillet.

"Here," she says, handing me a plate. "I made yours with egg whites and extra protein. Thought you'd want to keep it light with your fitness test coming up."

I take the plate, but my eyes are locked on the way she kisses her burned finger. Holding it to her mouth as if she didn't want to make a big deal of it but like it hurts more than she wants to show.

"Let me help you." I set the plate down and round the counter.

"I'm fine," she mumbles, but her eyes don't leave mine.

A bin of peeled potatoes sits on the counter, likely for whatever stew Aurelius had on the menu for today. I grab one without asking and slice off a cool piece.

"Let me see." I'm already reaching for her hand.

She lets me take it.

The burn is small, pink and angry. I press the cool slice of potato gently against the reddened skin, holding her steady in my palm.

"What kind of witchcraft is that?" she laughs quietly with relief.

"My mom used to do it when I was a kid. I'd always sneak bites out of the pan before they were ready." I meet her eyes. "Still haven't learned my lesson."

She blinks slowly, smiling. "Thank you, Nurse."

I nod, but don't move. My fingers still wrapped around hers, the potato slice cooling between our palms. I don't want to let go.

But after a second, I do. Slowly.

I bend down and kiss the crown of her head, then force myself to walk away. Rejoining Ari at the table, still feeling the shape of her hand in mine.

"So you guys headin' back today then?" Ari mumbles over a mouthful of pancakes.

"Yeah." I nod, chewing through a bite of mine. "But I looked at your team schedule last night."

His brows pull together. "You what?"

I hold up a hand, swallow. "Seems like we might be in Italy the same weekend in April. You're in Treviso then, yeah?"

Jasmine sits in the chair beside me, nursing a mug of coffee.

"I think so," Ari replies, rubbing a hand over his jaw. "I just go where they tell me to."

"Well, I'm in Imola that week. Figured if our timing lines up, we trade games. You come to mine, I'll come to yours."

He nods. "Fuck yeah."

145

Jasmine smirks between us.

"So romantic," she mumbles into her cup, raising her brows.

"Fuck, yeah," I echo, taking another bite.

"April's kind of far off," Jasmine says. Already standing to grab Ari's empty plate—the man ate like he was afraid someone would take it. "Christmas is in like three weeks. Why don't you two get together then?"

"I've never really celebrated it. "Ari shrugs his wide shoulders, then leans back and pats his stomach like he has a beer gut despite being built like a tank. "But I could come down to London, if you want."

My eyes flick to Jasmine, then back to him.

"I hadn't either. Not until last year. My mate's wife does the whole thing. She's doing it again. Big dinner, tree, the works. You should come. Stay at my place. We'll all go together."

He pauses as though he might say no, but the fight isn't really there. Just a moment of hesitation before he gives in. "Yeah, fuck it. I'll come. Long as they don't mind."

Jasmine snorts a laugh, rinsing a plate. "Alana will probably explode with excitement. And I'm pretty sure you and her husband will be arguing over who grills steak better and syncing your phone calendars before New Year's."

"That's probably true." I lean back with an easy grin. "Maybe we don't go, then. I'll lose my best friend and my brother."

Ari doesn't even blink. "Yeah, no offense, but I'm not competing for emotional custody. One brother's already exhausting."

Jasmine chokes on a laugh, nearly dropping a dish in the sink. "Noted. Just make sure I get front-row seats when you two start competing over who loves Kais more."

I look over at her. She swallows. Small, nervous. Still smiling. But not like last night. There's a hush in it now. A hesitation that wasn't there last night. As if she was keeping part of herself just out of reach again. But she looked at me anyway. Like maybe some piece of her still wanted to be seen.

And fuck, I see all of it. The retreat. The fear. The wanting. Even knowing she was pulling away, I want her just the same. Christ. I'm done for. And apparently spending Christmas in love with someone who's already halfway out the door.

After breakfast, we linger longer than necessary. Fumbling to-go mugs and bags at the doorway like none of us want to make the first move. Jasmine steps outside first, giving me space. As if she knows I'll need it before I do.

Ari doesn't say anything at first. Just pulls me into one of those one-armed hugs that turn into a full-force back slap. A moment passes before he steps back, chin ticking toward the car.

"Try not to crash it, Champ."

I scoff. "Try not to dry hump the goalpost next time you score."

He barks a laugh. "No promises. We Del Toros are emotional fuckers."

I shake my head. "Explains a lot."

"Poor bastard," he mutters, smirking as he reaches for his coffee. "See you in April, arsehole."

I clap his shoulder with a solid grip. "Or Christmas, ballbag."

He nods once. "Yeah. Christmas."

We don't say anything else. Don't have to. But something settles between us.

He isn't just Aurelius anymore. Not just some stranger

with my jawline and our father's last name. Somewhere between the pickleback shots, talking until we couldn't keep our eyes open, and pancakes, he became my brother. Like we'd been doing this our whole lives instead of barely twenty-four hours.

Apparently, that's all it takes for me. One night to know someone mattered. One night to realize they'd already changed everything.

Jasmine is already behind the wheel when I get to the car, adjusting the mirror like it doesn't already know her face. I climb into the passenger seat without protest.

I feel well enough to drive regardless of clearance, but I can't say I mind the view of her behind the wheel of my lorry. I stretch, legs long, arms crossed, head tilted just enough to watch her hands settle on the wheel.

She still won't look at me properly. Not when she reverses. Not when Aurelius waves us off. Not when we pull onto the narrow road that leads away from his place. Not even when I clear my throat like I'm about to say something, then don't.

Which she absolutely abhors.

The tension isn't loud. It doesn't need to be. It just lives between the seats. Itchy on my skin. And I don't know if I'm supposed to name it, or just let it hang there, yet another unspoken thing.

"Are you okay?" I ask quietly.

"Yeah. Just tired." She clears her throat. That nervous tick giving her away no matter how cool she tries to act.

"Should you be behind the wheel then?" I tease, trying to find a crack I could break the awkwardness with.

Her eyes meet mine for half a second before darting back to the road.

"James..." she sighs, then shifts like she's changed her

mind mid-thought. "I'm fine to drive. I'll probably just take a nap when we get back. You've got your test coming up. I have that meeting. Let's just focus on that for now."

Bullshit. But I let it ride. For now.

"You scheduled it?" I ask. "OneActive?"

"Day after tomorrow. Talked to the rep this morning."

Her voice lifts for half a second before flattening back out. Almost as if she'd caught herself being happy and snuffed it out like she wasn't allowed to want it.

Could be about us. Could be about the meeting. Hell, could be both. But she's shutting me out either way, and it's killing me. So, I try to find another crack.

"Have you told your family about it? Your mom had to have more adjectives for you this time."

"Yeah." She sighs a small laugh, eyes fixed on the road. "I'll tell her if anything comes from it."

I cut my eyes at her. That doubt she's wearing looks too much like mine, and I fucking hate it on her. She should see herself the way I do. The way millions of people who follow her do. But numbers don't mean shit when you don't have someone in your corner who actually knows you. Who sees you.

Whether she wanted me or not, I'm in her corner. That's not changing.

"Something will come of it, Jasmine. Whether it's with that company or not."

For the first time since we got in the car, she looks at me full stop. Those soft brown eyes holding mine with an expression that makes my pulse trip and my skin heat all over.

She sucks in a heavy breath before she turns away again. Then leans her head against the window, fingers twisting at the cuff of her sweater. Not mine this time.

And maybe that's the thing that hurts worst. A small, stupid gesture, but I want it back.

I wait, hoping she just needs space to wake up. But the farther we get from Bath, the more I feel it settling in. The pullback. The shift. Like whatever we'd been building was already out of reach. Like the longer I wait, the more compliant I am in the giving up.

"Jazz, come on..." I exhale a breath underscored with something I don't know how to say.

She keeps her eyes on the road like looking at me might hurt. I can't tell if she's protecting herself or me.

"James, please. Not now. We'll talk later, when I'm not running on two hours of sleep, okay?" She reaches for my hand, giving it a quick squeeze, then pulls away. It feels more like a goodbye than a 'we'll talk later'.

I shake my head, unsure what to do with the ache crawling up my neck.

Then, more gently, "You've got your test next week, are you ready?"

"As I'll ever be." I pause. "You'll be there, right?"

Her hand stills in her lap. She meets my eyes again. Just briefly. "Of course."

The words should be a relief. But they land flat.

Empty.

She drives a little faster, like speed can somehow outrun whatever's breaking between us.

I press my head back against the seat and close my eyes.

Kieran circling my seat. Jasmine pulling away. And I can't do a damn thing about either of them except show up and prove I'm worth keeping.

Jasmine

18

Penn: Please call me the second you leave. I need every detail.

Me: What if they don't want to work with me, Penelope?

Penn: Girl, please. The question is: do you want to work with them? And can they afford you?

Me: You are truly my spirit animal. I'll call you after.

Penn: Good. And just so we're clear I'll be asking invasive questions about that man too.

I ROLL MY EYES AND FLIP MY PHONE OVER ON THE table in front of me.

One thing I'll miss about Hampstead is the never-ending supply of aesthetically pleasing cafés. This one's no exception.

It looks like some Studio Ghibli–Nancy Meyers collab,

and I'm honestly living for it on a day like this. The kind of rainy, brooding London afternoon that makes you want to crawl under a blanket, put on Kiki's Delivery Service, and ignore the fact that you fell in love with someone you can't have and have been pretending not to feel anything for since you got back from his estranged brother's house.

"Vanilla cappuccino?" the waitress asks, setting a mug down in front of me.

"Yes, thank you." I smile and nod.

"Can I get you anything else? Clear these for you?" She gestures to the empty place settings across from me.

"No, I'm okay for now. I'm just early. They should be here any minute." I offer another polite smile that I hope doesn't look as fake as it feels.

I've wanted to work with OneActive since I started out on social media. Years of dreaming, building, staying consistent. And now here I am, in the middle of London, about to see it finally happen, and all I can think about is James.

God, I hate that.

The bell above the door chimes just as my phone buzzes against the table. I reach to silence it, already expecting a distraction I don't want, and freeze when I see the name.

> Travieso: You don't have to reply. Just wanted you to know I'm rooting for you. Whatever happens, remember you built something they want. Not the other way around. You've got this.

My heart leaps into my throat.

I start typing a reply—something dumb? Something mushy? I don't even know—

"Miss Lozano?" The voice is deep and overly polished, pulling me straight back to reality.

I rise quickly, slipping my phone into my pocket. The man standing beside me is barely taller than I am and cartoonishly buff, like he's bulking for a Popeye role.

"Hi, yes. You must be Mr. Hamilton." I extend my hand.

He grins wide and too white, shaking it. "Firm shake," he says, like he's impressed.

"This is my colleague, Mrs. Sanchez."

A tall woman with a blunt blonde bob steps forward. I shake her hand too, already trying to lock in. She has the kind of energy that doesn't wait for anyone to catch up and clearly, I need to pull my shit together.

"We were quite pleased to get connected with you," Mrs. Sanchez says as she sits down. "You've built something impressive. Over two million subscribers across your platforms and six million unique impressions a month."

Mr. Hamilton chimes in. "Honestly, I'm surprised you haven't taken on any bigger partnerships yet."

I shrug, slipping into the practiced version of myself I've been using for years on camera.

"I've had offers. I just haven't wanted to lock myself into anything beyond single-post deals, at least not until recently."

They both nod. Mrs. Sanchez reaches into her bag, pulling out a shiny black folder.

"Well," she says, smoothing her blazer as she opens it, "to be honest with you, we love that you haven't taken on anything major yet. It tells us your following is authentic. People engage with you because they like you."

She flips the folder open and turns it toward me.

Across the top of the first page was a clean, minimal logo: **OneActive** × **Jazz Lozano**

My breath catches.

"We want to design a full collection," she continues, "based on your style, your aesthetic, and the brand you've already built."

I turn the page. Then another. And another. They're mockups: sports bras, leggings, cropped jackets. Pastels, jewel tones, neutrals. The fonts feel like me. The silhouettes are already ones I wear.

"You'd have full creative input," she adds. "Our team would help with design and production, of course. But the direction would be entirely yours. Within reason."

I nod slowly. "This is actually... amazing."

Seeing my name printed on those pages, front and center doesn't feel like a pitch. It feels like proof. Proof that all the late nights, the edits, the consistency, the days I thought no one was watching... it all built something real. Something I could point to when people ask what I "really" do. Something my mom might finally understand. Maybe even be proud of.

Then James' voice cuts through the haze in my head. '*Don't take the first offer, even if it's shiny. Especially if it's shiny.*'

I sit up straighter and bite back my smile. Right. Not yet.

"This is amazing," I say slowly, "but I see here you're asking for trademark rights to my name. Is that just for the collaboration or indefinitely?"

They glance at each other. A flicker of surprise passes between them, like they didn't expect me to catch that.

Mr. Hamilton leans forward, elbows on the table.

"As it stands, it would be indefinite. Strictly to protect

us as a brand, of course. But we'd compensate you handsomely for the exclusivity."

I take a slow sip of my cappuccino. "So, I wouldn't be able to take other sponsorships or sell my own merch?"

"Not necessarily," Mrs. Sanchez jumps in. "You could still run your training programs and maintain compatible sponsorships in your content. They'd just need to be approved by our team."

I sit back in my chair, my confidence settling over me like an ill-fitted jacket. God, I want to just take it. To not make waves. To prove I'm easy to work with, grateful, not difficult. But something in me—maybe stubbornness, maybe James' voice, maybe just exhaustion at shrinking myself—won't let me.

"Right. That makes sense. How quickly are you expecting an answer?"

Mr. Hamilton raises his brows. "We were hoping today. Here."

I don't blink. "I hope you understand I can't give you an answer without having someone look over this."

He huffs, but Mrs. Sanchez places a hand on his leg and smiles, professional and tight.

"Of course. Have your people review it." She closes the folder and slides it toward me. "Give us a call by the beginning of next week?"

"Absolutely." I stand with them and offering my hand. "Thank you both so much."

I smile like I have every piece of this under control. Like I'm not already imagining all the ways this can go wrong. But I've worked too hard to hand over my name like it doesn't matter. Even if my voice shook the entire meeting, I have to look out for myself, get a second opinion.

Even if the truth is I don't have people. Not officially, at least.

Unless you count Alana holding my phone while I filmed in our tiny apartment, back when we split dollar ramen and called it meal prep. I've been a one-woman show through this whole thing.

But I do have someone. Someone whose opinion I need more than anyone else's, even if I can't quite understand why. Someone who sees through the shine. Someone who'd never let me sell myself short.

James.

He wasn't home when I got back. The apartment was still. Quiet and dark, the kind of quiet that felt too aware of itself.

I've never felt out of place here before. Not once. But without James, his apartment suddenly feels a little too big. A little too neat. Less like home.

I toss the folder from my meeting onto the coffee table, more dramatic than I mean to, and head to change out of my rain-soaked clothes.

I peel off my jeans with a full-body shiver and pull on the first pair of biker shorts I can find, followed by a hoodie I wish was James' but is definitely mine, even if I stretched the sleeves pretending otherwise.

I want his.

Want to wrap myself in something that smells like him, even though I've spent the last three days since Bath keeping careful distance between us. But then my brain supplies the lovely thought: *what if it smells like her instead of him? The ex.*

The woman who, without fail, has posted a new picture of her and James every day like a public love letter.

In pure frustration, I tug on the thickest socks I own—because my feet that are always cold somehow got icier with the thought of every smiling kissing selfie of them—then pad back out to the living room.

I'm not in the mood to doom-scroll or re-read that contract for the fifteenth time just to torture myself, so I hover in front of the shelf that housed what might've been the last surviving DVD collection in London.

James' collection is twice the size of mine. Half of it is British or Italian nonsense, some with titles I can't pronounce, but the other half is all classics. Comfort movies. Nostalgia in plastic cases. And perched right in the middle is *Kiki's Delivery Service*.

Just what I need: a peppy little witch with an existential crisis to make me feel less alone and distract me from spiraling into career doubt and emotional repression.

I pop the disc in, eternally grateful we both share the sacred calling to keep the DVD industry alive and cozy into the corner of the couch.

The elevator dings before Kiki even finds a job.

I freeze.

One second I'm perfectly content buried into the corner of the couch, half-asleep under a blanket, pretending I wasn't still replaying his last text in my head and dreaming it was more than friendly encouragement.

And now I'm suddenly hyper-aware of the fact that I've made myself comfortable in his space. Hoodie on. Socks wrinkled up my calves. Hair in a bun I hadn't looked at twice.

I sit perfectly still as I listen to him wrestle around in the foyer.

Maybe if I don't move, he'll think I'm a part of the furniture. But the folder from my meeting is still sitting on the table. And *Kiki's Delivery Service* is still playing. And I'm still wrapped in a blanket on his couch. Which means I've already made the first move. I'm just not sure if I'm brave enough to follow through.

"Good choice," James says, nodding at the screen as he casually flips through the mail.

"Can I watch it with you?"

He doesn't look at me as he says it.

"It's literally your house, James. You can do whatever you want," I reply, drier and more self-protective than I mean to.

"I guess that's true," he mutters, almost to himself.

He drops the mail onto the side table and sits at the far end of the couch. Close enough to be in the room, far enough to make me ache.

I know I've been avoiding him since Bath, but this? This strange, polite distance between us, it physically hurts.

He leans back, slinging one long arm along the back of the couch, eyes still on the screen. Still not on me. The silence sits between us for a while. I've always watched this movie for the aesthetic, not the dialogue, but now it might as well be static.

"How did your meeting go?" he asks finally.

I almost breathe a sigh of relief.

"Uh... fine, I guess."

I reach for the folder, hesitating for half a second, then extend it out to him.

"I brought this for you to look at. I can't tell if I'm

getting screwed or not." I pause, twisting the folder in my waiting hand. "I wanted to show you first."

His eyes flick to mine, and whatever is there in his expression makes me suddenly want to shrink back into the couch cushions.

"I mean—I guess I should've shown it to Alana or Kais." I try to cover my ass, walk what I said back. "I don't know why I didn't. Sorry."

His brow furrows, dark eyes searching mine. "You wanted to show me first?"

"Yeah." I nod, the truth of it pressing like a hand to my throat.

The corner of his mouth lifts and then he moves closer, gently taking the folder from my hand. He opens it without another word, scanning line by line, his focus intense.

But all I can think about was how beautiful he looks like this.

Quietly serious, sleeves pushed up, brows tight like he cares more than he should. How much I want to bring things like this to him. How much I wanted to belong to him. To be his person. To be the one he stayed up for, showed up for, looked at like this—like this matters. Like I matter.

But then I remembered the girl who keeps posting pictures of him like she already had that place. And just like that, my chest aches in a way that makes me want to fold in on myself and disappear.

He lets out a heavy sigh, his jaw working as he tosses the folder onto the coffee table.

Then, like some other language he needs to speak before words, he takes my feet into his lap, giving them a light squeeze, like he can warm me in all the places my socks have failed.

"Thank you for trusting me with that," he says, eyes locked on mine. "I know how much this means to you. And it means everything to me that I'm the person you trusted first."

My chest tightens. When did he become the person I can't do this without? When did his voice become the one I need to hear before anyone else's?

"With that said?" He nods toward the folder. "That's absolute shit."

Before I can laugh or cry, he keeps going.

"It's a leash. If you're okay with it, I'll give it to someone who can mark it up for a counteroffer. If you still want to work with them after they tried pulling that."

I hesitate, sawing my lip between my teeth.

"What do you think I should do?" I ask quietly.

"Honestly, Jaz? With those numbers? You could build it yourself. Keep every penny they're trying to take from you. Ten times over."

I sink deeper into the couch, overwhelmed. "I can't do that, James."

His thumb moves in slow strokes over my shin, soothing the panic climbing my ribs, even as it lights something else pulsing and off-limits between my thighs.

"Yes, you can," his voice is firm. "But do you want to? We both know you can. And they know it too. That's why they're offering you this garbage, wrapped in zeros and just enough praise to keep you from reading the fine print."

"You really think I could pull something like that off?"

He looks at me like he isn't sure if I'm being rhetorical or if I actually need the answer.

I do.

"Because I don't know if I can," I lean my head back against the couch cushion. "It's easier to play it small. To take what's safe. Let people underestimate me and act like that was the plan."

He doesn't say anything at first. Just stares at me with that quiet, unflinching intensity that always makes it hard to look away.

"I know you didn't come to me for the business answer," he keeps making those slow lines on my legs. "You came because you needed someone to remind you who the hell you are."

He leans in slightly, just enough to make it clear he isn't going anywhere.

"So let me remind you." His thumb brushes along the edge of my knee, slow and reverent. "You're not here by accident. You built this. You earned this. And you can outgrow every single person who thought you wouldn't."

He lets that sit. Lets it echo between us.

"If you want to play it safe, I'll support you. If you want to take the risk, I'll back you. But don't you dare doubt you can do it."

God, what I wouldn't give to belong to him. To be his person the way he's becoming mine. To stay on the receiving end of this look—the one that says I matter, that I'm not just passing through. Like he belongs to me and no one else. That when he says, "it means everything", he means it the way I feel it.

But that isn't reality. So, I remind myself to stop reading into things.

Letting out a slow breath, I shrug as if I'm not falling apart for a whole other reason now.

"Man, I could really use some junky snacks to go with all this emotional vulnerability."

He chuckles softly, flashing that perfect smile that always makes my stomach flutter. "If it wasn't absolutely pissing outside, I'd say we should go get some." He glances at the window, then back at me. "The animated bakery will have to do for now."

I smile, then—against what my brain says is safe—I pull his legs up to stretch out along the cushion beside me, flipping the blanket over us both.

"That works," I settle deeper into the couch, catching his grin as I turn back to the movie.

He doesn't say anything else. Doesn't push. Just sits with me. One hand resting on my legs, still tracing soft lines into my skin, like maybe he wants me to belong to him too. And for the rest of the night, I let myself believe it.

James

19

ANOTHER WEEK OF BRUTAL NECK-STRENGTH testing and sim work on the tech campus.

Sim work for test development? Fine.

Sim work to somehow "improve" my driving? A complete waste of time.

But I can't really argue in the state I'm in. After tomorrow's fitness test, I'm done playing the role of groveling, sidelined driver with something to prove.

For now, I have to walk into headquarters again and get thrown through another ring of hell: PR interviews.

I've gladly dodged every bit of press since the crash. But with the team days away from the final race of the season, Lamaire's decided it's not just necessary, it's mandatory if I want back on the grid next season.

As if sitting in front of cameras fielding questions about my crash and Kieran's contract negotiations is somehow going to prove I'm ready. As if this has anything to do with driving and not damage control—but sure, let's call it "good for the brand."

I sigh, tugging my hood a little lower over my cap as

Jasmine and I walk into headquarters for what feels like the fifth time this week.

I've basically lived in this place for the last ten years, but right now? I'd give anything for an hour alone with her and an honest conversation—something we haven't managed since Bath.

The timing hasn't felt right, even when we were buried under blankets a few days ago, watching every comfort movie we could agree on.

Having the "what are we" conversation while she's on the verge of the biggest career move of her life, and I'm still fighting for mine? Not ideal.

Still, I don't know how much longer I can ignore whatever the hell this is. Whatever it's turning into.

"Nurse Lozano!"

Patrick Holt.

My performance engineer and Alex Skarsgård doppelgänger from hell calls out across the lobby like he's been waiting all morning to see her.

Jasmine turns, smiling easily. Too easily. Could just been her being polite. Or it could be the jealousy already crawling up my spine.

She's been running half the testing sessions with Holt and the team doctor for the past month. And they've gotten irritatingly close.

"Morning, Patrick," she says as he approaches.

"Double shot, vanilla latte." He hands her one of the two cups in his hand, grinning like he knows exactly how charming he looks. "Don't ever say I don't pay attention."

He winks. Smiles at her like there isn't a single other person in the room.

Jasmine's eyes dart to mine, a reminder I'm still here as she takes a sip. And only then does Patrick glance my way.

"Morning, Del Toro," He lifts his cup in mock salute. "Nice to hear the Champ is finally getting back in front of the camera."

He sips as he says it, blue eyes narrowing just slightly. Like it's a compliment and not a test of my patience.

I huff a dry laugh. "Yeah, well, we'll see how well it goes since no one brought me coffee."

I smile, just enough to pass for good-natured. Jasmine swallows, then holds her cup out to me.

"Here, take this one. I'm still buzzing off that espresso you made this morning."

A slow smile pulls at my mouth. I take the cup from her. Not because I want it.

But because he's still watching. Because I need him to see it.

My fingers brush hers. My lips touch where hers just were. And yeah, I know exactly what it looks like.

I take a slow sip, never breaking eye contact with him.

"Mmm. Beans are burnt," I wince handing it back to Jasmine as if it wasn't a warning shot.

I watch him clock it. Quick, amused, like he'd expected it. Like it made this more fun for him.

Of course, he fires back.

Chuckling, he turns his attention right back to her. "Dr. Renaud's waiting upstairs," he says casually. "Wants to run through protocol ahead of tomorrow. Vitals, reaction windows, the usual. You know the drill."

Right. Of course she does.

He knows she does. Knows how close they've gotten running thorough pointless protocols. And that's the point.

Jasmine lets out a sigh, tipping her head back with a groan. "Did you tell Marcus that if he makes me recalibrate another reflex monitor, I'm never helping him again?"

Then comes his laugh. One of those slick, overly flirtatious ones that makes my jaw twitch. And just to twist the knife, his hand lands on her back. Light, guiding, like he has the right.

Fuck, I want to break his fingers. But I don't move. Don't blink. Because I can't do a bloody thing. She's not mine. And she doesn't technically work for him the way she technically works for me, so fair play.

The thought is still bitter.

"Wouldn't want that," he says, flashing teeth. "You're far too much of an asset around here. Maybe after the meeting, you'll finally let me talk you into coming on staff. Whip the other boys into shape the way you did Del Toro."

She gives him a polite laugh, but I can see it. The slight tension in her shoulders, the way her smile doesn't quite reach her eyes. She doesn't like it. And that makes the heat in my chest burn even hotter.

At the lift, she turns, glancing over her shoulder. "Good luck in there. Call me if you need me."

Her voice is light, but her eyes are searching. Like it isn't just something to say. A question.

I nod, once.

Holt says something else as the doors close, something I can't make out. But her eyes stay locked on mine. Even with Holt beside her, even as the doors slide shut, she's looking at me. Like she needs me to know she hasn't forgotten. Like that look is supposed to be enough.

And fuck, do I wish it was.

THE CONFERENCE ROOM IS DIM, only the center lit in that eerie, hyper-focused kind of way. Too-bright umbrella lights casting artificial shadows over a single couch and half a dozen cameras.

Adam Perry sits on the far end, bright-eyed and buzzing, answering questions like this is the highlight of his month.

Kid's only eighteen. Same age I was when I started here. But it looks a hell of a lot younger on him than it ever did on me. He's done well this season. Not great, not enough to keep the seat, but solid. Safe. And that's all the team needed him to be.

His face lights up when he notices me standing at the back of the room. The same expression he'd given me the first time we met, when he told me, "I've watched you race since I can remember." Which made me, at twenty-eight, feel like I had my birth year flipped.

"James! Come over here." He waves me over like we were about to catch up over beers, not sit under ten thousand watts of PR scrutiny.

I'm not in a rush to get in front of a camera, but a hair-and-makeup staffer intercepts me like she can't wait for me to.

She spritzes something vaguely herbal into my hair and mutters, "Well, you don't need much, do you?"

I give her the smile. The PR one I've been using since I was old enough to know people like me more when I keep things easy and don't show the cracks.

I step into the lights and drop onto the couch next to Perry.

"Where's Oliver? Isn't he meant to be doing this too?" I ask.

"Still in sim, I think. Should be done any minute," Perry

replies, practically bouncing. "I'm happy to see you back doing these things, mate," he adds, knocking his fist lightly against my knee. "Hasn't been the same without you."

I give him a half-smile. "You've managed well without me. Your run in Qatar was impressive. P4?"

He nods. "Yeah, well, that's not a podium."

"You'll get there," I say, meaning it. "Without a doubt."

The door swings open like it always does with Ollie. No hesitation, just his voice at full volume and zero restraint.

"Sorry I'm late, lads. Fuckin' sim rebooted on me halfway through," he calls, striding in full of energy as if he didn't just come from another five-hour stint on the tech campus.

"Hello, ladies," he adds with a quick grin to the hairdresser and makeup artist moving toward him. "Excuse the language."

They laugh like he just offered to buy them flowers. He can charm a room in his sleep.

"Right," the interviewer says, stepping up beside the camera, "should we get started then?"

One of the crew leans in to clip a mic to my collar while Ollie plops onto the couch beside me. Without missing a beat, he knocks his knee against mine. The same way he has since we were kids in karts, just with more cameras now.

"Good to see you suffering through this bollocks again," he mutters with a smirk.

I nod back, forcing a small smile of my own.

"Thanks for taking the time to sit with us, men," the interviewer says, settling into his stance like we're already rolling. "I'm Dan. Great to have you here. Let's start with Mr. Bisset."

Ollie sits forward, rubbing a hand over his jaw like he

hasn't been doing non-stop interviews since his win last Sunday.

"Oliver, you've had an incredible run the second half of the season. Helping Red Energy win the Constructors' fight while going neck and neck with Kieran Denune for what could be both of your first Drivers' Championships. How does it feel?"

"Feels good, mate." Ollie grins and adjusted his hat, all calm confidence. "I'm really proud of what Perry and I've done this last leg of the season."

Then he glances over at me, softening slightly. "But I wouldn't be in this position, and neither would the team, if James hadn't had the mega season he had."

It catches me off guard, how easily he says it. No fanfare, no expectation.

Ollie hasn't acknowledged much about my crash. He's kept things light since that night at Kais', deflects with sarcasm, goes quiet when things get too serious instead of ripping into me like he was before.

Can't really blame him for either reaction. I haven't let him in on the hell I've been going through mentally. And even though I know he means what he just said, part of me still has to swallow the lump it leaves in my throat. Because I couldn't feel further from the season he's talking about or who I am in this sport.

Dan turns to me next. "That must be nice to hear that kind of affirmation from your teammate. Welcome back, James."

"Glad to be back, Dan."

I lean back against the couch, careful with my posture. Relaxed, casual, pretending this isn't the most visibility I'd had in months. Every second of this will be clipped, posted, slowed down and captioned for reactions. They'll be looking for cracks. Signs I'm not ready. Proof that Kieran deserves to be in the car more than I do.

Welcome back to the circus.

"James," he continues, "you've accomplished a lot this year. Ten consecutive wins, scored the majority of your team's points in the first half of the season, set three new fastest lap records. Hell, you were even announced as a nominee for Sports Pictured's Sexiest Men Alive."

"Oh, come on," I groan, dragging a hand down my face. "That last bit can't possibly be true."

A woman behind him, helpfully, raises her phone and flashes the headline at me.

Ollie lets out a laugh. "Damn, just when I thought I was finally gettin' a bit of sparkle, we're back to glazin' Del Toro."

I shake my head, embarrassed.

"It's never been about any of that for me, mate. I love what I do and who I get to do it with. I stay off the internet as much as humanly possible. Mostly just use my phone to play solitaire."

That gets a proper laugh from the room. Even Ollie smirks like he doesn't totally hate me for being on that list.

Dan adjusts in his chair, the smile on his face just a little too pleased with himself. "It's no secret you and Ollie aren't just teammates. You're best mates. Some say that's what's kept Red Energy dominating these last few years. But how will it feel next season, seeing the number one plate on his car? Or worse, Kieran Denune's? Not because you lost it. But because you couldn't finish the season."

I exhale slowly, dragging a hand over my jaw. "Wow. You really know how to tee up a question, don't you?"

Dan smirks, like he knows exactly what he's doing.

I straighten a little, keeping my voice steady.

"I've always been sixteen in my heart. Picked it to remind me why I started racing in the first place: My mum, Lucia. That number's personal. It's why I race. Number one is a byproduct of the work. And seeing Ollie, someone I consider a brother, get his shot to wear it? That makes me proud. Not prideful."

Ollie smiles beside me, nudging my shoulder like he can feel the tension that's creeping into my voice. "Easy to say when the bastard's had it for the last four years."

I give him a genuinely appreciative smile. But my focus has already shifted.

Dan leans forward, zeroing in.

"And Kieran Denune?"

My jaw flexes.

"What about him?"

"Your crash at Spa, though ruled a racing incident, is still highly debated. Will it be hard to watch the man who some say ended the Del Toro era possibly wear the number one plate next season?"

I let the ensuing silence hang there. Needing a second to swallow the panic climbing my throat.

Ended the Del Toro era.

Four words that made this whole interview feel like an exercise in futility. As though tomorrow's test was just a formality before they hand my career to the man who put me in hospital.

As if my mum's sacrifices and Kais's bloody knuckles and Jasmine's faith in me won't matter, if I can't prove I was worth it.

I shake my head once, paste on the practiced smile everyone but Dan wants to see, and pretend to be someone I haven't been since the crash. "No. That sounds like giving the man too much credit."

My voice doesn't waver. My smile doesn't slip. But I can feel the tension in my shoulders rise.

"The results will speak for themselves when my tires hit the tarmac next season."

"Adam, how about you?" Dan glances quickly to his right, pivoting. "You've had a consistent run stepping in for James this season. What's it like, handing that seat back?"

Perry glances at me, then back at the camera. His expression calm. PR polished. But his words land with more steel than I ever had at his age.

"One thing I've learned from these two is: don't chase the seat. If you put in the work, if you stay grounded in the team, it'll come. I think that's shown in my performance this season. I'm proud of what I've done, and when I get my next shot, I want it to be because I've earned it. Not because I prayed for another man's career to end."

Dan blinks caught a little off guard. But he recovers quickly.

"Well. You guys really do have something special here. I look forward to seeing where this all goes."

Dan asks a handful more questions which we all breeze through with media-trained responses before calling it wraps.

By the end of it, I'm ready to claw Jasmine back from Holt and go home. I'll gladly sit through any dodgy American film she picks from my shelf if it means I can just be near her and shake this day off me.

We all turn over our mics as the camera crew packs up.

"Test day tomorrow, right mate?" Ollie asks in a hushed tone.

"It is," I reply, standing to put my arms through my jacket.

He rests a hand between my shoulder blades.

"Try not to sweat too much, yeah. And don't go replaying the crash in your head or anything. Just remember no matter how it goes, you'll always be a legend."

The words hit like a smack on a fresh bruise. Meant to reassure but cut with too much finality. He's already bracing for the version of me that might not make it back.

Ollie's always been like this. Says shit without thinking, without meaning it the way it sounds. I know that. I've known that since our helmets were too big for our bodies. But it doesn't matter. Because the panic is already there, burrowing into everything.

I don't wince. Don't blink. Just shove my hands in my pockets and keep walking.

Because what the hell am I supposed to say to that?

Thanks for the eulogy, mate?

I'm not dead yet.

Jasmine 20

THE ENTIRE RIDE HOME PASSED IN A BLUR.

James didn't say much. I wouldn't either if I'd just spent the day fielding questions from people trying to catch me cracking.

Usually, one of us would break the silence with a joke or a casual debrief, but I doubt he'd find it all that riveting to hear about the five different ways his performance engineer tried to ask me out.

Don't get me wrong. Holt is gorgeous. Polished, smart, good at his job.

But he isn't James.

And the second he placed his hand on my back, I was painfully aware of that. I told him, calmly but clearly, that I was seeing someone and to never do that again. Especially not in a professional setting. It wasn't even about the principle of it. It was about James.

Even if I'm not technically seeing anyone. Even if, in a few days, I'll be halfway to Miami to visit my parents and figure out what the hell I'm doing next.

The truth is I don't think I'll be seeing anyone for a while. I can't even stand the thought.

Not after this.

James barely said a word once we got back home. Just looked exhausted. When he said he was going to bed early, I didn't push. Not with his test tomorrow. Not with the way things have been between us lately.

I might've dreamed that night on the couch, because this past week? We've barely seen each other.

I haven't asked him about Francesca. I haven't brought up the pictures she keeps posting. I haven't asked him if they're talking again. If they're seeing each other again. Because I haven't even seen him.

Tonight's no different. I'm in my room. He's in his. And soon, he won't have to pretend anything with me. Or hide anything with her.

He can forget this ever happened, and I can start piecing myself back together like I always do. Which probably starts with finding another job.

I pull my phone from my pocket and sighed, tapping **Mami**.

She answers on the first ring, like she'd been waiting.

"Jasmine?"

"Hola, Mami. What are you up to?" I flop back on the bed.

"Well, mija, I'm sitting at the nurse's station playing Candy Smash," she replies, her voice heavy with fatigue.

"Sorry. I keep forgetting the time difference. I thought you'd be off by now."

"It's fine. I needed a break anyway." I can hear the familiar sounds of IV pumps and sneakers squeaking on the tile in the background. "I haven't heard from you in two weeks. Are you still in England?"

"Yeah. Just for a few more days, I think." I hesitate, then add, "I'm thinking about coming back to Miami instead of Dallas."

Her tone lifts instantly. "Sí! You know your father and I would love that. Your abuelita's getting older. You should see her more."

"I know." I sit up. "Is your floor hiring? Or do you know if the ED is?"

She clicks her tongue. "Ay, mija, you don't want to go to ED, do you?"

I don't want to go back to anything, but I can't say that. Not right now.

"I'm not going back to ICU or flight, Mama."

And there it is.

"Jasmine," she sighs, "you know it's the best place for you. Unless you like chasing twelve patients every shift. ICU is one-to-one, just like what you're doing now."

I huff. "That's what they say, until it's four-to-one because nobody shows up or someone floats."

"Mija," she sighs back, even heavier. "You're already starting to sound resentful."

"I'm not. I'm just dreading it." I fix my gaze out the window. Somehow the cool night sky seems warmer than this conversation I'm quickly regretting.

"It's like that sometimes. But this is what we Lozano women were made to do. You just push through it."

I pause, holding the phone tighter. "I've been thinking about taking a break."

I didn't plan to say it. But it's out. "I got a big offer. A sponsorship—"

"Jasmine Marisol Ortiz Lozano. Don't start this again." Her voice tightens. "That social media thing? It doesn't last.

You have a good, honest career. A legacy. Don't throw that away for nonsense."

I bite my lip.

"Yeah. Okay, Mami. Sorry I said anything."

"Don't be. Everyone has wild dreams at your age." She softens again. "I'll talk to Tina in ED. I'll get you a spot. Does that help?"

I swallow the lump in my throat. "Yeah. Gracias. I should let you get back."

"Okay, baby. Te amo."

"Te amo."

I hang up and stand there, phone still hot in my hand, waiting for something to hit. Anger. Tears. Fight.

Nothing comes.

Just this hollow, defeated feeling that settles in my heart and her words echoing in my head like I've been waiting to hear them.

Wild dreams.

Like everything I've built was just a phase I'd grow out of. Like I should be grateful to go back to twelve-hour shifts and call lights and pretending I wasn't dying inside.

I look at my scrubs, still crumpled on the floor where I'd dropped them every day after I was done pretending to be here for a job.

I should hang them up. Wash them. Prep for going back to Miami like a good daughter who knows her place.

Instead, I kick them toward the corner and head for the bathroom. Showers have always been my safe space. The place where I can breathe, reset, convince myself I can handle whatever's waiting on the other side of the door.

But tonight, even scalding water doesn't reach the knot in my chest. I stayed until my skin was red, until it ran cold, and my thoughts still won't stop spiraling.

In a few days, I'll be in Miami. Wearing scrubs I didn't want. Living a life I didn't choose. And James will still be here. Either getting his seat back and forgetting I ever existed or losing everything and needing someone to pick up the pieces.

Either way, it won't be me. I'll be gone. And maybe that's for the best. Maybe he'll go back to her. If he hasn't already.

I dry off and pull on the first t-shirt I find, then crawl into bed, staring up at the ceiling in a room that never really felt like mine. Except when he's in it.

"One in the fucking morning," I mutter, turning my head to glance at the clock.

My brain won't turn off. Not about going back home. Not about James' test tomorrow. Not about James.

My chest tightens with every thought, like I'm stuck in a loop I can't get out of.

"Water. Cold water," I say to myself, shoving the covers off and quietly slipping toward the door. Maybe if I get up, move around, I can shake this feeling off me.

I crack the door slowly, careful not to make a sound. He should be asleep. He needs to be asleep. But a narrow sliver of light is cutting across the dark hallway, spilling from under his door.

I stop. Of course he isn't sleeping.

My hand hovers over his doorknob, suddenly unsure. I should check on him. Just in case. But what if someone's in there? What if I'm interrupting something I can't unsee?

Frenchie posted another picture today. I saw it before I could stop myself. Her and James at some gala, his hand on her waist, both of them laughing. The caption was something about "second chances" and my stomach dropped so fast I had to sit down.

What if *that's* what this weird, silent week had been about? Him pulling away because she's back. Because they're trying again and he just hasn't figured out how to tell me yet.

Well, it is *technically* still my job to make sure he's adhering to his care plan.

That's what I tell myself, anyway.

I knock, light enough he could miss it if he was busy. Then I squeeze my eyes shut, like blindness might make me braver.

"Yeah?" His voice is quiet. Strained. Like it scraped its way up.

I clear my throat. "Uh, can I come in?"

He doesn't say anything for a moment before his voice finally cracks again.

"Sure."

I tug my t-shirt down a little, like that would somehow make this feel more professional, less like I was walking into his room half-naked in middle of the night.

I ease the door open. James is sitting on the edge of his bed, bare back to me, shoulders hunched slightly like the weight of the day still hasn't let up.

God. I should've changed. Something about seeing him like that, shirtless, vulnerable, quiet, made my own clothes feel thinner, even more revealing than they are.

Except it isn't about what I was wearing. It was about walking in here with my heart this exposed. With everything I'd been trying to hide sitting right on my face.

But I step in anyway.

"You alright?" he asks, shoving a hand through his hair without turning around.

"Are you?" I challenge gently. "Kind of late to be up partying, don't you think?"

He lets out a weak laugh, a broken sound, followed by a sniffle. And just like that, every instinct in me fires at once.

I don't think. I just move. Rounding the bed like my body already knows something my brain hasn't caught up to yet.

"You look nice," he tries for levity, wiping his cheek with the back of his hand like it might undo the proof already sitting there.

Too late. I see it. The shine. The red-rimmed glassiness. The way his shoulders barely move when he breathes.

"James," I whisper, crouching in front of him.

"I'm fine. Allergies." His voice is rough, the kind of rough that isn't about freaking pollen.

I arch a brow.

"That might work if I didn't know your entire medical history down to the molecule, travieso."

He lets out a small laugh, but it doesn't reach his eyes. Doesn't even try to.

"Yeah. I guess that's true." He clears his throat and sits up straighter, like posture might carry him through whatever he doesn't want to say. "I'm fine though, really. Just in my head."

I sit down beside him, my hand finds its place on his thigh without consulting my brain, clearly only taking orders from my heart.

"Remember what I said to you on my first day here? When you were in the shower?"

His eyes lift to meet mine and a familiar understanding passes between us.

"That seeing me naked was distracting?" He gives me a half-hearted smirk, resorting to humor like he always does when things get too close.

I don't take the bait.

"You don't have to be this for me," I say gently, my thumb brushing the fabric of his sweatpants. "It's okay to not be okay sometimes, James."

His jaw flexes. His gaze drifts to the far side of the room like he's weighing every version of the truth before picking one that won't sound weak.

"It's stupid," he mutters, running a hand over his face.

"Try me," I say, not letting go.

He exhales hard, elbows dropping to his knees. Shoulders folding in like a collapsing tent.

"Today just fucking sucked," he huffs, voice low and frayed. "And I can't get out of my fucking head."

I stay quiet, my hand still resting on his thigh, just holding space for him.

"I just keep hearing Ollie's voice, telling me no matter what, I'll always be a legend. " He goes on, jaw clenched. " Like it's already over. Like there's no fucking hope I come back from this shit."

His voice cracks near the end, just enough to slice through me.

"And I know it's Ollie," he adds quickly, like he's trying to give me permission to write it off. "He doesn't mean it like that. He just says shit. But I can't unhear it."

He swallows thickly, dragging a hand through his hair. "I can't stop seeing it," he says. "Can't stop feeling it, the second my car flipped into that barrier. It just won't leave."

I don't speak right away, instead I move my palm across his back, slow and steady. Feeling the tension coiled beneath his skin, feeling the fight still living there, balled up and waiting for a reason to spring.

"You don't have to unhear it right now. Or unsee it. Or pretend it doesn't still live in your body."

He lets out an extremely long, shaky breath that sounds like he's been holding it in since the crash.

"You've been trying to outrun it," I continue. "Like if you work hard enough, push far enough, it'll just disappear. But you can't, James. You have to feel it. At least a little. But you don't have to carry it alone."

He rubs his eyes with the pads of his thumbs, pausing there for a second. Just breathing. Just being. Then he looks at me. Really looks at me.

The way he always does when he forgets to guard himself. The way that makes everything inside me ache.

"You shouldn't have to worry about this shit, Jasmine," his voice thick and raw. "Not for me."

I stare at him, my heart aching for him.

He really believes that. That caring about him is some kind of burden I shouldn't have to carry.

But what he doesn't see, what he can't see, is that I'm not burdened by anything. I'm choosing him. Over and over. And I'd keep doing it even when he doesn't ask me to.

I hold his gaze. "I am though. Whether you want me to or not, James."

He turns toward me, red rimmed eyes flicking from mine to my mouth, then back again. His hand slides to the nape of my neck, and before I can think, my body leans in. Drawn to him like it's always known where to go.

Our lips meet, slow and searching.

His mouth is soft and warm, his kiss deep enough to send heat spreading through my belly and blooming between my thighs.

I wrap my arms around him, pull him closer, closer until I can feel every part of him pressing into me.

James groans into my mouth, his arm looping around my waist as he shifts us back, lifting me onto the bed with him like it's instinct. His mouth trails down my neck, setting fire to every nerve in its wake.

My hips move against his, seeking friction, like they don't belong to me anymore.

"James," I whisper, needing him to hear me.

Needing him to stop before I lose myself. But he kisses me again, deeper this time, and I let him.

For a moment. Because right now, I want him in any way I can have him. Even if my heart already knows it can't be like this.

Not as a distraction. Not as a way to drown out the things we're both trying to outrun. His test. His crash. My own heart, quietly breaking at the thought of letting him go.

"James," I pull back, breathless. "We can't."

He sighs, pressing his forehead against mine. "Jasmine, please," he whispers.

I reach up and press a finger to his lips. "Not like this, James. Not with everything you have ahead of you tomorrow."

His eyes search mine, uncertain but not pulling away.

"Lay down." I gesture to the pillow beside me.

When I slip beneath the covers, I hold them open for him too. He hesitates for a second, then sighs, resignation settling over his features, he slides in beside me.

I lean in and kiss him once more. Just one last time. Slow and lingering, longer than I should, considering how thin my restraint's wearing.

"I'll be right here," I whisper. "Today's over. There's only tomorrow. Just rest."

He nods, swallowing hard, then pressed a kiss to my forehead. I turn toward him, settling into his chest, his hand resting at my waist.

We don't speak after that. I don't close my eyes until I feel his arm get heavy and his breath slow.

And even if I never get another moment like this, even if Frenchie gets every moment after—every morning, every night, every version of him I'll never get to keep—at least I'll always have this one.

James

THE FIRST THING I FELT WHEN I WOKE UP WASN'T nerves. It was her. Still tucked against me, soft and warm in her t-shirt. Her breath steady against my chest like last night didn't crack us both wide open. One arm slung across my waist, fingers hooked in my waistband.

I could've stayed there forever.

But my alarm had other plans. 6:00 a.m. sharp. Test day.

So now I'm here, making a protein shake like this ritual matters. Pretending the biggest test of my career isn't in a few hours. Pretending the woman who slept in my arms last night didn't completely fucking undo me by just being there, steadying me with her words and her touch when I couldn't get a grip on myself.

I can't get my head straight.

We only slept together, even though I wanted to be inside every inch of her. That was still enough.

I've never felt closer to anyone in my life. And that might be the problem. Now I'm supposed to act normal. Forget I fell asleep with her body wrapped over mine.

Ignore that I woke up wanting to tell her every goddamn thing I'd been holding back. It's already killing me.

Francesca never got to me in my head like this. Not even when she cheated. The only thing that still gets to me about her is how Kieran weaponized her. Used her to take a shot at me before Spa even happened. But that's just mind games.

Spa was real.

The crash was real.

The barrier flipping my car, the impact that should've killed me—that's the hit that landed. That's the one I'm still carrying.

I've done everything right since then. Every rep, every test, every goddamn recovery protocol. My body's cleared, Dr. Renaud said so himself two weeks ago. The issue isn't strength or stamina or whether my hip can take the G-forces.

The issue is whether I can get in that car without seeing the crash. Without feeling the impact all over again. Every time I close my eyes, I see it.

And now Jasmine's in there too.

Last night, this morning, the way she looked at me like I'm someone worth staying for. I can't afford to think about that right now. Can't afford to think about Spa, either. I just need my mind to shut the fuck up and let my body do what it's trained to do.

"Morning." Jasmine's voice is soft as she steps into the kitchen in her usual black scrubs, her hair pulled back in a long ponytail.

Brown eyes meet mine, and suddenly the room feels too quiet. Like she can hear everything I'm not saying.

"You ready?" she asks.

I shrug, because the truth is too heavy to say aloud.

She steps closer, her hand sweeping lightly across my back. Just that, just a touch, but I swear to God, it nearly brings me to my knees.

Because a new thought presses its way in: *how the fuck am I supposed to do any of this without her?*

Her gaze holds mine. "You've worked really fucking hard, James. Don't throw it away by overthinking. Just be present. It'll all come together."

I don't say anything. Just watch her. The way she says it like it's obvious. Like I haven't been killing myself to believe that very thing. She believes it for me. God, I need that more than I realized.

I nod, the kind of gesture you make when anything more might split you open.

She offers a small smile, then reaches for the keys on the counter.

"Now come on. It's probably my last time driving your war machine, and I want to enjoy it."

I watch her tuck them into her pocket, calm and focused, like she has no clue she's the only thing keeping me steady. The pressure doesn't vanish. The noise doesn't stop. But for a second, it quiets. Just long enough to remember I can do this.

Just long enough to believe it.

"I'm gonna park and I'll be in in a minute," Jasmine says as we pull up to the front of the team headquarters.

She could leave the damn thing running and it would be fine, but I don't argue, especially with a very eager crowd of staffers and Ollie waiting at the door. No sense in making her deal with all this at six in the bloody morning.

"Let's fucking go, I'm so happy to have you back, mate," Ollie bellows, shoving my arm as I walk past him into the lobby.

"Let me get through the bloody test first, Oliver," I mutter.

"You're fuckin' James Del Toro. A busted hip's not gonna stop ya," he beams with all the confidence I wish I had.

"So what's the deal with you and French, aye?" He leans over the front desk while I sign in. "You two shaggin' again or what?"

I freeze mid-signature. "The fuck are you on about?"

He whips out his phone like it's a bloody press release, Francesca's social profile already pulled up.

"You know she can't keep her mouth shut. What made you think you could keep it a secret, you dirty dog?" he nudges me.

There it is. Not just a picture. A fucking campaign. Post after post, all from years ago, all of us. At races, at events, in bed for fuck's sake. Every caption vague enough to seem current. Every angle chosen to look intimate.

Recent.

My chest tightens. "How many of these has she posted?"

Ollie scrolls like it's show and tell. "Mate... daily. For like two weeks straight."

My jaw clenches, I shove the phone back at him. "I haven't talked to that girl since we broke up. So whatever that is, it's bullshit, yeah? She's probably just trying to piss on Kieran."

"Damn. Brutal." Ollie laughs as if it's nothing. "Well, at

least you're not shaggin' the nurse. She'd think you're two-timin' 'er."

My face goes hot. Anyone scrolling through that would think we're together. That we'd never broken up. All while I've been living with Jasmine. While she's been pulling away from me.

"Fuck," I mutter.

Ollie blinks.

"Oh, you are. Shit, James." His tone turns gleeful. "French is probably stalking her too. Did you know she's got, like, more followers than me?"

Jasmine, whose second job *literally* is social media, must have seen every single one of those pictures. That's why she's been distant. Why she won't look at me the same way. Why last night felt like she was already saying goodbye.

Fuck. No. Not now. I can't spiral about this right now.

"Yeah, I know. Ollie, shut the fuck up. You're taking me out of my head." I brush past him, heading toward the hallway.

He grins. "Not to worry, lad. She's coming in now. Can't be that bad, otherwise she would've quit, yeah?"

The doors slide open. Jasmine crosses through the lobby like she's memorized the layout, phone in one hand, unreadable expression on her face.

She doesn't look up. Just keeps walking until she stops in front of me on instinct.

"You're gonna be late," she says eyes locked on her screen.

"Good morning, Jasmine," Ollie chirps in an exaggeratedly sweet tone.

She looks up then. Cool and collected, not even blinking. "Fuck off, Ollie. He doesn't need you getting in his head right now."

I nearly laugh—because she says it like she's been defending me her whole life and knew I hadn't said it myself.

"Right." He blinks, clearly wounded. "Remind me to never talk to you two in the mornings."

"Don't talk to us in the morning," we both chorus, already walking off.

She didn't even need to look at me. She knew. Without me saying a word. And just like that, the static in my chest eases up. Like she reached in, found the short circuit, and flipped the breaker back on.

"Wait," she says, stopping just before we reached the recovery suite. Tucking her phone in her pocket she turns, planting herself in front of me, hands resting firm and steady on my forearms. Her voice gentle. "I'm not going in there with you."

I open my mouth to protest, but she's already raising that damn finger.

"I'm not leaving," she continues. "I'll find somewhere to wait. But you need to shake off whatever Ollie said, or whatever the hell you're saying to yourself right now. Go in there and be you. The results will speak for themselves. Screw everything else. Lock in."

I swallow, trying to keep something like emotion out of my voice.

"Is this why people like your exercise videos so much? You're very motivating."

She smiles. "That, and my ass."

I huff a laugh. "I'm a fan of that as well," I tease but she doesn't break her focus.

"I'm serious, James. We can joke through the pain another time. But this? This is the moment. Go in there and defend everything you've broken yourself for."

She squeezes my arms once, tight, reassuring, and nudges me forward.

She always knows exactly when to push. And exactly how. Now it's on me to show up.

THE RECOVERY SUITE is cool and sterile. Everything smells like sweat, eucalyptus oil, and recycled air. Like the calm before the lights go out.

I take a breath.

The moment I start, it's like everything narrows.

No Jasmine. No Ollie. No Frenchie bullshit or what-ifs. Just me and the numbers. The data. The work. The thud of my breath. The pound of blood in my ears, rubber mats beneath my shoes, fluorescent lights that never blink.

A monitor's clipped to my chest. A resistance sled rolls out, stacked heavier than I remember. My physio watches from the corner, arms folded, clipboard tight to his chest. No nod. No smile. Just eyes on every inch of my movement.

No one needs to speak. I already know the language.

Sprint intervals. Reflex drills. Core stability, strength testing, cognitive reaction time. Sim rig runs that pushes my body to edge-of-blackout focus. Every sensor's wired to track how fast I move. How much I strain. How far I can still go.

And I do it all. On instinct. On muscle memory.

On pain, if I'm honest.

On spite, if I'm being really fucking honest.

Every rep is a demand. Prove it. Prove it again. Prove it until they can't look away.

By the last circuit, sweat runs down my spine, soaks into my socks, and burns my eyes. My shirt clings to me like skin. My legs scream. My lungs burn. But I don't stop. Don't flinch. Don't fold.

I collapse onto the bench when they give the nod, chest heaving, vision blurry.

Dr. Renaud walks past without looking. "Stronger than before Spa."

He doesn't need to say shit else because that's a pass.

A fucking pass.

They don't clap. Nor cheer. That isn't how this sport works off camera. But I feel it.

I'm back. Maybe even better.

The rest will come later: the data analysis, the debriefs, the contracts. For now, they just step back and let me breathe.

"Bath's prepped," Dr. Renaud calls, already walking toward recovery.

I follow, nod, shake a few hands, but I'm not really here. My body's still processing what it just did. What I'd just proven.

"Fuck," I mutter, sinking myself into the ice bath.

The chill hits hard, brutally cold along my spine, numbing my legs as I sink deeper into the tub. I lean back, resting my neck against the edge, lungs working through the burn, letting it all settle—the pain, the pressure.

Then slow, deliberate footsteps echo across the tiles.

Lamaire.

He stops just short of the tub, hands clasped behind his back, blazer still buttoned.

"That," he says, voice smooth as a poured drink, "was a statement."

I don't look at him again. Just blink toward the ceiling,

breath still coming slow. I know better than to think this is congratulations. There's more.

There always is.

"You know they said it'd take another six months," he continues. "That you'd come back softer. Slower. You just shattered every one of their metrics."

He pauses. Then, quieter, closer. "You've always been a stubborn bastard. Thank God for that."

I tilt my head just enough to catch the way his eyes scan the data still scrolling on the monitor beside me.

"So, we good?" I ask.

He smiles. Not wide, but it's real. "You're cleared for the season. Contract's honored." He pauses. "But we need to have a conversation. About next year."

My chest tightens. "My contract's up next year."

"I know. And Kieran Denune's signing with Red Energy when his current deal expires. End of next season."

The words hit like a second crash. "For whose seat?"

"That depends." Lamaire's expression stays neutral. "You and Oliver are both up for renewal. Whoever performs better this season keeps their seat. The other..." He shrugs a shoulder. "We'll have options. But Kieran's a done deal."

I stare at him, water dripping from my hair, cold seeping into my bones in a way that has nothing to do with the sub-freezing water.

"You're telling me I just fought my way back to compete against my best friend for a seat next to the twat that caused my crash?"

"I'm telling you the grid's watching. Prove you're still worth it." He straightens. "Welcome back, James. Let's talk contracts and brand strategy next week."

Then he's gone, leaving me in the ice bath with the realization that passing the test was just the beginning.

My skin still feels like I'm on fire when I get dressed and leave the recovery suite. I run a hand through my damp hair, still buzzing from the ice bath.

My eyes find Jasmine before she notices me. She's leaning against the wall, staring at the ceiling as though she can't contain her anxiety.

Then her gaze lowers. Brown eyes, soft and a little glassy, meet mine.

"Congrats," she laughs quietly. "I believe I heard the doc say that was your best yet."

She smiles, rocking back on her heels as I approach.

"Couldn't have done it without you."

"You absolutely did do it without me." She waves a hand dismissively. "All I've done is drive you around, change some bandages, and talk shit when you try to cheat reps."

"I do not cheat reps." I nudge her side, catching a laugh.

The pride in her eyes nearly breaks me. I should tell her. About Kieran signing. About competing against Ollie. About how I just earned one more year to prove I'm not washed up. But I can't. Not when she's looking at me with so much relief.

Right now, I just need this. Her. This one moment where it feels like I've actually won something.

She twists away, still smiling.

"I'm proud of you, James. I knew you'd pull it off. I didn't think it'd happen this soon, but I'm happy for you." A quiet sigh follows. "Even if it means you don't need me anymore."

And there it is. I haven't even considered it. That

passing the test might mean the end of her being here. The end of her being mine in any way at all.

We never talked about what would happen after. After the test, after I was cleared, after she wasn't my nurse anymore. I've been so focused on getting through today that I hadn't thought about tomorrow. About her going back to a life that didn't include me.

Realization dawns on me then.

She's doing it again. Running.

Just like after that night a year ago. Except this time, it's been in slow motion and I've been too stupid to see it.

This whole time—living together, sleeping in my bed, holding my hand—maybe it was always just another night for her. Just drawn out over weeks instead of hours.

And now that the job's done, so is she.

But none of it felt like a job. It felt like something real. Something that would outlive the test.

Was I always just the patient to her?

I don't even get the chance to form a sentence before a voice, one I know too well, cut through the quiet.

"James."

Fucking hell.

We both turn. Francesca stands by the lobby doors, dressed like she's stepping out of a fashion editorial. Coat belted at the waist, heels clicking across the floor, sunglasses pushed into her hair like an afterthought. And she's smiling.

Right at me.

"Of course," Jasmine scoffs under her breath.

Francesca strides up like she's meant to be here. Her eyes sweep over me, lingering far too long, before landing on Jasmine.

"Oh my god. You're Jaz Lozano." A bright, sugary smile. "I love your workouts. I swear, I'd kill for your glutes."

Fake. So fake it practically echoes.

"With enough chicken and pain, anything's possible," Jasmine replies, cool as ice.

Francesca laughs theatrically like she's never heard a funnier thing in her life.

"You're hilarious. I like her." Then she turns back to me. "Leave it to you, James, to hire a fitness influencer as your nurse. So on brand."

I exhale sharply. "Don't be disrespectful, Francesca."

"Oh no. Full name?" She pouts, the thing she always did to get away with murder, except now it just makes my skin crawl. "Guess I can't be your Frenchie if you're still mad at me, huh, my love?"

She steps closer. Jasmine shifts, subtle but guarded.

Heat flares violently in my chest.

"I was hoping we could talk," Francesca whispers, like this is still her game to play.

Jasmine takes a step back. "I'll give you two a minute."

I catch her wrist before she can slip away.

"No, stay here."

Her eyes meet mine. Brief but searching. I hold them long enough to say what I can't out loud. And I see it then —the doubt. The assumption that I want Frenchie. That maybe the posts were real.

Fuck that.

I'm losing everything today. My seat, my best friend, maybe her. But I'm not losing her because of Frenchie's bullshit.

Not when I can do something about it. Not when the only thing I can control in this entire fucked-up day is making sure she knows the truth.

Keeping hold of Jasmine, I turn back to Francesca.

"Whatever you're looking for, it's not here. We haven't been a thing in two years. And I'm not interested in pretending otherwise."

I step aside, deliberately, making sure nothing about where I stand, or who I stand with, can be misread.

"This little routine? Playing daft. Ambushing me at work. Posting throwbacks like breadcrumbs? It's a bit strange. You want attention. From Kieran, from me, from anyone who'll bite. But I'm not biting. Disrespect your relationship all you want but stay the fuck out of mine."

Francesca shrugs, trying to look unfazed. She isn't used to being shut down mid-act. Good. Because I mean every word. Looking at her now—the pout, the performance, the way she expected me to fold—I can't believe I ever thought I loved her.

"I just wanted to say I'm sorry. That I—"

"Don't show up here again unless you're waiting for your boyfriend when he's groveling. And don't pull this shit at a paddock when you see her there either."

"Oh, come on." She scoffs. "How serious can that even be?" She gestures towards Jasmine.

"Serious enough that you keep embarrassing yourself." I'm already turning, my hand finds the small of Jasmine's back.

And then I walk her out.

Jasmine looks at me with those eyes that used to give everything away, except this time, I couldn't read a damn thing.

She pauses, like she wants to say something. Then doesn't. Only gets in the lorry, closes the door, and takes the warmth with her. And I stood there, praying I didn't just watch her slip through my fingers again.

Jasmine 22

"Jasmine," James huffs, almost desperate.

Headquarters is barely out of the rearview and its clear James isn't letting me ignore what just happened.

I keep my eyes on the blur of passing trees, arms crossed, pulse scattered.

What the hell am I supposed to say? That seeing her standing there like she belonged made every insecurity I'd been drowning in come clawing up at once?

That every perfect, pointed Instagram post felt like a countdown to the moment she'd tell him what he's missing. What he could have instead of me.

His eyes flick toward me, lingering. For a man who was just cleared to drive, he's being extremely reckless.

"James," I warn. "You're barely cleared. Can you please drive like it?"

He huffs, a pissy little exhale that says *Don't start*.

"I could drive this truck with my eyes closed, Jasmine. I wouldn't crash it." He flicked the blinker. "But if it makes you feel better, I'll pull over."

He starts merging.

"Do not." I shoot him a glare.

His jaw's clenched, but his eyes are doing that thing they do when he's trying to figure out how to fix something.

I know I can't avoid this conversation much longer, especially after whatever the hell happened back there and last night. Somehow putting it off has been comforting, like the longer I wait the longer until it's officially over between us.

But the look in his eye is telling me *Time's up*, so I relent.

"Fine. I'll talk," I say, finally. "Just drive. Please. And watch the road."

He waits patiently, just long enough for the silence to start digging under my skin.

I swallow hard, trying to dislodge the knot forming in my throat. I don't know when I got this emotional, this volatile, but lately, it feels like I'm always one breath away from unraveling.

"What do you want me to say, James?" I keep my eyes locked on my hands, even though I can feel him staring at me.

"Anything, Jasmine," he huffs, frustration threading through his voice. "You've shut me out completely since we left Aurelius'. And don't act like this quiet tiptoeing thing is about my test. It's not."

I finally look at him, brows tight.

"I'm not tiptoeing," I say sharply. "I didn't know what the hell to do about your ex and I didn't... I *don't* want to be another person who takes something from you. Especially when your entire fucking career is on the line."

I pause, watching the words hit him. Then I rush on,

before he can say whatever sweet, too-kind thing I knew he was holding behind those eyes.

"I'm done here, James. You don't need me anymore." My voice cracks: I power through. "Loretta can handle the rest from here. I'm going back home."

The truck slows at a red light. He lets out a quiet, shocked breath. "You can't be serious right now."

I turn, forcing my eyes to meet his.

"What's that supposed to mean, James?"

He flinches slightly, then looks at me. And damn it, he's hurt.

"You're running," he whispers like he's finally letting the words out. "And don't bullshit me, Jasmine. This stopped being about a job the second you walked through my front door, and you know it."

I scoff, turning back to the window. Crossing my arms tightly over my chest, as if that can shield me from him reading every thought I haven't said out loud.

"You keep pretending this doesn't mean anything," he continues, voice tighter now. "Like telling yourself you're just my nurse or some hookup, somehow makes it easier to ignore the fact that you want this. That you want *me*. Just as much as I want you."

The light turns green. He drives, slower now, but the tension between us is screaming.

"You don't know what I want," I mutter, defiant even against my own heart.

He sits up straighter, like he needs to see me.

"Okay, then say it."

He nods once, jaw set.

"Say you don't want me. Say you're not in love with me too." His voice breaks open. "And I'll let you go. I will." He looks back at the road, nostrils flaring.

"But don't you dare act like this is some favor you're doing me by leaving. Because I'll never stop fucking loving you."

I want to scream it, to tell him he's right, that I do fucking love him. But the second I admit it, I'll be doing what I always do. Wanting something so desperately that I convince myself it's real. That it's mine. And when it inevitably falls apart, I'll be the girl who was stupid enough to believe in it again.

We turn onto his street, slower than usual. My chest goes heavy, tight and aching, every warning bell in my body goes off at once. I press my fingers to my eyes, trying to calm the storm spinning out inside me.

"I'm not running," I say flatly, though my voice is barely above a whisper. My throat burning. My eyes stinging.

He keeps driving, slow and silent until we reach the curb. Then he parks. Kills the engine and turns toward me fully.

"Then what are you doing, Jasmine?"

I meet his eyes, and it undoes me.

"I'm fucking scared, James." My voice cracks right through the center. "There. Is that what you wanted to hear?"

The first tear hits my cheek before I can stop it. Hot. Heavy. More follow.

"Scared of what?" His voice is rough and heavy with hurt that mirrors mine. "I'm right here. I've always been right here."

He doesn't move. Those brown eyes pin me, his jaw flutters.

"That night wasn't meaningless." He tries to lower his voice, but it shakes with force. "It fucked me up."

He cards a hand through his hair like it's the only thing keeping him from unraveling completely.

"I looked for you, Jasmine. Everywhere. I didn't even know your last name, and I still tried. For months. Your face in every crowd, scrolling past hundreds of Jasmines on social media, till I felt like a fucking nutter. And when I couldn't find you, I convinced myself I'd made it up. That I imagined you. Dreamt of how good it felt to be with you. This insane connection with someone for one night, who I felt like I'd known my entire life."

He exhales hard, voice broken again.

"Then by some fucking miracle, you show up here and do it all over again. Drive the knife in even further by making me fall in love with you all over. Every. Fucking. Day."

His eyes find mine again, burning this time.

"If you're gonna walk away now, if you're gonna tell me this was just some moment for you, then do it. Just fucking do it. Put me out of my misery. But don't sit there and keep pretending this didn't mean anything. Because it means everything to me. Even if you tell me I'm nothing to you."

I blink fast, staring up at the roof of the car, because fuck, I don't cry in front of people. This isn't how I'm supposed to be.

"This does mean everything to me, James," I whisper. "You mean everything to me."

I turn to him, voice shaking.

"I just didn't want this." My hand motions between us. "This pain. This fucking thing where we give in just to break each other's hearts."

His eyes meet mine, and I see it, the exact moment he decides to lay himself bare. "Break my heart, Jasmine," he says, full of conviction. "Fucking shatter it. I don't care. It doesn't even belong to me anymore. It's been yours since the night I met you."

The air freezes in my lungs. I shake my head, barely able to speak as my tears stream.

"I... you don't mean that."

He doesn't answer. Doesn't argue. Just opens his door, steps out, and closes it with a decisive thud.

A second later, mine opens. He stands there, dark eyes unreadable now.

"What are you doing?" I ask as he leans in.

"Let's go."

I hesitate, blinking up at him.

"You ask me to talk, then kick me out of the car when I do?"

His hand reaches for mine with a kind of certainty that steals every snowballing thought from my head.

"We're done talking, Jasmine." He laces our fingers together and glares at me like he means every word.

He leads me inside the building without another word, his thumb brushing over the back of my hand like he doesn't want to let go. And I let him. Because I don't want to let go either. Not now. Not ever again.

We step inside the elevator and my heart slams against my ribs. The second the doors slide shut, like déjà vu: his mouth is on mine, claiming me completely.

His hand grips the back of my neck, guiding me into him as my spine meets the wall.

My body lights up like it's been waiting for him to call my bluff and stop me from walking away this time.

I pull at the hem of his shirt, my fingers trailing up his torso like muscle memory's dictating them, chasing every tight, flexing muscle with my palms.

He groans into my mouth, then drops to my jaw,

kissing his way down to my collarbone as he tugs my scrub top over my head.

"James," I gasp, "what if someone calls the elevator?"

He pulls back long enough to swipe his keycard, eyes never leaving mine. His hands stay firm on my waist, holding me steady before he reaches behind me, unfastening the clasp of my bra with a flick so smooth it sends a shiver up my spine.

The lace slips down my arms and hits the floor.

His mouth follows—hot, open-mouthed kisses down the center of my chest, then one teasing, lingering graze over each nipple. I gasp, arching into him with a soft groan, already unraveling.

Then he drops lower, his mouth tracing a molten path down my stomach. His tongue follows the dip of my navel as he sinks to his knees, hands already sliding beneath the waistband of my joggers.

"James—" My voice falters.

He doesn't answer.

Instead, he looks up at me from beneath thick lashes, and in one fluid motion, he pulls everything down—pants, panties, the last scrap of modesty—and strips me bare. Even my tennis shoes are gone, kicked somewhere behind him. The air hits my skin all at once.

I gasp, blinking down at myself. And he just stares for a second, in awe, like he's taking a mental photograph.

Then comes his mouth. Kisses over my inner thighs, slow and claiming, then higher. A hot, open-mouthed press of lips exactly where I'm aching for him.

"Mierda," I moan, my legs going soft beneath me.

He grins against me, smug and satisfied, before standing again like he only sampled what he planned to devour later.

I brace myself against the elevator railing, my chest still rising and falling, as the doors slide open to his quiet hall.

James steps in close, one hand slipping behind my head as he gently tugs out my hair tie. The silky black waves tumble free over my shoulders and down my back. His fingers linger at the nape of my neck, thumb stroking once as if he can't help himself. His mouth hovers just above mine, breath warm and ragged.

I can feel the restraint in him, the tension just beneath the surface. We're both stripped bare now, bodies and souls, and that makes everything all the more intense.

Still, after weeks of running away from the very thing I'm standing in, I feel impatient. As if a second more of waiting might break me.

Then he kisses me like he's memorizing my taste. His lips drag over mine before he sucks my bottom lip into his mouth and bites down gently, pulling a gasp from me.

"Walk." He nods towards the elevator door. I laugh under my breath, the sound unsteady.

"You just want to watch my ass, James."

"No, Jasmine." His gaze dips low, voice deep and possessive. "That doesn't belong to you anymore."

He follows me out of the elevator like he already owns the ground I walk on, then unlocks the door to his flat.

"K, take your clothes off now. Or do you want to reenact Titanic or something?"

Impatiently, I lean back against the table in the entrance, my arms braced behind me. James moves in fast—two long strides, and he's standing between my legs again.

His eyes lock onto mine, that stormy kind of focus that makes it hard to breathe.

"Are you mine, Jasmine?" he asks, dark and deadly calm.

I lean forward, lips grazing his, my voice a whisper against the heat between us.

"Yes, James."

His palms slide over my hips, lifting me easily onto the edge of the table. His mouth claims mine again, tongue sweeping deep just as his hand slides between my thighs and pushes two long fingers inside of me.

I gasp, my whole body reacting at once. His thumb finds the pressure point that has me twitching and breathless.

"Is this mine?" he growls into my ear.

A helpless sound tumbles out of me; I try to fight it to find my usual confidence and not melt within seconds like I had the first time we did this. But then he stills, just enough to make me whimper.

"You don't get what you want if you don't answer me, Jasmine," he warns, breath hot against my throat. "Are you going to be a good girl for me?"

And just like that, I'm gone. He knows exactly what he's doing—knows me—and fighting it will only make him more determined to prove his point.

"Yes." I nod furiously, barely catching my breath.

A slow, wicked smile curves his lips.

"Good." His voice drops even lower. "Then tell me what you want."

"You," I pant. "I want you."

"I'm yours, Jas." He kisses along the side of my neck, lips dragging over the places that make my spine bend. "Now what?"

I arch into him, voice trembling against his ear. "Show me you're mine, James."

A masculine grunt rumbles from his throat as he lifts

me from the table with startling ease, my legs wrap around his waist instantly.

The chill of the marble counter bites into my spine as he lays me back on the kitchen island. My legs dangle off the edge.

Through half-lidded eyes, I watch as he peels off his hoodie and shirt in one smooth motion. I don't hide that I'm completely turned on by the fact that every line of his beautiful, honed figure is about to be mine again.

"You're going to keep your eyes on me," he instructs, voice rough, already stepping between my legs. "Understand?"

I nod, chest heaving.

His eyes darken. "Use your voice, Jasmine."

"Yes," I whisper. "I understand, travieso." I giggle, the word slipping out breathy and teasing.

"What?" He tilts his head like he didn't hear me as his fingers slides between my thighs, pushing deep enough to make my body jolt.

"I said yes, I understand, travieso," I moan, louder this time.

His smirk is sinful. "Good. Keep that up."

Then he drops to his knees.

I watch as his mouth finds its mark over his working fingers, brown eyes locked on mine. The rhythm he finds is devastating; skilled, tantric, like he knows every nerve ending by name.

Tension climbs, starting low and fast, until it spreads like ice coursing up my thighs and into my chest.

"Sí, carajo," I hiss, head tipping back as my spine arches off the counter.

He stills.

"What did I say, Jasmine?" His voice is all heat.

"Fuck," I groan, fisting both hands in his hair as I force myself upright, locking my gaze back on his.

Then—only then—does he starts again.

And holy shit, watching him lap and lave, writing me a goddamn love letter with his mouth—it's better than any half hazy memory I've played in my head this last year.

I tremble at the sight, at the sheer intensity of him, of us.

It should be embarrassing how quickly I come for him. How wild and loud with a cry I can't hold back.

He works me through every wave of it—never letting up, never looking away—until the very last shudder, the very last breathless tremor, pulses out of me.

My vision is still hazy, nerves buzzing, when I feel his mouth on my stomach again—soft, soothing kisses trailing upward. His tongue flicks against one nipple, then the other, coaxing another wave of pleasure that rolls through me like an aftershock.

I sit up and pull him into a greedy kiss, tasting myself on his mouth and not caring for a second.

His palms flattened against my back, pulling me flush against him, and I feel the full weight of his erection, hard and insistent, pressed between my legs.

I break the kiss, needing more, needing him. My mouth trace along the curve of his jaw, down the strong line of his throat. I drag my tongue over the pulse beating wildly there, then nip his earlobe.

My palm finds him through his sweats—thick, throbbing—and the groan that rips from his chest sets me on fire all over again.

"What do *you* want, travieso?" I whisper, using his own word against him even though my voice is trembling with anticipation.

He presses his eyes close, exhaling like he's trying to cage something in.

But when he looks back at me—

God.

That fire I craved every second we were apart is right there. Dark and feral. This version of James that must be what he taps into when he's behind a wheel. No polish, no apologies, just taking exactly what he wants and making me desperate to give it to him.

His hand slides to my jaw, firm but tender, tilting my face up until our eyes lock. His thumb brushes my cheek, and I can feel it—this isn't just about sex anymore.

For either of us.

When he kisses me, it's gentle, reverent. Like he's trying to tell me something without words. Like he needs me to understand what I mean to him. I kiss him back the same way, letting him know I do.

Until neither of us can be gentle anymore.

"Turn around," he commands, just as possessive as I need him to be.

"I might not behave as well if I can't see you," I breathe, hopping down from the counter, my hands slipping into his waistband and pushing his sweats to the floor.

He catches my wrist with a smirk.

"What should we do about that then?"

Before I can answer, he spins me gently but firmly onto my stomach, forcing my palms flat against the counter.

"I'm sure you'll think of a fitting punishment," I giggle, biting my bottom lip.

A breath passes.

Then he steps in behind me, nudging my knees apart with his, one slow, agonizing glide through the slick heat his mouth left behind.

My breath shudders then turns into a strangled grunt as he pushes in deeper. His hands find my hips, grip rough, bracing me as he fills me to the hilt.

"Fuck," he growls, voice fraying at the edges. "I nearly forgot how well you take me, baby."

"She missed you," I whisper back, breathless and aching.

He lets out a strangled groan, both hands sweeping down my hips.

Then—rough, cocky, cracked down the middle with need—

"Yeah? She remembers who she fucking belongs to now, doesn't she?" He says as his hand circles my ass, delivering a sharp, biting smack to the underside—followed by a deep, punishing thrust that knocks a primal cry out of me.

"Siempre ha sido tuya," I reply breathlessly, locking eyes with him.

"Fuck—" he hisses. "Say it again."

I groan, trying to find the words, but the sheer ecstasy of him inside me keeps them from reaching my lips. My fingers grip tight around the edge of the counter as he rocks into me again, measured and addictive, every motion claiming more than just my body.

"Say it again, Jasmine." His voice is a growl now, thrusts deep and controlled as he brings his mouth to my ear. "Dilo otra vez."

His voice sends a chill down my spine that makes my eyes roll.

"Siempre ha sido tuya," I repeat in a soft cry, a plea to let me break for him again.

He sucks in a breath, just once. Then he presses his lips slowly and soft against my shoulder before hovering, his voice unwavering like he's making an oath, he whispers:

"Sei mia, tesoro. Sempre," as he sinks into me so deeply it takes my breath.

Each consecutive thrust comes with devastating precision—his precision. The kind no one else can ever replicate. My body is already dancing on the edge, strung tight like a wire. "You wanna come again, Tesoro?" he growls, a hard thrust slamming that need even deeper.

"God," I whimper, "Please."

"Then look at me, Jasmine." I don't. I can't. The tension is too much.

Another biting slap cracks against my ass.

"James," I gasp, nearly unraveling.

He slows, dragging his hips in deep. Taunting me. Punishing me in the most glorious way. "Look at me, baby."

I turn my head, cheek pressed against the counter, muscles burning as I force my gaze to meet his. His eyes lock on mine, dark and full of heat.

"That's my fucking girl."

His pace shifts: slower, deeper, more deliberate. Every inch dragged through every inch of me.

My pulse jackhammers. My vision blurs. Every nerve fires off.

"Whose are you, Jasmine?" he rasps, punctuating the question with another biting smack.

"Fuck. Yours," I cry, greedily arching back to take more.

He grunts, another deep thrust teasing the edge of release. "Whose am I?"

"James, I'm gonna—" I choke out.

Another sharp smack.

"Almost. Use your voice for me baby."

I whimper, voice shaking apart in my throat.

"You're mine," I gasp. "Mine, James. Only mine."

He lets out a guttural sound like the words broke something in him.

"Then come for me, baby," he snarls, voice wrecked and reverent, "Let it break you—I'll put you back together."

I bite my lip, fighting the flood, "Come with me, travieso," I beg, my last thread of restraint snapping clean.

That does it. He slams into me once more. I shatter beneath him, body clenching, crying out as my orgasm hits like a wave I can't outrun. His hips snap forward, his own release ripping out of him in a broken growl.

"Fuck Jasmine," he curses, voice torn as he spills into me, filling me like a signature to his claim. He thrusts through the aftershocks of my release, something only he'd ever drawn from me.

It's not just my body that feels claimed, it's every part of me. Every scared piece I'd tried to protect. He didn't tear my guard down, he waited me out. Steady and patient, until I let him in. And now he's everywhere.

And I'm so insanely in love with him that being anywhere else sounds like hell.

James

23

NEITHER OF US MOVE. I'M STILL INSIDE HER, STILL catching my breath, still trying to wrap my head around the fact that I might never be the same again.

Jasmine is quiet beneath me, chest rising and falling against the countertop, hair a mess, mouth kiss-swollen and flushed. For the first time in weeks, I'm not wondering if she'll bolt the second this is over.

She's here. Still here. Completely mine.

I stay braced over her, unwilling to let the moment break, unwilling to let her go. "Well," she breathes, a quiet chuckle catching in her throat, "that escalated quickly."

I laugh against her as I kiss the curve of her shoulder, slow and lingering. And just like that, I want to do it all over again—if only to prove it wasn't in my head.

"I think we're legally married now," I say, still breathless.

She lets out another laugh, catching her own breath. "Just don't make me wait ten years for a vow renewal."

"I wouldn't dare."

I peel her up from the counter and catch her when her legs buckle slightly. She doesn't even pretend not to be tired, just wraps them around my waist when I pick her up and tucks herself into me like there's no place she'd rather be.

"No way you're ready for round two already," she says, sliding her arms around my neck.

"If I hadn't virtually killed myself during that test, maybe."

I grin, kissing her hair as I push the bedroom door open...her room, now. Mine, technically. Or maybe ours. I set her down on the edge of the sink, start the shower, let the steam rise.

"Come on." I nod to the water.

She gives me that tired, sweet look that makes me forget there's anything outside this room. The season starting, Kieran, the whole bucket of shit to sift outside of this.

All of it just... stops.

She looks like she finally stopped fighting herself. No masks, no deflection, no planning her escape route. After weeks of watching her build walls, seeing her this open feels like a gift I don't deserve.

I step in behind her, pulling her into my chest as the rainfall shower soaks us in steady, rhythmic heat.

Her skin is warm, flushed from the high we still haven't fully come down from. She melts into me and I can feel the difference. No tension, no deflection, she wants to be here.

I reach for the shampoo, lathering it between my palms before working it into her hair, massaging in slow circles.

"Mmm, that's better than the salon," She lets out a relieved sigh, eyes fluttering shut. "Keep doing that and I might be ready to go again."

"Noted." I chuckle against her temple, fingers moving gently at her roots.

Once I rinse the suds from her hair, I run conditioner

through the strands, careful and slow. I press a kiss to each closed eyelid, just because I can.

Just because I want to.

One dark eye cracks open. A lazy, crooked smile tugs at her lips as her arms circle my waist.

"You know," she says, voice quiet but teasing, "you kind of told me you love me in the car."

I reach for the loofah, lathering it with soap, then tilt my chin down to look at her.

"That's because I do love you, Jasmine."

I squish her cheeks together gently with my freehand, turning her mouth into a puffy pout.

Kissing her once.

Twice.

Her big brown eyes hold mine, wide and glinting as I release her cheeks and start running the loofah over her chest and arms.

She catches my hand, holding me still. Her fingers wrap around mine.

"I love you too," she says steadily, meets my gaze head-on, for once, like she isn't afraid of what I might see there.

I swear it knocks the breath out of me.

She loops her arms around my neck and pulls me into a kiss. Unhurried, tender, like she's answering every question I haven't asked yet.

I pull back just enough to look at her, gently brushing a damp strand of hair from her cheek. My voice goes quiet, honest in a way that leaves me exposed.

"Hearing you say it out loud is even better than it sounded in my head."

She smiles softly. "You've been dreaming about it, huh?"

"Constantly," I admit, tracing a thumb over her jaw. "But reality beats the hell out of dreams."

"Then I'll make sure to keep reminding you." Her smile widens before she rests her head against my chest.

We let the quiet wrap around us while we scrub each other clean, stealing kisses between every rinse and lather, like the silence finally knows how to keep us safe.

By the time we finish, she's practically boneless in my arms, so I wrap her in a towel and scoop her up before her legs can give out completely.

"Will my feet ever touch the ground again?" she giggles as I carry her towel-wrapped body toward the bed.

"Only when your legs are steady enough to hold you," I grin and set her down gently. "Which, let's be honest, won't be often."

She sits back watching me, damp hair slung behind her shoulders, pinning me with that mischievous look.

"Arms up," I say, already fetching one of my old t-shirts from the dresser.

She rolls her eyes but obeys, lifting her arms overhead.

"You have some kind of clothing kink, I swear," she mutters as the shirt falls over her face and shoulders.

"Maybe." I watch the hem settle over her thighs. "You wear my clothes better than I ever have."

I step into a pair of boxers, then turn back just as she reaches toward the bedside drawer where she keeps her underwear. I catch her wrist before she can open it.

"None of those," I shake my head. "When we're home, they're not necessary."

She cocks her head at me, grinning. "Fine. No shirts for you then."

I shrug, brushing my fingers back through my hair. "Cheap trade. You know I don't wear them anyway."

She clicks her tongue and sits back onto the bed. The

soft glow in her smile makes me feel like I'm driving a victory lap, after everything it took to get here.

"Turn around," I spin a finger in the air.

"James Del Toro, you're an ass man—do you know that?" she giggles as she turns like she's about to offer herself up all over again. I grab her by the shoulders before she can get any ideas, pressing a kiss to the crown of her head.

"Just your ass," I say with a laugh, "but that's not what I'm asking you to do, Tesoro."

I run my fingers through her hair, separating the strands into three loose sections.

"Wait—are you braiding my hair?" she asks with suspicion and barely contained laughter.

"I am."

"I'm sorry—what summer camp taught you this?"

I smile, focusing on the braid.

"My mum had back surgery when I was in secondary school. Couldn't reach over her head for a while, so I learned a few things from a neighbor to help her out."

I tie off the braid with one of her silk bands from the dresser and let it fall down her back.

"And this is how you like to wear it to bed. Figured your back might appreciate a break too."

She makes a sound between a laugh and a snort, swatting at me. "God, you're such an ass."

I dodge her swing, smiling like an idiot, then pull her down into bed with me, draping the blanket over us both. She can laugh at me, curse me, call me every name in the book, and I'd still do this every night for the rest of my life if she'd let me.

She settles back into me, fitting against me like she was designed for this exact spot. My arm wrapped around her waist, hand resting in the warmth between her thighs.

This was what I want. Not just tonight, but every night. The thought should have terrified me. Instead, it feels like the most obvious thing in the world.

That's when it clicks.

Kais suddenly makes perfect sense. I'd called him mad for marrying Alana after knowing her for weeks, then rationalized it as some lottery kind of love that few ever get.

But now I understand. He wasn't gambling. He wasn't impulsive.

He was sure.

Because when it's real, undeniably real, there's nothing to wait for. You just reach for it and pray you're lucky enough that she reaches back. Now I just had to take a note from his book.

"Jas," I whisper.

"Mmm?" she hums, already half-asleep.

"When do we send for your stuff in Texas?"

She rolls to face me, brow furrowed.

"Send for my stuff?"

I shrug like it wasn't the most serious thing I'd ever said. "Or we can get new stuff. We don't need two couches."

She lets out a short laugh.

"James. Are you asking me to move in with you— halfway across the world?"

I nod once. "I mean, you've sort of already moved in. You just have to let me back in the bedroom."

She studies my face, looking for the punchline. There isn't one.

"I'm serious."

She shifts, hand resting on my chest, eyes scanning mine like she isn't sure what she'll find.

"And do what for work, James?"

I trace the pad of my thumb over the crease between her brows, smoothing it out.

"Whatever you want, Jasmine. We both know you're done with nursing, what's going on with OneActive? They need an answer soon, yeah?"

She twists her lips like she knows she wants more than that but is too afraid to say it out loud.

"Or we could skip all that and you could launch your own line like we talked about. Hell, we'll be in some pretty unreal places when the season starts. Perfect way to build a brand."

She rolls her eyes but smiles anyway. "I love how you say we like it's already decided."

"It is for me. You just have to tell me what you want,"

I rest my hand on her hip, tracing slow lines across her skin under her t-shirt.

She watches me, eyes searching mine. There's still fear there, just a flicker. But then she lets out a breath like it's been sitting in her chest for weeks. She runs her fingers through my hair before brushing them over my jawline.

"I'd be lying if I said this doesn't scare the shit out of me," brown eyes study me. "Moving here, leaving everything behind. My mom's already planning my life back in Miami, expecting me to come home and settle down with some nice Columbian boy who understands the value of a steady paycheck. She'll lose her mind if I tell her that I'm giving up nursing for something that feels like a pipe dream."

She pauses, her voice going smaller.

"I wouldn't even know where to start with my own line. It's not like they teach 'how to build a fitness wear empire' in nursing school. OneActive feels safer, even if it's not what I really want."

"Emilia could help," I offer without hesitation. "Ollie's wife. She's brilliant with that stuff—PR, connections, the whole business side. She'd love working with you."

"Yeah, no." She sighs heavily. "That's a whole other can of worms. I know you like to be a solitaire-playing hermit, but us being in a relationship wouldn't exactly be private. And the last thing I want is for it to look like I'm using you, or—if by some miracle I can launch a line successfully—that I look like Frenchie 2.0."

"Hey," I tilt her chin up to meet my eyes. "We'll never get anywhere if we waste our energy on what everyone else thinks. You know that. I may be private but I'm not naive. You've amassed a giant audience all on your own, and while yes, there will be more attention on you when you're inevitably labeled with the 'James Del Toro's partner' tag on race broadcasts..."

She laughs.

"What you build will be successful because of who you are and how hard you work. I just get the benefit of being the annoyingly supportive boyfriend. Fuck the rest. Use me. Use my connections. Just stay."

She gives me a watery laugh.

"You're insane, you know that? Relentless." Then with a sigh like she can't help but offer another rebuttal. "What about you, though? This season's going to be intense, right? All that pressure to prove you're back to form after the crash?"

She pauses, and I can see her already worrying about me, already considering what I need like it matters more to her than the dream that's right in her reach.

"I can't pile my shit on top of all of that. You need to focus, not be—"

I press my mouth to hers, stopping her spiral, and don't stop until she sighs into me.

I pull back, just enough to meet her eyes again. "Whether my season is shit or a championship, I want you there." I can see the war between her fear and taking the leap.

"Can I be honest with you?" she whispers.

I nod, placing a kiss on her palm.

"I don't want to be anywhere else."

If there was even a fraction of me still holding back—it just shattered.

"Then it's sorted," I mutter, pressing a kiss to her forehead and trying not to lose it all over again right here. Trying not to bury myself in her and show her a hundred more ways I don't want to be anywhere else either.

She touches my cheek, kisses me softly, then pulls back just enough to smile.

"One condition," she taps a finger to my lips.

"Name it." I kiss the tip.

"You have to meet my parents when we're in Miami in the spring."

I laugh, full and unguarded. "You really have to get better at bargaining, babe. You sell yourself too cheap." I shake my head. "Of course I'll meet your parents. Isn't that customary before the wedding?"

She scoffs and turns her back to me. "You've really got to stop saying that now that I'm your girlfriend. People aren't going to think you're joking."

I kiss her cheek, pull her closer, hand resting on her stomach as I press myself in behind her.

"Neh, I don't like girlfriend," I whisper. "That word doesn't even come close."

She snorts, muttering something under her breath

about me calling myself her boyfriend. Then laces her fingers through mine under the covers. I don't need her to say or do anything else. That says it all.

For once, she feels safe–and I can't even enjoy it because of the guilt crawling up my spine. I should tell her about the team drama; about how precarious everything really is.

But I'm not going to poison this with talk about contracts and team politics. She's taken enough risks tonight, choosing me, choosing this. The least I can do is shoulder my own shit and let her have this peace.

I just hope when everything hits the fan, I'll still be enough to make all her leaps of faith worth it.

Jasmine

24

"YOU DON'T THINK THE BOYS ARE A LITTLE YOUNG for this, James?" I ask, holding up the model-sized replicas of his race car.

He catches my eye from the bathroom mirror and shrugs. "It was this or their first karts. Pick your poison, Jas."

I sigh, eyeing my hopelessly crinkled wrapping job. "You're lucky it's Christmas Eve. Otherwise, we'd be at the store right now finding something less insane."

A heavy knock hits the bedroom door.

"You two decent?" Aurelius whispers like a kid afraid to walk in on their parents.

James peeks his head out of the bathroom with a smirk. "Should we tell him no? Squeeze in one more round before we go?"

I throw a wad of wrapping paper at his head. "Yes, Aurelio, come in," I call, rolling my eyes.

James grins, undeterred. "Not him, me."

A pillow flies next. He dodges it, laughing as Aurelius

223

opens the door and James ducks back into the ensuite bathroom like the menace he is.

"James is just finishing getting dressed. You okay?" I ask, clearing my throat, trying to appear less flushed than I feel.

Through the open door, I catch the warm scent of pine and cinnamon from the candles burning in the living room, where "Last Christmas" is playing, perfectly in sync with the lights from our tiny tree in the corner of the bedroom.

"We have to wear pajamas to this bloody thing?" Aurelius grumbles, still mostly hidden behind the cracked door like a reluctant teenager.

"That's the tradition, Aurelio," I reply with a teasing lilt. "What, you don't like the PJs I picked up for you?"

"Fuck no."

The door swings open to reveal him stuffed into triple XL plaid pajamas like a Christmas-themed sausage casing. The buttons are holding on for dear life.

I burst out laughing, clutching the edge of the gift table for support as James pops out of the bathroom, drawn out by the noise.

"Oi, lad, I can see your entire fuckin' knob in those," he wheezes, nearly doubling over.

Aurelius turns crimson and tries to tug the top lower.

"We don't have a male stripper scheduled tonight, but this could work for you," I add, choking on my own laughter.

"Come on, it's Christmas, innit?" he mutters, deadpan. "Can you two be merry without windin' me the fuck up for five minutes?"

James holds up his hands, still laughing.

"I'll take you to grab something else, mate. Just please get out of those pants before the neighbors file a complaint."

"Fine," Aurelius groans from the hallway, muttering something that sounds suspiciously like 'I fucking hate Christmas' as he disappears around the corner.

I click my tongue.

"Shit, I'm supposed to be there early to help Alana set up while she picks Penelope up from the airport."

I glance over at the window. Outside, snow is drifting in slow, lazy spirals, blurring with the fairy lights glowing in the sill.

James buttons his plaid pajama shirt halfway, the fabric clinging to his still-damp chest as he looks over at me.

"So go, babe. Take the lorry. I'll meet you there."

I pull my boots from under the bed. "You're not taking your F40 out in this weather, and that man is not fitting in there."

He laughs. "No, he absolutely wouldn't. We'll walk. It's like a quarter mile."

I start toward the door, but he steps in front of me, blocking it with his body.

"I'll walk," I insist. "You two need to hurry if you want to find anywhere open. Just bring the presents. And don't argue with me—I haven't worked out in three days, I need the steps."

"No." His voice dips as he closes the distance between us. "We can get as sweaty as you want tonight, but it's freezing. I'm dropping you off."

I open my mouth to protest, but he doesn't give me the chance. His mouth presses to mine, soft but sure, and everything I was about to say vanishes on contact. One of the wrapped boxes teeters off the bed as James lifts me, catching it just before it hits the floor with one arm while keeping me pinned to him with the other.

"Last time," I whisper, breathless against his mouth, tangling my fingers in his hair.

"Last time before we leave," he smiles into the kiss, "or last time today?"

I grin, brushing my lips along his jaw. "Depends if you're a good boy, travieso."

"No promises."

"BOLLOCKS, I miss it when you two pretended not to like each other," Aurelius groans from the passenger seat as I lean into the window to kiss James goodbye.

We both pull back laughing.

"Grumble any louder and the candlesticks in your cottage might start singing, Beast," James quips, still grinning as I reach for one last kiss goodbye.

I shake my head at both of them. "God, you wouldn't know you didn't grow up together with the way you two bicker. Next time we go out, I'm making it my personal mission to get you laid."

Aurelius scoffs. "Right, like anyone's rushing to bed the bloke who gasses up a pub bathroom after your cursed pickleback shots."

James and I both recoil in mock horror. "You're banned from ordering for him," James groans.

"Fair enough. I make bad decisions when I drink anyway." I shrug, smiling.

James leans in, voice low and loaded. "I seem to recall you making brilliant decisions. Like that one thing you do with your tongue—"

"Christ," Aurelius complains, slapping the dashboard.

"I'll take myself. Go on. Both of you. And take your unresolved sexual tension with you."

James chuckles. "Alright, alright. Keep your shorts on, we're going."

That's when the loudest, most dramatic whistle shatters the moment like a sitcom entrance cue.

"By all means, keep going!" Alana calls from the front door, one hand on her hip, long brown curls bouncing with every step. "We'll cancel the party and call it foreplay."

Her red satin pajamas shimmer under the porch light, and she looks entirely unbothered like she's seen this exact scene a dozen times and would again.

"Think she'll like my talking tea set?" Aurelius mutters under his breath, sounding both aroused and alarmed.

James snorts as Alana approaches the car, flipping her hair over one shoulder to pull me into a hug.

"Aren't y'all coming in?" she asks, glancing between us.

"Yeah, in a bit," James replies. "I've gotta take my brother here to find jimmies that don't violate international decency laws."

Alana smiles—one of those perfect, dimpled smiles that could get you to confess to crimes you didn't commit—and I swear I watch Aurelius melt like a snowman in July.

"Yes! Hi, I'm so happy you came." She offers her hand to Ari, the rock on her finger catching light. "I'm Alana Reinhardt."

The look of sheer, tragic devastation on his face at the name 'Reinhardt' is so tangible, James and I burst out laughing.

"What?" Alana asks, blinking. "What's funny?"

James shakes his head. "Nothing. Ari was just hoping you had a long-lost twin sister hiding somewhere."

Alana blushes and laughs softly. "Sorry to disappoint.

It's just me, my girl Jazz—clearly taken—and my cousin Penn, who's sworn off men like it's a religion."

Ari clears his throat, cheeks flushing as he gives her a polite nod. "Right. Lovely. Can we go get the fuckin' trousers now or are you hoping to flog me in front of Santa and the baby Jesus too?"

James grins, shifting the car into gear. "I'll be quick. Try not to fall in love with anyone else while I'm gone."

Alana hooks an arm through mine the second I step aside.

"I want every detail," she whispers, barely containing her grin as she hauls me into the warmth of the house.

It smells like mulled cider and cinnamon buns, with a hint of evergreen from the massive fir in the foyer.

The lighting is dim and soft, golden string glowing gently from the tree—twelve feet tall and dressed to the nines in red velvet ribbon, crystal ornaments, and dried orange slices.

A quiet instrumental version of "O Holy Night" plays somewhere in the background, just quiet enough not to wake the boys.

"Coat." She holds out her hand expectantly.

I hand it over, toeing off my boots near the hallway bench as she tucks the jacket away in the closet behind the tree.

"Don't you need to go get Penelope?" I ask, rubbing my arms for warmth, still caught somewhere between laughter and emotion.

"God, no. Kai won't let me drive in this weather. He sent Alonzo." Her tone makes it sound both like an inconvenience and a love letter.

I narrow my eyes. "I thought you needed me to watch the twins?"

"Nope." She grins, unapologetic. "I just wanted some alone time with my best friend on Christmas like old times."

My chest clenches. She doesn't have to say it twice. I already know what it means. What its meant since freshman year.

I follow her down the hall, toward the living room glowing with the light of another tree and the TV screen. *Christmas Vacation* is already playing with the volume just above a whisper and waiting on the coffee table: two bottles of hard cider, two bowls of caramel popcorn, and a blanket folded just so.

I nearly cry.

The same tradition we always did in college. One that used to highlight everything I was missing now felt like it was mine again. The shift is overwhelming.

I've spent so long protecting myself from wanting exactly this that actually having it feels dangerous. Like the universe might notice and take it away.

"You sappy bitch," I blink fast trying not to dwell on my emotions as I flop onto the couch beside her.

She smiles, tucking one leg under her on the couch. "Come on, catch me up—while the boys are sleeping and Kais is still at the gym." She glances at the baby monitor glowing faintly on the end table beside her.

I grab a handful of caramel popcorn, still warm from the oven.

"Well, my stuff came in from Dallas yesterday," I mumble between bites. "All of it. And Emilia's somehow got my launch scheduled for spring, so..." I shrug. "Guess I'm really not going anywhere."

Her head whips toward me like she wasn't expecting that. Then she squeals—quietly, so as not to wake the twins

—and clutches my arm. "Oh my god, Jazz! I'm so happy for you. And selfishly happy for me too." Her dimples deepen. "Your branding looks incredible, by the way. I sneaked a peek when I visited Emilia and the baby."

I huff a laugh. "I can't believe she's working already. Woman just pushed out a human."

"Keeps her mind off Ollie's contract drama," Alana shrugs.

My brows knit instantly. "Contract drama?"

"Oh, it's—" She catches herself, pivoting quickly like she said too much. "You know what? No work talk on Christmas. I want to know about you and James. Moving here means you're serious-serious, right?"

I shrug, trying not to smile like a lunatic.

"I think so..." I hesitate, chewing the inside of my cheek. "What did you say to me when you married Kais? That you loved him so much it hurt?"

Her expression softens. "Still does."

I nod slowly, heart thudding.

"Yeah, well... I thought you were out of your mind back then. But now? I fucking get it." I blink fast, my voice catching. "It hurts. Physically. Like if this doesn't work out, I'm shaving my head and smashing a car with an umbrella."

She laughs softly, instantly teary-eyed, as she squeezes my hand. "It'll work, Jazz. I know it will." Then her face shifts, lips tucking like she's biting back a secret too big to swallow.

I narrow my eyes. "What do you know?"

She throws her hands over her mouth like a kid caught with a present under the tree. The little shit can't keep a secret to save her life. She'll tell you what she bought you for your birthday six months in advance. But damn, is she trying her hardest now.

"Alana," I warn.

"I know nothing," she mumbles through her fingers, barely containing her glee. "I'm just saying... it's all gonna work out exactly the way it's supposed to." She hides her smile behind her cider like it might hide the sparkle in her eyes.

Before I can press her, the quiet chime of the front door echoes through the house.

"Ya Amar?" Kais' deep voice calls out.

The joy that lights Alana's face could power the entire street.

"Coming!" she beams, already on her feet.

I follow her out of the living room and into the foyer, where she launches herself into Kais' arms like they haven't seen each other in years. He catches her effortlessly, mouth on hers, hands around her waist, like nothing else in the world exists. Her giggle fills the air like music.

And God—just like that—I miss James with my whole chest.

"Lord, you two almost make me want to rethink my vow of celibacy," Penelope calls as she steps through the door behind Alonzo, shrugging out of a shearling-lined coat that looks way too chic for travel.

"Fuck yes," I whisper, already walking straight toward her with open arms.

She beams, bright blue eyes twinkling, freckles dusted across caramel skin that's somehow still glowing after a transatlantic flight. That perfect dimpled Cameron girl smile locked and loaded, like the last piece I needed to make everything about today perfect.

"Jazzy baby, I knew you wouldn't leave me alone with these PDA monsters," she says, wrapping me in a hug that smells like vanilla, expensive skincare, and just a whisper of exhaustion.

Alana snorts smugly. "Until her boyfriend gets here."

Penelope blinks at me, eyes going wide before a slow, crooked smirk curves her mouth.

"I told your ass. What happened to 'I'm comin' home single and emotionally unavailable'?" she says in a mocking tone, rolling her eyes.

Kais takes that as his cue to leave. "I'm gonna shower and check on the boys."

He presses a kiss to the top of Alana's head before disappearing like the emotionally intelligent husband he is.

I study Penn's hair in deflection, running my fingers over her long honey-blonde curls.

"This color? You're slaying. The blonde's giving first-class villain energy."

"Yeah, nice pivot." She bats my hand away with a half-scowl, half-smile. "Well, thankfully something's workin for me. Because I was startin' to feel seriously left behind by you girls."

"Not a chance, we're dying without you," I reply, linking arms with her.

"Oh yeah? lucky for y'all then," she says, smug as hell, "I've got an interview with a team here for a head trainer position."

"You what? Penn!" Alana's jaw drops. "Why didn't you tell me?"

"Didn't want to jinx it." Penn peels off her scarf, letting Alana fuss over her. "But since we're all out here spilling confessions like Christmas cocoa... now you know."

"What team? I didn't even know they had hockey here," I ask, popping the last piece of caramel popcorn from my hand into my mouth.

"Not hockey. Rugby. In some place that sounds like a shower." She's already slipping off her boots like she's over the conversation.

"Bath?" I blink.

"That's the one." She snaps her fingers. "Can I get a drink? That flight was long as hell."

I freeze in the doorway for half a second. "My boyfriend's brother plays for that team."

Both their heads whip around. Alana's eyes widen. "Wait—Aurelius plays for The Crusaders? That must be why Kais was watching them the other night."

"Yeah."

I follow them into the kitchen, still trying to make peace with how odd the word 'boyfriend' just sounded. James was right. It doesn't sound right. It feels too cheap.

"You must be *in love* in love." Penelope smirks over her shoulder. "You didn't even flinch when you said that word. Look at you—girl's practically glowing."

Alana hands her a cider, grinning like she's about to start wedding planning on the spot.

"When's the weddin'?" Penn teases, sitting on a barstool. "Or are you running off like this one did?"

"I did not run off," Alana huffs, clutching her chest like she'd been personally attacked. "I've just never wanted a big wedding."

"She's not lying, she always told us she'd do the small thing," I defend her. "But don't drag me into this. I do not want a big wedding either."

I chug the last of my cider like it might back me up. Penelope points her bottle at me with a cocky little wink. "See? Didn't even say she's not getting married. Just doesn't want it big. It's giving vows in two to four business days."

They both crack up. I flip them off just as the front bell rings again.

Smiling before I even realize it.

"Perfect timing," Penelope says, brushing her hair back. "Where is this man? I need to meet the guy who's got Jasmine freakin' Lozano talking about jumpin' a broom."

The front door opens. Alana turns to me, one eyebrow raised and full of mischief.

"There he is."

I smooth my shirt, heart stuttering just a little, hearing James' and Ari's voices carry down the hall.

25

"I look like a fucking idiot," Ari laments, tugging at the waistband of the cartoon Santa pajama pants like they personally offend him as we step into the Reinhardt's' front entryway—or, more accurately, onto the set of an American Christmas movie.

Hard to tell the difference.

"We did the best we could, yeah?" I reply to my growly brother, unzipping my coat as we move toward the boot room. "Least your lads are tucked up and not hunting for milk and cookies."

He grunts, knocking back the last of his coffee, the one he insisted we stop for like he couldn't face the evening without caffeinated armor.

A burst of laughter carries down the hallway from the kitchen, familiar and inviting.

"Fucking hell," Ari growls.

"What now, you Grinch?" I chuckle, shrug off my coat and hang it up.

"I really hope you're James and not him," a thick southern and unimpressed accent comes from behind me.

I turn to find a woman—short, freckled, and built like she could bench press me if I said the wrong thing—blocking the hallway like a security detail.

Same delicate features as Alana, but where Alana moves with warmth, this one has a steelier edge. Blue eyes bright as glass lock on me like she means business.

Jasmine and Alana trail in behind her, both wearing that look women get when they know the drama is about to be premium.

I give the blonde my best PR smile. "What's wrong with him?"

"He's an impatient ass," she snaps, cutting a look over to Ari.

"Says the pain in the arse who held up the queue to argue about milk," he shoots back.

I blink, realization dawning as I stare between them. "Ah. You're the coffee shop girl."

Her eyes narrow. "More like coffee-ruining hippie, if I recall correctly."

"This is James," Jasmine interrupts quickly, looping an arm around my back like she can feel me trying not to burst out a laugh. "And that's Aurelius, his brother."

She gives the blonde a pointed look.

"Guys this is Penelope Cameron."

Penelope thins her eyes at Ari before turning to me with a too-smooth smile. "Nice to meet you, James. I hope your manners are better than your brother's."

Ari grunts a humorless sound. "Yeah, well I hope they ban you from every caff in town."

Jasmine and I both blink. Same expression. Same wide-eyed *this is fine* energy.

"I really thought you two would hit it off. Ari here gardens," Jasmine gestures toward him, half-amused, half-regretting everything. "And Penn, you basically pray to your flower beds."

Penelope's lips twitch in a hateful smile. "I'm certain he's a carrots-and-potatoes kind of guy. Probably finds flowers pointless."

"They are," Ari volleys without missing a beat.

Jasmine sighs, leaning her head briefly against my shoulder like she's already exhausted. "Guys, play nice. It's Christmas. Don't make me put you in a time out before we've even had appetizers."

"You know," I add, watching them like a car crash in slow motion, "If you keep yelling at him like that and he's gonna think it's a proposal. Might want a matching set of pajamas by the end of the night."

Penelope blinks, looking vaguely horrified.

Before she can speak, Jasmine jumps in.

"Well, you better hope she doesn't have to work on your glutes next season."

Ari pales as if he just saw a ghost. "What, she's a physio?"

"Interviewing with the Crusader's as the lead," Alana chimes from the hallway, clearly enjoying the show. "So yes, she might be in charge of stretching you out if you're lucky."

Penelope smirks, suddenly enjoying herself far too much. "I've been told I'm gentle."

Jasmine snorts, then quickly claps a hand over her mouth in an effort to mask it.

"If this is your idea of gentle," Aurelius says with a slow grin, "remind me to piss you off next season."

Penelope's smile doesn't move, but something in her eye's changes. Just for a second. Like maybe she's enjoying this as much as he is.

And clearly, Ari is enjoying it. The stubborn git who hates small talk is practically leaning into her insults. Jasmine notices too, her gaze narrowing as if she's deciding whether to step in or let the match burn.

"Look who's up! My babies," Alana beams as Kais descends the stairs. One twin on each arm, all three of them dressed in matching red silk pajamas. I mean, of course they are.

"Oi, you couldn't have taken me to get some of those?" Aurelius mutters to me, eyes on the twins. "Maybe Azul here would think twice about yelling at me if I looked like that."

That earns him a blink of surprise and the faintest smile from Penelope. Not even a minute and she's already warming up to him. Hard not to like the stubborn bastard once you get past the growling.

Still, seeing him here, with these people who mean everything to me, it matters more than I'd expected.

"James," Kais greets, passing Rafi off to his mom before clapping palms with me.

"Let me have that boy, please, lad." I'm already reaching for Zayd, who melts into my arms with a warm cheek and a drool string.

"This is my brother, Aurelius," I nod toward him, still standing stiff by the door like he's debating bolting.

"Kais Reinhardt." Kais offers his hand. "I caught your last match. Hell of a tackle in the second half. You move like a bloke half your size."

Ari shakes it, giving a modest nod. "Bit of luck, that. Bastard slipped right into it."

He softens completely, stepping closer to get a better look at both boys before focusing on Zayd, who's doing his best impression of his father's intimidation stare despite still being in diapers.

"Suppose these are the big boys that stole all the good pajamas, yeah?" he chuckles, flashing a rare grin that wins him a gummy one right back. "Well, at least someone likes me."

"Yeah, they've got the run of the place. We're just the staff," Kais laughs, giving Zayd's belly a soft tap. "Don't let the drool fool you, he'll have you wrapped around his finger by the end of the night."

Then Kais moves—it doesn't even look like a decision —toward Alana. Hand to her lower back, a kiss to her temple. Smiling like the air in the room settled the second he touched her.

"Good to have you here, mate," he says to Aurelius over her head before returning to being focused completely on his wife. He looks at her like she holds his whole world.

I know that look. Because it's the same one I give the woman staring up at me like I hold hers.

"Here, I'll take him." Jasmine's voice is soft but sure, arms already open as Zayd lunges toward her.

She catches him with ease, holding him on her hip, and bouncing gently with the confidence of someone who's done this a thousand times.

Something in me seems to crack open.

Could be the warmth of the room, the cinnamon in the air, or the way the firelight catches the shine of her eyes, but I swear I can feel the shape of my future staring back at me. Barefaced. Flirty little bangs. Wearing the same idiotic pajamas as me. And looking up like I'm something worth softening for.

Yeah. Frame this. Bury me with it.

"After you," I kiss her on the forehead and motioning forward.

Behind us, Penelope exhales dramatically.

"Fine, I get it," she sighs, waving a hand as she walks past us. "You have my permission. Get married. Make babies. Whatever."

"That's what I'm sayin'," Ari mutters, trailing behind her like he can't help himself.

I turn back to Jasmine, dropping my voice. "Actually, I need to talk to Kais for a second. Can you keep your friend from making me an only child again?"

She gives me that indulgent smile—one that says she'd miss me but is trying to act chill about it.

"Be quick," she murmurs.

"Oh yeah?" I lean in, brushing my hand over the small of her back. "Should we find somewhere private?"

She rolls her eyes affectionately and waves me off before following Alana and Penelope into the living room. Kais nods me toward the door to his office, already halfway there.

I follow.

"So, what's the plan?" Kais asks, closing the office door behind us.

He moves to the bar cart without asking: two fingers of bourbon, same pour every time. We've been doing this for years now. Different houses, different cities, same damn ritual.

Only difference is we'd take the piss out of Ollie for getting married so young over takeaway and cheap whisky. Now they both have kids, Kais is married to my girl's best friend, and I'm one ring away from proving we were idiots all along.

"I don't know." I suck in a breath and sit in one of the

leather armchairs. "Talked to her parents last night. I just haven't told my mum yet."

He hands me a glass, arching a brow as he sits across from me. "You talked to her parents?"

"Yeah." I run a hand through my hair, laughing softly. "Her dad was easy. Happy I asked. Her mum? Not so much."

He smirks. "What, she make you run drills first?"

"Worse. Made me join her virtual book club." I knock back a sip of bourbon. "To prove I know how to commit."

"Fucking hell." Kais barks a laugh. "What kind of books?"

I shoot him a look over the rim of my glass.

"Self-help." I drain half my drink in one go. "Apparently I need to unlock my emotional intelligence before I get the green light."

He wheezes. "Oh, mate."

I sigh, slumping back. "Hell, maybe one of them will help me sort the whole money thing."

Kais' expression sobers, setting his glass down. "What money thing?"

"I've been covering her launch costs. The whole thing. Emilia's fees, production, everything." I rub my jaw. "She has no idea. Thinks she's doing it on her miracle budget."

"How much are we talking?"

"Enough that fighting for my seat and renegotiating with Lamaire just got a lot more complicated." I meet his eyes. "In no way do I want to race next to Kieran, but I can't take a pay cut for a smaller team right now. Not with Mum's B&B opening in the spring and Jasmine's business to think about."

Kais leans forward. "Does she know about Lamaire?"

"Fuck no. And I'm not telling her until after I put the

ring on her finger." I pull the ring box from my pocket, let it sit heavy in my palm for a second before handing it to him. "She's got enough on her plate without worrying about my shit."

He opens it. Lets out a low whistle. "Christ."

"Cost more than my fucking Ferrari did," I rub a hand over my jaw, pulse thudding. And worth it. Every bloody cent. Because she's the only thing I've ever wanted without a finish line.

He grins, still looking at the ring. "You're a proper tight lad. I'm impressed."

"Right," I say, leaning forward. "Keep it here, will you? I'm tired of carrying it around like a damn time bomb."

He nods, standing to walk it back to the safe wedged in the bookshelf.

"She's already suspicious," I mutter. "Keeps looking at me like she's figured it out."

"What about your mum?" he asks, shutting the safe door. "Why don't you just go see her? Do it there?"

"Winter in Ortigia?" I wince, setting my glass down. "Bit of a downgrade from midnight elopement in Monaco."

He huffs, shaking his head. "Place don't fuckin' matter. If she's gonna say yes, she'll do it just about anywhere. Just don't be lazy about it."

"Yeah, well I still don't know about going out there. The minute my mum sees me she's gonna start laying into me about my contract. She's got some special paddock mum access that gets the drama to her before half the drivers."

We both chuckle under our breath.

"It's only a matter of time before she finds out about my contract situation, she'll refuse any help with the B&B.

You know how she is about taking money when things are uncertain."

"All the more reason not to wait," he says simply, tipping his glass toward me. "Not 'cause you're rushing it. 'Cause you already know. And the longer you keep all this to yourself, the more likely it all blows up in your face."

A hard knock hits the door, then it swings open.

"Merry fucking Christmas, cunts," Ollie bellows.

"I second that. Merry Christmas, cunts," Montee's thick Scottish brogue follows as he comes in behind him.

Still looks like he can flatten someone with a handshake —shoulders that don't fit through doorframes, bronze skin mapped with tattoos, buzz cut going gray at the edges. The kind of face that makes you check your posture without meaning to.

The man is basically family, has been since he started training Kais when we were kids. He's somewhere between a father figure and a mate, which makes the brief period he dated my mum something I try very hard to forget.

"I'll have a bit of what you're having." Ollie nods toward our empty glasses.

"Nah, piss off. You're late," Kais grunts, already walking past him. "My wife made some mulled shite—cunted to hell with cloves or something. Come have a bit of that instead."

Montee lets out a deep laugh, clapping Kais on the back. "You get twitchy when you're away from dem boys for more than ten minutes."

"I'll be having two then," Ollie announces. "I've got the night off."

I turn, frowning. "The fuck does that mean? Your son's what—a week old?"

"Emilia's parents are in town. Hovering, rearranging the nappies, all that. She don't need me." He shrugs me off.

"She wasn't ready to leave the house, told me to enjoy myself. And I plan to."

Kais lands a heavy hand on Ollie's shoulder. "One drink. Then you're fucking off home to your missus and the boy, yeah?"

Ollie groans. "Yeah, yeah—keep your pants on. Christ."

The four of us make our way toward the living room, where the party is in full swing: voices mixing with jazzy Christmas music and the occasional burst of laughter.

"James!" Charles calls from the couch, raising a glass as we stepped into the living room.

Montee's raised the boy since he was twelve, and he now looks like he could take on my brother's entire team single-handed.

"Your missus made me the strangest drink—pickles and all—but it's brilliant."

"Of course she did." I laugh. "You're looking fit, mate. Kais working you hard?"

"Every bloody day," he grins.

Kais grabs my shoulder, voice low. "Didn't even correct him, mate." He smirks. "Let Alanzo know when you need the plane, yeah?"

Then he slipped past, already zeroed in on the blanket in front of the fire, where Alana, Jasmine, and the twins are playing with some wooden contraption that looks more engineering than toy. The kind of scene that makes you want to freeze time and never leave the room.

'Your missus'. Nothing about those words felt off. And God, if she only knew how desperately I wanted her to wear that title. To give her my name and earn the right to be called hers.

I drop into an armchair beside Aurelius and Montee's son, Tobias—smoother version of Montee with green eyes and that insufferable confidence that comes with being overpaid to play footie—half-listening to them bicker, half-watching Jasmine being her.

"Right, right. Big hits, no footwork," Tobias says, lounging in his usual cocky swagger like he owned the room. "Must be why you lot can't keep up with a ball unless it's shaped like an egg."

Aurelius leans back, gruff as ever. "Least it takes more than a stiff breeze to put us on the floor. You lot go down like folding chairs."

"Maybe" Tobias flashes him that smug rookie-white smile. "But folding chairs still get more airtime than rugby highlights."

Aurelius stands like a boulder getting bored. "Keep talkin', pretty boy. I've got boots older than your career."

"Yeah?" Tobias puts his hands behind his head, lounging. "They probably smell better than you too."

Charles, who's relaxed on the couch, nursing his pickle monstrosity like it's his day off, finally cuts in. "Tee, you're not wrong. But I'm not getting dragged into a fight with that fucking giant over it. Last time you ran your mouth, Kais made us flip tires till we shat."

"Character-building," Montee calls from the doorway. "And if you keep it up, I'll invite Aurelius to run your training next time."

Tobias turns, looking vaguely horrified. "That's abuse, Dad."

"That's accountability," Aurelius mutters, "I'm getting a beer." He waves, already walking off.

"They've been going at it since the moment that boy said he plays soccer for Chelsea," Jasmine laughs, sitting on my lap.

"It's football here, babe," I mutter, looping an arm

around her waist. Smiling like an idiot because apparently ten minutes without her is enough to warrant the glee I feel holding her again.

"Right, whatever," she teases. "There's no hot race car drivers in that, so I don't care."

Her arms slide around my neck, pulling me into a quick kiss that doesn't help me think straight.

I tip my head back, looking up at her.

"We've got a week or so before I need to be back at HQ. Want to go to Ortigia?"

"To see Mama Lucia?" she perks up, eyes warm, voice soft like she's always said it that way.

Something about hearing it, *'Mama Lucia'*, in her voice makes my chest ache in the best way. Like she's already part of all of it. Of home. Of family. Of everything.

"Yes." I nod. "And have lots of uninterrupted sex."

That earns me another kiss—slower this time, a smile pressed between us.

"Can we make it back before New Year's?" she brushes her hair behind her ear. "Emilia texted and said she got me a meeting with that sporting goods store. They might be interested in carrying a few test pieces."

"Already?" I try to keep the pride out of my voice. "That's moving fast."

"I know, right?" She smiles. "Feels surreal."

God, she had no idea how proud I was of her. Of the way she always showed up for everyone else—and finally, finally, was doing something for herself.

She gives me a subtle but pointed glance past my shoulder. "What's Montee's daughter's name again?" she whispers. "The one over there pretending not to flirt with her brother's best friend like she hasn't already practiced writing his last name next to hers?"

I follow her gaze to the couch, where Nadine sits with her legs tucked beneath her, laughing at something Charles is saying. He's leaned in, not too close, but closer than necessary—smiling in that effortless way that always gets a man in trouble.

"Nadine," I reply. "Montee's youngest."

Jasmine hums. "Yeah... Nadine. I was talking to her while you were with Kais. I think I want her to help with the launch. She's smart as hell. Got 100K followers and the kind of grit you can't coach. I think she just needs someone to bet on her."

I shrug. "If you can pry her away from Montee. She basically runs the gym when he and Kais aren't around."

Jasmine blows out a breath, thoughtful. "She doesn't want to do that shit. She just does it to keep her dad happy —and, if I had to guess, to stay close to that guy."

Before I can respond, Aurelius's thunderous voice cuts clean through the buzz of the room. "Azul says the food's ready."

"Please stop calling me that, *green giant*." Penelope groans, stepping out from behind him. "Everything's out of the oven, Lana," she adds.

Alana smiles from the floor where she's still cross-legged beside the twins and Kais.

"Then let's eat," she claps her hands gently. "Everybody to the table."

Jasmine

26

Emilia: Sample walkthrough is set for the third. Teaser clips roll out across all platforms this evening. Do you have a date in mind for the campaign shoot?

Me: You don't sleep do you Millie?

Emilia: I've got cabin fever and you're my favorite client. A girl can only take so many nappies and tears.

Me: Let me check schedules again with everyone. Hard to get these athletes to sit still for long. Let's pencil in week after next?

Emilia: Tell me about it. Looking forward to having you around the paddock this season, though!

Me: Just keep that crazy ass Francesca from my orbit and it'll be a good time.

Emilia: That woman's a nightmare. I've drafted a paddock prayer. "Dear universe, please bless Kieran with a DNS and Francesca with a locked hospitality pass."

Me: Toss in a demotion to Delancey's junior sim team and I'll light the incense myself.

Emilia: Consider it done. For now enjoy Sicily, you deserve a break. Just don't forget to snap a few pics for content. Your audience loves James.

Me: Yeah, the "Daddy James" comments are a bit unhinged though... Do I feed that beast?

Emilia: Oh the comment section is feral. But engagement's spiking and newsletter signups have doubled with each post. So... we're choosing our poison here. Let's keep your content with him faceless—the Ms. Bellum vibe works—mystery sells. So does that man's jawline.

THE SUN IS BARELY UP, CASTING A SOFT PINK HAZE over the ocean outside our window, and James is still dead to the world—sprawled diagonally across the bed like a Greek god in full repose.

We got into Ortigia late, long past his mother's bedtime. She left a note taped to the B&B door in loopy cursive:

Pick any room, I'll be here in the morning.

That was it.

The locanda, as the taxi driver had called it, is breathtaking. Thick stone walls, weathered beams, hand-painted tile in rich shades of cobalt and terracotta. Even in the dark, it felt warm—romantic in a way that doesn't try too hard. But in the morning light? It's a postcard come to life.

A breeze slips through the open window beside me, carrying the briny scent of the sea and something warm and savory wafting up from the kitchen downstairs. Pots clatter distantly, something scraping gently against cast iron.

The smell of yeast and citrus and something that might be garlic makes me suddenly aware of how long I've been sitting here pretending to work. Fiddling with my tablet while my stomach twists itself into knots.

James snores quietly behind me, blissfully unaware. The man sleeps like he's paid to ignore emergencies.

I glance toward the door.

Would it be weird if I just... went down there? Introduced myself?

"Hi, I'm the nurse who helped your son learn to function again, and now I live with him and sometimes steal his T-shirts."

God. Absolutely not.

But sitting here fully awake while I know his mom is downstairs? That feels worse.

So, I stand. Tug on a pair of sweatpants. Throw James' oatmeal-colored cardigan over my crop top. Hair in a messy bun. I look like I'm trying too hard to look like I'm not trying at all. But I'm not here to impress her with my looks —I love her son. That has to count for something.

It better count for something. And if it doesn't? Well, I'll fake a phone call and climb out a window.

The moment I open the bedroom door, it's like a memory hits me: fresh bread baking, and the metallic percussion of pans clinking in rhythm like a symphony warming up for sunrise.

The scent alone makes my chest ache. Not just from hunger, but from the quiet, unexpected tug of homesickness—of missing my mom more than I've let myself admit for a long time.

I pad down the stairs, drawn toward the noise.

The villa is still drowsy in the morning light, golden streaks casting long shadows over boxes, paint cloths, and the kind of half-finished projects that meant the place was loved into being, not designed for perfection.

I weave past tools and a leaning stack of frames, ducking through a low arched doorway into the kitchen at the heart of everything.

And it is exactly that—heart.

Hand-painted Delft tiles line the walls like patchwork art. Butcher block counters bear the marks of real use, and in the brick alcove ahead, a large butter-yellow AGA stove glows like the soul of the room. The heat from it creeps through my sweater, enough to warm my nose and feet at once.

In front of it, a woman stands with her back to me—barefoot, linen dress clinging softly to generous curves, a red apron tied tight around her waist, and a yellow bandana keeping thick brown curls swept back from her face.

One hand stirs something fragrant in a saucepan, the other moves instinctively to a salt pot—like this kitchen speaks a language she's been fluent in since birth.

She hasn't noticed me yet. I hesitate, nerves pooling in my throat, then I clear it gently.

"Good morning, are you Lucia?" I ask in a small voice.

She turns toward me, licking a bit of something creamy off her finger.

"Mmm, sì sì, bon giornu." Her smile stretches wide and for a split second, I'm staring straight into James' grin. Same dimples. Same mischievous sparkle. She flicks her wrist to wave me over. "I would come to you, my dear, but I'm just about to pull the ricotta."

I step into the warmth of the kitchen, drawn like a moth. Peeking into the pot beside her while she checks a thermometer and I inhale deeply, unable to help myself from taking in the heavenly scents around me.

"Bedda matri, you are beautiful." She laughs the rich and unbothered laugh of a woman who knows exactly who she is.

"And you are too, Ms. Del Toro." I smile, cheeks flushing.

"Technically, it's Marino," she corrects, waving the air. "But don't call me that—I'll feel like my mother. You can call me Lucia. Or mama, if you're feeling bold. Just nothing with 'Ms.' Unless I marry Massimo Torricelli... then you can call me whatever he wants."

She pulls the pot from the stove and begins pouring the curds into a cloth-lined strainer. I blink at her, stunned at her reference.

"Oh, trust me—for Massimo, everything's on the table. That man made every woman I know question their morals and their passport expiration date."

Lucia gives a knowing hum, hands deftly working the curds from the whey.

"Si. For him?" she tosses me a wink. "I have no morals."

I burst into quiet laughter, already smitten. The woman is impossibly charming, magnetic in that rare, unforced way. And now, I fully understand exactly where James gets it from.

"How can I help? James is still out cold." I glance around for anything I can jump in on.

"I'm just about done. But if you want to be useful, put on some coffee." She reaches for a moka pot perched on the windowsill and passes it to me with a smile. "It draws him from sleep like a beacon."

I turn it over in my hands, already moving toward the stove. "Do you have a grinder, or do you use Barbera?"

Her eyes sparkle before she opens a tin and hands it to me. It's unlabeled, old and dented like it's lived a dozen lives in this kitchen.

"My boy's been making you coffee?"

"That's what he calls it," I huff a laugh, scooping the rich grounds into the filter. "But honestly? It's more like jet fuel. I'm wired until dinner."

Lucia lets out a laugh that animates her entire face. "Must be strong enough to wake the dead—like that boy of mine."

I twist the pot shut and place it on the hot plate, the metal clicking lightly against the circle burner. The scent of the grounds bloom immediately, rich with the promise of being very awake in a few minutes.

"This place is a dream," I say, eyes on the moka pot as it heats.

Lucia smiles as she pulls a golden loaf of braided brioche from the oven, steam rising from its crust.

"It's been my dream since I was a girl," she replies, setting it on a wooden board with the kind of pride you can't fake.

"My family's from a rough town a few hours inland, but we visited Ortigia one summer... and I fell in love." She turns to slice paper-thin ribbons of prosciutto from a slab on the island. "With the sea. With the food. With a much older fisherman who gave me the greatest gift of my life."

Behind me, the moka pot begins to hiss, that telltale gurgle of bubbling espresso starting to rise. I reach for it, but she stops me with a wave.

"No, no—let it hiss. If it doesn't hiss, it's not real coffee," she instructs with a soft grin, placing an iron skillet on the burner and pouring in a generous splash of olive oil. The smell fills my nose instantly.

I glance around the sun-dappled kitchen, the sound of seagulls calling in the distance, and I understand exactly why she stayed.

"I see why you did," I say in awe. "There's something... magical about it."

Lucia hums in agreement as I finally pull the pot from the heat, the hiss tapering into a satisfied sigh.

"It's something, isn't it?" Her voice is softer now, reflective, as she watches the olive oil swirl in the skillet. "When you've spent your whole life surviving, you eventually crave softness. Ortigia is soft in all the right ways. And now—so is my life. No luxury. No noise. Just peace."

I still for a moment, the little espresso cups cradled in my hands. Ortigia is exactly that: dappled light, quiet corners, the scent of sea salt and rosemary in the breeze. And James... he's peace, too. The kind I never thought I'd be allowed to have.

"I understand that too well," I murmur, pouring the espresso as carefully as I can—as though the moment deserves ceremony.

Lucia glances back at me with a knowing smile, and I swear something unspoken passes between us. Something deep and woman-made.

"Well, look at you two," James' gruff morning voice cuts through the air like velvet and gravel, equal parts sleepy and amused as he steps into the kitchen.

" Amore mio," Lucia beams, pulling him into a hug like she hasn't seen him in years. She kisses both his cheeks, holding his face for a second longer than necessary, as if re-memorizing him.

"Bon giornu, Mama," James mumbles into her hair. "Sì, bellissima! You're glowing."

She swats his chest lightly. "Now you're trying to sweet talk me. What do you want, monello?"

He smiles like a boy, already eyeing the brioche on the island. "You know what I want."

She rolls her eyes. "Yes, yes—there's some already sliced in the basket. Ricotta's by the sink."

James starts to reach for one of the coffee cups, I catch his hand. "Doesn't have cinnamon in it yet."

Lucia lets out a burst of laughter, her eyes flicking between us. "Monello, you've taught her your coffee order?"

James ducks into the cabinet under me, pulling out a glass jar. "How else are we supposed to have a happy marriage, Mama?"

My cheeks burn.

"James," I whisper, nudging him.

He smiles that smug, slow grin and kisses my forehead.

"Aye, Tesoro... if she knows your coffee, the rest is just details," Lucia says, cracking eggs into her skillet without missing a beat.

James leans into my ear.

"Told you she'd love you," he says proudly, then pulls back with a wink.

"Too soon to know that," I retort, handing him the

espresso cups now dusted with cinnamon. "But she is really amazing."

James smiles big, passing one cup to his mom and keeping one for himself.

"What are we doing today, Mama?"

"Mmm, perfetto. Forte." Lucia takes a sip, her approval a quiet rumble as she sets her pan aside. "You want to help me paint? I'm too short and my back won't let me reach the top of the guest room walls downstairs."

James moves to grab a stack of plates, handing them to me. "I'll get it done, Mama." He grabs the ricotta from the counter. Then glancing over his shoulder, "You've got a few meetings today, don't you, Jas?"

"Uh—yeah." I nod, setting down the last plate. "Emilia's on me about finalizing the promo shoot. I've gotta lock down a date that you and Aurelius aren't bouncing around like molecules so we can shoot your bit for the men's line...and I need to approve the final mock-ups today."

Even as I say it, Emilia's words parrot in my head.

Your audience loves James.

I pause, suddenly loathing how much I'm asking of him and resisting the urge to shrink back.

"Busy woman," Lucia hums, bringing a painted ceramic plate over to the table, layered with fried eggs, tomato slices, and delicate roses of prosciutto. Turning back toward the stove, she adds, "What are you working on?"

I clear my throat, suddenly nervous. "Um... I'm launching a performance-focused activewear line this spring. James and Aurelius have kindly volunteered to model for the men's range. Helps to show how it fits on different body types."

James drops into the seat next to me, already piling his plate with enough food to fuel a full lap around Monza.

"Jam?" he mutters, eyes scanning the table like he's at home. Which, clearly, he is.

"Here, Monello," Lucia laughs under her breath, setting a small jar down in front of him then sitting across from us. She tosses back the rest of her espresso like a shot.

"So, this Aurelius," she says, looking at James over her cup, "You've told me so little."

I raise my brows.

"That's surprising," I glance between them. "I don't think they've given each other a breath since they met."

James keeps chewing, eyes on his plate, like he can ignore us and the moment might pass. Then finally—he swallows, wipes his mouth, and looks up.

"What, Mama?" he grumbles. "I didn't think you'd want to know about him. Because of Hernán, you know?"

Lucia crosses her arms, her dark brows furrowed. "Of course I want to know, James. You don't need to protect me. I love that you're connecting with your brother. I'm just sorry I never knew he existed. We could've reached out sooner."

James shrugs, mouth tightening.

"Chista è a vita, Mama." He scrubs a hand down his face, as if trying to shake the weight of it off. "You'll meet him in the spring. He'll be in Imola."

She exhales, something sweet flickering in her expression. "I'll hold you to that."

James just smiles at her then grabs another piece of brioche. "Don't worry. I'm certain Jasmine will make it her personal mission that you two meet."

"I don't even know that I'll have to," I add, swallowing my own food. "The man looks like a tree."

Lucia laughs, a rich, melodic sound that bounces off the kitchen tiles. "Sounds like he takes after Hernán. I have a thing for tall, dark, and questionable men, I guess."

"Mama, please." James groans. "I'm eating."

"Oh, don't act so innocent, James. I'm still a hot commodity, you know."

I nod, laughing mid-bite. "Definitely. Where do you think you get your looks?"

James winces, taking another huge bite, seemingly to mask his boyish pain. "I don't want to think about anyone looking at my mum, thank you."

Lucia shakes her head. "I don't know why he's like this. He's seen me date before."

"Yeah—when I was fourteen," James talks with a full mouth. "I've spent years trying to block it out, but thanks for the reminder."

I lean in, dropping my voice conspiratorially just to rib James. "Why? Was he also tall, dark, and questionable?"

Lucia tilts her head like she's flipping through a memory. "Tall and dark, yes. But very kind. Monello's best friend works with him still, I think... right?"

James sucks in a breath through his nose like he just stepped on a landmine.

My eyebrows shoot up.

"Who?" I beam, already bracing for the gossip.

He shoots me daggers, brushing his hands on a napkin. "Montee."

"Oh my god." I clap a hand over my mouth and burst into laughter. "Bravo, Lucia."

James drops his head back with a groan of pure despair.

"Is he seeing anyone?" she asks, completely unfazed, picking at her plate like we aren't detonating her son's composure in real time.

"Mama," James warns, dragging a hand down his face. "Please."

"No, he isn't," I chime in, not hiding my grin. "My best friend's married to Kais. Montee's been too wrapped up playing grandpa to their twin boys to date."

Lucia's hand flies to her chest, eyes sparkling.

"Twins? Bedda matri. I bet they're gorgeous. That boy was always devastatingly handsome." She sighs like she can still see him in her mind. "I can't wait to be a nonna. You have pictures?"

"Only about a million. I even have some of James napping with them."

She gasps, already reaching across the table. "Oh. My heart. Show me."

I pass her my phone, already open to the album. She snatches it with the enthusiasm of someone halfway in love with the idea already and starts swiping, cooing over every image like they're her own grandbabies.

James leans in closer, his breath warm against my cheek. "I've never heard her laugh this much before breakfast," he murmurs, grinning. "You've already got her wrapped."

I turn toward him, caught off guard by how much that simple line unravels me. The intimacy of it. The weight of his voice. The ease of us.

He kisses my cheek softly. "Love you."

"Love you more," I whisper, warmth blooming in my chest.

He stands, brushing his fingers along my back as he passes then begins quietly clearing dishes. The clink of ceramic and the scent of coffee fills the room again, grounding everything in something quietly domestic— something that feels a lot like home.

"If I do the painting mama, you're making the

parmigiana tonight, yeah?" James calls over his shoulder as he scrapes plates.

Lucia doesn't even look up—completely absorbed, still scrolling through my phone, eyes wide at every new picture of James cuddled up with Kais and Alana's twins. "I was already planning on it, Monello. But if you keep eating like that, you won't fit in your race car."

Then, without missing a thing, she adds, "And mamma mia, that 'I love you' nearly gave me whiplash. Should I start picking out dresses now or let you two pretend a little longer?"

"Mama," James groans from the sink.

Lucia waves him off without even glancing up.

"What? I'm just saying—you never bring anyone home, and now you're making me espresso, telling this beautiful woman you love her, and showing me pictures of babies. What am I supposed to think?"

He laughs softly, exasperated but clearly delighted. "Be patient, mama."

Lucia finally looks up, eyes crinkling with affection as she meets mine—her voice quieter, just for me.

"It's a beautiful thing... seeing someone love your child like that." She smiles. "You're good for him, Jasmine. Thank you."

I smile back at a loss for words. James looks over his shoulder from the sink, hands still wet, but his expression says everything. He doesn't speak, just smiles at me, like whatever he's feeling fills his chest to the brim like the look in his eye does mine.

James

"THIS WAS SO WORTH IT,"

Jasmine says around a mouthful of bruschetta, eyes half-lidded in bliss.

I lounge back in my chair, nodding. "Absolutely worth you two watching me paint all day."

She scoffs, indignant. "I painted half that yellow room, thank you very much."

"You painted for thirty minutes and spent the rest of the time taking pictures of my ass to compare with the baby photos my mum was pulling out of the grave."

"Monello," my mum tuts, rolling her eyes as she wipes her hands on a dish towel. "It was one picture."

I stare at my lying mum, agape. "Mama—it was three. And a full gallery of other ancient polaroids you resurrected like it was a séance."

Jasmine pushes herself up from the table, laughing while she starts gathering dishes.

"They were really cute though," she chimes in, tossing a smile over her shoulder.

I watch her carefully—how her energy has shifted now

that dinner's over, how the yawn she tries to hide almost swallows her whole.

"Go on, get ready for bed, Jas." I say, my voice gentling. "You've been non-stop today,"

My mum walks over, bumping her hip against Jasmine's with a grin. "Go. Before you try and tell a lie about not being tired."

Jasmine smiles, soft and sleep-heavy, her gaze flicking between us like she's locking the moment in.

"Okay, okay," she relents, stretching out her neck with a groan. "I've got to scrub all this paint off anyway."

She hugs my mum at the sink, a familiar ease between them already, then crosses the room to me.

"Goodnight," she mutters, kissing my temple.

"I'll be up in a second."

"No, you won't." She leans down, lowering her voice so only I can hear. "Spend some time with your mom. Just the two of you. It's a nice night and you both need it."

She steps away before I can protest further. The girl never stops trying to take care of me. Always seeing the space between things. Always putting me before her.

"Goodnight, Jasmine," my mum calls after her.

"'Night, Mama Lucia," she replies, her voice floating back down the stairwell like the tail end of a lullaby.

I sit back for a moment, letting the familiar clatter of plates and the steady tempo of running water fill the quiet Jasmine left behind. There's something comforting about it, like slipping into an old rhythm you didn't know your body remembered.

After a minute, I stand to help my mum dry. We don't say much. Just move around each other in sync, passing dishes and towels like we've done a thousand times before.

The silence is stitched together with years of closeness, lived-in, like the warm wood floors beneath our feet.

"You want to sit outside with me?" I ask her, drying the last of the wine glasses.

My mum glances up from her scrubbing, a mischievous glint already blooming in her eyes, "Vino?"

I grin, "Why not."

She shuts off the tap with a flourish and, within seconds, has a bottle plucked from the rack above the icebox and two glasses in hand.

"Come on, mio cuore," she calls over her shoulder, already disappearing through the glass patio doors.

I dry my hands, then follow her out into the night air, the chill biting at my arms the second I step outside.

"Maybe this was a bad idea," I mutter, rubbing at the goosebumps prickling down my forearms.

"Then heat your blood," She presses a glass into my hand—filled nearly to the brim.

"This is, what... a three-in-one pour?"

She shrugs without guilt. "Where do we have to be?"

She leans on the iron railing, her face tilts toward the sea. The moonlight spills across the water like silver ink, painting waves that look soft enough to sleep on. She looks peaceful. Really peaceful. I haven't seen her like this in a long time, maybe not ever.

For most of my life, my mother's face has been set with tension. That faint crease between her brows has been permanent since I was a kid. She was always hustling, always making something from nothing.

She gave everything so I could chase a dream most people laughed at. And now, here she is. Dream realized. Life quiet. Hands still full out of choice.

It reminds me (again) why I worked so hard to get where I am. Why I pushed. Why I never stopped.

So she could breathe like this.

"You ready to get back in that car?" she asks softly, her voice steady but enigmatic in that way that tells me she already knows the answer but wants to hear it from me anyway.

I let out a slow breath, watching it cloud in the air. "I think so. Everything looks good. I feel good. But I guess I won't really know until I'm back on the grid."

I take a sip of wine, letting it settle in my chest, pushing back the chill of uncertainty creeping into my bones.

Kais was right, keeping everything to myself will blow up eventually. Even knowing that, I've been trying to avoid this conversation since we landed. Standing next to her now, I realize how stupid that was. I've never been able to lie to my mum.

"Apparently, Kieran's in talks with Red." The words taste bitter. "Can't tell if it's for my seat or Ollie's."

She cringes, lips pressing into a thin line. "Is your contract up?"

I nod, eyes on the sea. "End of the season."

She turns her glass in her hands, the stem catching the moonlight. "Are you negotiating anything yet?"

"Not yet. It'll come... once they see that I can still drive."

She hums, thoughtful. Takes another sip of her wine. "You can. And you will. Just remember—when the time comes that you can't, it doesn't make you any less *you*, Tesoro. You're more than a car."

Her words land heavy, but gentle. Like they've been stored up in her chest for years.

"Yeah," I nod, my gaze unfocused. "It'll be fine. You'll see."

Even as I say it, I can feel the uncertainty gnawing at me. What if it isn't fine? What if the fear creeps in at 200 kilometers per hour? I take another sip of my wine, surprising myself by how close I was to finishing the glass. The fear, the future: maybe that's why I need to do this now. While I still can. Before everything gets complicated.

"I'm going to propose to Jasmine."

Her head snaps toward me, eyes wide and instantly bright, glassy with emotion. She smiles. "Amore mio, I'm not surprised. I've been watching the way you two love each other all day."

"That obvious?" I reply, half-laughing.

She nods slowly. "Like the sun on your face. Do you know when?"

I exhale through my nose, rubbing my thumb along the stem of my glass. "I was thinking here. After she met you. After this talk."

Her hand darts to her chest, overcome. "Dio mio, you're going to kill me."

I smile at her reaction, but my own gaze falls back to the sea. "I don't think I am now."

Her face falls. "Why not?"

"She's got so much going on," I breathe, feeling a knot ball in my chest. "She's finally on the brink of everything she's worked for with this brand launch. I don't want to pull focus... I don't want to take anything from her."

She moves in close, her hand settling on my back the way it used to when I was a kid too proud to cry.

"You've always been like this," she murmurs. "Putting everyone else first. Even when you were little." She glances up, eyes fond and far away. "Remember that year you came home starving for a month straight? Eating everything in sight. I was convinced your body had entered some kind of growth spurt apocalypse. I thought, 'How is this boy still hungry? I pack him enough to feed a grown man. And then —do you remember what you told me?"

"The lunch was for the kids who didn't have one. Said the crumbs were good enough 'til dinner."

She lets out a laugh, quiet and full of memory. "Dio mio, I almost cried into the pasta that night."

I look down at my wine, the warmth of her hand making me feel like a boy again, not a man holding the weight of every tiny decision.

"You and Jasmine," she says, "you'll figure it out. I know it in my body. You love each other. Deeply. And the fact that you can see her that clearly—can feel what she needs before she says it—that's what love looks like, mio cuore. That's what being someone's husband means."

She taps the rim of her glass, her gaze steady on mine now.

"You already think like hers...But I want you to remember something." Her voice quiet but firm. "It's okay to be fed. It's okay to make choices that are good for you."

I hold her gaze, that same fierce softness I grew up with is still etched in every line of her face.

"I can't just propose because it's what I want, Mama."

"I'm not talking about Jasmine." Her hand brushes my arm. "I'm talking about that team you race for. I know you've been friends with that boy a long time and I know you'll bleed for the people you love. But that doesn't mean you have to feel bad for fighting for what you want nor stay where you're not being fed."

Her eyes don't waver. "If they're stalling... if they're leaving you in limbo while they chase the next shiny thing —it's okay to be open to something else. Don't settle for scraps when you're the one risking your life every time you get behind the wheel."

She brings her glass to her mouth again but doesn't drink. "It would be good to do it for someone who actually cares what happens when you're out of that car too."

I look at her for a long moment, the breeze brushing through the curls she hadn't bothered to tame all day. Then I pull her in, arms wrapping tight around her shoulders.

"Maybe I'll just quit and move in here," I chuckle. "Be your doorman."

She snorts a laugh against my chest. "So you can see what time all the tall, dark, questionable men leave my room?"

I pull back, shaking my head. "Mama, really—it's out of hand."

She only laughs harder. "Oh? Is love only for you, then? Your mama's too old for a little cuddle?"

I roll my eyes and start walking my glass back to the kitchen. "You've got me, Mama."

She waves a dismissive hand. "Oh no, Tesoro, you're Jasmine's problem now." Then, cooing like she was already holding them in her arms: "But I do expect to get my hands on Kais' twins when I visit. Those cheeks... How have you kept them from me so long?"

"You'll get your own grandkids soon enough," I say, rinsing my glass. "We want four."

Her eyes nearly pop out of her head. "Quattro?! Amore Mio, you're going to break that poor girl's pelvis! Does she even know how much you weighed as a baby?"

I laugh, grabbing a towel. "No, but I'm pretty sure all those baby pictures you showed her clued her in."

She sets her glass on the island, arms crossed like she's

weighing blueprints. "Aye, I need a bigger locanda. Where will I fit them all?"

I lean in to kiss her forehead. "Just kick out the dangerous men, yeah? Plenty of room then."

She swats my arm. "Goodnight, Monello. Go kiss your wife before she falls asleep."

There's that crooked smile again—the one that always makes everything feel okay. "I've got a date with a book and a second glass," she adds, reaching for the bottle on the counter.

She wanders off down the hall. I turn off the lights and stand there for a second, listening to the quiet.

It feels like everything is just beginning again—new season, new stakes, new chances to get it right.

I just have to hold my nerve long enough to see it through.

Jasmine

28

THE HALLWAY OUTSIDE THE RED ENERGY hospitality suite buzzes with chaos. Team staff dart back and forth, radios crackling, espresso machines hissing, cameras flashing.

Everyone is energized for the first race of the season—everyone except me. My nerves gnaw at me like they have teeth.

James has been clinical in preseason training, surgically precise. I mean, the man puts a scary amount of confidence and craftsmanship into everything he does. I love that about him. His silent grind. His obsession with excellence. The way he's still somehow the best even with the weight of the world pressing against his ribs.

But not me. I'm barely holding it together at the thought of him climbing back into that car today. And my mother's passive disappointment bleeding through the phone isn't helping.

I press the phone harder to my ear, trying to drown out the surrounding noise as her voice crackles over the line. "I'm just saying, mija... your family is here. Dr. Ramos says

269

he'll put you on his critical transport team if you want. I also heard the Miami Hurricanes may be looking for a team nurse. Why don't you apply?"

There it is. The guilt, dressed up as concern.

"I don't want to work with basketball players, Mom," I counter, trying not to snap. "I have a real chance of building something. My launch is in a few weeks and—honestly—I think I have a shot at selling out."

She huffs, and I could hear her disapproval shifting through the line like static.

"Yes, I've seen the pictures. It looks fine, Jasmine. But it's not lasting. You have a good career. A real career. There aren't many women in your specialty. You've made a name for yourself. I can only imagine the doors that must've opened now that you've worked with... that driver."

I close my eyes and count to three, teeth clenched.

"Mami." I sigh. "Please don't call him 'that driver.' You know his name. You talk to him every week."

"Exactly, mija—he's not right for you," she pushes on like she's gearing up for a monologue she rehearsed. "You're always going to be chasing him across the world. How long until he gets in another accident, huh? And what if you're married? Or heaven forbid you have children and they don't have a father, what then?"

My chest burns. The air catches in my throat like a stone. I blink fast, willing away the heat pooling behind my eyes.

"Mami," I drawl, voice tight. "I don't want to talk about that. Not right now. Not minutes before he gets in the car."

"See? Look at you." She clicks her tongue. "Already hurt. You think you're in love, but you'll regret throwing everything away for this. Leaving your family for this."

I pat my cheeks carefully, trying not to smudge the

makeup I'd spent way too long perfecting this morning—trying to look polished, calm, in control for all the cameras that will be relentlessly shoved in my face today.

"I didn't leave you." My voice is a hard whisper. "It's no different than when I lived in Dallas."

She lets out a dry laugh that cracks over the line like a slap. "Yeah, well look how that turned out. You left a good job for that Milos."

I spot some of the Red Energy press team walking by their red polos and wide grins too cheerful for my unraveling. I force a smile, angling my body toward the wall like it can shield me.

"I didn't leave my job for him," I whisper, lowering my voice. "It was an internship. And it ended with me getting a real position in critical transport, Mami. Him playing for that team had nothing to do with it."

She sighs like I'd missed the point entirely. "I'm just saying, mija, you don't exactly make the best decisions."

And that's it. The last shred of my patience annihilated by the one insecurity I've been working to absolve for months.

The perfect excuse walks up the stairs.

Patrick Holt appears at the end of the hallway, his blue eyes finding mine in the crowd like it's nothing. He offers a small, easy smile—the kind that says he saw more than he lets on—and starts walking toward me.

"I gotta go, Mama. I'll see you in a few weeks when we're in Miami, okay?"

She sighs again, long and tired, like the disappointment of me lives in her lungs. "Bueno. Te amo."

"Te amo." I hang up just as Patrick reaches me, flipping my phone screen down hoping that can somehow silence the residue of her words still echoing through my head.

"You alright?" He asks, looking down on me with an easy smile.

"Yeah. Fine." I nod, too fast.

His eyes narrow on me briefly. Then he holds up a pair of headphones between two fingers.

"Came to bring you these. At the request of your... boyfriend." He says it like a teasing question.

"Yes, thanks." I take them with a small laugh.

"Thought you might want to hear team comms," he adds, still studying me with those unreadable blue eyes.

"How's he looking?" I ask, trying not to fidget.

He crosses his arms over his chest, shoulders brushing the wall behind him. "Brilliant, actually. Renaud says he's in top shape. Tuned in. He's got that blood-in-the-water look again."

I smile, small and tight, nodding to keep my throat from closing.

"Good," I manage. "Well, I better get in there before I miss the bite."

I start to turn, but he calls out, "Hey."

"Yeah?" I glance back.

He slides his hands into his pockets, cool and easy. "If it doesn't work out between you two... we'd still really love to have you on the medical team."

I arch a brow. "By we, you mean you."

He laughs, a warm, low sound. "I mean, of course me. But you're bloody amazing at what you do. Dr. Renaud's been teaching your data management system to the whole performance team. That's not just me flirting."

He steps back, pushing the garage door open with one hand, grin still tugging at his mouth. "Just something to consider, Nurse Lozano."

Then he's gone, swallowed up by the noise of the crowd outside.

Fucking whiplash. One minute my mother's telling me I've ruined my life, and the next, a gorgeous man in fireproof gear is telling me I'm a genius.

I need a drink. Or a sedative. Maybe both.

The moment I open the door, Emilia is already waving me over to her corner of the suite, thankfully holding two mimosas like an actual goddess.

"Hello, lovely," she greets me, kissing both my cheeks. "Figured you'd need this."

"Like you wouldn't believe." I drop into the stool beside her and take the glass, sipping fast enough to signal this isn't a social drink but a survival tactic.

The room buzzes with press, media managers, and a swarm of Red Energy staff I've never seen before, all laughing like they personally own the team.

Emilia raises a brow behind her flute. "He's looked really good in pre-race interviews. More cool and relaxed than I've ever seen him."

"Yeah, that's what Patrick said." I nod, eyes fixed on the screens looping footage of the pre-race chaos outside.

"Gorgeous man, that one," she murmurs, half to herself, watching the same screen with a smirk.

"Mmm." I hum, too tense to tease her back. "Hey—can you come to my room later or when you're back? The final pieces for the shoot came in yesterday. They're in my suitcase."

"Absolutely. Are you going back to Monaco or London?" she asks.

I set my glass down, still watching the broadcast, which is now rolling through highlights of James' career: shots of him as a kid, fresh-faced, wild-eyed, helmet too big for his frame.

"Monaco, I think. James is trying to hit that residency minimum during the season so we can spend more time in London in the off weeks, which I cannot wait for." I smile to myself. "But it's been nice being able to walk across the hall and knock on my PR agent's door. Though I don't think James loves it as much."

Emilia laughs lightly, but my eyes lock onto the screen. And suddenly, the air in the suite shifts.

A clip of the Spa crash plays across the monitors— James, airborne. The barrier. The smoke. The eerie stillness that followed. All the voices around us dull into static.

"Hard to believe it's only been six months since James Del Toro's crash at Spa..."

The commentator's peppy British accent clashes with the footage rolling beneath it—slow-motion b-roll of the rear clip, the car lifting, the curb launching him.

"...a crash that had him airborne after Kieran Denune clipped the rear going into La Source. That curb catching the car wrong and sending him straight into the barrier at nearly 200 clicks. Broken ribs, hip surgery, spinal trauma... most said it would end his career."

The image of James slumped in the cockpit, pinned between twisted carbon fiber and metal, lingers too long. I grip the arms of my stool, pulse hammering in my ears.

"But this is Del Toro we're talking about," the voice continues, *"A beautiful performance in pre-season testing. Now starting on pole after another stellar performance in quali yesterday. Maintaining a four-second gap on his teammate Oliver Bisset, and a fourteen-second gap on what some say is the much faster Delancey cars. Proving to everyone*

that it's not only the car but the driver that makes the race—
and he's not done with F1 yet."

The camera cuts to the live feed of James motionless in the cockpit, helmet down, locked into focus. Crew members swarming to ready his car.

I swallow hard.

"He's going to do fine," Emilia whispers as she squeezes my arm. "He looked really focused yesterday."

I force myself to speak. "I'm more worried about the rain. And Kieran."

"Oh please." Emilia rolls her eyes. "That little prick won't even make it past Ollie. And the rain will hold." She dismisses the thought with a flick of her wrist, like we were talking about bottom a ten rookie and not the guy who nearly killed James.

We both slide on our headsets as the boys rolled out of the garage, James first, the red glint of his car cutting into the blur of color and chaos on the track.

"Give 'em hell Del Toro," someone's voice buzzes through the headset.

My heart lurches as James comes through, staticky but steady: "I'll do my best, mate."

I lock in, suddenly wishing I knew more about tire degradation and pit strategy, and less about post-op hip recovery timelines.

The lights blink down in silence. The engines roar to life in a ripping vibration. A blur of red, silver, and black shoots down the straight like missiles, and the room around me surges. And I can't breathe. My palms press into the headset, clinging tighter as if that might help him make the first corner.

Patrick's voice breaks over the headset, "Clean start,

James. Holding P1. Bisset right behind, Delancey's are on the charge."

I lean forward, eyes flicking between feeds, trying to track every frame of him. James is already flying through sector one, fluid and mechanical. Not driving like it's his first race back, but like he never left.

"God, he's flying," Emilia reads my mind from beside me, almost reverent.

He is.

It's like watching someone conduct an orchestra at 200 mph. Every corner a brushstroke. Every acceleration perfectly timed.

Lap twelve. "Box, box." Someone commands.

"Negative," James replies, breathy but resolute. "Tires feel good. I've got margin."

"Copy. Maintain delta. Kieran's gaining."

I stiffen at the name. My stomach flips. The camera cuts to Kieran's Delancey, prowling just behind Ollie. His every move too antsy, too eager, like he's waiting for a window to take them both out.

Emilia exhales roughly. "God help me, if Ollie lets Kieran through, I'm putting his pillow in the freezer."

A photographer steps in front of us, snapping reaction shots like we aren't both seconds from cardiac arrest.

A few more laps tick by as James pulls further and further ahead, his car moving like it's part of him rather than something he was driving. Then Kieran's teammate spins out hard, kicking up gravel and nearly clipping the wall.

"Yellow flag, sector two. Hold position," Patrick comes over the comms.

James slows.

"All good?" he asks, calm as a surgeon.

"Clear now. Green flag. Push."

And push he does.

By lap twenty-four, he's seven seconds clear. Ollie is holding firm behind him, running defense like a man with something to prove. And suddenly, I like Oliver Bisset a whole lot more than I ever have before.

Kieran drops to seventh after an off-track excursion. Nowhere near James.

"He's got him bottled up," Emilia says beside me, grinning like she's orchestrated the whole damn thing. "Delancey's not even pretending to like Kieran anymore."

I can't speak. Can barely think, no matter how many conversations people have tried to pull me into today, I just need this to be over.

Lap fifty-seven. Final lap.

The entire suite holds its breath. Even the commentators go quiet for a beat—just the whine of engines piercing the air as James rounds the final corner.

I push my headset back, halfway out of my seat, eyes locked on the screen.

"Here's Del Toro," one of the commentator's shouts, voice barely containing the thrill, *"with a gap—nearly nine-point-six seconds now. Absolute dominance from the four-time champion! They said it couldn't be done. That we'd seen the end of an era. But James Del Toro has come back to show that this bull still has horns!"*

The checkered flag drops. The screen cuts to the team erupting in the garage.

"James Del Toro wins the Australian Grand Prix!"

The room explodes around me. I burst out of my seat cheering. Applause, cheers, champagne already spraying in the back corner. But I can't hear any of it, not really. My heart is pounding so hard it might crack my ribs.

"Fucking hell," Emilia breathes, clutching my arm pulling me into a tight hug. I let out the last breath holding my tears.

My vision swims. And then, through the comms—James' voice, soft but grinning:

"This was a good one, boys. Great to be back. Thanks, everyone."

"Come on," Emilia says, already halfway to the door. "You've waited long enough."

I don't need more than that. I toss off the headset as I bolt right behind her.

We weave through the crowd flashing our Red Energy badges through security. The moment we hit the stairs, the roar of the crowd outside punches through the glass. My chest tightens. The scent of rubber, heat, and fuel hits me even harder.

We shove through the last security barrier at the edge of the pit wall. Cameras flash. Crew members buzz in celebration. The smell of victory is everywhere.

Then I see him.

James climbs on top of his car, helmet still on, arms lifted. He raises both hands to his head and forms horns with his fingers, bucking like a bull in celebration.

The crowd loses it.

So do I.

He jumps down and dives straight into the pit crew, swallowed by red uniforms and roaring voices: slaps on the helmet, back-pats, fists in the air. He disappears into the noise, the energy, the chaos like he's born from it.

And I'm already running to him.

He hops down and yanks off his helmet. He looks like he just came home from war and won a crown in the same breath. His eyes search—only for a second—before locking onto mine.

He moves.

Fast.

Grabs my face in both hands and kisses me: hard, sweaty and full of adrenaline.

"Good fucking job, travieso." I laugh against his lips.

He pulls back just enough to grin.

"Del Toro, weigh in!" a voice barks behind him, some official already pulling him back into the post-win whirlwind.

And I let him go. I let him vanish into it again—into the chaos, the celebration, the blood and sweat and flashbulbs—because he bled for it.

Because he earned it.

And being here to see it all? Best fucking decision, I ever made.

James

Jasmine: You did great, travieso. I've got a plan for revenge on Ollie when we get back to Monaco.

Me: Does the plan include snapping his neck when he's in his resistance helmet?

Jasmine: Ooo, diabolical. I hadn't thought of that one yet. Where do we hide the body?

Me: Under the simulator. No one would check—he hasn't used it in months.

Jasmine: What are the odds you bring a race suit and helmet home? I think I've developed a kink. I have the sudden desire to bark every time I see you in them.

Me: Bark at me and I'll never wear anything else.

Jasmine: Woof

I GRIN AT THE SCREEN, BITING BACK A LAUGH that probably attracts a few side glances from the Red Energy staff still milling around the paddock. God, I fucking love her. I'm half a second away from ordering a custom helmet just to keep in our bedroom.

But the camera being shoved in my face dictates otherwise.

I turn my phone face-down on the table as the moderator nods toward a reporter.

He stands, mic already raised. "James, you've had an incredible season so far—four wins out of six races, and not a single podium missed. Such a brilliant performance today, it looked like you'd take the win again this week. Are you disappointed with the result?"

I bring the mic to my mouth with a clipped smile. "Yeah, I'm disappointed. We made some avoidable mistakes as a team that cost us the one-two. I'd like to avoid making those again."

A second voice jumps in before the moderator can shift. "You've got a comfortable twenty-four-point lead in the Drivers' Championship, but with Kieran and Fitz looking more confident in the Delancey cars each week—do you worry about holding that lead? Are you nervous when you see black in your mirrors?"

I huff a quiet laugh, shaking my head just enough to show it doesn't rattle me. "I feel confident in our car this year and in myself. No doubt, the Delancey cars are quick and pose a real threat. But I, by no means, tremble."

The room chuckles. Another hand shoots up. The moderator points.

"What's the status of your contract for next year? There's talk your teammate, Ollie, is heading to Apex.

Should fans expect to see you in Red again, or are you leaving too?"

I scrub a hand over my stubble, feeling the prickle of post-race heat from my suit clinging to my skin. "I can't speak for Ollie. I've been with Red since I was eighteen—it feels like home. There's loyalty in that."

The same reporter fires a follow-up. "Kieran Denune's been spotted speaking with your team principal, Lemaire. There's no love lost between the two of you after Spa. If he replaces Ollie...will you race with him?"

I sit up straighter, jaw tightening just enough to be noticeable. "I've never had a problem sharing the track, only when people forget how dangerous it is."

The room shifts: reporters scribbling, lenses adjusting, a few quiet exhales. Across the table, one of Red's PR handlers—Maya, dark suit and darker eyes—tilts her head with the faintest smirk. Approval. Relief. Like she's been bracing for impact, and I'd landed it clean.

I adjust the mic in my hand. Still in control. Still on message. Still here somehow.

A young, eager woman raises her hand. I nod her on with a laugh, already bracing for whatever headline she's about to write.

"You've been famously quiet on social media," she begins, "but your appearances on fitness influencer Jazz Lozano's page—very cuddly, by the way—have sparked a bit of a cult following. Fans are now calling you 'Daddy James.'" Laughter ripples through the room. "Do you find the attention distracting? And how are you handling such a public relationship?"

"I can't say I understand the nickname, but... I'm handling it," I say, lips twitching at the corners. Jasmine would be dying right now if she heard this.

"She's been a steady hand through all this. If anything, being with someone who sees past the podiums and press makes it easier to stay focused, not harder. The rest—fans, posts, all that—it's just noise. And I've never driven for the noise."

I run a hand through my hair, sweat still clinging to the base of my neck beneath the collar. "As for my relationship being public; we've kept the important parts for ourselves. What people see online is just a snapshot of the real thing. And it's part of her career, not mine."

A final hand shoots up. "Last question for you, James. I'm sure you're eager for a shower."

I laugh, low and hoarse. "Very much." I'm actually fucking sweltering.

"You've spent your entire career with Red Energy, but is there another team you ever dreamed of racing for? Or is this the dream for you?"

"The first dream was just getting to F1," I unzip the collar of my race suit, letting out a breath as heat pours off my chest. "But yeah, I think every driver romanticizes Delancey or Fargo at some point, for the legacy, that history."

I pause, eyes scanning the row of reporters for a second longer. "My focus now is just to be the best at what I do... no matter the team."

I thank the room, step down from the platform, and go to find Ollie.

The second I slip out of the press zone, the noise breaks. Still loud, still chaotic, but farther away. Like the volume dial of the day is finally getting turned down.

I should feel proud. P2 after falling back seven fucking places. Still on top of the driver standings. Still ahead of Delancey. But all I can think about is how easily we could've had the win. How close we came before it slipped through our fingers because of a teammate I trust like family. Or used to.

And now I'm meant to smile through it. Keep it together. Be the face.

I'm fucking tired.

The air in the hall is cooler, but it doesn't do much. Not when I'm still wound so tight I feel like I might shatter if anyone touches me the wrong way.

And I knew exactly where to find the twat responsible.

Hours of media had been the only thing that saved Ollie. If he'd held his position—if he'd just kept his fucking head—we'd be walking out of here with a clean one-two. Instead, he finished P7, and I'm left carrying second like it's a goddamn participation trophy.

He's in the lounge, drink in hand, watching the replay like he didn't just throw the whole thing away.He exhales the moment he sees me.

"Oi, don't start fucking laying into me, yeah?"

The screen in front of him flashes, my car slicing through the final corner, Kieran's smug-ass face taking the podium.

"What the fuck happened, Ollie? You were supposed to hold position. Why the hell did you go for a pass when you didn't have the clearance?"

He swats the air. "Oh, fuck you. I had the pace. You were backing us into Kieran."

I scoff, stepping in close. "Don't be daft. You couldn't hold that position on those tires and you know it."

He rubs the towel over his face, jaw tight.

"You were trying to prove something," I grit.

"And you cost us the race. You cost the team points. P2

would've looked fucking brilliant for you right now. Not bloody seventh."

He stands then, blue eyes narrowed. "Yeah, well maybe I'm fucking tired of being your number two, James."

I blink. "When the fuck did we start a hierarchy? We've always been in this together."

He lets out a bitter laugh. "Since Red wants to give my seat to Perry."

His face flushes, voice rising. "I'm out. This is it for me. I needed to show something, anything."

I drag a hand through my hair, my pulse pounding behind my eyes.

"That's just rumors. You know they put that shit out there to distract from what's really happening. You don't think I hear things too? We both know no decisions get made this early in the season." I shake my head. "You're consistent, Ollie. You won Drivers last year. You're not going anywhere."

He looks me in the eye.

"You're fucking delusional, mate. Loyal to a fault."

He exhales, jaw tight, something his eyes twists my gut. "These fucks don't care about you. Or me. Or what we've done the past ten years. It's always about the future—and it's not me."

He claps a hand on my shoulder. Firm. More serious than I've ever seen him.

"And if that cunt Kieran keeps it up... it won't be you either."

The door creaks open behind us.

"Debrief, gentlemen," Holt calls.

"No." I shake my head. "I'll catch you Tuesday. I've got somewhere to be."

Patrick sighs, but he doesn't push. Can't.

I've given everything to this team. And for what?

If Ollie's being replaced by Perry and Red's dead set on signing Kieran, that means Lamaire's already made his choice, I'm gone. Or he's turned this into a cage match between me and the driver who nearly killed me.

Either way, I'm fucked.

Jasmine's parents' house is alive. Music vibrates through the cracked windows, laughter spilling out onto the front lawn. Chatter rolls down the driveway as thick as the grill smoke. Balloons are strung on the mailbox, and cars pack both sides of the street. It's a full-blown house party.

And my quick post-race shower and protein bar didn't prepare me for any of it. I'm already running on fumes. All I want is to lie down with Jasmine, bury my face in her neck, and let the weight of the day bleed out of me.

But I promised I'd come. And she's worth every ounce of effort it took to pull myself out of the car, out of press, and now out of my own head.

The screen door bangs open as a group of women burst onto the porch in a flurry of perfume, laughter, and long acrylic nails. One of them clocks me immediately.

"Damn, papi," she says with a grin, practically licking her lips. "¿De quién es este güero?"

Before I can speak, Jasmine pushes through the girls like a force of nature.

"Mine, Rosella. Fuck off." She wraps an arm possessively around my waist, shooting her a withering look.

"Call me when you get bored, papi chulo," Rosella calls out, brushing past us with a laugh.

I smirk. "No mames."

The group erupts in laughter.

"Damn, Jas," one of them wheezes, wiping a tear. "You been teaching him? That rolled off the tongue too smooth."

Jasmine rolls her eyes and pulls me through the door, her hand warm and steady in mine.

We step inside, the bass of a reggaetón beat thumps through the walls. The air is thick with heat and spices—garlic, onion, slow-cooked pork. The kind of scent that hits you in the chest and plants hunger in your stomach.

Voices overlap in fast mixed Spanish dialect. Kids dart out the door. Somewhere in the chaos, someone's yelling something about la lotería.

We pause just inside the entryway. Jasmine looks up at me, a hint of apology in her smile. "My cousins are feral. Ignore them. Actually, ignore half the people here. I only care that you meet my parents."

"It's fine, they were just taking the piss."

She brings her arms around my neck and pulls me down for a kiss that melts every knot of tension I've been carrying. She lingers for a second, brushing her nose against mine.

"You do look really fucking good in this shirt," she murmurs, fanning the loose fabric of my button-up. "Very Miami."

I chuckle, my hands slipping into the back pockets of her cutoffs. "I've been fucking boiling since the race, I couldn't stand the thought of putting on something that wasn't loose."

Those plush lips curve into a grin.

"Your ass in those fireproof suits is still top tier, but

this..." she gives my shirt another little tug, "...this is some primo boyfriend material."

"Well..." I smirk, leaning down. "Your ass in these shorts might give me a fucking heart attack."

She laughs, pressing another kiss to my lips. "You okay?" she asks, her voice softer now. "I know this is a lot. We don't have to stay long."

I shake my head, letting my forehead rest against hers. "I'm good, Tesoro. I want to be wherever you are."

Her eyes shine, warm and wide and full of that easy kind of adoration that's become the lifeline I've clung to for months.

"Use the signal if things get too crazy," she whispers. "Don't worry about me. We're a team. Where you go, I go, okay?"

I give her the exaggerated finger-to-nose move we'd jokingly agreed on, just to see her smile again. She laughs, then kisses me all over my face, fast and dramatic.

"Aye! Are you two going to come in or make out in my hallway all night?"

Jasmine flinches like she's been caught sneaking out. "Aye, Mamá. We were just—"

"I know what you were doing," her mom says, arms crossed in the archway her mouth holds the shape of a smile, but her eyes don't carry it through.

Jasmine sighs. "I just wanted a minute alone before you guys try to tear him apart."

A roar of laughter and overlapping Spanish comes from the living room. Gloria—arms crossed tight, mouth flat now—looks like she's never told a joke in her life.

"We will do no such thing," Gloria replies, turning to me. Her tone polite but clipped, eyes hard.

"Good to see you, James. Thank you for letting us come to your race today. It was... interesting. Very fast."

I offer a smile and release Jasmine. "Thanks for coming, Mrs. Lozano. And for having me here."

"Yeah, of course" She doesn't return the smile. "Come meet Fernando. He's in here with the men."

She turns and disappears toward the living room.

Jasmine hooks her arm with mine, leaning in and whispering, "You'll love my dad. He's not as scary as Angry Gloria."

I exhale. "That's... comforting."

But it isn't her dad I'm worried about. It was the woman who hasn't smiled once, who seems to be measuring me for the exact size hole I'll leave in Jasmine's life.

The scent of roasted meat and garlic intensifies as we passed through the kitchen. There are trays and trays and *trays* of food stacked high on every counter. Empanadas, arroz con pollo, tamales, sweet plantains glistening with oil and syrup.

The whole place is a feast. And my stomach is doing flips while also begging for a bite of something.

We round the corner into the living room.

"Fernando, this is James," Gloria calls.

A dozen men turn to look at me. Jasmine's dad—dark-haired, glasses, a round belly, and Jasmine's exact dimple—stands with a bright smile.

"Bueno. Bueno," he says, extending a firm hand then pulls me into a hug before I can properly shake it. "I'm so happy you made it, mijo. What a race today. Reminded me of your F2 days."

I blink. "F2?"

"Oh yeah, I've been watching F1 since I was a boy. But you've been top of my card since you started."

That catches me off guard. For a second, I just stand there. My shoulders ease a little. The tension behind my ribs softens. Jasmine mentioned her dad maybe watching the sport once but Fernando comparing me to my F2 days— when I was hungry, scrapping for every tenth—that's exactly who I'd been trying to prove I still was.

Jasmine laughs, surprised. "I had no idea you watched James that long, Papi."

He lifts his beer with a sheepish grin. "That's because I usually have to watch the races at work. And your mama's still bitter that Mexico has a track and not Colombia."

Gloria glares at him from across the room. "I don't have time to watch your silly cars on my only day off, Fernando."

Jasmine steps in like a pressure valve, "There's actually rumors they're trying to have a GP in Colombia. So maybe you could get into it, Mami."

I cock my head at her. "How did you know that? You didn't even know what a Grand Prix was a few months ago."

Jasmine smiles up at me, placing a hand on my forearm. "I guess that changed when someone I loved was in one of those cars."

The room tilts just a little. She says it so casually. So publicly. And she means it. Every fucking word.

My chest pulls in the best way.

Gloria stands stiffly, cutting her gaze at Jasmine. "Ah yes, so exciting, putting someone you 'love' in a death machine." I stare for a moment, searching that hard scowl for some signs she's joking, She isn't.

Jasmine cuts her eyes at her mother but shrugs it off as if she already decided it isn't worth the energy tonight.

"Why don't you sit?" she asks me, like there's no one else in the room. "I'll make you a plate. Hungry, right?"

"Starving." I press a dramatic hand to my stomach. "And whatever's going on in there smells amazing."

I smile politely at Gloria, who of course smirks coldly in return, giving me a flat, "Cerveza?"

Before I can answer, Jasmine's fingers tighten around my arm. "Water, Mami. He just got out of a race."

Her voice is tight, and so is the air between them.

I've been in Gloria's damn virtual "Book Club" for three months now and I still haven't gotten her to crack. If anything, she's just gotten colder. And clearly tonight meeting me in the flesh has solidified something.

But Jasmine doesn't flinch or bend. And for the first time tonight, I'm not thinking about the crash or the press conference or Ollie.

I'm just watching the way she stands between me and the world, realizing she's been doing that since the moment she showed up in my flat six months ago. While I've been hiding contract negotiations and team drama from her like she's too fragile to handle it.

She isn't. She never has been.

I settle into a plastic folding chair next to Fernando, the kind that creaks if you breathe too heavy. The living room is buzzing with conversation and the occasional burst of laughter, but my focus keeps drifting. Not to the conversation. Not even to the race replay on the TV.

But to Jasmine. Tense in the kitchen, her shoulders stiff as she stacks plates and fields a dozen questions at once from her family. Her smile is still there, but it looks tighter than usual. More for show.

I try to turn my attention elsewhere, just to give her some space.

"So who else do you follow, Fernando? Are you a driver or a team man?"

Fernando chuckles, his beer balanced on one knee. "Drivers, for sure. My heart'll always be with anyone from Mexico—so right now, I'm rooting for Marco Ruiz to pull something better than P12." He shakes his head with a laugh. "I like your test driver too. Adam Perry, right?"

"Yeah. Perry's talented. Really locked in last season." I lean back a little, a bit more at ease around Fernando. "Smart, too. Keeps his head down and listens."

He takes a swig from his beer, nodding with quiet approval. "Of course, all the talk is about silly season. Everyone's wondering if Red's gonna lock you down or if someone else might snatch you up. You wouldn't want to let an old man know where you're going early, eh?"

He taps me on the knee with a laugh, and I force a smile that I know doesn't quite reach my eyes. If only I had that answer myself.

Jasmine appears at my side before I have to respond.

She sets a heavy paper plate down in front of me: arroz con pollo, tostones, empanadas, more than I could finish in one sitting. But the moment her hand brushes the back of my neck and her lips press to the top of my head, I feel like I could breathe again.

Then she's gone—back to the kitchen—before I can even thank her.

Fernando watches her walk away with a small, private smile. Then he turns back to me.

"You love my daughter?"

All the men around us stop mid-sip, mid-chew, mid-sentence, every eye landing on me. Like whatever I said next would determine if I ever get invited back. Or worse, if I get to finish the plate in front of me. Doesn't change the truth.

"With everything I've got."

Fernando grins, pleased. A few of the others nod and go back to their drinks as I take a bite of rice—fuck, it's good. Jasmine wasn't kidding about her family being the best cooks. They're right there with my mum.

"Then you should let her go."

Gloria. She almost says it under her breath, almost conversationally, but it hit like she thrown something at me.

She hands Fernando a plate and doesn't look at me. Just keeps her eyes on her husband. Like if she can just make him understand, maybe she wouldn't have to say it to me again.

There goes my appetite.

"Let her come back to where she belongs," she continues, finally meeting my eyes. "Here. With her real career. With her family. Not chasing you around the world holding her breath that you don't crash again."

Fernando's face pinches. "Gloria."

But she shrugs him off like he's a breeze and not a barrier.

"No, Fernando. I watched the blood leave my daughter's face today every time another car got close to his. I watched her mouth prayers I know she hasn't said in years. I saw the fear in her eyes. That's not love, that's suffering. And it breaks my heart."

Her voice doesn't rise. She doesn't yell. She doesn't have to. Because every word punches the air out of me.

What do I say to that? Would anything I say even matter? Because she's not wrong. Not entirely.

I stare at my barely touched plate, swallowing over the lump in my throat.

"I'd walk away tomorrow if she asked me to," I say

quietly, looking between Gloria and Fernando. "Nothing I do out there means more than her."

Gloria's brows shoot up. Her eyes narrow, lips quirking like she has something loaded and ready to fire but before she can let it go, Jasmine is at my side, her hand firm on my shoulder.

Spanish flies from her mouth—angry, clipped, like her anger has been waiting just beneath the surface all night. Her grip tightens as Gloria responds, matching tone for tone. Too fast for me to even try to translate.

But the wobble in Jasmine's voice is killing me.

Then she switches to English, as if sensing my worry.

"I don't want him to give up anything. I am happy with what I'm building, and who I'm building it with, Mami. I didn't bring him here for your approval—I brought him here to include you. Because you're my mother. And this is my life. One you can choose to be a part of or not. But I won't sit here and let you disrespect him. Or me."

The silence that follows is like static in my ears.

Then she looks down at me, her voice low and resolute. "Come on. No need for a signal. We're leaving."

I press my hand over hers, catching the storm still brewing in her eyes.

"Jas, it's fine."

"It isn't, James," she says, barely above a whisper. "You've got a flight in the morning, and this is the last thing you need after a race." She gives my shoulder another squeeze. "Let's go."

She crosses the room and pulls her father into a hug. "Sorry, Papi. I'll see you tomorrow."

Fernando gives her a small nod, lips tight. He doesn't say a word. Neither does anyone else.

Gloria turns and walks out of the room without another glance.

Jasmine shakes her head, swiping a tear from her face. "I'll wrap your plate up," she mutters, turning back toward the kitchen.

I stand, reaching to shake Fernando's hand. His grip's steady, apologetic in that silent way that says he doesn't want to stir the pot.

"She'll come around," he says quietly. "She's just... protective. Jasmine's our only baby." His voice cracks on the last word. "Take care of my girl, okay?"

"Yes, sir. I will."

And I mean every word.

Jasmine 30

THE AIR OUTSIDE HITS COLD AND DAMP. FLORIDA rain has rolled through like a thief; the humidity is thick enough to choke on. James opens the passenger door without a word.

I climb in, balancing a warm stack of foil-wrapped plates in my lap. My hands are shaking, not from the chill, but from the adrenaline still burning through my bloodstream.

He climbs in beside me, and I keep my eyes forward, focusing on smoothing the crinkled foil like it matters. I'm too full of embarrassment, hurt, anger to even look at him.

I should've known better. Should've never brought him here. Should've protected him from her. From this.

I was an idiot to think she'd come around. That she'd see how far I'd come and just...be happy for me. Even if she didn't agree with the choices I've made.

What a joke.

It's quiet except for the faint ripple of tires on wet pavement. The silence doesn't bother me, it feels like a small mercy. My throat's too tight to speak anyway.

Then James reaches over, his hand settling warm on my thigh. Just the weight of it's enough to ease the pressure in my chest.

"I'm really fucking sorry," I breathe. My voice sounds raw, cracked.

"Don't do that." His grip tightens, voice gentle. "You didn't do anything wrong. I knew it might be rough before I even walked in. That doesn't scare me away."

God. He says shit like that and it's like he knows exactly where the cracks are and how to hold them together.

I let out a shaky breath. "It just really fucking sucks for you. Especially when you've got a mom like Lucia."

That's more honest than I mean to be, out loud anyway. But I don't take it back.

"Yeah, well... I also had a dad like Hernán. And your mom's nowhere near that. So let's call it even."

I huff a quiet laugh, the sound catching on something tender in my throat.

"James..." I clear it, needing him to really hear me. "I meant what I said in there."

He nods, eyes still on the road but fully present.

"I know what I signed up for when I fell in love with you. I am fucking terrified every time you get in that car. But I'm also completely lit up when I see your face after. I don't want you to stop. I just want you to come home to me when you're done."

He exhales, the kind of sigh that holds too much for words. His thumb traces slow, soft lines over the inside of my thigh.

"I'm trying, Jasmine," he says quietly. "Every time I get in that car, I'm thinking about you. About how badly I want to come home to you. Not just in one piece—but proud. Like I earned the right to walk through that door."

He glances over at me, and in the passing glow of the streetlights, I see how much it cost him to admit that. How much he's carrying, quietly.

"I don't take what you said lightly," he adds. "And I don't want you ever thinking you have to apologize for me. I've never been more sure of anything in my life than I am about you."

I slip my hand over his, lacing our fingers tight.

"You don't have to earn shit," I whisper. "You own the whole house. There's nothing in my life that means more than this. What we're building. What'll someday be our family. Just me and you, when there's no more champagne and no more photoshoots."

He blinks a few times, jaw working, like he's trying to hold something back.

"Fuck," he mutters, voice thick. "You say shit like that and I..." He shakes his head, trying to laugh it off, but it catches in his throat.

His thumb brushes slow and steady over my leg. "I want all of it with you. I think I always have. Even before I knew it."

He goes quiet for a moment, just the hush of tires on wet asphalt filling the silence. Then, softer: "I haven't told you how much this has been eating at me. But I'm nervous as hell about next year."

He lets out a breath like he's summoning courage. I swallow hard, waiting.

I'm not blind—I've seen all his fake smiles, heard every time an announcer pushes the rumors about Kieran joining the team next year and how James' contract is still up in the air. I let it fall into the background as noise until I saw the look of defeat in his face when my dad asked about next season.

I knew then there was more he was shouldering and that I'd stand by his side until he was ready to let me in on it. And looking at him now, I can see he's cracking the door for me.

"Everything's shit," he huffs. "Ollie's spiraling and seemingly going to another team while Perry takes his seat." He shakes his head, grimacing with frustrated confusion. "Lamaire's playing some game between me and Kieran. Dangling my contract in my face to see which one of us wants to kill the other more."

He pauses as if the words are bitter in his mouth. "Feels like I'm playing poker with half a hand. And if I lose... if Red brings in Kieran and I'm left scrambling..." He exhales hard, shaking his head. "I just don't want to fuck this up. Not my career. And definitely not us."

"James, you're not playing with a half-hand. You've got champagne from Delancey and watches from Fargo the two best teams there are. It's not even a secret that Delancey wants you—hell, how many times has their principal invited us to dinner like we don't notice what he's doing."

He slows behind a line of backed-up traffic.

"That feels fucked though, doesn't it?" His tone is almost apologetic. "Like poaching."

"No," I huff. "What feels fucked is you busting your ass to come back from the brink, lighting up every race since, and Lemaire still can't pull his head out of his ass. What more does that asshole need to see?"

He stares ahead, jaw flexing, like he's chewing glass.

"I don't know," he says almost to himself.

His stomach growls loud enough to break the tension. He drops his head back against the seat with a groan. "Fuck, I'm starving. And we're gonna be here forever."

"Pull off here." I point toward a side street. "There's a park up ahead. I brought you a fork."

James looks at me like I've just handed him a winning lottery ticket. "I was heartbroken to leave that plate behind."

"I know." I smile. "I still don't understand how you make weight with the way you eat. Magic genetics or a deal with the devil."

He laughs, turning down the quiet road. "Kais is gonna kill me for eating in his lorry."

I blow a raspberry, waving him off. "I'll get it detailed before I leave. He'll never know."

James looks over at me, the teasing fades. Something heavier in his dark eyes as he pulls into a parking space.

"I know it's only a week," he drawls with a wince. "And it's completely irrational. But I'm gutted you won't be in Imola."

A smile creeps up on me without warning. Not because I want him to be sad, but because he has tried so hard to keep it light for me for months. Always carries the weight alone. The fact that he's saying it out loud, that he isn't trying to swallow it? That feels like real trust.

"I am too," I reply, gently unwrapping the foil and handing him his plate. "But Ari and Mama Lucia will be there. And I'll be right back with you for Belgium."

He tenses at the name—just enough for me to feel it in my chest. I don't push. Just run a slow hand down his back as he hunches forward over the food.

He doesn't say anything for a few bites, then mumbles, "Maybe I'll actually go to one of those dinners Delancey invited me to. Couldn't hurt, right?"

I stay quiet, just listen. But inside I'm fucking cheering.

"Ollie's going to Apex," he continues. "Other than some

fucked up loyalty to the team, I don't even know why I'm staying anymore."

His voice is light, like it doesn't matter but his eyes are far away. "I think Lemaire just wants to see how Spa goes. Maybe I do too."

I give his bicep a squeeze. "It'll go like every other race has gone this year, James. It's no different."

Then, because I need to see that smile again, I add, "And I swear to God, if Kieran's engineer even thinks about pulling a bullshit call, I'll walk straight to the pit wall and choke the life out of him."

James snorts, mid-chew. "You're so fucking feisty. You've gotta stop watching those true crime docs."

"Over my dead body," I grin, catching the slow tilt of his smirk just before he breaks.

We both laugh. And God, I need it.

"This food is so damn good." he stares at his plate almost hurt. "I wish Gloria didn't hate me, so I could've told her that myself."

I roll my eyes, sinking back into my seat.

"She doesn't hate you. She's just... perpetually disappointed in me." I shrug, trying to keep heat from creeping up my neck again.

"Which is insane, considering one sold-out launch made me more than I earned in years as a nurse. You'd think that would mean something. Or the fact that the biggest sports store in the States wants to carry my line—like, that should count for something."

I shake my head. "But no. If it's not what she pictured, it doesn't count. And I'm done living like that."

James sets his plate on the dash, turning toward me. "She'll come around."

Ever the optimistic. Did he not see how foul she acted all night?

He waits a second, then adds, "And if she doesn't, maybe I'll lightly suggest a parenting book for her next book club read."

I burst a laugh—one that cracks straight through the ache building in my chest. "It's completely ridiculous that you do that, even with her acting the way she does."

A half a smile tugs at his perfect lips. "It's really helped me find some inner peace. And not commit a dozen crimes against Ollie after that race today."

"I guess," I laugh, picking a chip off his plate. "But you never told me why you actually do it. Is it to get her to like you? Because honestly, we'd need an exorcist for that."

He chuckles, but there's something heavier behind it, something that makes his smile falter. He scrubs a hand over his jaw, sheepish.

"Uh... not exactly."

My brows pull tight.

"What do you mean?"

"She told me I had to," he says slowly. "If I wanted her blessing to marry you."

"What?" I blink, turning to face him fully in my seat.

He raises his brows like it's no big deal. "Yeah. I asked your parents. Back around Christmas."

My mind blanks for a second—like someone unplugged me. He asked my parents? He's been in this stupid book club for months and she still...

"She still acted like that," I almost yell, "after you..." I cut myself off, anger catching in my throat. "That's fucking insane, James."

My chest is buzzing now. "You've been killing yourself trying to earn space in a room she never planned to let you in. And you did it anyway. You've done everything right. She just refuses to see it."

The heat behind my eyes finally spills over. I blink fast, wiping at my cheek with the backs of my hands, but the burn stays lodged in my throat.

James leans over, wiping my tears. "What did you say to me a little bit ago? 'Nothing in your life means more than this?'"

I nod, throat tight.

"Well, a fucking book club is chump change. I'd have done anything she asked if it meant I could ask you to marry me without any extra weight."

"I would've said yes regardless of what she thinks."

His brow furrows, like he isn't sure I mean it.

"Even if that's true... I know how much your family means to you. And I figured... if it gave us even the smallest chance at peace, it was worth the shot."

He's fucking impossible. And sweet. And selfless. And stupidly good. Damn, I want to give him everything—every last piece of me—until there was nothing left to give.

I respond the only way I know how in this moment.

I climb into his seat.

"What are you doing?" he laughs as I straddle him, his hands automatically finding my hips.

I press my finger to the button and slide the seat back. "There's no way you think you can tell me you've not *only* asked my parents for permission to marry me but *also* joined a fucking book club to prove your loyalty and think I'm not going to fuck you."

"Jasmine." He snorts. "In Kais' car? In a park?"

"It's a fucking G-Wagon. Plenty of room," I slide my hands up under his shirt, tracing the taut line of his abs. "I won't make a mess. And you don't have to do a thing."

He groans, head falling back against the seat.

His fingers meet the back of my neck, thumb brushing along my bottom lip. For someone protesting about Kais' car and public parks, his hands are already pulling me closer.

"You would have said yes, Tesoro?" he asks, voice breathy against my mouth.

"Guess we'll find out when you ask, travieso,"I whisper, closing the space with a kiss that doesn't ask.

He pulls me in deeper, sucking my bottom lip between his teeth until I whimper into him.

"Fuck," he growls, trailing his mouth down my neck. "You've got the prettiest fucking cry."

My hands are already working his zipper, frantic and unsteady. He grunts, deep and satisfied as I wrap my hand around him, hot and heavy in my grip. I tug my shorts down, one leg free, the other caught in the loop. Neither of us care how graceless it is.

His fingers glide against the slick heat between my thighs and he hisses, "I'm not going to last a fucking minute in that, Jasmine."

"That makes two of us" I smile, kissing him hard. "I've been aching for you since I saw you in this fucking shirt."

His hands grip my ass, fingers spreading wide to hold me open while I sink onto him with zero patience.

My breath catches at the sting, forehead falling to his shoulder as my body adjusts.

"Fucking hell," he growls in my ear.

I bite back a moan, kissing him again, deeper, letting my tongue trace the edges of his mouth while I roll my hips over him, slow and greedy.

His hands set the rhythm, guiding me with unrelenting control. He shoves one hand up under my top and pushing it up until my nipple meets his mouth—his tongue hot, purposeful, circling in perfect sync with the tension building between my legs.

"Fuck, James," I whimper, stuttering against him.

He keeps going. Moving his hand back to my ass, giving it that biting smack—the one that lights me up every fucking time—and grips tight.

It's quick, desperate and completely lacking in finesse. But even screwing like teenagers James knows my body. When to slow down when to speed up. How to find that magical little spot in my belly that seems to have his name written on it.

The tension snaps in no time, my rhythm faltering as everything in me surges forward, unraveling in shivering waves. James meets me there, hands firm on my hips, guiding me through the last few desperate slams that send both of us spiraling.

He pulls his mouth from my breast just in time to catch my cry with his lips, swallowing it whole as his body goes rigid beneath me.

A deep, guttural growl rips from his chest as he comes, his grip seizing, his breath stuttering in sync with mine.

I rock my hips slowly, gently, drawing out the last tremors while kissing him softer now. Grateful. His fingers stay locked around the back of my neck, pulling our foreheads together, the tips of our noses brushing as we laugh through the comedown.

"Now you just have to drive me home so I can sneak in through a window, and we'll have officially completed the teenage boyfriend role-play," I mutter, brushing my nose against his.

He chuckles, voice hoarse. "I just want you to know that if whoever details this car does a shit job, you're the one explaining to Kais why his seat smells like sex and empanadas."

I laugh so hard it hurts, already shimmying back into my own seat. "If you want to put a ring on my finger, I'll do no such thing. You'll have to figure that one out all on your own," I volley, still breathless, re-buttoning my shorts.

He shoots me a look, eyes still dark with satisfaction, but lazy now, sated.

"If he asks," he says, tugging his waistband into place and scanning the parking lot like a man on the run, "I'll just tell him it was a religious experience. Because holy fuck."

He fixes his clothes like someone might've seen us during our spiritual sixty seconds.

"Good news is the traffic's probably clear by now," I joke, resting my hand on his thigh as he backs out of the space.

He laces our fingers again, tightly this time, like he doesn't want to let go and is already dreading the week we're spending apart.

My eyes catch the flutter in his jaw like there's something more sitting behind his teeth, but all he says is, "Maybe do your nails red before you fly back to me."

I thin my eyes at him, suspicious. "Red?"

He shrugs, way too casual. "I don't know... might look nice in pictures. Complement my racing suit for Spa. You know content and all."

I smile slowly, letting the warmth in my chest stretch wide as we pull back on to the street. That wasn't a suggestion. That was a heads up. The sweetest kind.

And now I've got seven days to get a manicure and keep my shit together.

James

31

THE LIGHTS IN THE BRIEFING ROOM BUZZ LIKE A migraine waiting to happen.

I sit with one leg bouncing under the table, eyes fixed on the screen showing weather models and tire degradation charts like horoscopes. The room carries its usual smell of stale coffee and tire rubber. Normal. Everything looks normal.

But it isn't.

The chair next to me is usually taken by Ollie, whose inappropriate jokes and nonchalant manner made race day less intense. But today, his chair is occupied by Adam Perry, our test driver and the nineteen-year-old kid who filled in for me at the end of last season.

"Ollie should be rejoining us for Spa if his respiratory infection clears up by then. If not, Adam, you'll sit in on that one too," says Carlos, Ollie's race engineer.

I sit back in my chair, fingers tapping a slow rhythm on the arm rests as the team runs through final prep. Pirelli has them leaning softs to mediums, classic Imola gamble. Grip early, margin late. Risky—but I like risky when it's clean. When it's controlled.

"James. We'll keep you on the softs through Lap 18 unless temps spike," Donte, the chief strategist says, eyes bouncing between telemetry feeds. "Mediums should hold to the flag. And the DRS issue from quali's been sorted— ran diagnostics twice this morning. No faults."

My jaw pops. That glitch nearly cost me pole. Which is the last fucking thing I need after that shit show in Miami. Especially when I can't tell if this rookie's sudden prominence means Kieran's off the table or I am.

"You'll have Perry lining up P5," Carlos adds, glancing briefly at Perry.

Adam is a solid driver. Not a hot head like a lot of the incoming rookies, wants to learn, hungry but not desperate enough to lose his head.

Honestly, the kid reminds me a lot of myself. Could be because me and Ollie have spent so much time mentoring him that he's just adapting to how we are, or it could be that he's just a decent teammate and that's refreshing in this fucking spiral Ollie's going through.

The man's really struggling with the whole idea of slowing down. I don't know if it's the new dad thing or if he's quietly disappointed that I came back this year the way I have while he's struggling. Whatever it is, he isn't the teammate he's been and that stings more than a little.

"Perry, priority's to protect the start gap and give James clean air through the first stint," Donte continues. "Eyes on the Delancey's. Watch for undercut attempts by Lap 10."

Perry nods once. No nerves. Just focus.

I let my eyes meet his across the table. Not measuring or doubting; I don't have time for hesitations or nerves. This isn't about trust, not yet, but it could be the start of something. A proper alliance between the two of us.

"Let's not make me regret this, yeah?" I say, low enough only Adam can hear.

His mouth twitches. "Wouldn't dream of it."

I rise from the table to head to the pit, checking my phone on the way. A string of messages awaits me.

> Mama: Texting you as a reminder to myself to give Aurelius my pasta alla norma recipe before he leaves.

I scroll.

> Ari: Your mum is now my mum, that's not a question. Congrats we're full-on brothers now.

He's lost his mind if he thinks I'm not asking questions about that.

Scroll.

> Jasmine: How many times can you work the word empanadas over comms today? I need some excitement when you start lapping people again.

> Me: At least once. Good luck with your shoot today Tesoro.

> Jasmine: Will send pics. Wouldn't suggest you show Mama Lucia. Te amo.

God, I miss her. I don't know what kind of sick dependency I've developed—not even a week apart and I already feel like I'm crawling out of my skin.

It's not healthy.

I lock the screen and toss it onto the bench. Time to suit up.

"It was a clean race, babe. Looked like you had it until whatever happened with that first pit. Between Delancey, Fargo, and you guys—the top six are milliseconds apart. I don't think there was anything else you could've done, James," Jasmine says from my phone screen, swiping on eye shadow in a vanity mirror.

I hold the phone way too close to my face, hoping proximity might soften the distance. "You know, if you ran debrief, I'd probably listen a hell of a lot more."

She pauses, that slow smile ticking at the corner of her mouth as she cuts her eyes toward the screen. "Don't act like you don't already take ten-page notes and beat yourself up over every micro-second, travieso."

I rake a hand through my hair, huffing a laugh.

"Not this time. I didn't make a single mistake. Neither did Adam. I didn't realize how much that kid's grown into the role." My voice drops a little. "I kind of get why Red would want him to replace Ollie."

Her eyes widened. "Ooo, don't say that too loud. Emilia's floating around here somewhere."

She glances over her shoulder, then comes closer to the camera, dropping her voice anyway.

"Honestly? You two looked solid out there. He's got that cool, quiet focus about him. Wouldn't be the worst thing in the world to have him as a teammate next year."

I nod, trying not to let too much slip. Because the truth is, Kieran's shadow is longer than anyone's admitting. Red might already be committed and I'm starting to feel the floor shift beneath me.

A knock at the door of the driver's suite, followed by the telltale creak as it swings open. Fredrick Lemaire.

"Hey Jas, Lemaire just walked in. I'll call you back." I'm already starting for the end button.

She raises a brow, kisses the camera lens, and disappears.

"Clean race, James," Lemaire announces, stepping inside with his usual commanding confidence. He sits in the chair across from me. "Team's already sorting the DRS fault, it won't be an issue at Spa."

"I hope not," I mutter. "That ten-second lag cost us the podium. We've never missed here."

He shrugs like it isn't personal. "Yeah, well... we only have the future. Not what's already done."

The words hang there, loaded. This is clearly going to be more than just a debrief. So, I don't dance around it.

"So Ollie's really out next season?"

His expression is smug, crossing his arms at his chest and looking me over with a bit of surprise at my curtness, "Oliver is signed with Apex. We see Adam as the future— should have his contract locked in the next few weeks."

He leans back, still sizing me up. "You know you're the face of the team, James. I won't downplay what you bring but I've got real concern."

I'm leading the Drivers' Championship. Carrying this team on my fucking back. Am the most consistent, marketable, dominant racer on the grid and instead of protecting that, he's prepping for my replacement. Red isn't just slipping. It's rotting from the top down.

I narrow my eyes. "About what? I'm still leading Drivers. The last two races had nothing to do with me."

"True." He gives a single nod. "But you're missing the edge. That hunger you had before the crash."

His eyes flick to the side, then back to me. "We're not saying the car's perfect. But with a driver who doesn't flinch? The gap between us and Delancey disappears."

Heat flares in my chest. There are teams that would build a car around me as a lead driver. That would offer blood to keep me. And here I am being scrutinized like I'm the liability.

"You mean a driver like Kieran?" I don't hide the edge in my voice. "So that conversation we had after my test—that's still where we're headed?"

"Maybe." He bounces his shoulder, casual as ever. "The kid's not afraid to go for blood when it counts. That's what we need while we're developing someone like Perry. Kieran's shown us he'll take risks. Big ones."

He stands then, looking me dead in the eye. "Maybe at Spa, you show us you're still that guy. That you're willing to do what it takes."

I don't blink. I know exactly what he means. I'd been right to suspect this was coming: Dirty moves. Brake checks. Taking risks that flip cars and wreck careers. The kind that fills headlines and fuel investigations.

He doesn't want better machinery. He wants controlled chaos. Dominance, no matter the cost.

And I don't know if I'm angrier at him or at myself for hesitating. But either way, I need to get out of this room before I do something irreversible.

"I understand you perfectly, sir," I reply coldly, then give him a firm handshake and walk out.

THE PADDOCK IS STILL a buzzing war zone—technicians shouting over engine cooldowns, reporters dragging trailing wires, crates rolling by like aftershocks.

My body's heavy, overheated, wrung out. I haven't had a proper post-race nap with Jasmine since before Miami and I'm starting to feel it. I need out. I need quiet. I need something that doesn't reek of corporate bullshit and barely disguised threats.

I duck through the back corridor to the hospitality suite, shoulders tight, jaw still locked from that conversation. I keep hearing Lemaire '*Maybe at Spa, you show us you're still that guy*'. Like I haven't been *that guy* since I was a rookie. Like clawing my way to the top after a near career-ending crash doesn't count. Like loyalty and clean racing made me soft.

The moment the door opens, the noise shifts.

I spot them instantly—my mum, Ari, and Penelope—huddled around a small table, laughing over something, faces lit up and easy in a way mine hasn't been all day. My chest loosens just seeing them.

"Amore mio," my mum calls out, warmth in every syllable, arms open.

"Hi, Mama." I step into the hug. Her embrace is instantly grounding; a balm I didn't know I'd needed until I was wrapped in it.

Ari is next. He slaps a hand against my shoulder hard enough to rattle my teeth.

"I'm fucking impressed, mate," he says, all gravel in his voice and a wide grin on his face. "You fought like hell to claw back. That champagne should've been yours. Not that cunt who gave you the finger."

"Yeah, well..." I force a smile. "That's how this thing

313

goes. Mistakes happen. And yeah, Kieran is a proper cunt. Sorry mama."

My voice is tight. Not bitter yet. But damn close.

"I agree with you boys. But speaking of champagne," my mum says, reaching into the tote bag at her feet. "You do have some." She pulls out a sleek black bottle and holds it up. "Can't remember the man's name, but he insisted."

Penelope leans in, already smirking. "Otto Costa."

"Yes!" My mum snaps her fingers, beaming. "Otto. Wore a Delancey jacket. Very handsome, by the way."

"Mmm. Very," Penelope adds, nodding with mock solemnity.

I blink, straightening a little. "Wait, he gave you champagne?"

Before I could say anything else, Ari cuts in with a scowl. "That's disgusting, Penn. He's old enough to be your dad."

She hums, unconcerned. "Boring stuff like that only matters to you, green giant."

My mum laughs, throwing her head back like she's been waiting all day for that exchange. "I should charge tickets with the way they go back and forth. They've been at it all afternoon."

She smiles at them—at whatever inside joke they're still riding the high of—then her expression shifts. Like a switch flipping. Her hand moves to her back pocket, pulling out a small envelope.

"Here." She presses it into my palm. "He left this too. Says he wants to take us to dinner."

I give her a look. "Mama, you can't date Delancey's team principal."

She swats my arm before I can even open the note.

"Not like that, Monello." Her voice drops low, meant just for me. "He wants to talk to you. He sounded serious."

Otto Costa has been sniffing around me forever, doubly so since Australia, trying to pin me down for a conversation. Like every other team principal worth their payroll. It isn't new. Every year there are rumors.

James Del Toro might leave Red!

James Del Toro might shake up the grid'.

But I never bite. Not because I haven't been tempted but because what matters more than flash or money is loyalty. Relationships. Driving for a team that feels like mine.

Only lately... Red doesn't feel like mine. Not anymore.

I slip the card from the envelope. The handwriting is sharp and clean.

> Red is fading. You deserve a car that matches your talent—and a team who sees it.
> 20:00. Casa Bianco.
> We'll keep it discreet.
> -O.C

"A team that sees you." God, the idea of that shouldn't feel so far-fetched. And yet here I am, being courted by a rival feeling like I'm the one who needs to prove something.

I exhale slow and deep, tucking the note into my pocket.

"Well..." I glance at my mum, "you wanna be my date to this?"

She smiles, warm and full of something deeper than just amusement.

"Yes, Monello. But I can't promise I won't flirt with that man just a little."

I scoff, and she raises both hands like she's innocent. "I'm kidding. I'm kidding," she then turns her head ever so slightly toward Penelope and shakes it—not subtle in the least.

Pennelope stifles a laugh. The two of them burst into a fit of quiet giggles like teenagers.

I shake my head and turn to my brother who's doing a shit job of hiding his jealousy. "Thanks for coming, Ari, You two wanna come out with us tonight?"

He cools his expression. "Least I can do after you suffered through my terrible fucking match last night."

I smile, but my attention drifts to Penelope, who's already whispering something to my mum.

He turns to her, gruff as ever. "Oi, you wanna go to dinner?"

She cuts him a death glare that could freeze the tarmac. Then she looks at me and with a long-suffering sigh. "I'd love to, but it seems personal. And probably a bit unprofessional to take your team's physio to dinner, Aurelius."

"You came here though, didn't ya?" he grunts, unbothered. "What's the difference? Starving or eating?"

She rolls her eyes, crossing her arms. "You told me you were driving me back to the team hotel, Aurelius."

"And I am," he says, as if that settles everything. "Just needed to stop here first. Next, we stop for dinner. Don't see the problem."

She blinks at him. Once. Twice. Then slowly turns back to me. "Your brother is insufferable. If you weren't dating Jasmine, I think I might've already killed him. Maybe next time. I need to get back."

I grin. "Well, thanks for not killing him. And for coming, even if it was against your will."

She laughs.

"I need to go get ready for this. Ready, Mama?"

My mum grabs her purse and stands with a flourish. "I am. Rellino, Penn, I'll see you both on Wednesday."

My brows pull. "Wednesday?"

"Sì, mio." She smiles like it's the most natural thing in the world to hang out with my brother without me. "Rellino's team has a special event near the locanda. I've invited them to dinner. I'm going to teach them to make my pasta alla norma."

Penelope lights up. "Yes, I wasn't tricked into this one. No way I'm missing your mom's cooking not after how Jasmine described it."

I look at Ari, raising an eyebrow.

"Told you, it's not a question." He says with a shit eating grin.

Then I turn back to my mum with mock seriousness. "Just remember I was here first. You're already cooking for him, giving him nicknames... don't go stuffing him in my old clothes too."

She scoffs. "Dio mio, you're so needy. Let's go."

And with a dramatic push to my chest, she's tugging me out of the room like she didn't just casually schedule my emotional unraveling and a recruitment dinner in the same breath.

Jasmine 32

Papi: You're comin to dinner tonight right? Give us a chance to see you before you leave?

Me: Probably stuck in this shoot late. Sorry papi. Also, can't talk to mami right now.

Papi: I'm proud of you Estrella... So is your mother, she just wears it differently.

Me: And by different you mean not at all...

I TURN MY PHONE OVER BEFORE HE CAN REPLY with whatever excuse he was going to make for her. It's been a week since that dinner, seven days of silence. No call. No text.

I won't pretend my heart isn't broken by it because it is. She couldn't even make eye contact with me when I was sitting across from her at the table.

I kept showing up to her 'family dinners' this week,

hoping she might look at me, ask how I'm doing, say anything and she just... didn't. Being a part of my life should matter more than what I decide to do with it.

I can understand her hesitation with James. I really can.

His job is terrifying.

I know what it's like to sit there watching, holding your breath, not blinking until he steps out of the car. I know she can't stand seeing that fear in my face and knowing she can't protect me from it. But even if she hates the risk, even if it twists her stomach the way it does mine, I wish she could find comfort in what's behind it.

Because I've never loved anyone the way I love James. And I don't mean that in a past-tense, old-boyfriends kind of way. I mean—ever. It's not some wild spark or perfect fairytale.

It's deeper than that.

Quieter. Like... I finally met someone who fit. Like I've spent my whole life trying to explain myself in another language, and he's the first person whoever just understood.

So, when she rejects him, when she talks to him like he's some mistake I'll soon wake up from—it feels personal. As though she's rejecting a part of me, the one that finally makes sense.

"Ready for you on set, Jazz," Emilia calls from the door, all towering heels and a Carmen Electra blowout that defies the Miami humidity and logic. I nod at her reflection and stand, smoothing my top.

"How's Ollie?" I ask, falling into step beside her.

"Oh, he's fine. Man turns into a baby over the slightest sniffle. Honestly, I think he's playing it up. His ego's still bruised from the last race."

I let out a low whistle. "Oof. Harsh, Millie."

She glances back, not slowing. "I don't mean to sound

cruel—he's just been impossible lately. OJ's teething, and Ollie's allergic to anything that looks like a middle-of-the-night diaper." She shakes her head, exhaustion softening her edges.

"Why don't you let me take OJ tonight? Maybe you two can talk before the flight—or you can just sleep."

She pauses mid-stride. "It could be my sleep-deprived mom brain or the start of an aneurism, but weirdly, I don't want to say no."

I loop my arm through hers. "Then don't. I could use the company anyway."

She smiles, a little glassy-eyed. "God, I'm so unprofessional. What kind of PR rep makes her client babysit?"

I roll my eyes. "Please. On paper, sure. But we're friends. That may be bad business, but I don't give a shit. I wouldn't change it."

She nods, visibly exhausted.

"God, I wish this wasn't our only season together. Just when James is settled down and can rub off on Ollie in a positive way—poof. New team. Hopefully the next couple months is enough time for him to learn how to support someone without needing credit for it. The launch thing was so sweet—Oliver would be screaming it from the rooftops if he helped me like that."

"Yeah... the launch," I repeat, trying to sound casual.

"Right?" she gives another watery laugh.

"It's been such a relief since you've blown up. No more James calling me every day about those invoices—'*Don't let her see this one, I've got it handled.*' So sweet but so stressful." She clutches her chest. "Did you absolutely melt when he finally told you? I mean, James has always been careful with money, living in that modest flat and all. But then just covering all those startup costs without blinking? Oliver would never."

"Yeah," I say softly, trying to keep my voice steady. "That's James. The man's never needed fanfare."

Her grin brightens as she pats beneath her eyes to stop any tears from smudging her liner. "Right then. Let's get you in front of that camera. This first look?" She gestures to the fitted technical bodysuit I was wearing. "It's a damn slay."

I laugh and walk toward the set, lighter and heavier all at once. The numbers have never quite added up with this whole thing. Invoices I expected never came. I let the details turn to background noise, but hearing it confirmed changes everything.

Him calling Emilia daily? Managing costs behind the scenes? This is who James is—shouldering his mother's B&B debt, practically giving away apartments.

Part of me wants to swoon while the other part aches for him. Always carrying everything alone when I'm right here. He's making decisions that benefit everyone but him, like he isn't worth considering.

UMBRELLA LIGHTS GLARE from every angle, bouncing off industrial beams and scattered equipment. The warehouse looks abandoned from the outside—inside, it's transformed. The perfect backdrop for the launch campaign of my collection across Ross Sports stores nationwide. The whole thing feels surreal. Like I blinked and landed here.

After I turned down OneActive and launched the line myself, things snowballed.

Everything sold out.

Then sold out again.

Then Ross came calling, offering to carry a staple collection in stores while letting me keep full creative control online. Kais helped with the numbers. I handled the vision. A few rounds of negotiation later, here I am. Succeeding in every way I dreamed of.

And still... falling apart a little on the inside. Because no matter how big this gets, part of me would rather be trackside—smelling rubber and gas, surrounded by adrenaline and chaos.

The version of me from a year ago would probably slap the shit out of me for even thinking that.

But the truth is, with this deal in place and a solid team behind me, I'll finally have time to breathe. To be present. To watch my hot-ass boyfriend spin around a circuit at 200mph and build whatever life we want together.

We work through a handful of looks, posing with the other models, then directing a few sets of them on their own. Hours fly by in a blur of flashes, smiles, sweat and a lot of spandex. We're nearly wrapped when they call me back for my last solo session: a wet-look set, showcasing the bra and underwear collection.

"I'm gonna sneak a few of these for James," Montee's daughter, Nadine, whispers, crouching behind the photographer with my phone.

I laugh, trying not to break focus. Having her interning has been everything I hoped it would be. She's smart as hell —manages my socials so well I barely have to lift a finger beyond approving posts. It's been the biggest weight off my shoulders.

"Pull your chest up a little more. Really dig those hips and shoulders into the floor without losing the arch," the photographer coaches.

I adjust, holding the tension in my core.

"Yes, beautiful!" He fires off a rapid burst of shots.

"You should do a handstand," Nadine chirps, still snapping pictures. "Your abs look insane and it'll show how secure the bra is."

The photographer whips his head toward her, eyebrows up. "That's actually a brilliant idea. Why didn't I think of that? Your assistant's a genius, Ms. Lozano. Want to try it?"

I let my back relax into the floor, grinning. "Yeah, why not. Let me braid this mess first."

I push upright, running my fingers through my damp hair—

And it hits me. The aching pang of homesickness. Not for a place. For a person. For James: kneeling behind me on our bed, hands steady and gentle as he braids my hair like he does almost every night. His touch. His voice. His quiet patience.

Shit, I need to pull it together.

"Jazz, your mom texted. Says she's here..." Nadine says cautiously.

My attention snaps to her. "What do you mean, *here*?"

Before she can answer, I catch a glimpse of my visitor over her shoulder.

My mother, walking in next to Emilia. Small frame swallowed in blue scrubs, hair slicked into a low bun like she came straight from work.

I sigh in resignation. "Nadine, will you sit with her while I get this last shot? Just take her to my dressing room."

Nadine hurries across the room. I watch as she approaches my mom—gently, way too gently for a woman like Gloria—and tries to coax her toward the back. My mother shakes her head. No.

Nadine turns back, her usual playful green eyes wide and a little panicked. She clears her throat when she reaches me. "Um, Jazz... she says she wants to watch. She won't let me tell her otherwise."

I roll my eyes, irritation tightening my chest.

"Fine," I grit out.

I turn back to the set, nodding at the photographer. "Let's get this done, baby doll."

The photographer lifts the camera in silent understanding. I step to the center mark, brace my hands on the floor, and kick up into the handstand. Toes pointed. Core locked. Smile soft. Face relaxed.

Pretend it doesn't matter that she's here.

Somewhere behind me, I hear Emilia holler an "Ow ow!"—cheering me on like always. I can't even glance her way. I can't afford to break. My arms start to wobble under the weight of everything brewing in my head more than my body.

"I think we got it," the photographer calls.

"Oh yeah, that's the one," Nadine chimes in proudly.

I lower myself carefully to the floor, blood rushing back to all the parts of me it's supposed to be in. My body steadies faster than my heart does.

A crew member hands me a robe, and I tie it around my waist as I pad over to the monitor.

"Wow," I mutter, blinking at the screen. "That is one hell of a shot. Good suggestion, Dean."

The side profile looks almost unreal like someone etched it from marble. Every line of muscle, the clean arch of my back, the sheer control. It doesn't just look strong. It looks like art. It looks like freedom. Like proof I'm standing on something solid—even if it's just my own two hands.

"That does look good," my mother whispers behind me, almost reluctant.

My soul nearly leaves my body. I turn slowly, like her confession might vanish if I move too fast.

"Can I talk to you for just a second?" she adds.

I sigh, my breath pushing up through tension I didn't realize was sitting between my brows.

"Yeah," I reply quietly. "I'll meet you in the dressing room."

She turns on her heel and walks away. I nod at the crew, thank everyone quickly, and follow her back.

"Alright," I huff as I step into the room, dropping on a bench and reaching for my sweats. "What's up?"

She leans against the doorframe like she can't quite decide how to hold herself. "I came..." she hesitates, then squares her shoulders. "I came to apologize to you, Jasmine. Woman to woman."

I freeze, one leg halfway into my pants.

"Apologize for what, Mami?" I venture cautiously, standing and pulling them all the way up.

"Oh come on, Jasmine. You know what."

I scoff, yanking my hoodie over my head. "No, Ma. I don't." My fingers tug a little too hard at the hem as I smooth it down.

"I only want what's best for you," she says in a hush. "I wasn't trying to hurt you. Or that man."

I roll my eyes, flopping back down on the bench to pull on my socks.

"That man has a name," I mutter. "Which you should probably learn because it's about two seconds away from becoming mine too."

She exhales hard through her nose. "Yeah. I know..."

What the hell?

I expected a fight. An argument. Another backhanded comment. But she doesn't. And somehow, that almost makes it harder to breathe. I shove my feet into my sneakers, ready to get the hell out of this room, but something keeps me rooted.

"I shouldn't have spoken to him the way I did. I should have talked to you first instead of letting my frustration control me."

My head snaps up. She isn't being sarcastic. She isn't deflecting. She actually fucking means that.

"You learn that in one of those books you make James read or something?"

"Actually, yes." She huffs a dry laugh. "But it's true. I mean it."

I roll my lips under my teeth, watching her—this rare, cracking version of my mother—standing here trying. Trying in a way she never has before.

"Look," she starts again, voice lower now. "I may not agree with what either of you do for work. Or love that you've moved an entire ocean to get away from me. But none of that matters as much as being part of your life. I don't want to push you farther away."

Her voice breaks at the end, becoming thin and raw, and something in my chest buckles.

I stand, feet moving before my brain catches up.

"I didn't move an ocean away to get away from you, Mami." I stand right in front of her, holding her gaze. "I moved because I found the person I want to build my life with. Like you did with Papi."

Her eyes soften, breaking open in a way I'm not ready for.

"I've always just wanted to make you proud." My voice is barely steady. "But I'm at a point now where... I want to build the next part of my life for me. Not for what you expect. Not for what you force."

"Yeah," She nods slowly, swallowing hard. "I get it. I know that feeling."

She looks smaller suddenly. Not weaker—just human. Not Mami, the brickhouse. Just her.

"I was exactly like you once," she says. "But I chose the opposite. I played it safe. And it built me a good life—with you, and your father. But I guess..." she exhales, shaking her head, "I thought if I pulled you the same way, I could keep you safe too."

Fuck. I've never seen her like this.

For so long, I only ever saw her one way: unyielding, unreachable, already finished. But right now, she's just a woman, standing in front of her daughter, scared and proud and grieving all at once. And it cuts straight through me.

I pull her into a hug. Her body's tense at first, stiff like she doesn't know how to let me in. But then, slowly, she gives in, her arms tighten around me, her breath hitches in the hollow of my shoulder. A faint, broken sob slips out of her, like it cost her everything to let go.

I hold my mom until she pulls away. The hug barely lasts more than a few seconds. But for a woman like my mother that's a lifetime.

She swipes at her cheeks, smoothing her scrub top back into place like she can tuck the whole messy moment away with it.

"Well. It's settled, right?" she says, straightening her shoulders.

"Yeah. Settled." I nod, wiping my running mascara off with the cuff of my hoodie.

She clears her throat, her voice thick but determined. "Good. Let me know when the—" she catches herself, a faint smile starting. "When *James* pops the question. Not that he needed it after the way your father acts around him, but... I texted him. Gave him the okay."

I huff a wet laugh. "Does that mean he can stop reading those stupid books?"

She smirks, already stepping back into the hallway. "Joke's on you. He told me he's still going to."

Before I can chase her down, she's gone. Only Nadine stands in the hallway, pretending she didn't hear the entire thing.

"Your phone, my dear," she sing-songs, handing it over with a playful curtsy.

"Thank you *my dear*." I smile, unlocking it. "Will you grab OJ from Emilia? I'll meet you back at the hotel."

"Nanny Dean to the rescue." She beams, giving a dramatic little twirl before disappearing down the hall.

The second she's gone, my phone buzzes.

A new text from James.

A photo: his hand, holding a sleek black cap embroidered with the Delancey logo and the number sixteen stitched below it.

My whole face splits into a grin at the message that follows:

> Travieso: Think we'll look good in black, Tesoro?

God, I could fucking float right now.

He's fucking doing it. Choosing himself. Choosing

what he deserves. Choosing us. After all the times he's put everyone else first, he's finally choosing what's best for him.

I thumbed out a reply, my heart pounding.

> Me: Mmm. I like dark James. Looks like I was already a step ahead of you.

I attach the black-and-white shot Nadine had snapped of me mid-handstand, the one we were saving for the socials drop.

One last message:

> See you in Spa.

Jasmine

The sky is grey, streaks of light crack through the thick billows of clouds, moody and unpredictable just as it'd been during practice and qualifiers.

Whispers of mist kiss my cheeks as I head to the garage to find James before his formation lap. Chaos swarms around me, noises overlapping in dueling layers. A crew of cameras is set up just outside the Red Energy garage, interviewing Ollie who's finally making his way back into a car.

James stands next to Holt, eyes locked on the screen in front of him. I sneak in around the pit crew and his eyes find me in an instant. He plucks off his headset like he isn't about to climb into a car in a matter of minutes.

"You okay?" he shouts, raising his voice over the noise as he rests his hands on the sides of my shoulders.

"Yeah, fine. I just wanted to see you one more time before you got in."

He smiles, leaning in to brush a quick kiss to my lips.

I smooth my hand over the zipper of his race suit, my

manicure black instead of his suggested red in celebration of his signing to Delancey next season and taking Adam Perry with him. He covers my hand with his, catching my gaze.

"We gotta move quick once this is all over. I've got something planned tonight."

A smile twitches at the corner of his lips.

It's painfully obvious what he's referring to, but I'll play clueless because it's cute watching him think he's sneaky.

"Clear the grid!" a series of loud voices shout.

I lean in and kiss him once more, whispering "Shake and bake, baby"—pulling a wide grin from him—before I saunter back into the chaos.

"Excuse me, excuse me," I say under my breath, brushing through the thick crowd of visitors and press.

"Jazz!" a melodic voice calls from beside me.

Francesca.

Dressed to the nines like every other paddock princess and grinning from ear to ear.

I give her the fakest fucking smile I can muster.

"Frenchie."

That seems to piss her off a little.

"You look amazing." Her tone is sarcastic. She falls in step with me as if she's also heading to Red's hospitality suite. "I ordered some leggings from your company, they're like butter—and no camel toe, truly a miracle."

I stop dead in my tracks. "Can I help you with something, Francesca?"

I try not to sound irritated but let's be real this is the worst day for her to pop up.

"Oh no, I'm just headed in this direction to get a feel for next season and say hello to an old friend," she says with a sugary smile, stepping past me and into the Red Energy suite without an ounce of shame.

I trail behind her, watching as she breezes up to Lucia like they're sorority sisters.

God, Kieran is such an idiot for staying with someone who's spent half the season posting about her ex-boyfriend. Everyone knows her "making Kieran jealous" excuse was bullshit—anyone with eyes can see she's still hung up on James.

Exhibit A.

"Darling," she coos, arms open.

Lucia smiles politely, but it doesn't reach her eyes.

"Hi," she replies stiffly, shooting me a look like: *Do you know this lunatic?*

"I heard you were here today," Francesca goes on, "and I just had to stop by. I can only imagine how hard today must be for you."

I take a seat at the table where Alana is sitting, whispering behind my hand, "That's James' ex."

Alana's posture snaps straight like she's about to launch out of her seat. I put a calming hand on her lap, biting back a laugh. "Down, girl."

She narrows her eyes at me but settles back down.

Meanwhile, Francesca is still talking, stringing together a sob story about the good old days or whatever, when Lucia finally cuts her off.

"I'm sorry," she drawls. "I'm having the hardest time— could you remind me of your name again, miss?"

I snort into my drink. Alana does too. And the blood drains right out of Francesca's face.

"Frenchie?" she says, disbelief and horror in her voice.

"Frenchie?" Lucia echoes, like the name itself is an insult. She shakes her head. "Doesn't ring a bell. I'm sorry.

My son's about to race and I need to get back to my daughter-in-law. You understand, I'm sure."

She smiles with gracious finality before turning her back to join Alana and I at the table.

Looking pissed as hell, Francesca spins around so fast she nearly body-checks Emilia, who catches herself with a laugh.

"Oh, French!" Emilia blurts, faux-surprised, adjusting her glass. "Didn't realize Kieran was driving for Red today. I thought he saved his groveling for after the race."

Francesca's face flushes the same shade as the bull logos plastered across the hospitality suite walls.

"Very funny, Emilia," she snaps. "Let's see if your husband can actually stay on the track today. God knows I'll see him at the bar tonight if he doesn't."

She tosses her hair and storms out, leaving the air thick with tension and the unmistakable smell of bitterness.

Emilia blinks, utterly unfazed.

"Terrible woman," she mumbles, sliding into her seat like nothing happened.

We all crack up.

"You really didn't recognize her?" Alana asks Lucia, eyebrows lifted.

Lucia laughs quietly into her drink. "Of course I recognized that awful girl. I just thought it'd be funnier if she thought I didn't."

Another round of laughter ripples through the table.

"Wasn't she in Imola?" I ask, shifting my gaze to the pre-race footage rolling across the monitors. The cars are lined up now, mechanics and engineers making their final tweaks. Nerves start to thrum under my skin.

"Not that I saw," Lucia answers, her attention following mine back to the screens. "Although I'm certain that beautiful friend of yours would've knocked her down a few sizes, the way she handles James' brother."

She smiles at the thought.

Beside me, Emilia leans over, clinking her glass against Alana's. "Nadine's got the boys tucked away in a quiet room for their nap. We should have time for one drink before duty calls."

"Nanny Dean to the rescue," Alana says, lifting her glass with a grin.

I smile too, but my focus keeps drifting to the race feed, to his car, to the sponsor logos stamped across his helmet. My heart is already racing like I'm the one about to take off. I've gotten better throughout the season. But today, I can't pull it together.

"Where's Kais?" I ask Alana, half-watching as the cars pulled out the garages.

"Wiggled his way into the garage somehow," Alana sips her drink. "Left with some pretty guy named Patrick."

"Of course he did." I lean back in my chair, eyes glued to the screen now.

Cars glide through the warmup lap, weaving back and forth in long, lazy curves to put heat in their tires. The mist hasn't thickened yet, but it slicks the track just enough to stir a knot of nerves in my stomach.

James is right there at the front on pole. Kieran isn't far enough behind him at P5, and Ollie slotted in between.

The camera pans back to show the cars lined up in their positions, engines rumbling, drivers making final adjustments. I watch James at the front, checking his gloves one last time. Even with the mist rolling across the track, he looks steady. Focused despite the threatening weather.

Rain or shine, chaos or calm—he'll find a way forward. He always does.

I grip the edge of my chair hard enough that my knuckles ache. Five lights blink at the top of the screen.

"And it's lights out in Spa" the announcer says.

The engines roar loud enough to rattle the glass.

The world blurs forward.

James launches clean, maintaining the lead with the kind of confidence that only comes from surviving your worst nightmare.

The conditions are nearly identical to last year: wet track, low visibility, every corner a potential disaster. The same recipe that put him in the hospital.

My heart climbs straight into my throat but I don't let my eyes budge from him.

"Good start," Lucia celebrates under her breath, arms crossed tight across her chest like she can keep James in clean air through sheer force of will.

The field thins through the first few turns, engines screaming, the mist spraying off the tires. James continues to hold the lead, clean and crisp, a sight that makes breathing come easier. The kind of driving he does that makes it look easy when it isn't.

The wet track magnifies every tiny mistake the drivers make. Every second feels like a coin flip of who would crash.

Kieran claws forward, desperate not to let the gap stretch between him and James. I can see it even before the commentators catch it—the way Kieran's car darts too wide into the corner, tires spitting water sideways instead of gripping.

A mistake.

Not huge, but enough to make my stomach turn inside out.

The camera cuts away before I can see what happens

next, flashing to drivers in the back of the pack that may as well have been static to me.

I barely breathe until they cut back to the track and by then, the mist is too thick, swallowing the back half of the grid in a shroud of silver. A cluster of cars appear out of it and suddenly one is spinning, too fast, helpless.

My body lurches forward in my chair even though my mind screams at me to stay still. Safety car boards flashed. Yellow flags everywhere.

"Oh no," Emilia whispers.

The camera jumps to Kieran's car.

It's sits backwards against the barriers. Smoke and steam hissing up from under the chassis. I immediately look for James. Scanning every glimpse of the lead cars until I catch the sleek flash of black and red, still pointed the right way. Still alive.

But my heart isn't steady. Not even close.

Without thought, I push up from my seat, bolting for the stairwell leading down to the pit lane. Lucia calls my name once, but she doesn't try to stop me.

I know it isn't normal protocol, but I also knew how this team works. How James works. His comms channel is open to Patrick and today if I could help it, I'll use whatever pull I have to get to him.

I just need the headset. And if I have to muscle my way into the pit wall to get my voice through to him, I will.

I just need to hear that he's okay. That he's still James, not lost in whatever memories that crash is likely dragging up.

By the time the safety car rolls out, I'm already at the pit wall.

"Get her a headset!" someone barked—maybe Patrick,

maybe Donte. I don't know or care. A tangle of hands shove a headset into mine.

I yank it on, fumbling with the strap as my eyes lock on James' car still weaving, still going.

Static crackles in my ear, and then I hear it—not words, just James' breathing.

Heavy. Fast.

"Safety car, James. You alright, mate?" Patrick's voice comes through the comms.

James answers in a hoarse voice. "Yeah, mate. I'm in front of it."

"Any damage?" Patrick replies.

"Right wing maybe," he rasps, breathing quick and shallow. I know that feeling—the edge of panic.

"You need to box?"

The silence after nearly breaks me. His breathing speeds up, sharp and ragged, the same way it did in the dark before his fitness test. The same way it does any night the memories try to take him down.

I clutch the mic tighter, like I can moor him with just my voice.

"No," I answer Patrick, steady where he can't be.

"James." I press the headset harder against my ears. "You've already won this. Just bring it home."

James

I CAN'T SEE. CAN'T FOCUS. THE CAR IS MOVING, but only by muscle memory. I keep seeing it—feeling it—the moment I flipped off this same track, pinned against the barrier I keep passing.

I can't breathe.

My body's on fire.

The air's too thin.

My fucking drink isn't working.

My chest is way too heavy.

I can't breathe.

I hear Holt's voice crackling through the comms, something about a safety car. No shit there's a safety car.

How the hell am I even in *this* car right now?

My brain is a blind, wet mess. This track is soaked. My mind is worse. I can't fucking find a way through the panic.

Then her voice breaks through the static, like a hand pulling me from the deep—

"James, you've already won this. Just bring it home."

Jasmine.

How the hell did she get on comms? My hands clench

tighter on the wheel, and something in my chest eases—just enough that I can feel my body again.

It isn't enough.

Not yet.

I hit my comm button.

"Where's Ollie?" My voice is tight.

"Behind the safety car, untouched," Jasmine answers quickly, knowing exactly what I need.

My lungs finally drag in a full breath. Enough for me to feel the engine vibrating around me again.

Still my race. Still my track.

"Copy," I rasp into comms, feeling the wheel in my grip.

The safety car peels off. One flash of lights, and it's gone into pit lane.

I drop the clutch. Setting the pace, my car lunges forward, slick asphalt tearing beneath me.

The rain eased a bit under the safety car, but the track is still greedy. Still lying in wait for any mistake. I shift gears, letting the tires bite into the damp patches just enough, keeping the throttle easy until I can open her up fully.

Turn by turn, the world stitches itself back together. The track blurs beneath me in long gray ribbons.

Nothing else matters.

Not the crash, not Kieran, not Red.

Just this.

Just bringing it home like she asked.

The gap widens. Half a second. Then a full second.

"Purple sectors, James. Keep this pace. Five laps to go," Patrick says.

I stay quiet. Every ounce of me is locked into this— feet, hands, lungs, blood.

The final laps blur past in a rhythm my body knows better than breathing.

Throttle, brake, feather it out of the turn.

My eyes lock forward, my brain is already running the next corner before the wheels even catch it.

Fucking beautiful.

I glance in the mirrors: empty.

It hits all at once: I'm okay. I'm not fucking damaged goods. I haven't lost a bloody thing.

The noise of the car—engine screaming, tires chewing up asphalt—blurs into something familiar rather than haunting again. Leaving this overwhelming knowing sitting in my chest. And for the first time all season, it isn't rage or pressure or fear that moves through me.

It's peace.

I can finally see it. I'm not running anymore. Not from the crash, not from expectations, not from myself. I was always meant to end up here, better than I was before with the rest of my life on the other side of the checkered flag.

And somewhere under all of the noise, another thought settles in my gut: *Do it now. Fuck waiting. Fuck timing. This is the whole damn point. Coming through the fire and finding something worth building after it.*

Her.

I thumb the comms button, holding it for half a second longer than necessary. I can almost feel her hand pressed to mine through it.

"After the line," I correct myself. "Clean it first. Give her something to remember."

I drop into the last turn; eyes locked on the flash of checkered flags ahead.

The finish line blurring up to meet me. "That's the flag. P1. You did it mate. Good fucking day in the office," Holt says over my comms, a roar of cheers muffling his voice.

"Thank you, everybody. That was a rough one."

I swallow hard, nerves thick in my throat.

"Holt," I say, my voice cracking. "Is Jasmine still there?"

"Hasn't moved a muscle," he replies, grin audible in his voice.

I close my eyes for a beat and hold the comm button. "Col cuore in mano, sei mia, tesoro." *With my heart in my hand, you are mine, darling.*

I take a breath.

"Will you marry me?"

Static, followed by a roar of cheers swelling through the pit. Then—Patrick's voice, popping in and out—"Lots of tears and a yes, mate."

I can't get to parc fermé fast enough. Can't get to her fast enough.

The spot should've meant everything. P1, redemption after this track nearly broke me. But none of it compares to the reason I'm running now.

Helmet off.

Weigh-in a blur.

My eyes lock onto her, the only thing in the chaos that feels real.

Kais is waiting at the edge, grinning like a fucking maniac, handing me the little black box without a word. Good man. Always knows exactly what I need.

I cut through the sea of cameras, heart battering against my ribs, every nerve humming. There she is.

Red-rimmed eyes. That big, breathless smile lighting up her whole damn face. Like she can see right through the noise to me.

I pop the box open with shaking hands, gloves still on. She doesn't even hesitate. Sticks her hand straight out, like she's just as desperate to close the distance.

A perfect fit. My perfect girl.

She doesn't look at the ring for more than a second before she's pulling me down into her kiss.

The whole world narrows to this one blazing point—us.

A dozen kisses. Breathless *I love you*'s exchanged in time with our heartbeats. Until she whispers against my lips—

"Go get your champagne. I'm not going anywhere."

I kiss her again, feeling certain and unhurried.

"You are the champagne, Jasmine."

James

A FEW MONTHS LATER...

Smoke and jazz fills the cigar bar, amber sconces cast long shadows across the leather booths. My drink sweats against my palm, nearly gone, the last bite of scotch burning warm at the back of my throat.

"Can I get you gentlemen anything else?" The waitress asks, with a voice like velvet and a walk that says she knows exactly how good she looks under this kind of lighting.

She's been eye-fucking all of us most of the night, though I doubt she would've had the nerve if Montee and Ollie hadn't been so into it.

"Yeah, you can, darlin'." Ollie tips his chin up with a wink. "Let us snag another one for the road. Got a long night ahead." He lifts his cigar like it's a toast.

I tap the ash from mine, take one last pull, then lean back against the booth, eyes on her. "What's your name?"

She smiles, coy. "Corrine."

343

I offer a polite smile, then point to Montee and Aurelius.

"Corrine, those two right there are the only ones still on the market. Don't let that one's charm suck you in." I gesture toward Ollie, who grins like the devil and lifts his drink.

She turns to Kais. "You have a wife too?"

He exhales a slow puff of smoke, one eye narrowing as he reaches into his inner pocket. Doesn't say a word, just holds up his phone. Flashing his lock screen: Alana tucked between their boys, all three tangled up in white linen and sunlight.

He gives it a second—long enough for the image to settle—then slips the phone back into his jacket, lifts his scotch, and turns just enough for his gold wedding band to catch the light.

Corrine huffs a laugh. "Right. Message received." Then her gaze cuts back to me, eyes glinting with amusement. "Where's your ring, then?"

I tip back the rest of my drink, the scotch warming its way down.

"Waiting at an altar in Sicily," I reply, flicking a thick stack of bills onto the tray to close the tab.

She lets out an appreciative sound. "Mmm. I like the loyal type." Her attention settles on my brother and Montee. "You two share that same quality?"

Ari stands first, stretching slow like something dangerous coming out of hibernation. He adjusts the collar of his jacket, shoots a glance at Montee, then looks her square in the eye.

"Can't speak for this prick," he jerks his chin toward Montee. "But yeah, I'm spoken for."

My brows shoot up—Kais straightens too, though his

only tell is the way his thumb drags along the edge of his jaw, hiding a knowing grin.

Corrine blinks.

"You?" she asks, turning to Montee.

He just chuckles, easy and unbothered, as he buttons his jacket. "Sorry to be the last to disappoint, lass. I'm a granddad now. Got two boys to see before they're off to bed." His smile gentles. "Lads, hell of an evening." He gives Ollie a pointed look. "Keep this one out of trouble, yeah?"

Then he turns to me, reaching out to clasp my hand with a firm shake. "Congratulations, Son. Tell your mother I said hello when you see her."

"I will, sir." I nod as he gives Kais a final squeeze on the shoulder, before heading out to be with the twins back home.

I exhale, dragging my hand through my hair before turning toward Ollie—who, naturally, is already up to no good.

"What?" he whines, throwing up his hands as the waitress walks away. "I was just being nice."

"Don't need to be nice, mate. Just respectful," Aurelius says, slinging an arm around Ollie's shoulders and giving him a jostle as we step outside. "Nice'll get you divorced from that pretty missus of yours."

Ollie brushes him off with a grin. "Yeah, well—speaking of my missus... her itinerary says we're meant to head there next." He points across the street to a brick building glowing red under a flickering neon sign:

Black Cat Club – Tables and Dancing.

I squint at it, recoiling instinctively. "Yeah fucking right, you cunt."

"No, seriously! Look," he flashes text from Emilia.

Sure enough, there it is.

Kais stares at the building, then at Ollie.

"I'm not going in there," he announces flatly.

"If Emilia planned it, how bad can it be?" Ollie shrugs.

Kais doesn't respond. Just pulls out his phone and taps a few buttons, already dialing.

"Oi, babe. Why's this fuckin' schedule sending us to some dodgy club?" He pauses, listening. A few pointed nods. Something muttered in German. Then he hangs up.

"Missus says it's part of the plan." His sigh is loud. "Pull any more of that shit like you did in the lounge, Ollie, and I swear—"

"I'll behave!" Ollie holds up both hands. "Come on, let's just grab a bite and see what it's about, yeah? We're celebrating our boy's last knee-up before he takes the collar."

Kais turns with a grunt and starts across the street. Ari throws an arm around Ollie again.

"Oi, lad, Mr. Wife Guy is gonna absolutely knacker you if you keep talking like that."

Ollie just laughs as Ari steers him toward the entrance.

I follow after them, dragging my feet with the feeling I'm walking straight into some kind of trap.

The scent of perfume and cheap liquor hits like a wall the second we walk in, mixing with the pulsing throb of bass that vibrates through the floorboards. A velvet curtain frames a stage, drawn tight. The dim lighting paints the room in sultry shades of crimson and gold.

"It's a proper burlesque gaff, innit?" Ollie mutters, grinning like he's won a bet as we step through the doors.

A woman in feathers, pearls, and absolutely no shame saunters past us, tossing him a wink that should come with an antibiotic.

"Right, I'm off then," Kais says brusquely, pivoting like he's actually about to leave.

But then—"Hey boys!"

Penelope's country twang cuts through the haze, halting him mid-step. She stands down the hall, perfectly poised in tight black pants, still wearing her coat like she's just come out of the cold, one hand cocked on her hip like she's been waiting for us.

"What the hell are you doing here, Azul?" Ari asks, eyes narrowing.

"We came here for dinner," she replies innocently. "We were supposed to miss you guys. Must've came too early. Wanna come sit with us?" Her grin is pure trouble. Something about it says she's far too pleased with herself.

I glance at Kais. He exhales hard, jaw flexing as he stares her down. After a long moment, he gives a single nod. The man's got instincts like a bloodhound for bullshit. If he's following her in, so am I.

How bad could it be?

Penelope leads us to a table dead center, right in front of the stage. Velvet ropes cordon it off from the rest of the room—VIP seating. It's clear a soul hasn't touched it all night. She turns to Ari with a smirk. "Did you bring me a cigar?"

"You're serious?" He eyes her like she's grown horns.

"Deadly." She holds out her hand expectantly.

"Oi, give me the bag," Ari grumbles to Ollie.

He hands over the cigars with a flourish, still riding the high of being the chaos engine who got us here. He passes two to Ari, who hands one to Penelope with a grunt. She takes it with a victorious smile.

They say something else but my eyes are moving, scanning. The lighting is too dim to make anything out clearly, the velvet shadows wrapping around every corner of the room like they had secrets to keep.

"Lads," Ollie says, tossing the rest of the cigars our way before settling into his chair with far too much comfort, legs spread wide like he lives here.

I catch mine midair, light it, sitting back but my gaze keeps drifting. The stage still curtained. Tables around us filled with people. But no Jasmine.

Kais unbuttons his jacket as he sits, fingers tapping once against the glass in front of him. He's scanning too.

"Where's my wife, Penn?" he asks dryly.

"I'm not sure, Father Bear," she replies, already smirking. "I'm sure you'll see her in a minute."

Penelope flags down the waiter with her unlit cigar still wedged between her fingers. "Hi, let me get five of the strongest thing you have, over ten years old and from Kentucky. Three fingers. Neat."

Ollie chokes on a laugh. "Fuck, order a porterhouse and Ari might fucking erupt."

We all crack up, the table tipping into warm, low-lidded laughter.

"Nah. Restaurants always disappoint me," she volleys, glancing at Ari. "I make 'em better at home."

I glance sideways, noting the way Ari hasn't taken his eyes off her since we walked in. It's like watching a bear try to decide if the fire is too pretty to burn him. But it's Kais I lean toward.

"She knocks back bourbon like it's sweet tea," I mutter. "And you and I are sitting here like two fuckin' bloodhounds trying not to panic."

Kais gives a quiet huff of a laugh, shaking his head and sipping his drink. "That obvious?"

"Only to me." My eyes land back on the stage. "I'm doing the same thing."

I sink deeper into my armchair, lighting my cigar with a flick of my wrist, the glow catching in the haze above us. I take a pull, let the smoke twist past my lips.

I'm surrounded by velvet, smoke, and women walking around in various states of undress like it's all part of the furniture and still, the only thing I can focus on was the empty stage and the very obvious absence of my fiancée.

Then the lights dropped to black.

Conversations cut mid-sentence. A collective hush rolls through the room like a tide pulling back. Penelope snaps to attention beside Ari, spine straightening as she turns toward the stage like she's been waiting for this exact moment.

A single spotlight cracks on, stage right.

And there's Emilia.

Posed like a centerfold from some forbidden magazine, sprawled across a velvet lounger in a floor-length fur stole that barely concealed anything. I don't know whether to shield my eyes or keep looking for Jasmine. Emilia's lips contort into a smile as she locks eyes with Ollie and tosses him a wink. She brings the mic to her mouth, voice sultry and smooth.

"Oh, Mrs. Del Toro."

Heat twists in my chest. My pulse kicks.

No fucking way.

The spotlight cuts. Then another snapped to life—stage left.

Alana. Reclined in a mirrored pose, legs crossed, one hand draped over her stomach like she's toying with the idea of committing sin just for the thrill of it. Wrapped in white fur, lit like a goddess, and looking like everything that might make Kais commit actual felonies. She lifts her mic, lips glinting under the stage light.

"Won't you come out, Mrs. Del Toro?"

Then, darkness again. Everything goes quiet. Then the center stage explodes in gold light.

And there she is.

Jasmine.

I forget how to fucking breathe.

Standing tall, alone in the spotlight, her entire body glittering like stardust, catching the light in places I didn't think light could reach.

Rhinestone thigh-high heeled boots catch every flicker of light, hair wild and full, her eyes smoky and that... thing she's wearing—chains and rhinestones arranged like some wicked daydream of a bodysuit—isn't even pretending to be modest. It's temptation built from chains and glitter and every dirty dream I've ever had.

My chest pulls tight. She looks like sin and salvation all at once.

And she's mine.

The rest of the room ceases to exist. The crowd, the stage, the smoke: gone. All I can see is her. All I can feel is the slow, rising thrum of heat crawling beneath my skin, winding its way through every pulse point. And I haven't even seen her move yet.

The lights go dark again, longer this time. The air buzzes with smoke and anticipation. Then a wash of blue light bathes the stage. All three of them stand in formation now: legs parted, posture poised, each with a chair in front of them like they'd summoned them with a spell.

"Oh fuck, are they going to do some kind of chair dance?" Ollie says half-rising from his seat. "I don't know if I can handle a minute of that."

Me either.

Jasmine steps forward, raising a mic to her glossy lips, gleaming under the lights like the rest of her.

"Mr. Del Toro," she purrs, "could you report to the stage please?"

I blink, hard. A slow, disbelieving grin breaks across my face. I point to myself, as if she could mean anyone else.

She nods, smiling like she knows I'm a puddle already.

"Mr. Reinhardt," Alana calls, her voice soft but commanding.

Kais sits frozen, jaw locked, like he doesn't trust himself to stand.

"Mr. Bisset," Emilia giggles, crooking her finger in Ollie's direction.

He's out of his seat and bounding toward the stage before either of us can blink.

"Do I get mine here, then, Azul?" Ari mutters behind us.

Penelope answers with a pointed elbow to the ribs.

I stand, pulse pounding—mostly in my fucking pants —and look over at Kais. He exhales through his nose, finally rising like a man preparing to walk into battle.

"You good?" I murmur, as we start toward the stage.

"No," he says flatly. "You?"

I laugh, "Absolutely not."

He gives a short huff, something that might've been a laugh in another life.

"Keep your cool, mate," I add under my breath. "She's already won."

"Don't remind me," he mutters.

Jasmine meets me at the steps, takes my hand, and leads me to the center chair as if she's crowning me for slaughter. Kais takes the seat on my left like he's restraining a weapon.

Ollie's on my right, already flushed and beaming like a kid on Christmas morning.

I lean into Jasmine, unable to help myself.

"What is all this?" I whisper in her ear.

She kisses my cheek, slow and agonizing, then steps away without an answer.

The lights drop again plunging us back into darkness.

Then some smokey rendition of 'I Put a Spell On You' starts to play. The crowd behind us roars, whoops, howls—but the second Jasmine steps forward, everything else drops away. She locks eyes with me like there's no one else in the room.

My breath catches. My pulse goes nuclear.

She walks toward me in slow, measured strides—hips swaying in time with the beat, mouthing every word like they're hers. Her hands skim down the length of her own body, fingertips dragging over glittering skin and rhinestone curves like she can't decide where she wants me to touch her first.

Then she lifts her leg and presses the point of her heel into my chest. A command.

I don't dare move.

Her fingers slide down her thigh, catching on the top of her garter. She starts to peel it down—I stop her. Take it from her hand and pull it off myself.

She smirks—spins—and lowers herself onto my lap with fluid, practiced ease, her back pressed to my chest.

Her weight settles over me as she finds my hands. Guiding them across her hips, down every curve like she's etching the memory into my bones.

Then she leans back, mouth brushing my ear, hips rolling in time with the music.

"Siempre ha sido tuya, papi," she whispers.

"Shit" I hiss, nearly losing my cool entirely.

And then she's gone again. Walking away with the same devastating grace as the other two, all three of them falling into a choreographed rhythm so tight and hypnotic it could be an actual fucking spell.

Hip rolls. Hair flips. Legs splitting over stools like they were born to be worshipped.

The woman could be a fucking professional. I'm impressed. I'm in awe. I'm in love. And I'm *starving* to be inside her.

The song slows. The lights shift. She comes back.

Every move she makes stays just out of reach—an arm's length away, a breath past touch—as if daring me to break. She pulls my hand. Lets it hover at her waist. Tempting me. Daring me.

If this room were empty, I would pull her into my lap and shatter every last rhinestone on this fucking bodysuit. I would make her feel what she was doing to me with every inch of me.

The music softens into something raw. A slow, aching moan of sound. And that's when she does it. She rolls her ass right into my knob. Grinds against me in one slow, perfect curve. Then she looks back.

And fucking—*smiles.*

The moment she feels me throbbing beneath her, that smile goes wicked. I'm one hand slide away. One more ass drop into my lap from completely losing it—right here, in front of God and everyone else—like a fucking teenager.

And then the song ends.

The lights drop. The crowd roars. The girls are gone. Vanished like a fucking fever dream. My heart is somewhere in my throat as I sit here like a man freshly baptized in sin.

Kais doesn't speak. Ollie looks like he just stumbled

upon his first dirty magazine. Then Ari's voice cut through the silence behind us. "Well, that's one way to bless a marriage."

Ollie finally exhales. "I think—I think I blacked out for a second."

I run a hand through my hair, "What the hell have we done to ourselves?"

Kais sits forward, elbows braced on his knees, eyes still locked on the now-empty stage like he's trying to burn through the curtain.

"She planned that knowing I wouldn't be able to touch her." He runs a hand down his face, exhaling through his nose like a bull. "She's not making it out of here in that outfit."

"Nope," Ollie agrees, shaking his head slowly. "We are so fucked."

"Speak for yourself," Ari says behind us. "I'm the only one here still capable of rational thought."

I look over my shoulder at him. "You're sweating through your shirt, mate."

"Fuck off," he groans.

Then Penelope appears, strolling in front of us like fucking Willy Wonka. She claps her hands together.

"I'd say they did their jobs well. You boys look like you've seen the face of God and forgot how to blink." She laughs, hands on her hips, nodding in satisfaction. "Hot, right? Took me three months to choreograph that. Little taste of Texas for you London boys. You're welcome."

Kais' jaw flexes. "That was strategic warfare. You're lucky you share blood with my wife."

Penelope swats the air, delighted. "Come on, Romeos," already turning on her heel. "If you want your girls back, you'll need a backstage pass."

Jasmine

"GOD, THAT WAS LIBERATING," EMILIA CALLS, fanning her face as she follows behind me into the dressing room.

"Did you see Ollie's face before the lights went off?" Alana says, then does a perfect impression of his slack-jawed, wide-eyed reaction.

We collapse into laughter, the kind that's breathless and a little unhinged—the aftershock of a high we aren't ready to come down from.

"Kais looked like he was going to fucking detonate at any minute," I add, tugging my robe off the back of a chair and slipping into it. My skin is still buzzing, my rhinestone bodysuit squeezing against my every breath.

"Yeah, and you single handedly fulfilled all of James' dirtiest fantasies in that thing," Alana flicks at the delicate chain running across my sternum. "What kind of magic pasties are even covering your boobs? There's no fabric."

I take a long sip of champagne.

"New product launching with my spring line, gel stickers. Industrial strength and morally questionable."

Emilia holds out her glass, eyes sparkling. "I'm so glad you guys adopted me as a friend. I mean it. You're both brilliant women."

Alana and I exchange a look, then wrap her in a warm, chaotic tangle of silk, glitter, and friendship.

"We love you, Millie," I say. "And you shake ass like you're from Houston—so if you ever leave PR behind, you'll make a killing."

Emilia snorts mid-sip, nearly choking.

"God, that's brilliant." She catches her breath, eyes flicking to the door. "You think it worked? Might I finally get laid?"

Just then, a knock echoes against the dressing room door.

"Only one way to find out," Alana says giddy as hell, already stepping toward it.

Aurelius stands in the doorway, one hand shielding his eyes like he didn't just watch us strut around in rhinestones and a whisper.

"Oi," he grunts, dry as usual. "Just popping in to say that was amazing. On a talent level. Not that I was staring at your bits or anything."

He clears his throat, adjusting his jacket.

"I'm taking Penelope home—we're off to Sicily first thing in the morning. And frankly, I'm not convinced any of you are making it out of this dressing room alive. I'll catch you lot on the plane... if you survive what you've done to those poor lads."

We all burst into laughter again, Emilia wheezes into her champagne.

Penelope slips in behind him, a satisfied glint in her eye.

"I come bearing very wound-up gifts." She pushes the door wider to reveal them.

Ollie, Kais, and James.

Each of them looking varying degrees of undone. Ollie is flushed and jittery like he had too much sugar. Kais looks like someone lit a fuse and then dared him not to explode. And James—

God. James is just staring at me, that slow, knowing smirk pulling at the corner of his mouth like he's still trying to process oxygen.

"You did me proud," Penelope says softly, stepping back out. "Now deal with the consequences of your actions. Goodnight."

She shuts the door behind her with a soft click that feels louder than it should.

"Right," Kais says, stepping forward. "No use fuckin' about in here. Babe, car's outside."

Alana tilts her head, playing innocent. "You don't want to stay and have a drink with everyone?"

He blinks once, then holds out a hand like it's non-negotiable.

"Ya Amar," he says, voice low and full of promise. "Consider yourself lucky to make it out that door without me ripping you out of the three straps you're calling underwear. The partition in the car's the only privacy you're getting before I do."

Alana's mouth lifts, but she bites down on the smile, eyes sparkling. "Goodnight, ladies. See you on the plane tomorrow," she says sweetly, slipping her things into a bag.

I can't tell if her excitement is about the wedding... or the threat Kais just growled like a promise.

Kais doesn't wait. He scoops her up without warning— straight over his shoulder—and carries her out the door like a man on a mission. Alana's giggle echoes faintly from the hall.

I blink after them, breathy with laughter. "Twenty bucks says she turns up pregnant next month."

James, still standing near the wall like he doesn't trust himself to move yet, gives a slow nod. "Absolutely."

I hold his gaze for a moment. The look in his eyes isn't just heat. It's certainty. Like he made a decision and was just waiting for the world to catch up. My skin prickles under it.

Ollie clears his throat, stepping toward Emilia with mock-serious reverence.

"Em, my love. My darling. My undercover stripper of a wife."

"Oliver," she laughs, shoving his shoulder as a flush creeps over her cheeks.

"I am not as poetic as Kais Reinhardt," he says solemnly, "nor as patient. I would very much like to shag you in the toilet. Would you be interested in that?"

Emilia chokes on a laugh, setting her glass down. "I've been advised to make you beg, Oliver—and that's exactly what you're going to do for me."

She takes one last slow sip of champagne like she already knows how the rest of her night is going to go.

Ollie's eyebrows shoot up. "Yes, ma'am," he replies, clearly delighted.

"Follow me," She grabs her coat and ties it with a dramatic flourish. "I have a few ideas." She gives us a wink over her shoulder. "Goodnight, you two. See you in Sicily."

Ollie trails after her like the smitten puppy she just turned him into.

James shuts the door behind them, turning the lock with a soft click. I lean back in my chair, letting my robe slip open as I sip from my glass, watching him over the rim.

He smiles, crooked and devastating, his dimples flashing as he squints at me. "You worked on that for three months?" he asks, disbelief threading through his voice.

"Mhm, you're not the only one who can keep a secret."

He crosses the room, dragging a chair in front of me, and unbuttoning his jacket as he sits. Then he reaches for my chair, gripping the sides and pulling me quickly into the space between his legs.

I set my glass down on the vanity, pulse already hammering.

He trails a finger down my sternum and unties my robe the rest of the way; his eyes drinking in the sight of me, glittered and glowing.

"There's no fabric to this at all, Jasmine." His voice is barely a whisper.

He stares.

"No, James," I murmur with a soft laugh. "There isn't."

I drag my fingers down the swell of my breast, peeling away the flesh-toned adhesive that covers me. He gasps—quick and involuntary—as I remove the other, his gaze locked on every movement.

"Is this bad luck or something?" he whispers, eyes still glued to my chest.

Without a word, I drop to my knees in front of him, my robe falling wide at my sides, the cool floor kissing my skin. My hands slide up his thighs, slow and certain, before I tilt my head toward his watch.

"Nope," I reply softly. "Still thirty hours until the wedding."

I catch our reflection in the vanity mirror: me on the floor, him seated like a king with his eyes glued to me, chest rising with hunger. But it isn't just lust written across his face. It feels like devotion. Something primal but still impossibly gentle.

"Stand up," I husk.

A slow smile pulls at his lips. "You want to be on your knees for me, Tesoro?"

I tilt my chin up, meeting his gaze without flinching.

"*I am* on my knees for you, James."

He stares like I just broke something inside him, something he isn't in a hurry to fix.

Then he stands, slowly.

I watch as his eyes sweep the room until they land on a pile of feather boas tossed over a chair. He crosses the room, grabs a handful, then stands in front of me.

"No, baby." He shakes his head. "You think I'd let you touch the ground?"

He lays them down beneath me. Then let his hands sweep into my hair, pulling me into a kiss. It isn't soft. Not at first. It's hungry. Claiming. The kind of kiss that says I've waited long enough and I'm going to make you feel everything.

He pulls back, breath hot against my mouth, his eyes devouring me.

"This thing you did tonight..." His voice cracks, dark with awe. "Fuck."

He drinks me in chains, glitter, nothing hidden. Then kisses me again slower this time, like his breath has finally caught up to his heart. His hands stay in my hair, holding me there, close enough to feel the tremble in him when he pulls back.

"But more than how bad I want to fuck you right now..." His voice barely scrapes out.

"I need you to know how much I love you. And how much I see you." His eyes don't waver. "All the shit you've had going on—your launch, my races. There's no way this was easy." He shakes his head once, jaw tight, like he doesn't trust himself to say more than the truth.

"But I know you did it for me. Because you wanted this to be something bigger than just a bachelor party." He exhales hard. "And it is. Fuck, Jasmine, it is. You just branded yourself onto my fuckin' soul."

I lean in to kiss him again, aching for him. Every word, every soft touch turning my need for him primal.

Our lips crash together hungry, claiming. My hands finding the ridges of his torso, slow and sure, unbuckling his belt. He groans into my mouth as my palm finds him, thick and throbbing like he's been tortured for far too long.

I can't have that.

I pull back from his kiss, our noses brushing.

"Stand up, James."

He obeys without hesitation. I stare up at him through my lashes—tall and towering, eyes burning. He'll let me do anything to him. Fuck, he'll do anything to me that I ask. But that's not what I want.

Not tonight.

"James," I whispered, "I do feel seen. I do feel loved by you. I know how much you love me. But for tonight—for right now—I need you to feel how much I love you."

I hook my hands into the waist of his pants, easing them down his hips, pressing soft kisses along the scar from his accident on my way down. When I look up again, his eyes hold mine.

"Starting with my mouth."

I push the last of the fabric away, letting it pool at his ankles. Then I kiss a slow path down the length of him, thick veins pulsing beneath my lips. Every soft press of my mouth drawing a jolt from him.

When I reach the base, I wrap my hand around him and pause. My eyes rake over him; every inch etched and aching.

"I want you to give me every thought and fantasy you had on that stage," I murmur. "Got it?"

Those dark eyes smolder, voice fraying as he lets out a helpless groan. "Jasmine..."

I squeeze gently. "James. I know you. I can take every last bit of it. I want every last bit of it." I meet his gaze fully now, my voice steady and commanding. "Show me but call me by your name when you do."

He bends, catching my jaw in his hand, forcing our eyes to meet.

"Siempre ha sido tuya. You just had to come take it, Mrs. Del Toro." He kisses me, ravenous and full of heat. Then his mouth brushes my ear. "Stick out your tongue."

I obey. He grabs the champagne bottle from the vanity, taking a shallow drink, then tilts my chin back. Hovering over me, he lets the chilled champagne pour from his mouth into mine.

I swallow hard, the cool rush sliding down my throat as my hand presses over the skin it travels. He watches every movement like it's a podium ceremony.

"Now do that again," he whispers, "but swallow me instead."

Then, gently, he wipes a drop from the corner of my mouth with his thumb and pushes it to his lips like a dare. He shrugs off his suit jacket, tossing it over the back of the chair, eyes never leaving me.

I grin and sitting up to my knees, wrapping my palm around him again but not claiming him.

I tease—dragging my champagne-slicked tongue down his length, letting the cool meet the heat of him. Then I lay the tip against my tongue, holding his eyes watching him shudder with anticipation. I kiss the drop of excitement waiting for me.

Then lick it slowly from my lips.

His hand rakes through my hair, fingers tightening as he releases a groan. "If you don't take me in your mouth right now, I swear I'm gonna lose my fucking mind."

I smile up at him, wicked and sure. "Siempre ha sido tuya, mi corazón. Just take it."

I open my mouth, inviting him in.

His jaw flexes. His breath hitched. Then his hand finds my jaw, thumb brushing my bottom lip.

"You're gonna kill me," he mutters, then feeds himself into my mouth with a groan that sounds like it came from the base of his spine.

His hands smooth my hair back with aching tenderness, like I'm something sacred, something he doesn't want to miss a single second of. I feel his palms cradle the sides of my head, steady but trembling. Then he starts to move. Hips rolling, slow at first, then deeper with each pass.

His body coils tight above me while I let him hit the back of my throat, again and again. my hands anchor on his hips, coaxing him to go further, take more.

I breathed through my nose, jaw relaxing, tears pricking as I let him have all of me. This man who gives everything, finally feeling free enough to be greedy is the biggest turn on of it all.

He's so close: his grip turning desperate, his moans ragged, a tremor runs through every muscle of his thighs. Then stills for just a beat, one broken sound leaving his lips...

Before hot, thick salt spills into my mouth in a violent pour.

I swallow, letting him empty into me, working him

through every wave of it as he comes apart against my lips. Hands fisting in my hair, chest rising like he can't find air.

He shudders and I keep him in my mouth. Soft licks, gentle sucks, until the aftershocks make him hiss from the sensitivity. Only then do I pull back. Lips slick, slightly parted, breath warm and heavy, as I look up at him.

His eyes are still dark. His chest rises slow and deep, the edge of his release still taut in his shoulders.

He braces himself on the vanity, catching his breath. I swish the last sip of champagne in my mouth and wait.

Whatever relief he'd found moments ago doesn't last long. The heat in his eyes says so. And the way he's already hardening again in his hand? Proof enough.

He sits, pulling off his boots, then kicking free of the pants still pooled at his ankles. His shirt is next. He unbuttons it slowly, then folds it with the rest in a neat pile.

Then he stands.

Completely bare.

Stepping in front of me and silently offering his hand. I take it. And the second I stand his mouth is on mine.

Hot and urgent.

His arms wrap around my waist, muscles coiled like steel, chest pressed tight to the soft swell of mine. His tongue teases mine, coaxing, as if he needs to taste what I'd just taken from him.

His hand fists in my hair, tugging my head to the side, his mouth latches onto the soft spot beneath my jaw. He sucks hard. A deep, aching pull that sends a shock straight down my spine and tears a whimper from my throat.

His hand moves down the center of my belly, finding the edge of the adhesive underwear. He tears it off like a Band-Aid and tosses it aside.

Then his fingers trace the slick path of my desire.

"You're fucking soaked," he groans against my lips.

I smile into his mouth. "We both know how I get when you look this damn good."

He kisses me again, then parts me with two fingers, scissoring gently along the swollen, throbbing ache between my thighs.

"What do you want me to do, Mrs. Del Toro?" he whispers against the curve of my neck.

I moan, grinding my hips into the rhythm of his hand. "Keep doing whatever the fuck you're doing with your hand," I whimper, the sensation building, tight and hot and crawling up my belly like a fuse being lit.

He smiles, turning me around to face the mirror. One arm wraps around my waist, the other stays between my legs; calloused fingers still working me, slow and precise. With his free hand, he smooths my hair to the side, brushing it over one shoulder. Then his breath fans against my ear sending goose bump down my neck.

"I want you to watch. And when you touch yourself... I want you to think of this." He kisses my bare shoulder.

"James," I breathe. "I only want you to touch me. I'll burn waiting if I have to."

His fingers don't stop. He just holds me tighter, coaxing me deeper into it. "I'll only come for you, travieso."

He inhales sharply.

"Fuck, babe..." he growls, his forehead pressing to my shoulder. "You say shit like that and expect me to stay in control?"

I meet our reflection in the mirror. His body is molded to mine, chest broad and heaving behind me, hand buried between my thighs. My lips are parted, cheeks flushed, glitter dusts across every inch of my skin like I've been kissed by starlight and claimed by something darker.

But it's his face that makes me tremble. The way he looks at me like I'm his entire fucking religion. He'd die with a smile as long as I was driving the knife, and I'd gladly plunge myself at the end of his blade.

I shake my head. "No, I don't. I want you to lose control for me, James. Let me see you inside of me... so I can lose it too."

He lets out a ragged breath. "Keep those eyes on me then..."

His hand moves from my throat, the other still working me as he hooks a finger under the chain acting as a thong around my waist—his eyes flick up to meet mine in the mirror, dark and deliciously possessive.

"I'm the last man who ever gets to see you like this, Mrs. Del Toro. No more shows unless they're private. Understand?"

I nod. And with one quick tug—he snaps it. The chain shatters, the gems scattering across the floor like fallen stars.

"You're mine," he growls against my neck.

Dark eyes lock on our reflection in the mirror. Then he grabs my thigh, lifting it onto the vanity with force and reverence all at once, angling me open just enough to give us both the full view.

"Look at yourself, Tesoro," he praises, glazing the tip of himself in teasing patterns over my swollen center. "Look how fucking beautiful you are. You did this to me."

Then—He slides in. One long, slow, devastating thrust.

I cry out, head falling back on his shoulder, body arching into his hold. The stretch of him makes my vision blur. I clutch my muscles around him.

"Oh fuck," he growls, "Keep milking me like that and those pills won't matter."

"I stopped them last week," I breathe, arching into him

ravenously. Needing to feel everything he's giving me as he starts to move.

I meet his thrust with another hard squeeze of my core.

"Fuck Jasmine," he hisses, "You want to carry me, don't you?"

He holds my throat with one hand, my thigh with the other, his hips rocking into me in deep, measured thrusts. I watch through heavy lids; every glistening inch moving inside me. His eyes tracking every flutter, every gasp like I'm a symphony he's memorized.

"That's it, baby. Take it just like that," he growls against my throat.

"Pon tu nombre dentro de mí..." I cry.

He grabs my jaw forcing my eyes to his, "What the fuck did you just say?"

Moans continue to rumble from my chest as he thrusts. I can't think. Not in Spanish, not in English.

He slows, bringing down the wave begging to crash over me, making me desperate.

"I said, put. Your. Fucking. Name. In. Me. Travieso."

His rhythm shifts—picking up with the boil of my climax. I feel him angle just right, hooking his hips into me with purpose.

His eyes lock on mine. "Then watch while you take it from me."

That's it.

My body convulses, a cry tears from me as my orgasm hits. Raw and sudden and all-consuming. I contort against him, violent and greedy, my eyes rolling shut as I shatter with him inside me.

He moans against my neck, licking and sucking sloppily as he lunges into me over and over. Driving every last drop of his release deep into my body until every last bit of him found a home in my belly.

We both pant, our bodies still tangled in the heat of what we'd just done. My legs refuse to move, still frozen in place, stretched wide as I lean back against his chest—full of him, marked by him, claimed in every way that matters.

"Beautiful," he whispers, eyes locked on the mirror as he looks at himself still inside me, then watches as he slowly pulls back, a warm slip of his release following in the wake.

He reaches down, runs his fingers over the trail, and gently pushes it back inside.

"You beat me to it," I whisper, not breaking his gaze.

"I love coming in first." He smiles, that devastating dimpled grin, presses a kiss to my shoulder and adds, "Time to catch that plane."

Chicane

BONUS CHAPTER

James

ABSOLUTELY NOTHING ABOUT THIS DAY HAS GONE to plan.

The photographer dropped out last minute. The singer I hired came down with bronchitis. And I'm fairly certain it's going to rain—even though the sky looks clear now, which feels like a trap.

Not ideal when your entire wedding is being held in a garden that's currently glowing under about four hundred candles and one very expensive arch of imported flowers.

But the real issue is Jasmine. She decided to uphold that ridiculous tradition of sleeping apart the night before the wedding.

And honestly? If there's a petition going around to make that illegal, I'd sign it.

Twice.

What is the actual point of that? To remind me what it felt like to be without her? Because trust me, I remember. I spent a whole bloody year learning that lesson before she came back to me and I've got no intention of doing that again. Not for a single night.

The girls pulled a full-on miracle. One hurdle after another, and they handled it like a Formula One pit crew on espresso.

Emilia's been on the phone with magazines all day, Nadine's been bossing vendors like she owns them, and Jasmine—God, my Jasmine—has been tucked away with the twins and Alana, calm as anything, as if she didn't just fix everything with one well-placed call and a prayer.

And Penelope (quiet, steel-spined, unexpected Penelope) offered to sing. I've never heard her sing a note, but my brother swears she's got the voice to back it up. He even volunteered her before she did, which... says something, doesn't it?

I pray to every patron saint of wedding days that she pulls it off. Not just because we need her, but because there are three magazine reps scattered around the property pretending to be subtle while they take notes. And one of them's bound to turn her performance into some kind of headline if it goes sideways.

But I've got a gut feeling she'll be brilliant. Could be instinct. Could be the way Ari looks at her.

I don't know what's going on between them, but it's not nothing. She doesn't curse him anymore. Doesn't roll her eyes. Just looks at him like he's holding up the sky. And he watches her like she might disappear if he blinks too slow.

Pretty sure I'll be getting a wedding invitation from them before I know it. Then he really will have made himself family in every possible way. The man would literally be the twins' uncle, not just by heart like me.

I'll give him shit about it, of course. But truth be told? I'd love that.

I'd love that a lot.

It's almost been a year since we met, but it feels like he's always been my brother. And having him here today—him and Kais and Ollie—does something to me I wouldn't admit to anyone but Jasmine. Something warm and aching. The kind of gratitude you can't put words to without your voice cracking.

A soft breeze pushes through the open French doors behind me, fluttering the corner of the letter where my hand hovers.

From where I sit at an antique desk facing the window, I can see the sun dipping toward the waterline, the Ionian Sea glittering like a jewel beyond the stone wall of the garden.

I can also see the blur of bodies moving below, chairs being adjusted, glass clinking against glass, someone dragging a table just slightly too loud.

It's chaos.

Beautiful, buzzing chaos. And I'm trying to recenter myself in the only part that really matters, her.

I duck away from the lads for a few minutes just to finish this letter. Not my vows, those are scrawled on a folded note card in my pocket, waiting. This is something else. Something just for her.

All the bits I can't say in front of everyone. The quiet promises. The memories I never want her to forget. Just to remind her that while the world spins around us today, I'm right here.

Waiting.

And always will be.

"Oi," Ari's voice breaks through the quiet as he taps his heavy knuckles against my shoulder. "You about finished yet?"

I finish the last line, sign it with a quick *Ti amo, sempre*, and fold the page neatly before slipping it into the envelope. My heart's already thudding.

"Yeah, yeah, I'm done, you big bastard. Back off, yeah?" I say, trying to sound less emotional than I feel.

He ignores that completely, holding out a small emerald green box tied with a crisp white bow.

"Don't get sassy with me, twat, or I'll just pocket the gift she told me to give you."

I reach for it instinctively. "Give it up then."

He raises his eyebrows and holds it just out of reach. "Letter first."

I huff. "You're a damn child, you know that. I could take the letter to her myself. I want to. Just to check on her."

Ari shakes his head, smug. "You know you can't do that, mate. Bad luck. Plus..." he shrugs casually, "I need an excuse to go back there anyway."

"Oh yeah?" I raise a brow at him, a slow grin creeping across my face. "Someone you want to see?"

He doesn't even blink. "Yeah. I need to check on Penelope. Make sure she doesn't need anything before she sings you down the aisle."

I stand from the desk, the letter still in my hand, watching him. He's trying so hard not to look obvious. Failing miserably.

"Why do you need to check on Penn?" I bite back a smirk. "We could just send Ollie or Kais. Their wives are in that room too. Bet they want to see them just as badly."

Aurelius rolls his eyes. "You want the fuckin' box or not, James?"

He's grinning now, doing a bloody terrible job of hiding it.

I start to hand him the letter slowly. He drops the green box onto the desk with zero ceremony and snatches the envelope from my hand before I can change my mind. But instead of leaving, he pulls something else from his pocket.

"Here," he grunts, voice a little rougher now, "before I forget or some shit—this is for you too."

He passes me a small wooden box. Nothing flashy. The grain is old, darkened by time, smooth at the corners from use. I blink down at it in my palm, brows furrowing.

"This from Jas too?" I ask, still expecting some cheeky gift that would make my ears go red.

Ari shakes his head. "Nah. Me. I know you've got a ton of 'em from racing or whatever, but I thought this one might mean something to you."

He shrugs, like it doesn't matter.

"Or not. I don't give a shit. Just thought you should have it."

I open the lid slowly, the little brass hinge creaking with age—and there it is. A vintage Rolex with a green face, restored to gleam like new.

It looks out of place in this quiet evening light, like something that traveled too far just to end up here. My fingers hover over it before I pick it up, heart already hammering.

"You bought this for me?" I ask, voice quiet.

"No. It was in the Del Toro family lockbox. Belonged to our grandfather. He wore it on his wedding day."

He pauses, something shifting behind his eyes.

"Has his initials on it."

I turn the watch over and there they were—**J.D.T.** etched into the backplate in elegant script. Jovanni Del Toro. A name I'd clung to when Aurelius was three sheets to the wind off pickle backs last year, showing me every family photo he could unearth in his tiny house.

He's watching me carefully now, shoulders stiff, face unreadable.

"Good man. Would've loved you like hell."

I don't know if it's the weight of the day, or that name, or the simple fact that this man—my brother—just reached into our bloodline and handed me a piece of it... but my eyes sting instantly. The tears come too fast to stop.

I clear my throat, turn my face toward the open window for a second like the sea might be able to swallow the lump in my chest.

"So you and Kais are both sappy bastards now, yeah?" I mutter, voice shaking as I blink it away.

Aurelius steps in, wraps one arm around me in that hard, bone-jarring hug men like him give. He slaps my back with enough force to rattle my spine, then leans in and mutters:

"Fuck off."

I laugh, wobbly and grateful. I clapped a hand to his back, steadying both of us.

"'I love you' works too, twat."

Then softer: "Thank you."

His voice dips just above a whisper. "Yeah, yeah. I love you too, you bastard."

He steps back, brushing something invisible off his jacket, and nodded toward the emerald box on the desk.

"Don't suggest you open that other one in front of anyone, by the way. Penelope told me what's in it."

He raises an eyebrow with a knowing smirk before turning on his heel and disappearing into the hallway, leaving the door slightly ajar.

I slide the watch onto my wrist and cross back to the

desk. The emerald green box waits where Ari left it, tied neatly with a white satin ribbon innocent as if it wasn't just passed to me with a warning. I pull the ribbon loose and lift the lid.

Inside is a small black velvet book, the kind that looks too expensive to touch, with the word *Travieso* etched in gold script on the cover.

My heart slams. I pick it up carefully and open the cover.

And there she is.

An entire boudoir shoot. Jasmine in nothing but silk, and sheets, and—God help me—nothing at all. Curves I know by heart but somehow look new. That look in her eyes that says she isn't just trying to turn me on, she's claiming me. Reminding me exactly what I'm coming home to. Exactly who I belonged to.

This woman might actually kill me.

I have no idea how she loves me like this. Like she's been waiting her whole life to give it all away to me. It makes no sense. She could inspire her own religion.

Hell, she kind of does already with that cult-like following of hers: her brand, her presence, the way she makes people feel seen.

But still... she looks at me like I'm the whole damn universe. Like the only thing that will ever matter is taking my name and then multiplying it.

Fuck, if that isn't humbling as hell.

I scrub a shaky hand down my face, heart still thudding, and close the book before I get any ideas. Sliding it under the bed, our bed for tonight, knowing full well I'll be pulling it back out the first moment I can.

We barely get time for a honeymoon—just a few days

before I'm back on the track—but neither of us wanted to wait any longer.

I shut the bedroom door behind me and cross the hall to the room where the lads are getting dressed. It's all dim lighting and scattered laughter. Old hardwood floors creaking underfoot, that ocean air floating through the open window, and the quiet thrum of pre-wedding nerves that no one will admit to.

Kais and Ollie are already in their tux shirts and trousers. The two of them lounged in armchairs, cigars in hand, half-drunk glasses of something rich and amber resting nearby.

They look like some old Hollywood promo shoot. Whatever they're talking about has Ollie wiping his eyes with the back of his hand.

I cross to the bar cart sitting under the tall window and pour myself the smallest glass of scotch.

My hands still a little shaky as I reach for a cigar from the polished humidor beside it, my fingers brushing the lighter, then pausing.

"Any minute now, right?" Ollie calls, his voice rough like he'd been up half the night—or possibly fighting off tears again. He wanders over to me, tie askew, holding an untouched glass.

I nod, exhaling a deep, shaky breath. "Yeah. Should be any time. Can't lie, my stomach's doing backflips."

Kais looks over from the corner; cigar perched at the edge of his mouth like he belongs on the cover of GQ: Wedding Edition. His eyes hold that same steady calm they always did before one of his fights. He's built for this kind of tension.

Meanwhile, Ollie pours himself a glass that was... not small.

The door flies open, and Aurelius steps through. Montee's daughter Nadine follows hot on his heels, already lifting her camera as she calls out:

"Hello, handsome men! We're about five minutes to showtime. Jazz wants some candids of you lot getting ready."

Click. Flash. She's already snapping shots of Kais, who looks up from his cigar like he could've been auditioning for the next Bond—if Bond had a softer side and two toddlers calling him Baba.

I drain the last of my scotch, then set my untouched cigar back down on the tray. There'd be time for that later.

Right now, I need steady hands.

"How are the girls?" I ask my brother, heading over to the clothing rack where our tux jackets are hanging.

He steps beside me, his tie half-knotted and a crooked smirk forming.

"You askin' about the lot of 'em, or your wife?"

Hearing her be called my wife does all kinds of crazy things to me that would probably be more fitting for a honeymoon than this moment.

"All of them," I say, pulling my jacket from the hanger.

Aurelius chuckles putting on his own. Lad looks polished, enough to pass for a mob boss with those tattoos and that constant resting glower, but there's no denying he cleans up well. Could give me a run for my money if he smiled once in a while.

"Girls are fine," he replies. "Whole lotta gigglin' and cryin' goin' on in there. Jasmine looks excited." He pauses, adjusting his cuff. "It'd be scary if the woman could get any more beautiful than she already is."

That makes me smile, wide and helpless.

But damn, that smile lights a fuse. Because suddenly my nerves are back, crowding into my chest all over again.

Kais steps in beside us, easing his jacket over his broad shoulders with a cigar still perched between his teeth. He glances over at me, then at Ari, then back at me.

"Good to be nervous, mate," he says, voice steady. "Don't have to pretend to be made of stone. Doesn't make you any less of a man."

Aurelius nods in agreement.

"Yeah. No fightin' back the tears, mate. They'll fall the second you see her, whether you want them to or not."

They share a knowing look, two men who have already walked through their own kinds of fire. It settles something deep in me. But, of course, I can't let it pass without giving Ari shit.

I clear my throat, needing to deflect before I get misty-eyed in my own damn dressing room. "Still sweet on your ex or something?" I toss toward Ari.

Ollie snorts from across the room, yanking on his jacket and striking a pose the second Nadine lifts her camera. Man wouldn't understand the concept of candid if it slapped him.

"Fuck no," Ari shoots back, visibly offended. "Completely forgot about 'er 'til you just brought her up."

He chuckles as he straightens his lapel, but before I can dig in any further, a soft knock on the doorframe pulls all our heads around.

My mum peeks in. The moment I see her face my heart drops clean through the floor.

"They're ready for you," she says softly, her eyes already glassy.

I stand there, throat tight, the scotch turning to mist in my chest. This isn't nerves about Jasmine. Not even close.

I'd never been more certain of anything in my life. It's the bigness of it all. The way it swells up inside me, too full to hold.

There aren't many moments in life where you get to see the change coming. Most of the big ones, good or bad, just slam into you like a freight train. But this is different. I'm walking into it. Step by step. Getting to take in the scent of the room, the shape of my brother's silhouettes in the light, the warmth of my mother's voice.

And fuck, if that doesn't wreck me.

The boys file out one by one, each of them tapping my shoulder or squeezing the back of my neck as they pass; small, wordless rites of brotherhood. I barely meet their eyes. My chest is too tight, my throat a raw knot of emotion.

Then my mum steps forward. She crosses the room quietly, her heels whispering against the old wooden floor, her perfume the same she'd worn since my carting days. She reaches up instinctively and fusses with my bow tie, even though I've checked it a dozen times in the mirror and a dozen more in my reflection on the window.

"My boy," she breathes, and it's over for me.

Her voice unleashes the tidal wave I've been trying to hold back all day.

She takes my face in her hands, gentle but steady. Her thumbs brush the edges of my jaw like I'm not a fully grown man with a lifetime already behind me.

"I'm so, so proud of you, Cuore Mio." Her voice fracturing right down the center as tears slip down her cheeks. "You are an amazing man, James. And I'm so happy I got to be your Mama."

My own tears come fast—hot, shameless, and completely uninvited.

She holds tighter, voice barely a whisper now. "And I am so very, very happy for you. I couldn't have picked a better woman for you than your Jasmine."

She pauses to collect herself, but it doesn't stop the tears.

"You take care of each other, amore mio. Hold on with both hands. You don't get a love like this twice. Treat it like the precious gift that it is."

I nod, crying openly now. A full-body kind of sob that makes my shoulders shake.

She laughs through her own tears, brushing them away with a shaky hand. "And you call me the minute you two decide to start making little ones. I'm on the first flight to wherever you are."

We both let out a wet, quiet laugh. She pulls a handkerchief from her purse—lace-edged, monogrammed, probably older than me—and dabs at my face with the tenderness only a mother can get away with.

"I figured I'd be the one needing this," she says, wiping beneath my eyes. "But I should've known my sweet boy would be crying just as much."

I lean into her touch, eyes closed, grounding myself in the smell of her, the brush of her fingers, how unbreakable but warm she's always been.

"I love you, Mama," I whisper.

She nods, her smile watery but bright. "I love you too, Tesoro."

Then she steps back, smoothing the front of her dress and tucking her handkerchief back into her purse.

"Now," she clears her throat with a glimmer of mischief in her eyes, "let's get you down there before my daughter starts wondering what's taking so long."

She slips her arm through mine, and together we walk out to the garden.

It feels like walking into a dream. The kind of dream you try not to wake up from, just in case it's the last good thing your heart ever gets to hold.

Most of the space is situated behind tall hedges and flowering bushes that sway in the breeze like they're part of some slow choreography. The air smells like salt and jasmine and fresh-cut stems, the kind of perfume that clings to memory.

The sky is finally clear, thank God, and the sun is just beginning to dip, casting everything in that fleeting, perfect light before it turns amber. The kind of light that turns skin to gold, eyes to honey. The kind of light Jasmine always looks most herself in.

At the far edge of the garden, the ocean stretches out like a painting: deep, endless blue crashing softly against the cliffs. The altar sits just before it, framed by a willow branch arch wrapped in cream roses and wild olive leaves, as if the sea itself had come in and whispered *yes.*

The aisle is a narrow stone path lined with hundreds of glass cylinders, each one cradling a flickering candle. Warm light shimmers up from them like tiny suns, dancing at our feet. Most of the guests are already seated, their anticipation tangible in the air.

The priest steps forward first. My mum squeezes my hand gently—maybe for her nerves, maybe for mine—but it helps.

Then the guests rise. All of them.

My heart thunders.

Penelope sits off to the side on a simple white stool, a Spanish guitar perched on her knee, a small mic set just in front of her mouth. Her long blonde curls loose and her dress fluttering in the breeze like something out of a country fairytale. Her eyes meet mine and she tilts her head, asking without words if I'm ready.

I nod once.

She drops her gaze, adjusts the neck of her guitar, and then she begins to strum. A simple melody at first, but already my throat is closing around it. *Home*. She hasn't even sung a word yet, and still it hits. Soft and aching.

The wedding party starts to walk.

Kais and Alana led the way, the picture of quiet joy: his hand resting protectively at her lower back, her smile shining like she just invented love.

Then Emilia and Ollie, who look like they just stepped out of a black and white film reel, polished and glowing.

Then comes Aurelius and the twins.

And Christ.

Both boys are in miniature tuxes, cheeks round and flushed, grinning and fully aware they're stealing the whole show. Rafi waves with both hands. Zayd stares at the candles like they're magic.

I'm barely holding on. My eyes are already watering, the lump in my throat is getting harder to swallow by the second.

Aurelius hands the twins off to Nadine at the end of the aisle, giving one last look over his shoulder.

Then everything changes.

Everyone stands.

My breath catches somewhere between my ribs and my heart, and suddenly the whole garden goes still. Even the sea feels like it stopped crashing for a moment.

Penelope starts to sing. Her voice has that sweet country twang that sounds like both love and heartache stitched into a lullaby.

"Alabama, Arkansas, I do love my maw and paw, not the way that I do love you..."

My chest cinches tight.

The melody wraps around me, delicate and devastating, and just as the words settled on the air, there she is.

Jasmine.

She steps into view at the top of the aisle, and the world drops out from under me.

God.

'Ethereal' doesn't even cover it. She looks unreal. Like something the sun itself had conjured up just to watch me fall to my knees.

Her veil, floor-length and sheer, catches the golden light, making her glow from the inside out. It's pinned into her hair, done up in that polished, sexy way only she can pull off. A few strands in soft curls falling around her neck, framing her face like they were sculpted there.

And that face, fuck. Her makeup is simple, glowing, perfect. Doesn't hide a single freckle or flaw, just lets her shine through. Every inch of her looked like she belongs to another realm, but still somehow... still mine.

Then there's the dress...Christ, the dress. Satin that clings in all the right places, then softens and falls away at her chest and shoulders like it's melting. I swear my hands ache to touch her. Ache to pray to her. The rhinestone thing she wore the other night doesn't even come close to this.

She pauses at the end of the aisle; her arm hooked with her dad's and smiles at me through trembling lips. Tears brimming.

Mine are already falling.

Brown, glassy eyes lock with mine and in that one look, everything we'd been through rushes back—every almost and every forever. I couldn't have picked a better song. Every lyric wraps itself around her like it was always meant for this moment. For her.

"Man oh man you're my best friend, I'll scream it to the nothingness, there ain't nothin' that I need..."

Penelope's voice carries Jasmine down the aisle like a whispered prayer. Like my mums garden itself has hushed to make room for her.

And I—weep. Blubber, actually.

Like a damn baby.

Don't even care that everyone can see.

My mum presses a handkerchief into my palm, the one she'd used on me not fifteen minutes ago, and I wipe my face with it before passing it back, hands trembling.

Jasmine reaches the end of the aisle, kisses her dad on the cheek, and turns to me. I take her hand and I know I'll never let her go again. Not even for a second.

Her cheeks are streaked with tears, her fingers daintily trying to wipe them away, but it's useless. Neither of us can stop.

Penelope sings the final lines like she's placing a blessing over us. Jasmine turns her head, mouths a thank you to her, and smiles again; eyes shining, lips trembling.

The priest starts to speak. But I don't hear a single word. Because I can't take my eyes off her.

Suddenly the priest asks for my vows. I blink, pulling myself back into the moment. My hands fumble at the inside pocket of my jacket, fingers shaking as I pull out the folded piece of paper I've read a hundred times in secret but still feel completely unprepared to speak aloud.

I clear my throat, barely, and look straight into her eyes.

"Tesoro," I start, my voice already catching. "My beautiful, fiery girl."

She lets out a watery laugh, the sound soft and golden. Like she's trying to hold me up with just that.

"I told you you'd be my wife from the moment I met you," I smile through the emotion that's crawling up my spine. "How does it feel now that I've tricked you into loving me?"

Laughter ripples through the garden. Jasmine laughs too, her eyes glimmering.

"What can I say," she whispers, "you're the hottest stalker I've ever met."

The crowd chuckles again, but all I can feel is her hand in mine. I look back at my paper, the words blur for a second. My breath stalls but I push forward.

"I love you without reason," I say slowly. "Without a plan or conditions. I love you as my own body. So much so that I don't even know the difference between your heartbeat and my own anymore."

Her lips part, trembling. Her eyes fill again. And my voice—fuck—it cracks right down the middle.

"You came into my life like an angel in my darkest hour. And healed me in more ways than I ever realized were broken."

I swallow, hard. The sound echoes in my ears.

Out of the corner of my eye, I see my mum: hands clasped to her chest, crying openly. But I can't stop now.

"More than the love of my life," I continue, "you're my best friend. My home. My reason for dreaming again."

Jasmine wipes at her cheeks with one hand, holding mine even tighter with the other.

"I promise to love you with every part of me," I read, voice shaking. "To braid your hair every night without question. To crawl out of every car and find you in the crowd first. To watch every dodgy movie you have committed to memory—as many times as you want."

She lets out a full, messy laugh through her tears. And I smile, because that sound—that laugh in the middle of all this beauty—is everything I ever wanted.

"But more than anything," I finish, "I promise I'll never let you go again. That I'll hold onto you until this life takes us both. Through tears and joy, love and hurt. Through our youth and into our golden years... I'm nothing but yours." I pause. One breath. Two. "Forever."

She drops my hand and cups my cheeks, her thumbs brushing the tears off my skin. Then, with no ceremony and no hesitation, she pulls me into a kiss.

The crowd groans and grumbles like someone just spoiled the final scene of a movie, but I can't stop smiling into her mouth. I kiss her again before she pulls back with a flushed laugh.

"Sorry, sorry," she says to the crowd, hand raised in apology. Then she turns to me, eyes glinting, and mouths '*not really*'.

The priest clears his throat gently, and then it's her turn.

Jasmine pulls a note card from the bouquet that she'd dropped to the ground kissing me. I watch it shake. Feel her breath stutter. My chest clenches all over again.

"James," she begins, huffing a breath already thick with tears. "I have been completely gone for you since the moment I met you at that concession stand at Kais's fight, trying to convince me to try your disgusting British snacks."

Laughter breaks through my tears. Her hand trembles in mine, so I rub gentle lines over her knuckles with my thumb, steadying her. Her lip quivers as she blinks up at me through thick lashes wet with tears.

"It's just me and you, Tesoro," I whisper, low enough for only her. "Take your time."

She nods and breathes deep, shoulders dropping.

"Some girls dream of houses," she says slowly, voice catching, "and cars. Some dream of becoming mothers or doctors. But me?" She pauses, eyes filling. "I dream of you."

She looks up at me not reading anymore, going from memory.

"You are everything. You are my person."

Her voice breaks, and so do I.

"You are my safety. My laughter. My joy. You are my sorrow when you're away too long. You are... my Mr. Bingley."

We both laugh—completely us. Knowing no one else would understand it. That's the point.

"I will love you in every form," she says, wiping tears from her cheeks. "The ones you show the world... and the ones you only trust with me. You and you alone, will always be enough for me."

My grip on her hand tightens, like I can keep her words right there in my palm.

"I will follow you to the end of the earth, and around every track you choose to spin circles on. And I will make my home wherever you lay your head."

I don't wait. I pull her into my chest, arms wrapping tight around her as the crowd groans and laughs and someone (probably Aurelius) mutters something about us being hopeless. But I don't care. Not one bit.

The priest clears his throat again, amused. "Alright, alright. You think these two are ever gonna say 'I do' or what?"

The laughter ripples again. We break apart, just barely. Our eyes never stray. And then—

We exchange rings. Our fingers tremble. Hers barely fitting mine because my hands are shaking so damn much, and she laughs through another round of tears. And finally —*finally*—we reach it.

The priest smiles, voice clear and steady.

"I now pronounce you husband and wife. You may kiss the bride... again."

But I'm already there. Mouth on hers. Arms around her.

Home.

About Marie

Marie Allen writes swoon-worthy romance with emotional grit. Known for her perfectly imperfect heroines, unapologetically possessive heroes, just the right amount of spice, and found families you'll want to be part of.

Based in the Rockies, she's a first-generation organic farmer who believes love stories don't need perfect people—just the right kind of messy. When she's not writing, you'll find her planting something, building the perfect playlist, or daydreaming about her next fictional crush.

𝕏 x.com/AuthorMarieAllen

♪ tiktok.com/@AuthorMarieAllen

▶ youtube.com/AuthorMarieAllen

Cant get enough?

The *Unchained* series continues with:

Aurelius ♥ Penelope

in

Offside

www.Marie-Allen.com

www.ingramcontent.com/pod-product-compliance
Lightning Source LLC
Chambersburg PA
CBHW021954130726
47903CB00014B/1283